More praise for *First Friday*

In this debut novel, Hartmann takes what appears at first to be a romantic comedy and turns it, unexpectedly, into a thriller. As a result, there are many slapstick and laugh-out-loud funny moments throughout the tale, such as an elaborate prank in a church, but there's also a darker undercurrent—a constant dread that Anne's misgivings about Bruno might actually be right on the money. Still, the novel is filled with hilarious misunderstandings and moments of family strife, including a disastrous dinner in which Sheldon first meets Anne's family. Overall, this fast-paced, plot-heavy tale is as riveting as it is cheeky. A witty, sensitive story that will satisfy discerning fans of family dramas.

I0645652

Kirkus Reviews

Meet the O'Neils, a good-hearted, Irish Catholic family. But the O'Neils are so opinionated, so married to Church dogma, that they cannot connect with their daughter, Agnes Anne, on a human level. And so Agnes leads a life of guilt, selfy-doubt, and awkward rebellion—a life in which her only true solace comes from Jude, her metaphorical pet snail. But all is not lost. Throughout the pomp and bravado, throughout the arguments and put-downs, the Virgin Mary is there, her presence as soft and subtle as dew upon amountain. This book succeeds on many levels. Five stars!!!

James Hanna,
The Siege: A Prison Uprising Redefines Justice
Call Me Pomeroy; A second, Less Capable Head and Other Rogue Stories

While laughing out loud at Agnes Anne's efforts to grow beyond the low expectations of her family, I began to realize that a great mystery was developing. As her quest for independence from her family and her truly villainous brother-in-law become more and more desperate, Agnes Anne grows in self-confidence and determination. However, Hartmann has created a three-dimensional character, who never loses a shade of her vulnerability. Anyone who has ever spent an hour, a year or a lifetime trying to get away from the clutches of controlling family will appreciate her dilemma. And in today's world, the portrayal of faith/religion gone from sustaining to abusive, here in one particularly bizarre family, will strike an eerie note. Hartmann knows how to handle it all with a deft touch that keeps us nervous, reading eagerly, and occasionally giggling, beginning to end.

Elise F. Miller
The Berkeley Girl: In Paris, 1968

First Friday

How virginity almost killed me

Copyright ©2016 Tory Hartmann

Published by Sand Hill Review Press
www.sandhillreviewpress.com,
P.O. Box 1275, San Mateo, CA 94401
(415) 297-3571

Library of Congress Control Number: 2015904009

ISBN: 978-1-937818-06-7 Case Laminate
ISBN: 978-1-937818-42-5 Paperback
ISBN: 978-1-937818-51-7 Ebook

Cover design by Tory Hartmann, Sand Hill Review Press, LLC
Graphics by Backspace Ink.

Edition 2, cover change, January, 2017

First Friday: How virginity almost killed me is a work of fiction. Its characters, scenes and locales are the product of the author's imagination or are used fictitiously. Any similarity of fictional characters to people living or dead is purely coincidental.

SHRP
Sand Hill Review Press

For Bill

I wish you had lived long enough to see *First Friday*
as a book and not just a crazed stack of papers.
Hopefully, they have a library in Heaven.

First Friday

How virginity almost killed me

Tory Hartmann

1. Out of Obscurity

I CONSIDER OBSCURITY AN ART FORM. The hidden nook in the back office of my father's San Francisco real estate company has been my cocoon. I've worked in this small neighborhood business since high school and throughout my college years and never left. Three steps up from the sales floor, I'm still an observer. I've marveled at what the women wear, seen the guys in their long sleeved shirts and button-down collars, as well as the ones who look too casual in their Polos and leather jackets. I know who works hard, who makes cold calls, who takes every rejection as a personal failure. Yes, I've watched guys snivel. Really. Maybe that's why I decided the bar was low enough for me to jump over, that this shy person with a stutter could leap from the anonymity of back office and into the cubicles where the real money is made.

Last year I made a plan. A no-holds-barred, pedal-to-the-metal plan to catapult myself out of my parents' crazy, Catholic household and launch myself into a new life. All my brothers and sisters had left, but here I sat—28, not the youngest, yet somehow stranded. I had no boyfriend, no career, no prospects for anything but the same-old, same-old.

When I heard Ma say, "Agnes Anne will be a blessin' t'us in old age," my hair stood on end.

I had to leave. I had to do this.

Hail Mary, full of Grace, please help me to not screw up.

The day of my titanic leap, the day I would tell my stick-in-the-mud uber-Catholic father that I wanted to say good-bye to the escrow department and instead join the sales team, I felt sick to my stomach. I said a quick prayer to the BVM (Blessed Virgin Mary) and lurched toward my closet. My younger sister Fiona says that every day you should wear something that makes you feel good. I had never bothered to take her advice until today.

I peered into the thicket of hand-me-downs and

shopping mistakes populating my closet, and pulled out at least a half dozen tops and pants, blazers and skirts. Some matched. Most didn't. One after the other, I rejected each of them and tossed the failures into a giant heap across my slipper chair. They looked like sins.

Hail Mary, full of Grace, please help me to pick out a dynamite outfit. And not to screw this up.

I climbed into my new-old poplin suit, which I bought a long time ago but had been saving—for what I don't know. I tried to check myself in the mirror. Too many holy cards had been slipped into the frame. I snatched them away. Finally, there I was: Agnes Anne O'Neil, the girl with an enormous hook in her nose, a bulbous chin, and an anvil jaw. Yuck. I didn't have time to riff on what God gave me. Nerves made my stomach hurt even more. *Not now,* I thought.

I raised my chin, took a few deep inhales and exhales and forced myself to practice what I was going to say downstairs. My spiel sputtered and stuttered. Furious, I paced back and forth reminding myself what my speech therapist told me about breathing. It was getting late. I had to get down to the kitchen. I went over to my statue of the Virgin Mary in the dish garden on my desk, and reached out to touch her and make a blessing. Yikes. There was something on her skirt.

I came closer. It was a miniature mollusk, its two front tentacles waving around like tiny arms, its light brown shell speckled like a tweed coat. I watched it glide up Mary's skirt. *How sweet*, I thought. *I have a living thing in my dish garden.* Backing away, I made the sign of the cross without my customary touch to the statue and hustled out the door.

Hail Mary, full of Grace, please help me to not screw up.

"Yer late," my father said, without looking up from his breakfast. "This's First Friday. The train ta heaven waits fer no man."

"I know," I mumbled, taking my seat. "Sorry."

In my parents' house, First Friday was practically a sacrament, their own family-enforced Holy Day of Obligation. My father, the last of the Neanderthal Catholics, believed that if you attended Mass on nine first Fridays in a row, you received a Special Indulgence. It's sort of a Get Out of Jail Free Card you could use in Purgatory, if you happened to find yourself stuck between Heaven and Hell.

I had quite a number of completed Novenas, not an easy task, as doing anything nine months in a row was chancy. And, like Sisyphus pushing a rock up the hill, if you missed one month, the ball rolled back down. I always thought that was unfair, but I don't make the rules.

As though the giant, elongated pancake in front of my father might scamper away, I watched him stab it, roll it up and cut it to pieces. Meanwhile, my mother shuffled back to her skillet to create another masterpiece. No one had noticed how dressed up I was today. My parents were like salt and pepper shakers. They belonged together, but they were very different. I took a deep breath and tried to remember what I'd rehearsed.

Hail Mary full of Grace, please help me to not screw up.

"Da?" I said.

His mouth bulged on one side like a bagpipe filled with air. Ma came over from the stove and tapped her spatula on the edge of the table.

"Malachi," she said, "ya never told m'what i'twas."

"Oh golly, Irene, I'm sorry. It was a picture of... let me t'ink..." Da gazed down at what was left of the scene on his plate, any hope of deciphering it ruined. His rheumy eyes rolled to the ceiling. "Saint Patrick sendin' tha snakes out 'a Ireland?"

"Nah." Ma's face took on a vague sense of hurt.

Ma ran back to tend her restaurant-style skillet. Her brown hair, peppered with more and more kinky gray each month, fell stiffly to her jaw line. For years she'd been drawing with pancake batter. Over time, she moved beyond Mickey Mouse ears to doves, and when she ladled an enormous Valentine heart onto her skillet and called it the Sacred Heart of Jesus, it was a turning point. Ma was addicted. She even gave up her ladle and, for more accuracy, squiggled entire Biblical scenes on her skillet using a discarded mustard container, pausing to let each aspect cook before she added the next, each scene tinted in deepening shades of creamy tan to nutmeg brown. Every time she made pancakes, we were supposed to "know" what she had drawn with the bubbly batter. Pancake breakfasts had evolved into a game of Biblical Jeopardy.

"Y-yesterday?" I continued, trying to regain Da's attention. "In the m-mail? I got..."

My breath nipped off as though someone had pinched my windpipe. No air moved in or out. I had to relax or this would take forever.

"Did'na ya see tha hole in tha center?" Ma said, coming back to the table.

"Agnes's talkin', Irene. Go on," he said, returning his attention to me. "What did'ja get in tha mail, Agnes Anne?"

I watched him stuff a great wad of pancake into his mouth.

"I would t'ink, Malachi," Ma said, "ya would'a recognized tha Angel a'tha Tomb."

"Right. Right," Da said, speaking and chewing at the same time. "That's what i'twas. A big rock, hole fer tha cave, and an angel standin' tall. I got it, Irene. Now Agnes, get on with it."

I inhaled. "I have my r-real estate l-license."

There. It was out, stutter and all. Da's jaw dropped like a drawbridge over a moat, which enabled me to glimpse the revolting contents of his mouth. I swallowed hard and took another breath the way my speech therapist, Miss Allison, had taught me. She said my stuttering stemmed from the fact that I thought too hard about everything and then forgot to breathe, which caused my throat to lock up.

"Yer what?" Da said. He swallowed so hard I could see the lump of pancake pass his Adam's apple. "Did'ya say real estate license? Agnes Anne, is that what yuv been doin' all these nights at school? You've been studyin' fer your license and ya never told me? *Never told yer Da?*"

Throat frozen solid, I could only nod.

"Ya said ya were takin' business classes."

"Real estate is business," I whispered.

Even though I knew whispering might make me seem tentative, it was better than being caught up in a spasmodic stammer. Then my subterfuge made me blush. Miss Allison told me that no one stutters when they whisper, so I tried to whisper in a gushy sort of way like Marilyn Monroe, my idol and, to me, the most famous stutterer there ever was.

"Fer a quiet girl," Da said, jamming more pancake into his mouth, "yer pretty sly. Ther'r not supposed ta be any secrets in this family."

In apology for this Sin of Omission, I glanced at the enormous picture of the Virgin Mary hanging above the sink. Mary stood in a rose garden, her crimson heart bulging dangerously out of her body. This picture was a grand old catechism tableau Ma had rescued from the trash at the rectory some years ago. My eyes locked on the white dove flapping around inside Mary's heart. I felt sorry for it.

"An' just wha' d'ya think yer going ta do wid a real estate license?" Da said, his Irish accent more pronounced than usual.

I used Marilyn's technique and pushed the words out through a gushing sigh. "I want to go into sales, Da."

"Ya do, do ya?" Da braced his hands on the table, his elbows stuck out like oars on a rowboat. "I want ta tell ya somethin', Agnes Anne, yer not tha salesman type. Yer too shy. I know yer tryin' very hard *not* ta be shy—even goin' ta tha' woman—that stutterin' class or whatever i'tis and it's true yuv improved, but trust me, ya don't have tha moxie. It takes fortitude ta be in sales, a boldness that's not in yer nature. Face it, darlin', ya couldn't sell a bowl of milk t'a cat. So let me stop ya before you get started 'n end up disappointed 'n frustrated and then Ma 'n I will hav'ta pick up tha pieces."

Cutlery clanked against his plate as he mopped up a puddle of syrup with a piece of pancake. I bit my lower lip and commanded my face to remain blank. I would not show how much this hurt me. Shy people are very good at this.

"Remember yer spell in high school?" he said, holding a dripping wad of pancake on the tip of his fork.

Ouch. I flashed back to my collapse, the two weeks I didn't speak. It started after my Junior Prom.

"That was nearly twelve years ago," I whispered, angry that this one incident still clouded the way my family saw me.

Bruno had been my boyfriend until the night of that dance. There was a terrible scene in the back of his car; I was so ashamed, I never told on him. I realize now, I should have. The following week, Bruno took up with my sister Katie. I went into a dizzying funk, didn't speak for days. My family came to the conclusion that I was jealous of my sister's happiness and probably thought it amusing that a boy had gone from one sister to the other. But the only emotion I felt for my sister was sorrow. Bruno Stark was a first class creep.

"Yuv never accepted failure well, Agnes," Da continued. "Failure comes from God." He pointed his fork up in the air, then at me. "We all can't be everythin' ta everyone. Accept what God 'as given you 'n be grateful. Stay where ya'are, Agnes Anne. Ya do a bang-up job in tha back office. Don't try ta become somethin' yer not."

Words swarmed in my head. Unfortunately, none made it from my brain to my mouth. I thought about Marilyn Monroe. Surely she would have said something. She would have charmed her audience, blinked her eyes and had a clever comeback. But I just sat in rueful resentment.

"Here ya're, love," Ma said. She presented me with a platter. "Guess what i'tis." Her gush of pride nearly popped the snaps on her pink, checkered housecoat.

I gazed down at the twists and turns of the pancake. Wavy lines from east to west usually meant water.

"Washington crossing the Delaware?" I couldn't help my sarcasm.

Da guffawed. Inwardly, I chided myself for being mean.

"Aggie, ya know I only make religious pancakes."

"Sorry, Ma." I tried to concentrate on the tan squiggles. "I see water..."

"Right."

"And is that a fish over here? And big waves? Over there, is that a boat? And is that blob Jesus?" I snapped my fingers. "Jesus calming the sea!"

"Yer right, m'darlin'!" Ma giggled with delight. "Someone recognizes my talent!"

"Ah, yes, Irene," Da said, rolling his eyes. "If drawin' with pancake batter were an Olympic event, yud 'ave a gold medal."

Merrily, Ma went back to the stove to squirt out another holy scene, this one for herself. Da tucked a smirk at the side of his mouth. The spewing batter over at the stove sounded like baby farts. I wondered how long it would be before Ma went completely nuts and took me with her.

Da's head twitched from side to side like he was about to

say something, but he didn't. I reached for the syrup, slathered on a generous amount and began to eat.

Soon Ma came over, tilted her own platter toward us and said with pride, "'N this?"

Da and I stared at the pancake rendition of some famous biblical scene. Tiny yellow and tan puddles of cooked batter ran in an even row across the top. Our silence made her huff.

"Canno' ya see it?" she asked.

Bubbles? Stars? My mind went blank.

"It's tha Las' Supper!" she exclaimed.

I saw it then, the circles were their heads. The lines down, their bodies.

"Nice." Da nodded.

Ma poured syrup over the twelve apostles. A feeling of loneliness engulfed me. Maybe I would never get out on my own. Never leave this house. My stomach tied in knots just knowing my Big Plan had stalled on the kitchen table and I would have to live with my nutty parents forever.

"Malachi, if th'angel wants ta try sales, what harm is there?"

I perked up. That was so sweet of Ma to say.

"I don't need another salesman, Irene," Da snapped. "Business 's crap right now. 'N I especially don't need another woman weepin' 'n wailin' on tha sales floor 'cause there's no business. It's commission only out there." He stared hard into my eyes and dropped his voice. "Agnes Anne, if ya do this, ya won't make a dime."

Ma forked the heads of three apostles and paused before she ate them. "I thought yer best salesmen 'er women."

"They may be. But Agnes Anne isn't tha type. She's far too shy."

"I'm not shy. I'm r-r-reserved," I said. Damn. Why didn't I breathe out like I was supposed to?

"I'm tryin' ta protect ya, love." Da leaned over the table and shook his fork in my face. "The Virgin Mary never worked outside tha home, ya can bet yer boots on tha'." He forced one eye into a conspiratorial wink.

What was he talking about? We both had a Special Devotion to the Blessed Mother, but just because the Bible didn't mention that Mary ran Joseph's construction office or sold Avon on the side, how were we to know if Mary worked or not? What did that have to do with me?

"But wha'bout that German woman?" Ma said, slicing into the bodies of the apostles.

"Verna Korbel is a ball-bustin' steamroller," Da shouted. "Ha! I bet right now that woman's eatin' tacks fer breakfast and chewin' them inta bullets. All day long she'll be spittin' 'em out of 'er mouth. Now, d'ya want to be like tha', Agnes Anne?" He shuddered as though his head popped up out of a pool of ice water. "Do ya?" His ruddy face came over the table, his whisper hoarse. "Tha Holy Water will freeze over before I let one of m'daughters become coarse 'n tough like her."

"I would never become abrasive, Da," I said, using my breathy voice. Verna Korbel was magnificent. I could only hope to be as sophisticated, as well dressed, and as competent as she. "I think I'd be good at sales, Da. I'm a good listener and—"

"Sales is *sellin'*, Agnes Anne." Da pounded the table. "It's not standin' there like a stone post. It's convincin' someone to do somethin' they don't have tha nerve t'do! Buyin' a home is tha biggest purchase anyone ever makes and t'sell real estate ya have ta be confidence itself. No, no, no, no. Yer not a confident person." Da leaned his porcine face down into his coffee cup and slurped. "Believe me, yer not cut out fer a life in sales." He wiped a drip off his chin with the back of his hand, then grabbed his napkin and finished the job.

"Oh, Aggie," my mother said. "You want to be a lady, not some career girl with a chip on her shoulder. We'll pray to the Virgin Mary and see what she says, dear. If you want a change, God will have somethin' wonderful in mind for ya. We'll pray ta Mary and ask her ta reveal it."

"I've been praying to her for months, Ma. Mary wants me to succeed. Mary wants me to achieve my full potential."

The two of them stared at me as though I were an apparition.

"I can't live on what I make in the back office," I blurted.

"What?" Da screeched. "Ya live here quite nicely, young lady."

"But I can't afford to go out on my own, Da. I'm the only kid left." My voice broke; tears stung behind my eyes.

I looked around at the cavernous kitchen, the dusty

catechism tableau over the sink, the old stove with the trash burner on the side. Nothing ever changed. All my brothers and sisters had escaped. They found their lives, married, had kids, my younger sister, Fiona, even had a career. But here I was, still stuck in a religious museum surrounded by statues and wrapped in a peculiar guilt that stemmed from that terrible night of my prom, a guilt I could never seem to shake.

"Why should ya go out on yer own when ya can live in a ten room house wid us?" Da said, cleaning his plate. "Ya have it mostly ta yourself."

If they couldn't figure it out, I couldn't answer this question. I imagined myself leaving now, packing up, and hiring a truck. I'd send my furniture to a new apartment, say good-bye to Ma's religious pancakes and statues of Mary. But I couldn't leave just yet. I had to save more money for my plan. Inside the folds of my napkin, my hands trembled.

"I n-need to be ou-out on my o-own."

Damn. There it was, that stutter again. What did Miss Allison say? Speak through an exhale. Be breathy.

Hail Mary, please help me to be more like Marilyn Monroe.

"Mary told ya that?" Ma craned her neck toward me, her head tilted one way then the other, her hair as inflexible as a roll of steel wool. "The Blessed Mother *told ya* to leave us?"

My mother's face blanched to oatmeal gray; her freckles darkened like the spots on a giraffe. Would I resemble her in 30 years? In 30 years would I be squirting biblical scenes onto a skillet? Oh God, surely I'd have my own apartment by then. I should have it by next year. But did I have her nutty genes? Somewhere inside me were these genes ticking like a time bomb?

"We'll be late fer Mass." Da pushed back from the table. "Mary, Mother of God, what's tha world comin' ta?" He quickly crossed himself and threw down his napkin. I heard him mumble as he left the room, "Agnes Anne has a real estate license. Now I've heard everythin'."

"M-maybe the D-Doheney G-Group will take me on," I called after him through clenched teeth. "O'Neil isn't the only real estate company in San Francisco, you know." Anger singed my insides.

Next year, I won't be here. Next year I'll be gone.

That thought was a comfort. That thought had spurred me on through the darkest of nights and the most boring of days. If I had to, I would go outside the family to succeed. I didn't want to work for someone else, but I would.

"Did you hear me, Da?" I shouted. "*The Doheney Group!*"

A spasmodic cough blustered out of the hallway.

"Oh for godsakes, Agnes Anne," Ma said, as though Da's cough were my fault. "Tha' would be disloyal."

"Agnes Anne, don't ruin m'day," Da yelled, from the hallway. "Hurry up, both 'a ya. 'Tis a sin to be late for First Friday mass."

"It is not," I said, under my breath.

"Don't argue with yer father." Without moving her lips, my mother murmured, "Doheney Group..." The rest was unintelligible.

I helped Ma clear the table, then left the kitchen to fetch my purse. I stopped next to the front door where a statue of Mary stood on top of a ring of stiff china clouds. At Mary's feet was a pretend lake that Ma kept filled with Holy Water. I gazed up into the Virgin's delicate porcelain face, dipped my first two fingers into the Holy Water, crossed myself and whispered, "Hail Mary, full of Grace, please help me to not screw up."

2. Meet You by the Statue

DA LOOKED LIKE AN ANGRY EAGLE as he headed up the street, his tweed sport coat flapping in the wind. Ma and I moved our legs as fast as we could to catch up with him.

He turned to Ma and me as we hustled along. "Where are tha roses? Didn't ya pick tha flowers?"

Ma and I looked at each other. We had both forgotten. As children, it was the youngest girls who picked flowers for Mary. On First Fridays, Ma would lead us around the yard and even to the yards of neighbors to gather blossoms and sprigs to lay at Mary's feet. Roses were always our favorite. We knew they were Mary's, too.

The statue was a neighborhood shrine and stood on a stubby pillar sheltered by a nook cut into the thick adobe cemetery wall next to Old Mission Dolores. This common-faced Mary wore a crown that looked like Ma had made it on her skillet, small doughy blobs protruded around a circle on Mary's head. This Mary had the hands of a farm girl, the right one so large it looked like she wore a baseball mitt. Fiona nicknamed her Our Lady of the Belgian Waffle, as we gave every Mary around us its own moniker. Sturdy and robust, her features were not unrealistically delicate like the statues in church. This Mary seemed strong enough to plow fields or sweep streets and just might, at any moment, step down off her pedestal and get to work. I loved her.

"Mary will just have to do with only our prayers today," Ma said.

"And how can ya be a good agent, Agnes Anne," Da asked, "if ya canno' even remember tha flowers?"

"Sorry, Da. I was distracted."

Camellias and mums, roses and daisies were shriveled to leggy brown stems and desiccated petals around the statue's base. Three votive candles, flames low in their tall hurricane glasses, still burned at Mary's feet, the wax melted to golden oil at the bottom. Ma stepped up on the riser and reached forward to start cleaning. She swept the dead flowers off the pedestal and fluttered a tissue around the statue's base, slapping at dust and causing more dried petals to fall to the sidewalk.

After a brief bow from the waist, Da walked up to the statue and gazed up into Mary's face as though she were the most beautiful person in the world. I knew my father's Mary was an ideal, the perfect woman. I could see so much love and tenderness in him at these prayerful moments that I sometimes wondered if he wished he were married to her instead of to Ma.

My mother's Mary was the keeper of penance, a strong woman who carried her burdens silently and without complaint. Ma relished her personal suffering. She thought the more one suffered in this lifetime, the higher in heaven you'd go.

My Mary was a girlfriend, someone who encouraged me, someone I could turn to. Sometimes I saw Mary as a white woman dressed in her traditional Mary blue, eyes either peering up into heaven or downcast and staring with resignation at the ground. But I also saw Mary as an Hispanic woman with a braid down her back; or I'd picture her hair in cornrows, her skin cinnamon brown. Sometimes my Mary was a Hindu woman with a bindi on her forehead and a lilting accent that could rock me to sleep. This Mary sat at the foot of my bed and listened to me practice my speech lessons, urged me go to back to school and told me over and over not to give up.

"If you think ya have a job on tha sales floor waitin' for ya just because ya snuck around and got yer license, yer wrong, Agnes Anne," Da said, after his prayer. "I need ya 'n tha back office. Understand?"

"Hire s-someone else," I said, surprised that I was capable of such a retort.

"I donut want the expense now," he bellowed. "This isn't tha time to be flittin' around dolin' out jobs."

A few parishioners, the regular ones who came to mass each day, not just Sundays and first Fridays like most O'Neils, were walking by gape-mouthed. My father went to mass every day and everyone knew him and knew this was another O'Neil show, something my family had become quite famous for. I could probably make money if I sold tickets to these episodes. Trouble was, I never had advance notice.

"Business is slower 'n watchin' mold grow on cheese," Da exclaimed. "Ya know that. Ya see how few escrows are 'n the office right now. And here you are, standin' 'n front of God and Mary, dissatisfied. We're still in a recession, Agnes Anne, tha worst recession since tha 1930s. Ya should be grateful ya *have* a job."

In emphasis, Da's hand gestured sideways and slapped into one of the tall candles at Mary's feet. It careened into an empty jelly jar. I watched the tall votive candles fall like dominoes. Shards of glass, stems and petals fell onto the sidewalk beside the base of the statue. The candle oil ignited, and the flame hopped from the spill to the dried flowers.

"Now look what yuv made me do!"

His face blotched with red, Da began to stomp on the small fire next to the statue's base. The stems and dried petals were perfect fuel. Several parishioners rushed in from the sidelines, all of them stomping in a sudden community Saint Vitus Dance of Doom. The small blaze was out in seconds.

"Donut get cut, now," Da said, warning people and waving the smoke away.

"Are ya all right?" Uncle Jimmy came out of the crowd.

"Of course we're all right," Da said, brushing off his sleeves. He made quick bird-like jerks at his coat cuffs while rolling his shoulders, as though shaking off droplets of water. "A candle knocked over. Accident." He gave me a look of rebuke.

"Do we have the makings of a miracle?" Uncle Jimmy's eyes were bright with mischief. To him, everything was a joke.

"I swear, Jimmy," Da said, nodding hello to my Auntie Lucy, "my eighth born could piss off tha Pope." Da turned away and strode up the street toward the church, his arms swinging at his sides as though he led a parade.

"Don't b-blame it on me," I called after him. "I didn't knock it over."

Da turned around and pointed at me. "Yuv ruined m'day, Agnes Anne. Ruined it! I hope yer proud of tha'."

He continued his march and disappeared into the Old Mission. Passers-by eyed us with curious pity and moved on.

"Wha' the hell'd ya do, Agnes Anne?" Uncle Jimmy turned to me with great interest. "You've gotten him goin' right well this mornin'. I'll say that for ya."

As usual, Uncle Jimmy looked like an overgrown leprechaun. Today he had on a green sports coat with quarter inch orange stripes running through it both horizontally and vertically. Fun-loving and a jolly drinker, my uncle was a regular Irish cliché.

"Good mornin'," my Aunt Lucy said. She pecked Ma on the cheek and then me. Our problems seemed to make her sapphire eyes dance with delight. "Malachi havin' a spell, is he?"

"Wha' tha hell'd ya do, Agnes Anne?" Uncle Jimmy asked again.

Miss Allison told me to look people square in the eye, which I did. And so I wouldn't stutter, I took a hearty Marilyn Monroe breath and gushed, "I got my real estate license."

Uncle Jimmy inhaled so fast he began to cough.

"Good for you, Aggie," Auntie Lucy said, giving me a friendly elbow. "That's showin' the boys. Don't worry about yer da. Malachi's never set well with change. But he usually comes 'round." She busied herself rearranging a blue and red silk scarf draped around her coat collar.

"If ye don't mind me sayin', Agnes Anne," Uncle Jimmy said, recovering from his coughing fit and shaking his head like I was a gonner. "Yer not exactly tha salesman type. It's not just yer stammer, luv, but ya don't meet people easy."

"The Virgin Mary's been talkin' t'her," Ma said, her tone matter-of-fact, like Mary was our next-door neighbor and we'd had a chat over the fence.

"This statue's been talkin' ta ya?" Uncle Jimmy said, glancing over his shoulder. "Our Lady of tha Belgian Waffle?" His forehead became a mass of pink furrows that disappeared into his washed-out red hair.

"No," I whispered. I didn't like the way this was going.

"She said tha Blessed Mother told 'er ta leave home," Ma chimed in.

"And 'ow does tha BVM appear ta ye, Agnes Anne?" Uncle Jimmy said, suppressing a grin. "Like a ghost?"

"She doesn't appear, Uncle Jimmy," I said, trying to keep my indignation in check. Ma started to snivel, and I watched her search for a tissue, first up one sleeve, then another. Opening her coat, she fished inside her dress and pulled two tissues out of the top of her bra.

"Agnes Anne's goin' ta leave us. I know she is." Ma shook her head and blew her nose. "But I donut t'ink she's ready. Nah yet. It's true she's been makin' progress wid her stutter 'n her shyness, but..."

"Now, now, Irene. That's wha' children are supposed ta do," Auntie Lucy said. "Someday they leave. Look 'ow old she is. It's time, I'd say." Auntie Lucy glanced at me as though she needed to make another assessment. "Yes," she said, giving me a quick nod and a wink. "'Tis time."

"How would ya know?" Ma snapped. "Yuv never 'ad any children and I've 'ad nine!"

"It wasn't fer lack of tryin', was it, luv?" Auntie Lucy looked at her husband with flirty amusement. Uncle Jimmy rolled his eyes.

"Nine," Ma said, again. She straightened her coat, tossed

her head and walked toward the Old Mission.

"Just 'cause yuv popped out babies like they were hen's eggs," Auntie Lucy called after her, "donut mean ya know anythin' more 'bout human nature."

"Is everything all right?" Father Mac said, coming up to us.

I wondered if Da had said something. Had Father made a special trip out here to calm the arguing O'Neils?

I glanced over at the mess next to the statue, the broken glass and the burned flowers. I fished a plastic bag out of my purse, went over to the jumble next to the wall and started to clean it up. This wasn't entirely altruistic. I didn't want to speak to Father Mac right then, and besides, I was embarrassed. Uncle Jimmy was going to make a big deal out of my real estate license, or the way I ticked off my father, or something else.

"This one's been talkin' ta tha Virgin Mary, Father," Uncle Jimmy said, pointing to me with his hitchhiking thumb.

"That's wonderful," Father Mac said, smiling. He draped his hands over his paunch, looking like a kindly Friar Tuck. "I wish more people would endeavor to have a relationship with Our Lady."

"Oh no, 'tisn't like tha'," Uncle Jimmy continued. "Irene said she's *talkin'* ta tha Blessed Mother and Mary *told* her ta leave home."

There it was. I had become his new stand-up comedy partner. I couldn't take it anymore. I would be leaving home soon, I reminded myself. I was going to get away from my family. Stop letting them use me as the butt of jokes. I crouched lower over the broken glass and resisted the urge to cover my ears.

"Your brother's family has always had a Special Devotion to Our Lady," Father Mac said. The wonderment in his voice made it seem like miracles happened all the time over at our house.

"Well, Father," Uncle Jimmy continued, "tha Special Devotion over there 'as turned inta Mary Mania. No wonder Agnes Anne is all bollixed up. There are Marys in tha kitchen, in tha hallways, 'n bedrooms. Not a square inch over there doesn't 'ave a Mary in it. There's even a couple of Marys in

tha loo." Uncle Jimmy leaned close to Father Mac's ear, but I
could hear him plain enough. "I don't mind tellin' ya, Father,
it's hard to pee in there wid Mary watchin'." Uncle Jimmy
laughed like a demented leprechaun.

"Bruno! Katie!" Uncle Jimmy raised his arm in greeting.
"There ya are!"

Uncle Jimmy began his small talk all over again. How I
had ticked off my father. How the flowers started to burn.
How Mary told me to leave home.

"Good morning, Agnes," Bruno said, his voice deep and
resonant. I stood up and tried to walk around him. "New
suit?" he said. "I love you in blue! You look fantastic." He
kissed my cheek, I turned my face away and tried to move
toward Katie, but he held both my hands fast and squeezed
them. "You haven't been answering my messages," he
whispered.

Our eyes met, mine hostile, his inquisitive and probing.
Before I lost my breakfast on his feet, I broke away and went
to my sister, Katie.

"Hi," I said, giving her a hug. "Feeling better today?"

"Didn't sleep," she said. "Cramps."

Katie's face, the color of bread dough, sent a pang
through my heart. Was she wearing her old plaid high school
uniform skirt? Was that how thin she had become? Before I
could quiz her on what she thought was causing her cramps
and insomnia, Bruno took my sister's hand and walked her
toward the Old Mission. Stunned at his rudeness, hurt that I
couldn't have a word with her, I watched them stroll away
from me.

"What's wrong, luv?" Auntie Lucy said.

I shook my head. Everything was wrong. Why didn't
anyone else see it?

"Katie will be all right," Auntie Lucy said, watching them
walk towards the Old Mission. "After all, she lives with a
doctor. Bruno-god-love-him will see what's best. Don't ya
worry about tha'."

A cold early morning wind blew down from the fog and I
regretted I hadn't put on a coat. I turned around to gaze up
into the Virgin's face and quickly made a blessing. Auntie
Lucy followed suit.

"Where is everyone this mornin'?" she said. "I 'aven't

seen Luke 'r Fiona. I know Darcy 'n Domenic don't come up much from tha Peninsula on First Fridays, but why don't Matthew and Mark come over tha hill 'n 'ave mass wid us anymore? The family's fallin' apart, I tell ya. Well, come on, dearie, 'r we'll be late." Auntie Lucy grabbed my hand and tucked it around her arm. We started to walk up the block together.

"I t'ink it's grand you've got yer license, Aggie, but I wan' ta know. Just what did tha Virgin say ta ya?"

I looked at my aunt, at her puffy face, at the powder that didn't quite hide the fine squiggles of broken veins around the base of her nose.

"Was it Our Lady of tha Belgian Waffle who spoke to ya?" Auntie Lucy asked, with a quick jerk of her head. "Or one of them in the house?"

"It w-wasn't l-like that."

"Listen, luv," Auntie Lucy said, shaking me out of my misery. "Just one thing. If some night yer in communication with the Blessed Mother and... well, you have the chance... can you ask her somethin'?"

Auntie Lucy's face turned somber, her eyes serious. I wondered what she would possibly want me to ask the Virgin Mary that she couldn't ask herself. Her lips came close to my ear.

"Will ya be a dear," she whispered, "'n ask 'er fer some lottery numbers?"

3. Mass at Mission Dolores

EARLY MORNING MASS was held in the original Spanish Mission next to Mission Dolores Basilica. Auntie Lucy went to the pew where Uncle Jimmy was already seated. I walked by Bruno and Katie, who were chatting with Father Mac and slid in next to Ma. I turned around and waved to Katie, but she didn't see me. She walked straight up the aisle where Da was, looked up into the eyes of Father Junipero Serra, a doll-like statue on the side in the front, and said a prayer. I wanted her to sit with me. Even hoped Da would slide in, but he was up there as well, drifting around the small chapel, visiting saints like they were old friends.

With anything religious, Da's attention was fanatic. As though the journey to Heaven were an ecclesiastical football game, Da even made charts and graphs showing how many times we had attended mass on First Fridays. The record book went back to before I was born. There were a lot of pages leading up to 2012. It's pretty strange to look through his Novena Book and note that in 1990, the year we emigrated from Ireland, the whole family missed First Friday mass. Or that Uncle Jimmy blew it off in the summer of 1991. Of course, Da and Ma were the hands-down winners of what my brothers called The Novena Game. Uncle Jimmy and Aunt Lucy held a close second.

If Da didn't see us at Mission Dolores, he asked each one of us if we had attended mass that morning. Each month, if my brothers didn't come over to Mission Dolores, they would recite both the church and the hour of the service they had attended. I was probably a bad person for even thinking this, but I wondered if they sometimes lied to please him.

I knelt in the pew and said my prayers, entreating God to make either Katie or Da hurry up and get in the pew, be a buffer between me and Bruno. Oblivious to my needs, Da still stared into the eyes of one of the saints up at the front of the chapel, his lips moving. Katie was up there too. Finally, both of them came back down the aisle.

Come on, Katie, I thought. *Hurry up.*

My heart sank. Bruno didn't wait for Katie. Instead, he slid in beside me and kept sliding. Bruno came so close I could feel the heat of his arm next to mine. Hot breath flowed across my ear.

"I need to see you today," he whispered. "Call me."

I ignored him and tilted my chin at a haughty angle. Bruno took a couple of knee-steps closer. I felt the warmth of his thigh seep through my skirt. Alarmed, I moved three knee-steps closer to Ma.

Ma munched at her prayers rabbit-like, her lips buried in her tented hands, her rosary festooned like a garland across her enlarged knuckles. She stopped her frenzied litany and gave me a sharp elbow. Bruno closed the gap I'd opened. The heat of his thigh burned into me. Choices had to be made. I took another knee step toward Ma.

"Stop it," Ma hissed. "I'm sayin' this rosary for *you,*

Agnes Anne... Career girl, indeed."

I wiggled away from her and ended up cuddling with Bruno, who now had the opportunity to coo in my ear, "When can we meet?"

My temper boiled. I was sick of Bruno always finding a way to humiliate me, even in church. I closed my eyes and prayed to the Blessed Mother to take this burden from me, a practice my parents called "Offering It Up."

As children, we were forced to do this Offering Up business all the time. It was their favorite punishment. "Agnes Anne O'Neil," my mother would say to me, "You've made Mary cry. I want ya to go ta yer room, pray ta tha Virgin Mary, 'n Offer This Up." As I grew older, I found I liked this practice. I liked getting rid of whatever bothered me and sending it up to either Jesus or Mary.

When I was ten, I pictured Jesus and Mary living together in a huge heavenly mansion. I wondered what they did with all this pain and suffering everyone kept sending them. I imagined it seeped up through their floors and rushed in through their windows. Could Mary somehow sweep it away? What if one day, Jesus needed his skis or something and he opened a closet and all the pain and suffering built up over the ages came thundering out like a raging river? What would Jesus and Mary do then? Could they send it along to someone else? Did Gods have Gods? My parents could never answer these questions. "Agnes Anne," they'd say, "don't t'ink so much. Accept tha' God loves ya. Simple as that."

Bruno's hot breath wafted across my neck. "So are you going to call me?"

I shook my head and pretended to pray, if only I had the power to make him disappear. My eyes found Saint Michael the Archangel, the largest statue inside the old Mission. Saint Michael stood center stage way on top of the reredos, the ornamental screen covering the wall in back of the altar. I wished I had a sword like his and had permission to use it. I would stab Bruno the way Saint Michael stabbed the devil rising up under his foot. Yes, that was it. I'd stab and stab and stab.

"I've got to see you, Agnes. It's about Katie."

Something in his tone made me look into his eyes.

"What's wrong?" I whispered.

"Later," he mumbled out of the side of his mouth.

I knew Katie was still depressed about her miscarriage. Why wasn't she snapping out of it? Why was she losing so much weight? Why was she so pale?

My mind wandered through all sorts of scenarios. Did Katie have cancer? Could Bruno be protecting us by not telling us her diagnosis? Doctors are like that. People were so obsessed with privacy now. Could it be against the law for him to tell us? No one in our family ever had any privacy so I didn't see that it was necessary now. I leaned forward so I could see Katie, maybe catch her eye, but she was praying. Her blonde hair drooped forward, covering her face like a silken scarf.

Bruno leaned his head down until he interrupted my gaze, his eye blizzard-blue. "Coffee," he mouthed. "Today."

I felt the jab of Ma's elbow, the sound of a snake hissing in my ear.

"Shhh," she said. This time she meant both of us.

The congregation stood. Mass had begun. Father MacBean sang as he came up the aisle and the gathered faithful picked up the tune. It was Tantum Ergo, a real 13th century hit. Probably tipped the top of the charts back then. The assembly sang it like a dirge, as though they slogged painfully through knee-deep molten cheese and were too polite to scream.

Bruno was still staring at the side of my face, so I gazed up above the crucifix, back up to Saint Michael the Archangel, and admired his sword. Gross to be thinking of killing in church. And I don't mean to imply that I would actually kill Bruno. That would be a terrible sin. Although not, in my opinion, a particular loss to mankind. But meditating on Saint Michael's raised sword was almost comforting. It meant one could confront enemies and succeed.

I thought about my mistake, about not telling my parents what happened that teenage night in Bruno's car twelve years ago. I imagined the sword impaling the secret. Deflating it. I wished I could turn back the clock. Say no when he had asked me to leave the dance and go out to the parking lot. Shame still engulfed me when I remembered coming home and repairing the rip in my dress, terrified that someone—my mother or my sisters—would realize that I had returned without underpants.

I had wanted to tell. But when I tried to, or even hinted that Bruno wasn't the person he pretended to be, it sounded like I was jealous because two weeks after the prom he had chosen my sister Katie over me. The two of them began to date. Bruno was quite a catch, he was in college and pre-med. On weekends they walked around like they were joined at the hip. I heard words like "sour grapes" and received lectures from Ma about the Sin of Pride, as well as a good teasing from my family that I had been thrown over by my sister.

When the congregation sat down for the first reading, Bruno wiggled toward me again, his butt next to mine. I squirmed toward Ma until she delivered another elbow to my ribcage. Why couldn't she see what was happening? Why didn't Katie care that Bruno wasn't paying attention to her but kept moving toward me?

I turned to Bruno and met his stare and conjured up the worst frown I could muster. The back of his hand deliberately grazed my thigh.

"Stop it," I said, under my breath. I pushed him away with the side of my arm.

"Stop botherin' Bruno," Ma hissed.

I tried to distract myself by listening to the readings, but my mind drifted away and I imagined myself at work in the not-so-distant future. I tried to picture myself as the top salesman. I would be sitting in the prized corner office surrounded by elegance. No hand-me-downs. None of that this-will-do-for-now stuff for me. My office would have expensive furniture arranged by a decorator. I pictured myself sitting in that office and doing deals. Big real estate deals. Verna Korbel, the current top salesman, would be out in cubicles with the other agents and giving me the stink-eye.

We stood. It was time to hold hands and say the Lord's Prayer. Ma grabbed my right hand. I reluctantly gave Bruno my left.

After the Lord's Prayer, we're all supposed to greet each other. it's called the Sign of Christ's Peace. In our family we give kisses to family members, shake hands with strangers. I kissed Ma, then immediately shook hands with the people in the pew in front of us and the people behind us, always saying the customary, "Peace be with you." I shook hands with an Hispanic lady and her husband, two Anglo ladies who looked like ex-nuns, and greeted Mr. Fiori, a neighborhood gentleman who comes every day to mass like Da does. I could feel Bruno's hand on my shoulder. He turned me around and hugged me tightly, kissing me behind my ear. Over his shoulder I looked into Katie's vacant eyes. What was wrong with her? When Bruno released me there were only a few seconds left to give Katie a quick hug. To outsiders we must have appeared like a normal family. A family without secrets.

4. Coffee with Bruno

MID-MORNING AT O'NEIL & CO. and Da still avoided me. Every time I walked his way so we could have the Big Conversation and iron out the details of my transfer to the sales department, he turned his back and slammed his office door. I tried to be casual on my way back to my desk, but actually I was obsessing that I would be stuck at that green Formica-topped desk for the rest of my life. The phone interrupted this miserable daydream.

"Hey," Bruno said.

"Hey," I said back, surprised, and yet not, that he called.

"Can you get away? I'm up the street."

I was an hourly employee and wasn't supposed to leave the office. Was I going to wait for other people to give me permission to live? To work? To breathe? Seeing Bruno was a poor excuse to go AWOL, but when I thought of Katie's pallor, her terrible thinness, I hung up the phone, grabbed my purse, and left my desk.

When I marched by Pansy the receptionist, she blinked in that stupid Betty Boop way of hers. She probably expected me to tell her where I was going, but I didn't say anything. Soon I wouldn't be an hourly employee. Anyway, it was none of her business.

The coffee shop was on 24th Street, one of those trendy places with biscotti for sale in cellophane bags and singles looking for a date. On the way, my mind went into hyperdrive. I tried to stay positive, but the more I thought about Katie's pale face, the more apprehensive I became. Did Bruno want to tell me that she had a major disease? For good luck, I said a quick prayer to Saint Agnes, my namesake and patron saint of young women. I said another to the Blessed Mother.

The aroma of fresh brewed coffee surrounded me the moment I entered the shop. I spotted Bruno. His broad smile made a current of electricity, the dangerous kind, run through me. If I didn't know him and this had been the first time I let my eyes glide over his strong jaw or the shock of blond hair edging over one eyebrow, I might have been intrigued. But I knew him too well. To me, his looks seemed reptilian, like the monster on that other Holy Card of mine, the one with Saint George.

Bruno, now out of his sports coat, wore a golf sweater over his white collared shirt. He motioned me over to a tall table and had already ordered. Not coffee in cardboard cups, but two lattes with sprinkles in thick brown china cups sat on the tabletop.

"Everything okay?" I said, climbing up on the stool, dreading the reason he had called this meeting. Bruno's skin looked waxy and his granite-blue eyes didn't seem to blink. I thought of Katie, and a pang knifed through my heart. What terrible news would he tell me? Did she have chronic fatigue syndrome? Lupus? Cancer? Another doomed pregnancy? While the heady odor of coffee swirled around me, my fingers trembled. "What's wr-wr-wrong?" I asked.

"Nothing's wrong," he said, smoothly. "At least, not anymore." His smile slid up one side of his face like he was the cat burglar and just scored a heist.

"What's wrong with Katie?" I asked. "She looked terrible this morning."

"A morning like all others," he said. I noticed the flick of his eyebrows, the strain in his jaw. Bruno tossed a shock of hair out of his eyes and tilted his head to one side.

His stare made me uncomfortable. I avoided his gaze and picked up my coffee and took a foamy sip. The heady flavor of newly roasted coffee filled my senses. I wished I could enjoy this latte all by myself.

"What does Katie have?" I said, putting down my cup.

"Let's just say," Bruno said, stirring artificial sweetener

into his latte, "she's really not very well right now and there's not much we can do about it."

I watched the foam in his cup swirl like something a television weatherman might draw to indicate a class five hurricane. He licked his spoon and I winced at his bad manners.

"So what is it?" I asked. "W-what's g-going on?" My stutter had returned. I flashed on my next appointment with Miss Allison and how I would tell her about this recurrence.

Bruno didn't speak, but his eyes were on me again, so I looked elsewhere and said a quick prayer to Saint Raymond, patron saint of secrets. San Ramon, as the Spanish called him, had a hot poker put through his lips and a lock snapped through them. Sometimes I felt the weight of that lock, not only on my lips, but on my heart. If Katie had something terminal, I had to be strong enough to bear it with her.

"*You* know what's wrong," he whispered.

Bruno's smile revealed no teeth and the broadness of it made me again think of a dragon. I didn't know what he was talking about and a kernel of embarrassment took root. Was there information that went around the family that I missed? Did everyone else know except me?

"No, I don't know," I stammered. "W-what's wrong with her? Tell me."

Bruno let a long beat of silence stretch languidly between us. What could a person have that would make them look as pale, skinny, and sickly as my sister? When I was just about to burst, Bruno interrupted and said one, blunt word.

"Us."

For a second, I thought I misheard. Us? His expression told me I had heard correctly. Us meant us. *The two of us.* My tongue became the Sahara Desert, my throat, a dry well. He leaned forward over his latte and tried to catch my eye. Humiliated, I looked at spots of dried coffee on the tabletop.

"You've changed, Agnes," he said. "I don't know what it is about you lately, but you've changed."

"That's stupid," I said, still avoiding his eyes. "Tell me what's wr-wrong with Katie, right now. Quit beating around the b-bush. Just tell me."

He shook his head in a way that made me feel dim-witted.

"I wouldn't mind beating around a couple of bushes with *you*."

Anger bubbled in my midsection. I couldn't look at him.

"I'm sorry," he said. "I'm playing with you. You're upset about Katie and I'll tell you, Agnes. It's pretty simple. She's just not coming out of her miscarriage funk. That's all it is. She's on hormones now to correct the imbalance. She also has digestive problems. Eating problems." He shrugged again, dismissing my concern. "She has to want to get well. I can't do it for her."

"Why don't you take her to a—" I stopped myself from saying "doctor," because, after all, he was one. But Bruno was an Emergency Room doctor, not a specialist.

"Christ, Agnes, lately I find myself dreaming about you! Did you know that? You and your goddamned perfect body and the chance I had... " He shook his head.

I could feel my face gathering color. I turned away. I longed to be the girl behind the counter who ran the espresso machine and pulled that big arm down and listened to the noise, got to see the froth bubble up in the pitcher. I wanted to be that woman over in the corner reading the newspaper. Despite these efforts to distract myself, my face ignited into crimson flames. I stammered again, my words tripping over each other as I asked him if that's why he had come here, to tell me this nonsense.

"You're twenty-eight years old," he said, his voice runny and smooth as melted chocolate. "And you're still a virgin, aren't you?"

"It's none of your business," I snapped. His smirk turned my stomach and reminded me of everything bad that had ever happened between us.

"God," he moaned. "Do you know how you torture me? Every First Friday I have to look across the dinner table at you and remember that night. I could have had you that night! I had the chance... and I blew it." His fist lightly pounded the table. "Things could have been so different."

"You're nuts," I hissed. "I would n-never be with someone who... s-s-someone who... "

"I never forced you." His eyes darted around to see if the other patrons had overheard, then he put his hand to the side of his face to shelter his words. "You wanted it, Agnes. Don't blame me. That was a long time ago, but you wanted it, too."

I clamped my teeth together so hard my jaw ached. I would not cry. I would never give Bruno Stark the satisfaction of seeing me break down. Why did something that happened twelve years ago still bring tears to my eyes?

"You pushed me into the back of your car like I was some cheap—" My words must have had some impact on him, because this time, it was Bruno who looked away.

"I was only sixteen!" I hissed. *"I trusted you."*

Memories of struggling, of hitting him, of him hitting me, of twisting and thrashing boiled to the surface. I thought I had put all of this to rest. I had certainly worked hard at it. Had all this emotion merely been lurking below the surface? I remembered how the stain of sin had loomed over me after that night. Having sex in the back seat of a car was not what I had wanted. I felt it was my fault, even though I knew it wasn't. And yet I was the one who had agreed to go out into the parking lot. So it was my fault, too. *My most grievous fault.*

Boys had come out to have their smokes and someone must have spotted us because they surrounded the car and began to bounce on the bumpers.

"Ride 'em cowboy!" someone had whooped.

Then all the boys picked up the chant. Bruno cursed at them, which gave me the chance to wriggle away and throw myself on the floor of the car and hug my knees, my spine curled over like I was practicing for an earthquake drill. I prayed no one could see me in my shame and in my mind I called out for Jesus, for Mary, for Joseph, for any saint who could hear me. The boys jeered, rocking the car as they jumped up and down.

Odd as it might sound, I actually gave thanks for those horrid boys. They were the distraction that ended this unfortunate ordeal and, in a way, split my life in two. From that day on, there was always a Before and an After. I ended up stuck somewhere in between, imploring Mary the Blessed Virgin to heal my broken heart and San Ramon to help me keep my secret safe.

My prayers to the Blessed Virgin had been incessant. I prayed for Bruno to apologize. I prayed to go back in time and for him to love me the way he had at the beginning of the dance, before everything had gone wrong.

"Agnes," Bruno whispered, "we were just kids. I'm really, really sorry for what happened that night. It was all bungled up, but that was a long time ago—back in the Dark Ages. You know, guys at that age don't have a completely developed dorsal lateral prefrontal cortex."

A dorsal lateral what?

While I choked on fury, I watched Bruno calmly take a deep swallow of his coffee.

"Oh," he said, with a disconcerting chuckle. "I guess you're still mad that I married your sister."

I nearly threw my coffee in his face.

"Lately," Bruno said, his voice turning into a milky foam, as slick and sweet as the top of my cooling latte, "I feel like I'm back in school or something. I can't stop thinking about you. All day long, you're on my mind."

Had that been the way it was? Had he once thought about me all the time? But for me, high school had been lost in a tangle of scars and bad memories.

"Hey," he said. "Are you even listening to me?"

The sprinkles on my latte were melting. They made pockmarks in the foam, the chocolate bits disappeared into the froth like insects burrowing in white sand. I longed to go with them.

"Look at me, Agnes," Bruno said. "Look at me. Where are you? Talking to your saints? Praying to your namesake?"

Ire prickled across my skin. This time I met his gaze, dead-on. "Saint Agnes is also the patron saint of rape victims," I said, glaring at him, daring him to contradict me.

"Wait a second. I never—" He leaned over the table, his whisper, hoarse. "We didn't consummate anything that night. How could we? You started to panic and your hymen was bolted shut." He saw my disgust and quickly added, "Okay, okay. It turned out all wrong. I'll say I'm sorry *again*. Is that what you want to hear? Is that better? I'm sorry. I'm truly sorry, Agnes, but I never—"

My look silenced him.

"Is that why you've never gone with anyone else all these years? Why you're so inward? So shy? After all this time, you're still blaming me?"

I had never thought of it that way. When I had confessed to Father Mac, the terms I had used back then were broad.

Since I thought it was my fault too, I told the priest I had engaged in "inappropriate behavior." I received the perfunctory dollop of absolution and a small lecture, my penance a few Our Fathers and a couple of Hail Marys.

"Hey, we're consenting adults now." Bruno sat up straighter. He leaned the side of his face on his fist, as though he might be posing for a portrait.

"You d-disgust me," I whispered.

"Don't take it like that." Bruno fought with his paper napkin. "Look, I'll admit I was stupid and clumsy back then. I was a screwy college kid and you had the best tits around. Jesus," he mumbled, "can you blame me? You still have a great bod. Hey," he said, moving his head around, trying to get me to look at him. "It's a compliment. Why can't you lighten up?"

What did he expect me to say? That everything was forgiven? He ripped my prom dress, assaulted my body like I was a worthless whore, and when I ran out of the parking lot to make my way home, he came after me. I wouldn't get in his car, but while I walked alone for a couple of blocks, my chiffon prom dress dripping from the heavy fog, he coasted beside me in his Mustang.

He kept calling to me to get in and when I wouldn't, he stopped, got out of the car and physically threw me in. He said if I ever told anyone what happened, he would deny it. He was applying to med school and nothing was going to ruin his chances. He said if I told, he would run me over in the street. One look into his icy blue eyes and I believed him.

The next day, I couldn't get out of bed. I thought about the way everything had turned upside down. Ma thought I had the flu and kept me home for a few days. When I started school again, I found that Bruno had picked up with my older sister, Katie. She chatted on the phone with him five times a day and when she passed me in the hallways at school, she grinned like she had one-upped me in a game of badminton.

I stopped trusting boys. Stopped trusting Katie. Trusting anyone. Even I, myself, had proven to be unreliable. I couldn't seem to find solid ground. I started to stutter. My grades fell. I got a case of acne that should have made the medical books. Now years later, after all the turmoil had been settled, Katie and I were close again. Now Bruno thought all he had to say was, *Oops. Sorry. Nothing I've ever done counted because my freaking lateral cortex was out of whack?*

Bruno cleared his throat and sucked at his lips as though they were coated with sugar.

"Agnes, I come home each night to a sickly woman who constantly complains. We haven't had sex in months. I need a little cheering up. Why can't you be nice to me? You used to be fun."

Had I once been fun? Did I laugh and make jokes back then? Was I ever a giddy teen who did silly things? I stared at his face and noticed the way he was aging. Bruno's hair was thinner now, his forehead deeper and higher, his cheeks fuller. Someday he would have jowls.

Bruno reached out and covered my hand with his. I resisted the warmth that flowed down from his broad palm and slender fingers, the hand of an ER doc, the guy who sews people up after accidents.

"What I wanted to say to you... is that... I'm sorry for everything that happened between us. I know now... I married the wrong sister."

My entire body jerked and I expected to hear the sound of shattering glass. Bruno was still speaking because I saw his mouth moving, but the sound fell somewhere else.

"You don't love Katie anymore?" I said, through trembling lips. "And you don't care that she's sick?"

"I didn't say that."

"Yes, you did."

He picked at small balls of lint on the sleeve of his baby blue sweater. It made him look like a regular person, someone who was normal, who might be having a casual conversation. But before my eyes, Bruno had morphed into that old monster, that dreadful fiend I still saw in my dreams.

"You don't love her anymore."

"That's not entirely true." He flicked the fluff ball he'd been picking at and watched it drift away.

"So which part is true and which isn't? You love her sometimes, but not when things get tough?"

Bruno's face pushed forward into a pout and he blinked in rapid succession. "I do my best," he said. His eyes filled with mist. "I do my—"

I grabbed my teaspoon from my saucer and with all my might, hammered it down on the table as though I pounded a nail. Several patrons turned our way.

"Try harder," I whispered between my teeth. "Take her to a specialist. Take her for a complete examination. For godsakes, find out what's wrong with her."

"You don't think I have?" he said. His voice rose, his face a snapshot of fury.

I stared into his steely eyes and watched a muscle at the hinge of his jaw throb one, two, three, four times.

"It's you I love," he whispered. "Did you know that I still have your panties from that night?"

Gross! I jumped off the stool. I couldn't look at him. I picked up my purse and darted for the door. An explosion of hate and old emotions fizzed and popped inside my head. I didn't care that hate was a sin. I welcomed it. And if that burden of vile thorns sent me to Hell, I would go willingly. I would never give up my disdain for this man, for hate was the cloak that covered my shame.

5. Sanctuary

I MARRIED THE WRONG SISTER. I married the wrong sister. I married the wrong sister. The words echoed in my head to the rhythm of my clicking high heels. At times I ran. Then I walked. After a block, I was out of breath. I stopped in front of a manicure shop. The sign read, "Walk-Ins Welcome." I glanced up the street, worried that Bruno might come out of the coffee shop any second. Run after me.

Gazing past the glare of the windows, I could see open stations. I needed sanctuary. I glanced up the block. Bruno was coming out of the coffee shop. In a panic, I grabbed the door handle, twisted it, pulled it, pushed it, shook it like a burglar and when the door finally opened, I practically fell inside.

The sound of jangling bells heralded my entrance. Closing the door with a bang, I fought the urge to throw the lock and lean against the door with relief. A lady in a flowery apron smiled and came toward me drying her hands.

"Welcome to Pretty Nail Town," she said. "What culla?

What culla you want today?" She took my trembling hand and examined my fingernails, then looked up into my eyes. "You very nervous lady."

I swallowed hard. She had no idea.

"We take care of you. You sit down, you poo' ting. Relax."

I glanced at the window. Could Bruno see me in here? If he did, would he come in?

"Manicure and pedicure today? That what you need. Look at your nails," she said, clicking her tongue and inspecting my hand more closely. "You a mess."

I felt myself blush, ashamed that I bit my nails, chewed on the cuticles, and picked at the nails that split. Then I heard a familiar voice.

"Zo, Agg-nez, you are finally taking care of your nailz? Goot. Goot for you. Zey are in bat shape. Dizgusting, az a matter of fact."

It was Verna Korbel, the top salesman at O'Neil & Co. She was originally from Germany and when Verna spoke, all of her s's turned to z's, all of her w's to v's, and d's to t's. At first, I had a hard time understanding her, but it's like Pig Latin, once you know the rules it's easy to catch on.

Perfectly groomed, expensively dressed, I always admired the number of contracts she closed. I followed her career the way some people admire baseball or football players and longed to have some of Verna's abilities, even prayed for them. If I could be one tenth as successful as Verna Korbel, I would have all the money I ever needed. Actually, I wanted to be her assistant, but she was so frightening, so fearsome and intimidating that I didn't know if I would ever have the nerve to ask her. Besides, she hated me.

"Aren't you going to zay hello?" Verna said, shifting her weight in the overstuffed salon chair.

I watched the way her long legs stayed parallel to each other, the way her black hair never seemed out of place. I wondered how she accomplished it. I was lucky to keep my dropped ponytail together. I couldn't imagine sweeping my hair up into a French twist and making it stay there all day.

"Um. Hi, Verna. How are you?"

"Perfect. But I am alvays perfect," Verna said, holding her head unnaturally high. "It's everyvon else who is imperfect.

But I manage to tolerate everyvon." This, I knew, was Verna's sense of humor.

The nail lady brought me over to a salon chair opposite Verna's. I was grateful that if Bruno did walk by the front window, he wouldn't be able to see me.

The nail lady massaged one of my hands and the sweet scent of jasmine wafted around me. Her undulating touch, so comforting and gentle, nearly brought me to tears.

Verna admonished her manicurist not to get nail polish on her cuticles. I hunkered down and tried to be invisible, which was pretty difficult. We were the only two customers in the shop.

"Zo, Agg-nez," Verna said, raising her voice. "Vy are you here during zee day? I never zee you here. I never zee you go out at all. Dit you tell Pansy zat you hat a doctor's appointment? Had to zee Dr. Nailz?" Her throaty laugh filled the room.

I knew what she was really saying. I wasn't supposed to leave my desk during the day. One of the agents might need me. They might be searching for me right now. I thought of fabricating an excuse, but the cyclone of fury from coffee with Bruno rolled like thunder inside my head.

"Vell?" Verna said. "How did you escape?"

"I-I—just walked out," I blurted. "I was sick of sitting there." I should have divulged the news about my real estate license, but the urge to tell her dried on my tongue.

Verna's violet-blue eyes held onto my face.

"I just n-needed a m-m-manicure," I fumbled.

"You hav alvayz needed a manicure," Verna said. "So zis turned out to be zee big day, eh? Manicure Day. Ve should write it up in zee O'Neil Newsletter. Agg-nez Ahnne Haz a Manicure."

"As good a day as any," I said, mustering up merriment from the pit of my acid stomach.

"Goot. Goot for you, Agg-nez. Unt I von't tell your fazher zat you are here entjoying yourself. If you don't take zee initiative, you know, you never get anyvere in life."

I nodded, surprised that now two manicurists, each holding one of my hands, rubbed my nails with polish remover, even though I didn't have any nail polish on.

"What culla?" the chief manicurist said, again.

I stared into her deep almond brown eyes and envied her clear skin, her high cheek bones, the perfect oval of her face, as well as her small nose and delicate chin. I was born into the wrong race. Why couldn't I have been Asian?

Another lady brought me a tray of colors, some of which were disgusting. Green. Orange. Brown. I wouldn't even wear those colors for Halloween.

"Try two thirty-two," Verna commanded.

One of the manicurists handed me a fire-engine red bottle. I winced. It was so not me.

"You muzt try it. It iz vonderful." Verna's R's rumbled from the back of her throat. "It makes me feel powerful to wear zuch a bright red."

"Pedicure?" one of the manicurists asked.

I don't know why, but I nodded. Two more ladies trotted over and rolled up my pant legs, removed my shoes and my knee-highs, then each lady grabbed a foot and began to massage my feet. I gave thanks that I had at least shaved my legs.

All this attention made me feel helpless and somewhat out of control. I had to relax. Stop my heart from pounding. Verna would have to leave soon, wouldn't she?

"What culla? What culla, lady? So many. You see?" The head manicurist wouldn't give up. "You still shaking. I have little doggie like you," she said, patting my hand. "Always nervous."

I married the wrong sister. Bruno's words still reverberated in my head. What would Da and Ma say? My brothers Matthew, Mark, and Luke? Would they be outraged at Bruno? Or blame me? And that thing about my underpants. Unspeakable. My sisters Fiona and Darcy, what would they think? The tale of Bruno dumping me for Katie still followed me like a shimmering ghost and somehow defined me in the family as the one who lost, the one whose feelings could be disregarded and trivialized. What made me think things would ever change?

"Relax, lady." She tapped me on the back of my hand. "You just rob a bank? You so nervous! Think about culla. What culla you want? This one nice." The manicurist raised one of the nail polish bottles and shook it like a bell. The pink iridescence seemed to pulse. Maybe it was radioactive.

"Round or square?" another manicurist asked.

What was she was talking about?

"Tip of nail round like this? Or square like this?" She tapped her nail file on a demonstration board. I stared at the huge fake fingernails. One with a rounded tip. One squared off.

Then I recalled Pansy the receptionist had round nails. My sister Darcy's were square. I remembered why I hated salons. All this silliness over trivia. I craned my neck and glanced over at Verna's nails. They were round.

"Round," I said.

"Good." The chief manicurist seemed pleased she had made progress. "Now what culla?"

I wanted to shove a pie in her face.

Someone placed another long tray of nail polish bottles beside me the shades of Christmas candy. Someone else passed another tray with brighter colors reminiscent of gum balls. Each color bore a number. I stared at the myriad of colors and I wished that Bruno would clutch his heart and die.

Mary mother of God, wishing someone dead was a horrible sin.

My parents said there were mortal sins, venial sins, sins of commission and sins of omission. All of them disappointed our Lord and his mother, Mary. On the good side, every problem also has a solution, which frequently could be gained from a particular saint who dealt specifically with that arena of human nature or occupation. If you didn't want to bother Jesus, all you had to do was ask a saint for their intercession. I couldn't help it. I wanted Saint Michael to step on Bruno's back and shove his sword clear through his square head.

"This culla very populah." The manicurist held up a purple bottle, which seemed to be half full of glitter.

"Gott im himmel! No!" Verna said, peering now over my shoulder at the rows of polish.

"One twenty-one," I said, quickly.

"Goot choice, Agg-nez," Verna said. "Zee you back at zee office."

I turned to watch her leave and admired her black tweed suit, the way the vent pleats at the back sprung out like a rooster tail. I loved her two-tone black and silvery grey shoes. Everything about Verna screamed expensive. I turned away and handed the nail polish bottle to the manicurist. I expected trumpets to blare.

"Very pretty," she said, dipping her brush first into a foul smelling chemical then in white powder and bringing it over to my hand. I watched her create a new nail, a longer nail, gliding over a fake nail she had already glued into place. Fake on fake. Is this what I was becoming? Hiding my brother-in-law's advances, pretending they didn't exist so I could protect my sister?

The manicurists and pedicurists continued their treatment, filing down my calluses, washing away the dead skin on my feet when the head manicurist flipped a switch and my chair began to vibrate and warm me like a hot bath. I closed my eyes, took a deep breath and let the heat penetrate, let it thaw my leg muscles, and soothe my aching back.

I wondered what advice Mary the Blessed Mother might give me now, now after Bruno had verbally abandoned his marriage vows. A thought came to me in a blaze of inspiration. *What if I could convince Katie to leave Bruno?*

Dreams of the apartment I would have one day danced not in shimmering fantasy, but now took on an urgent need. If Katie left him, she could move in with me! But would she blame me for breaking them up? I must have drifted off to sleep at this point, because the next thing I knew, the lady in the flowery apron gently slapped my hand.

"Coffee, lady? Man want to know if you want Stah-buk. He regula' customah. Buy for whole salon." She winked. "He nice man."

I opened my eyes. The salon chair had been leaned back into a chaise and I had fallen asleep. My nails were gigantic berry-colored claws. I gazed over at my raspberry toenails. A nerdy guy with curly hair and glasses seemed to be leaning over me, his mouth moving. Was he speaking to me? It sounded like he might be asking if I wanted a cup of coffee. I worried that while I was asleep, my jaw might have fallen open and, at this very second, drool could be running down my blouse. I shivered with embarrassment.

"Would you like a cup of coffee?" the curly haired guy said.

A jolt of caffeine sounded too good to pass up. I certainly didn't get much coffee when I saw Bruno, so I nodded.

"What kind would you like?" he asked.

I knew I was supposed to rattle off some lingo like "Bring me a frappa-frappa, mocha grande with a soy back-flip." But I never went into that coffee shop because it humiliated me to stutter and stammer with a line of people behind me listening. I like to go into a shop where, "Small coffee to go, please," makes perfect sense.

"Latte?" he prompted.

A latte would have reminded me of Bruno. "Coffee with cream," I said. Then I remembered to say, "Please."

"Grande? Tall?"

"Just... n-n-normal," I said, knowing there was a difference, but not sure of what it was.

"Tall," he said.

"No, small."

"Tall is small," he said, smiling. It was a kind smile, but I thought he might be laughing at me. "What's your name?" he said. "I haven't seen you in here before."

"A-Anne." I gulped and took a breath. I didn't know what possessed me right then to try out a new name, my middle name, the name I secretly always wanted. Blame it on my ridiculous raspberry nails. Blame it on my real estate license. Blame it on Bruno making me want to be someone else. Anyone else but Ugly Agnes, sister-in-law of creepy Dr. Bruno Stark.

"Anne O'Neil," I repeated, embarrassed that my words came out too loud.

"O'Neil? Like the real estate company up the street?"

I smiled and nodded. I wondered if he noticed my blush.

"They helped me buy a parking pad a couple of years ago."

Not knowing what to say, I nodded again.

"Small deal. No one probably remembers. I went in there several times. I don't remember seeing you," he said, over his shoulder.

How could he? I was in the back office.

Somehow it surprised me when Curly returned laden with coffees for all the women in the shop. I had been asleep so long that the shop had filled up with people. Was he one of the manicurists too? The owner? His extravagance stunned me.

"Here you go, Ginny," he said to the head manicurist. Then he passed out the other coffees to the rest of the ladies, calling each of them by name.

I worried that my claws weren't quite dry and, to grip the cup, I stuck my fingers out like they were coated with something that smelled bad. Curly pulled up the chair that one of the manicurists had vacated and sat down next to me. He asked me for my business card, but I wasn't an agent yet and didn't have one. To get past this humiliation, I pretended that to even search for my card would ruin my nails.

Maybe that was why I chattered so much—I wasn't myself. Or maybe I went on because I was afraid Bruno might be lurking out there on the street and like some filibustering senator, I kept the conversation going by asking questions. Answering his. It wasn't like me to be talkative. Wasn't like me at all. But it wasn't like me to have brightly-colored fingernails and toes either.

To my utter surprise, this guy, who told me his name was Sheldon, asked me out to dinner. I didn't care that he hung out in a nail salon and might be gay or that he was complete stranger. I wanted to go out with him, but Mary, mother of God, how could I accept? Tonight was First Friday.

6. Dressed for Success

WHEN I LEFT PRETTY NAIL TOWN, I felt like Dorothy starting off on her journey to Oz, skipping down the Yellow Brick Road. My nails were long and the color of summer berries. Someone called me Anne instead of Agnes. And that same someone asked me for a date. I was so giddy that I actually wasn't thinking about that dreadful coffee scene with Bruno. When I passed a store with a bunch of briefcases in the window, I stopped to gaze. I saw a feminine one that resembled a long purse and I couldn't stop admiring it. I stared at it for so many minutes that the shopkeeper came outside.

"If you're looking at something that long and that hard," he said, through a chuckle, "I think you owe it to yourself to come in and check it out."

Even from the window, the smell of new leather practically intoxicated me. As though I had fallen into a leather-induced trance, I followed the salesman inside.

"Black, brown, cordovan, or aubergine?" the salesman said removing the briefcase from the window.

"What's aubergine?" I asked, remembering my Marilyn Monroe gush so I wouldn't stumble over my words.

"Eggplant," he said, opening the window case with a key from his pocket. He paused and turned back to me, waiting for my instruction.

I had already made too many color decisions today. In the silence, the salesman eyed me up and down.

"Try this," he said, bringing out the aubergine briefcase. "It goes well with your nails."

"Oh," I said, my eyes flicked from the case to my nails and back.

He set the case on a low counter before me. I practically salivated as my hand ran along the side of the case, the leather so supple it felt like silk. My hand gravitated to the zipper tab and I felt the smoothness of the ride down the center channel where the zipper lay recessed. Inside the case, I inspected the two velvety compartments, one for documents and another slot for a laptop computer, not too wide and yet not too small. There were rounded puffs blossoming out of one of the inside walls for pens and another place for business cards, even a place for ID and credit cards. I became captivated by the fine workmanship, hypnotized by the extra pockets for tablets and the little poufy netting topped by a zipper for odds and ends.

In a sudden lurch of excitement and daring, my right hand dipped into my own bag, located my wallet, and extracted my only credit card. I avoided credit.

The trouble with credit cards is that you have to pay the company back and if I used my credit card this month, I wouldn't be able to save as much. A pang went through my center and I thought of thanking the clerk and leaving the store, but when I imagined myself leaving behind this gorgeous briefcase, this high fashion purse with its retractable handles, long thick strap, and golden zipper fob, I felt even worse.

The credit card moved toward the clerk. What was I doing? I couldn't afford this luxury, and yet a voice inside me said this purchase wasn't an extravagance. It was a *professional* expense. Just inhaling the air around this briefcase was enough to stimulate me into the fearlessness of launching my new career. I had to use my real estate license and if my father wouldn't let me become a salesman, I would hold my head high and carry this beautiful briefcase into another real estate company and apply for a job.

As he rang up the purchase, I asked the salesman if he could please clip off the tags. Then I carefully slipped my pens into the small fitted loops, my wallet and makeup bag into one of the compartments for folders and stuffed my collapsed purse where the laptop computer should be. Hoisting the long flat strap onto my shoulder, I thanked the salesman.

"Looks nice," he said, with a wink. "You can have that zipper fob engraved, you know. It's gold plate." He smiled like he was advertising toothpaste. "You look like a million dollars."

I smiled back, my face only blushing slightly, not out of embarrassment, but out of a keen sense of excitement.

"Wait," he said. He slid the scarf from my neck. "May I?"

Surprised that he did something so personal, yet curious, I watched him fold it longwise and in a wink, he re-tucked it around my neck, then adjusted my collar so that a strip of the scarf stuck out below either side of my lapel.

"That looks better." He turned me around so I could see into a mirror behind a display of handbags.

"Thanks," I said, wondering why I had never thought to do this myself. "I love it. You have a flair for this."

"Yes, I do," he said, with a wink. "Now you're set. Great briefcase. Nice outfit. Go out and conquer the day."

Hail Mary, full of grace, thank you for this briefcase.

I marched up the street, entered O'Neil & Co. like I owned the place, and blew right by Pansy the receptionist. She looked so surprised to see me, she might have swallowed her gum. I strutted straight into Da's office, plunked my new briefcase on top of his desk, and leaned toward him.

"So," I said, "when do I start?"

"Agnes Anne, you don't really except me to—"

From behind me, there came a voice.

"Nize caze, Agg-nez." As though the fragrance of new leather had put Verna Korbel into the same trance I had just experienced in the store, she strolled into Da's office and began to run her hands over my briefcase. She picked it up and turned it this way and that, admiring it from all angles. All the while, Da's eyes seemed to blaze bright as burning coals. I half-way expected to see smoke come out of his nostrils.

"I didn't zee zis before—" Our eyes met in silent conspiracy. "Goot color," Verna continued. "It vil go viz black unt viz brown."

"Did I tell you I got my real estate license?" I said to her, unable to stop myself, yet cringing inside as I took a sideways glance to watch the effect of my words on Da.

"You? You?" Verna's violet eyes grew even larger and her eyebrows rose in two identical black hoops. A look of conspiracy came over her, as though now she understood why I had come into the nail salon this morning. She probably thought I was in there to get a Good Luck manicure.

"Crazy as a cuckoo, this one." Da said, standing up. "She's not the sales type and look what she does—she gets a license."

I know he wanted to shoo us both out of his office, at least get my briefcase off his desk and rid himself of this female invasion.

"No, Mel," Verna said. "Not crazy. It iz shmart. Very shmart. Goot for you, Agg-nez. You didn't tell me." Verna tilted her head from one side to the other, looking at me with newfound interest. "She vil do vell, Mel. Agg-nez iz a hard verker."

I turned to Da and grinned without showing my teeth.

"Ach, the market is crap right now," Da said. "No time ta start a real estate career. And who has time ta train 'er?"

"I vil train her. I need zomeone to help me viz my listingz."

I thought Da's knees would buckle. Maybe they did because he sat back down into his big chair with a hefty plunk.

The timing of this was so wonderful, I nearly grabbed

both of Verna's hands and genuflected.

"Thank you, Verna. Thank you," I said, somewhat embarrassed that I was gushing.

Verna reached out and took hold of my dropped ponytail and held it out behind me like it was a head of celery.

"Rrrrreally, Agg-nez, you zhould do zomething vis zis hair of yourz. It iz boring. It iz tedious and unexziting. To be in zales, vee must drrrress for succeszz. You hav zee briefcase now, zo let zis ponytail be your next project."

"I-I-I'm planning to do something with my h-hair th-th-this weekend," I said, having had promised my sister Fiona that I would let her take me to her hair stylist, one of the many items on my list.

"Goot. Any style vil be a tremdouz improvement over ziz." Verna scowled again at my dropped ponytail with its neat black bow and turned to leave. But after a few steps, she turned around and smiled, not at me, but at my briefcase. I think I saw envy in her eyes. "Nize," she said, again, looking at the case. "Really nize."

I turned to my father, triumph dancing across my face. It felt like we were playing a game of gin rummy and I had just gone out and he still had a fistful of cards he could never play.

"Don't get cocky," he said, waggling a finger up at me. "Ya still have ta continue in the back office. I can't afford ta hire anyone right now an' I can't have everythin' go all sour because yuv gone off the beam."

"Okay." I nodded. "Then I'll get my salary *and* commission."

I watched Da turn purple.

"Yer makin' a mistake, Agnes Anne O'Neil. Yer tryin' for somethin' out a' your nature. This sales business is wrong for ya. I donna' want ta see ya crash."

"I won't crash, Da."

Da waved his hand like his office had suddenly filled up with horse flies. I reached for my briefcase, spun on my heel Verna-style, and did my best to imitate her confident walk.

"Agnes Anne," Da called after me, "yer becomin' proud and haughty. Yu'd better say yer prayers."

7. First Friday Dinner

I WAS LATE GETTING HOME. Once in the door, I proudly planted my new briefcase in front of the Holy Water font. It had been quite a day. An amazing day. Also a crappy day. All at once.

I dipped my first two fingers into the lake at Mary's feet and blessed myself, forehead to chest, left shoulder to right, my mind a jumble of successes and failures. New nails, the nice guy at the salon who asked me out, Verna offering to train me. I wanted to forget about Bruno, but I couldn't. He might be here tonight. How would I act? Who could I tell?

I gazed up into the Blessed Mother's calm and placid face and murmured, "Thank you, Mary. Thank you. Thank you. Thank you."

"Agnes Anne! Yer late!" Ma said, coming into the foyer. "I t'ought ya were goin' ta help me. Wher'ave ya been?"

"Got delayed, Ma." I ran upstairs to change, past the Mary on the bottom landing, the one where her baby looked like an old man with a big head. My sisters called this Mary Our Lady of Postpartum Depression.

The Mary on the top landing gazed out at us with such worried pinched eyes, we called her Our Lady of the Migraine. I fled to the Mary statue in my room. This Mary had a faint smile and looked happy. I checked the dish garden for my little snail. I had decided his name was Jude, like the patron saint of lost causes. I found him tucked into his shell and sleeping contentedly at Mary's feet. Maybe Jude was my new good luck charm.

Darcy and her brood of four came through the door just after I had ironed the napkins and was laying the tablecloth. Her husband, Domenic, carried a dish swaddled in quilted fabric.

"Look out, it's hot. It's hot," Domenic said, as he maneuvered through the hallway and headed to the kitchen.

"Wha'd ya bring?" Ma said, wiping her hands on her apron, and greeting her grandchildren.

"Scalloped potatoes."

"I'm boilin' spuds fer tha mash," Ma said, the pride in her voice unmistakable.

"I told you I'd bring scalloped," Darcy replied. "We don't need two kinds of potatoes, Ma. You do this every time."

"Tha more spuds, tha merrier," Ma said, turning her attention to her freckly-faced grandchildren.

The kids didn't follow their father, but gathered in front of the Holy Water font next to the door. All of them stared up at the Virgin Mary atop her porcelain cloud.

"We want a blessing, Grandma," they said, jumping up and down. The little ones raised their arms and tried to reach into the high bowl. Domenic Jr., the eight-year-old, could reach it, and dipped into the Holy Water to bless himself. It only made the rest of them want it all the more. Brennan jumped up and down like he was playing basketball and tried to slam dunk.

"Hold on, there," Ma said. "Mary doesn't like ta be pestered. Stop jumpin', Brennan. Girls first."

She lifted up Penelope, the youngest, and helped her touch the Holy Water and make the Sign of the Cross. Then she lifted Angela. Darcy rushed over to stop Ma from lifting Brennan, who was now seven and far too heavy.

I went back to setting the table, giving Darcy sideways glances and wondering if I should tell her about what Bruno said to me today. Darcy fetched the stack of plates from the china cabinet while I got out the silver. We both set up the knives and forks, and when we were finished, I dragged the ironing board back to the utility closet.

"Two kinds of potatoes again," Darcy said, under her breath, as she followed me into the utility room. The heady smell of earth surrounded me as I walked in. This was where Ma kept her root vegetables, onions, potatoes, turnips and beets. The washer and dryer were here, as well as an old slate wash tub. Ma called this room "her larder."

"I had coffee with Bruno today," I blurted.

"Oh?" Darcy looked at me quizzically, and I could tell she was confused as to why I said this.

"He... um... " I watched my sister's eyes search my face. I lost my nerve. "Katie isn't well."

"She never is," Darcy whispered. "Every time they come,

she looks worse than the time before. Did he tell you what she has?"

"Darcy!" Domenic shouted from the kitchen. "Can you get me a lime?"

We both looked to the bins Ma kept for produce. Darcy picked up a lime and I ended up following her out to the kitchen, my opportunity for a private conversation lost.

Domenic stood at the makeshift bar, which was a collection of colorful bottles blooming like a garden at the far end of a kitchen counter. Darcy handed her husband the lime and he sliced it, wrung it out like a rag and dropped it into his glass.

"What do you ladies want to drink?" Domenic asked.

The doorbell rang, but the door was unlocked and my brothers, Matthew and Mark, bounded in with their wives, Jennifer and Susan. They were sisters as well as sisters-in-law. Honestly, the four of them looked like interchangeable game pieces. Matthew and Mark, the Irish twins, as we called offspring less than a year apart, wore matching O'Neil Roofing polo shirts and helped themselves to beers. I knew they would swagger around drinking as though they were pleased with themselves. For what, I have never known.

The volume picked up. More food was set on the counters, some for eating, some to be served cold, some for snacking while having a cocktail. Now that Matthew and Mark's kids joined Darcy's, they spread out like a flock of wild birds.

Da, Uncle Jimmy, and Aunt Lucy came sauntering in next. I could tell that Da and Uncle Jimmy had already had a drink on the way home as Uncle Jimmy's eyes were unnaturally bright, and my father's cheeks had the hue of ripened tomatoes. Aunt Lucy toted a bottle of whiskey, which she set down with the liquor on the side counter. She then put two apple pies Uncle Jimmy had been carrying on the hot shelf above the oven. They weren't homemade. They came out of pink bakery boxes.

"My favorite night of tha month," Da bellowed, raising his beer and spinning around. "Ta all of ya. The last First Friday of the year!"

"Cheers!" most of them said.

"Sláinte," cried Auntie Lucy.

"Salude," Domenic said.

"Be they kings, 'r poets, 'r farmers," Da went on, relishing the audience before him, "tha Irish are a people of great worth. They keep company wid tha angels, 'n bring a bit 'a heaven here ta earth. May all of us be reminded that we are from tha' stock. We 'ave tha luck of tha Irish 'n in God's path we will walk."

"Amen!" came the cry. Glasses clinked. Ma turned back to her work.

Fiona came in with a tray of stuffed mushrooms and began to pass them around. With her bright red hair, Fiona was the most colorful sister of all. She took after Da, where I had Ma's dull hair gene. Darcy, who had it too, dyed her hair. I had to think about that. Tomorrow I could come out of the salon a brighter shade of brown—or even an entirely different color.

"So, Domenic," Da said, taking a swallow of beer, "how's Tombstone Territory?"

Darcy's husband, a large Italian fellow, came from a family who owned a cemetery marker business out in Colma. Da always called it Tombstone Territory, even though Domenic had gone off on his own and started a kitchen and bath granite countertop business. A very successful one. They lived in a Hillsborough mansion and had a kitchen the size of a tennis court.

I poured myself a white wine and stood near-by Da's conversation, hoping that he would announce that I was his new salesman. Tell everyone that Verna Korbel was training me. Then I heard a familiar voice. Bruno and Katie had arrived. Bruno carried a salad bowl as big as Ma's oven. Katie's pallor took my breath away. Fiona saw it, too, for she literally hovered by Katie's side.

What a rat he is, I thought. My stomach felt sour. I ditched my wine.

Fiona and I were the only single girls left, except for our sister the nun, the eldest, who stayed in Ireland and joined a convent. Katie was the only married sister who didn't have children.

Darcy stirred her gin and tonic and raised her glass to me. I found my wine and we clinked glasses.

"Your nails! Oh-My-God! Your nails!" she said, practically in a shout.

In a blush of realization, I looked down at my new fingernails. The color was too purple, my nails, too long. My hands didn't seem go with the rest of me.

Katie came over to admire my nails. When I gave her a hug, I could practically count her ribs.

"Very pretty, Agnes," Bruno said, in that slippery voice he used today in the coffee shop. He reached out and took my hand in his. I withdrew it. "You have lovely hands."

His tone made me shudder. I wondered if everyone heard how inappropriate his voice was, how sexy and bad it sounded. But my sisters continued to chatter about nail shapes and styles, French manicures and nail wraps.

Bruno slipped his arm protectively around me like it was normal and expected because, after all, we were a close family. It felt like ants were crawling over my arms. I looked for an escape.

Ma tugged a steaming roasting pan out of the oven, and I flew to her side, grabbed an oven mitt, and helped her move it to the top of the stove. I stayed right beside her, helping to move the roast onto a platter, and transfer the chicken to another big dish, start the gravy, and mash the potatoes.

"Ah, bless this lovely roast," Ma said. "We should all give t'anks tha' this blessed beast gave his life fer us, like Christ gave his life on tha cross so we all might live. That's wha' this lovely cow did fer us, God rest her soul."

"Animals don't 'ave souls, Ma," my brother Matthew said, backing the beer bottle out of his mouth.

"Tell that ta Saint Francis," Ma snapped.

"They do too have souls," Da said. "All God's creatures must have some sort of soul. A lesser one, perhaps."

"Just get tha meat ready fer me ta cut, eh?" Matt knocked back the rest of his beer and shuffled over to take up the knife. For several years now Matthew had been given the job of carving the meat. Mark always stood near-by as though he needed to learn this mystical art.

They had always been like that—Matthew and Mark—two peas in a pod, nearly twins. What one did, the other followed. It always amazed me that their brogues were still strong. Stronger than Da's. Maybe they kept talking that way because they were in high school when the family came over from Ireland and now they hung out with other newly emigrated Irish in the trades. I mentioned it to Darcy once and she said she tried hard to lose her accent. There was no way she was going to sound like an immigrant. I never told her that she still has the Irish inflection. Katie, Fiona and I came when we were in elementary school and in a couple of years had no accent at all. I suppose that linguistically, our family could be seen as dynfunctional. Probably in other ways, too.

The girls brought the side dishes out to the dining room, served up the food for the children at their own table and called them over. My brother Mark and Bruno brought up more chairs from the basement for the kids' table and soon we were all standing, each behind a chair the same way we did in our childhood, waiting for Da to say grace.

Grace was always a long extemporaneous prayer of thanksgiving, which he sometimes used to praise achievements or chastise sinners. I hoped he would remember to announce that I was now a salesman at O'Neil & Co. and give me a special blessing. I held my breath.

"God bless 'r first born, Sister Margaret Mary," Da intoned, in his best radio announcer voice, "who serves Our Lord 'n dignity 'n faithfulness. May this family receive tha blessings of another Margaret Mary, Saint Margaret Mary Alacoque, who has promised through tha Sacred Heart 'a Jesus tha' every person who attends mass 'n tha first Friday of tha month and receives communion fer nine consecutive months will receive a Plenary Indulgence."

Da looked around and forced his right eyebrow to meet the upturn of his cheek, which covered his eye with a fan of eyebrow hair. We called this scrutiny "the hairy eye." Then he closed his eyes again and blessed "Bruno-god-love-him" for taking care of Katie, and prayed that she soon would feel better. I thought I might be next in line for a blessing, but when he didn't say anything about my real estate license and we all said, "Amen," my heart dropped to my knees.

It was Ma's turn. She stood to Da's left, at the first seat on my side of the table. She raised her hand toward us, showing her palm. "Bless m'children, Lord. Matthew, Mark, Luke and 'r dear baby John-God-love-him-may-he-rest-in-peace. Bless m'daughter Margaret in Ireland, who chose tha religious life. Bless Darcy, Katie, Agnes Anne, 'n Fiona, 'n all my grandchildren. Keep everyone safe from harm, safe from sin, 'n forever honest. Amen."

Matthew and Mark shouted their usual, "God is a Gael!" and started to sit down.

"Isn't anyone going to congratulate Agnes?" Fiona asked.

Those in the process of sitting, quickly tried to stand up again. Everyone ended up bent at half-mast, either on the way to down or on the way back up. It looked like a slow-motion version of Whack-a-Mole.

"Thank you dear Lord," Fiona said, bowing her head and giving my hand a squeeze, "for Agnes's wonderful achievement. May she enjoy financial success in her new career. Amen."

"What career?" "Wa'd ya say?" "Who?" One after the other, everyone seemed not to hear what Fiona had said.

I took a big breath, Miss Allison-style, and tried to relax my throat. "I have my real estate license," I whispered. There. It was out. And I had said it without a stutter. Emboldened, I took another breath. "I'm leaving the back office."

I glanced around the table to see the reaction. Next to me on the short side of the table opposite Da, Uncle Jimmy and Auntie Lucy shared the piano bench. Auntie Lucy raised her whiskey, toasted me, and clinked my glass. "Well done, Aggie."

The room exploded with congratulations from my sisters and sisters-in-law. Da said nothing, but I noticed his face reddening, like pressure was building up behind his eyes. He began to resemble one of those bug-eyed gargoyles at the entrance to China Town.

Matthew sat down with a plunk, reached for the nearest platter and stabbed a piece of chicken. "That's a bit of a waste, id'n it?"

I didn't want to ask why because I knew I'd be walking into a trap, some sort of joke at my expense. I pretended not to hear.

Darcy wanted all the details. Katie clapped her hands and leaned over the table to give me a high-five. Jennifer and Susan, Matthew and Mark's wives, smiled merrily, but down at the other end of the table, Da still looked like a bilious ghoul. Before he could ruin my moment, I took an extra-deep breath and used my best Marilyn Monroe whisper to say,

"I've decided to change my professional name to Anne."

No one spoke. Maybe they hadn't heard me. I tried to make eye contact with everyone, except for Bruno, but I only managed to glance sideways at Fiona and then down to the roast beef, the chickens, the two kinds of potatoes, the fading peas and carrots languishing in a thick coat of mushroom soup, and the gargantuan salad bowl.

"What bullberry 'tis this?" Da shouted. "I named ya Agnes!" The scrape of his chair against the hardwood floor sounded like the bellow of a wounded beast.

"My name is Agnes *Anne* and now that I'm a real estate agent, I'd like to start using my middle name. Lots of agents change their names. I-it's m-my ch-chance." Shoot. I was running out of air and stuttering again. I should have taken another breath. I made a mental note to practice long extemporaneous sentences.

"Lord God," Ma said, from the other end of the table next to Da. Her head bobbled like it wasn't quite attached. "How will we ever remember? And what about Saint Agnes?" She leaned forward to look down the table at me. "She'll feel bad ya don't like her anymore."

"Ma," my sister Fiona whined, "Saint Agnes died seventeen hundred years ago. And Anne's a saint, right?" Fiona leaned into me and whispered, *"Who was Anne, anyway?"*

"Anne was Mary's mother!" Katie said, clapping her thin hands. "Anne is perfect." Katie turned to the rest of the family. "Why not? If Agnes wants to change her name now that she's an agent, why shouldn't she? People call Da, Mel. His card doesn't say Malachi O'Neil, it says Mel, not even Mal. He changed his name. Why can't she?"

My eyes started to fill with tears. That was so sweet.

"Won't change anyt'ting a'tall, now will it?" my brother Matthew said, shifting back and forth in his chair. "It's like rearranging tha deck chairs on tha Titanic, eh?" Matthew's brogue made him sound older than his thirty-nine years. "Yu'll always be Aggie," he said, plopping down a big load of scalloped potatoes onto his plate.

"How rude!" Darcy said, her plate still empty. "How absolutely caddish and uncouth to say that, Matthew. She's your sister. Look what she's accomplished! She got her real estate license! Can't you be supportive?"

Matthew unhinged two slices of roast beef and flopped them on top of his potatoes, then passed the platter. "Well, where's she goin', eh? Where's she been, eh? Aggie will always be Aggie. In tha corner by 'erself. No more, no less. Call 'er whatever you like. Agnes? Anne? A rose by any other name..."

"Load of thanks to *you*," Fiona said, tossing a roll on her plate and passing me the basket. "You could introduce her to someone, Matthew. Invite her somewhere."

"I 'ave fer godsakes. She did'na say a word. How can she get a boyfriend, let alone sell property, when she donut talk? If ya ask me, 'er license is a fekkin' waste."

"Language." Ma said, sternly.

I couldn't believe it. They were having a conversation about me like I wasn't in the room. Through all of this Da just put food on his plate and scowled down the long table, giving us the hairy eye like we might be thieves here to pinch the silver.

"Congratulations, Anne," Bruno said.

I looked up. He gave me that evil, greasy grin I knew so well. Revulsion roared through me like thunder. I couldn't take it anymore. Either I was going to cry or throw up. Maybe both. I ran for the bathroom.

When I returned, I pretended that nothing was wrong. Probably no one realized that anything was wrong—that Bruno had been eyeing me like a piece of steak.

Da pushed back and reached over to the sideboard for his Novena Notebook and his reading glasses. He flipped through some pages and found his Saint Margaret Holy Card, then dramatically cleared his throat. The chatter stopped.

"Lest anyone forget why we observe First Friday," he intoned, "there 'r twelve promises of Jesus connected ta tha Sacred Heart."

A symphony of groans rose from the table.

"Number one," he read. "*I will give 'em all tha graces necessary fer their state of life.*"

"Don't read it again, Da," my brother Mark begged. He glanced around the table at all of us, as though trying to find a quorum. "Has anyone told him it's 2012 and not tha fifties? No one does this sh—" He stopped and tried to find another word than the one he was going to say.

"Then don't listen," Da snapped. "Number two." As though he was playing a trombone, Da brought the holy card in, then out, squinting hard. *"I will establish peace in their families."*

"Well, tha' hasn't 'appened yet," Matthew said, winking at our side of the table. "Da, stop readin' this muck. You do it every month. No one does this anymore. We know why we're trapped inta this. Do'na rub it in."

A few laughed. I could hear Matthew chew his food.

"Three. *I will console them in all their troubles.* Four. *They will find 'n my heart an assured refuge 'n life and especially a' tha hour of their death."*

Mark reached behind his wife and hit Matthew on the shoulder. "If looks could kill, buddy, I'd say yer a gonner. Ya might need tha' one."

"Five. *I will pour abundant blessin's 'n all their undertakin's."*

"Pass tha gravy, Darcy," Mark said. "I need some blessin's on me beef."

Darcy clicked her tongue, yet passed him the gravy boat anyway. Mark glanced at Da and rolled his eyes.

"Six. *Sinners shall find 'n My Heart an infinite source of mercy."*

"Come on, Da," Matthew pleaded. "Put a cork in it. We hear this ev'ry month. We know this by heart. Yer preachin' ta tha choir."

Da raised his voice and spoke over him. *"Tepid souls shall become fervent. And fervent souls shall speedily rise wid great perfection."*

While my brother sighed, their wives, Jennifer and Susan, looked somewhat uneasy, as though their loyalty was being tested. Domenic and Darcy had placid expressions. Perhaps they were pretending to be somewhere else. Like on a train.

"Nine. *I will bless the homes where 'n image of My Heart shall be exposed and honored."*

"Hey, Ma," Mark said, "wid all tha pictures of tha Sacred Heart around here, you'll shoot straight up." Chewing with his mouth open, Mark pointed to the ceiling with his knife.

"Ten," Da shouted, over him. *"I will give ta priests tha*

power ta touch tha most hardened hearts."

"Hardened what?" Mark said. Both my brothers snickered.

"Tha' will be enough!" Da yelled. "Eleven! *Those who propagate this devotion shall have their names written in My Heart, never ta be effaced.* And finally, *Tha all-powerful love of my heart will grant ta'll those who shall receive Communion 'n tha first Friday of nine consecutive months...* Do ya hear me everyone?" Da shouted over the cross-conversations. *"...the grace of final repentance; they shall not die under my displeasure!"* Da looked up and down both sides of the table and once again, gave us all the hairy eye.

Everyone concentrated on his plate, the sound of the cutlery like small tinkling bells.

"So," Da said, setting the well-worn holy card aside. "Let's see wha' we've got this month, shall we, boys? Now, I saw Agnes Anne, Bruno 'n Katie, Luke, 'n of course Ma, a'mass this mornin'." He made checks on our lines. "As well as Jimmy 'n Lucy." More checks.

"Tha' we were," Uncle Jimmy said, looking up. The way my uncle ate like a hungry vulture, I wondered if Auntie Lucy ever cooked for him.

"Matthew?" Da said, "how come ya boys don't come down ta Mission Dolores anymore?"

"Don't 'ave time, Da. We 'ave tha kids ta get ready fer school. By then it's too late. But I nipped inta Saint Emydius at noon."

"Ah, Emydius, Patron Saint of Earthquakes, he is." Da's finger followed today's column down to Matthew's line. He made a check. "I hope ya said a prayer 'bout the Big One."

"That I did, Da."

"Good boy," Ma said. "Earthquakes are terrible t'ings."

I looked hard at Matthew. I didn't think Saint Emydius had a mass at noon.

"Mark?" Da prompted.

"Emydius," he said, quickly.

Mark's face took on an angelic aura of innocence. I didn't believe him. Not for a minute.

"Good." Da looked up at my sisters-in-law, Jennifer and Susan.

"Saint Cecilia's at eight," Jennifer said. "Both of us."

"Glory be, that's wonderful, girls," Ma said, peering over at Da's notebook to see the long line of check marks. "Yer almost ta nine."

Jennifer and Susan traded smiles. I watched their cheeks flush. They didn't know I knew Saint Cecelia's only had a daily mass at seven and another at nine.

"Good, good. Saint Cecilia, Virgin 'n Martyr," Da said, making checks on their lines and moving his finger down the row. "Fiona?"

"Did the 7:30 at Saint Vincent's, Da," Fiona said, looking up from her plate.

"Wonderful," he said. While making the check on her line, he mumbled, "Patron Saint a' Bricklayers 'n Vintners, Saint Vincent is. Did ya know tha'?"

Fiona shrugged. Bruno stared at me. There was longing in his eyes. I glanced at Katie. She didn't have a clue that her husband was a cheating liar.

"Darcy?" Da said.

"Domenic and I did the eight at Saint Bart's in San Mateo," Darcy said.

"Excellent. Saint Bartholomew, one a' tha Twelve Apostles," Da said. "So! We're all accounted for! Good job!"

Bruno's eyes were still on my face. Loud and clear, he said, "Can you pass the rolls, *Anne*?"

I had to admit, it was nice of someone to use my new name, but when I handed Bruno the basket, he put his lips together and blew me a kiss. I wanted to scream, but instead, I dropped my eyes and spent the rest of the meal staring at my plate.

8. Another Secret

THE NEXT MORNING, I could hear my sister Fiona's voice echoing up the stairs. Full of life and quick wit, she entered the house like a whirlwind and when Da teased her, she laughed it off, shooting him a smart remark to make him chuckle. All their disagreements became the Wimbledon of retorts and snappy comebacks, a wonderful game the two of them obviously enjoyed. Fiona had authored two travel books and was even on television, sometimes as a reporter, sometimes she hosted travel specials. I couldn't believe we came from the same parents.

I had overslept, and while Fiona and Da were verbally sparring downstairs, I ran around my room leaping into my underclothes and trying to choose something fashionable to wear. I didn't want to be the odd-looking, badly dressed sister of the glamorous Fiona O'Neil. She was taking me to her hairdresser today, who, if you believed her, could work miracles. I understood the implication: I needed a makeover, and possibly a miracle as well.

Fiona burst through my bedroom door just as I was pulling on a pair of brown tweed slacks.

"Let it be known," she said, finger poised in the air, "that this date shall be named The End of the Ponytail Day and shall live forever in infamy." Fiona put her hand over her heart and bowed her head. Her perky red hair slid forward and covered her cheeks. "May Agnes Anne's ponytail rest in peace and may we all enjoy this Feast Day forever and ever. Amen." She made an elaborate Sign of the Cross.

I did not acknowledge this drama, but ducked into the closet to find either a sweater or a blouse. My wardrobe was a mishmash of things Fiona and Darcy had given me and only recently had some nice additions. I kept telling myself it was "in transition," along with everything else in my life. There were five areas of improvement on my master list. This was one of them and I would force myself to change.

"What's wrong? Don't tell me you have the Mean Reds. I don't have time today to buy a bag of donuts and window shop at Tiffany's." She began to hum *Moon River*.

"Very funny."

"Geez, Agg," Fiona said. Her eyes roved around my room, a room we used to share. When we were little, Katie, Fiona and I were all in here. Darcy had her own little room down the hall, the old "fainting room," small as a closet. In our room we had bunk beds against the wall and a third twin bed next to it. Actually, we had a blast, the three of us. Now the bunk bed had been removed and there were just two twin beds side-by-side. I was by myself.

"When are you going to get outta here? With all these Holy Cards plastered everywhere, this place looks like a church. Give 'em up for Lent or something. Donate the Holy

Cards to charity. Or put them into albums. But pasting them all over the place looks—aaack! Are you going to become a nun or something?"

She acted like my collection caused her gastric distress and she began to twist and gyrate around the room as though she had been gripped by an alien that would soon burst out of her belly.

"Of course not," I said, "I'm going to move out sometime this year."

"I'll believe that when I see it." Fiona spied my small display of laminated Marilyn Monroe photos stuck in the base of my vanity mirror and came over to take a better look.

"When did they make Marilyn Monroe a saint? Is this a shrine, or something?"

"Of course not. I just like her, that's all."

"Has Ma seen this?" Fiona whispered.

"I guess."

Fiona lost interest in my Marilyn Monroe corner and turned away. She picked up the stack of fashion magazines from my desk chair. She had given them to me last week with instructions to study the photos and pick out a hairstyle. "Did you pull out some photos?"

"Oh," I said, vaguely. "I didn't find anything in there I liked."

"Out of this entire stack of magazines you couldn't find any haircuts you liked?" Fiona yelped. "Are you nuts?"

"Stop belittling me."

"I'm not! Look at you, Agnes. You're the tallest of all of us, you have a great figure, but you hide yourself behind baggy clothes and dull colors. Geez, Agg—I mean *Anne*, you could look like a lot of women in here." She slapped her hand on *Marie Claire*. A sly smile came across her lips and one eyebrow went up. "Wait until I get through with you."

"I don't want to look weird, Fiona. I'm going into sales now. Verna Korbel is going to train me. I've got to look professional. That's all I want today, a nice professional hairdo that's easy to care for."

"Get out of those horrible pants. Wear tight-fitting jeans."

I looked down at my tweed slacks. They suddenly seemed shabby and ill-fitting.

She waved me away like I was a bothersome moth, then turned her attention to my dish garden. "Jesus Christ! What's that?" She jumped back and pointed at something crawling up the Virgin Mary's skirt.

"It's a baby snail," I said, as casually as I could.

"Kill it!" Fiona screamed. She jumped around and poised her fingers to flick my snail into oblivion.

"No! Stop!" I yelled. "He belongs there." Half way into the jeans, I waddled over to take a look. Fiona had a point. If you weren't expecting to see the critter, it was somewhat disgusting.

"Now you have a pet snail? *A snail?* This is—" Fiona's face screwed up into a mass of pleats and wrinkles. "Oh, Jesus, you're turning into a nutcase. Between the Holy Cards and the statues of Mary—and now this?" She exhaled in a huff and pointed to a small reddish mound in the garden. "And what is that? Snail poop?"

"Dried cat food," I whispered, zipping up. "Jude likes it."

"You've actually named a snail? Jude? Patron saint of Lost Causes? And you feed it cat food? Holy Mother of God! I am so glad I moved out. This place drives me crazy!"

"Who's takin' tha name a' our Lord in vain?" Ma's head popped through the doorway. Her face reminded me of my own, only Ma's nose was smaller and straight. Through some twist of the genetic helix, I ended up with her turned-up chin and dull hair, as well as Da's huge hooked hose and anvil jaw. I called it the double whammy.

"Fiona O'Neil, yer choice a' words is disappointin' ta the Holy Mother as well as ta God. Yer makin' tha Blessed Mother cry."

"Yeah, Ma. Sorry. It's just that... Anne here is turning into a... I don't know. An old woman. A weird old woman."

"She certainly is not! She's an upstandin' young woman wid high morals, 'n her devotion t'Our Lady is ta be admired, not ridiculed. Ya could take some lessons from her yerself, Miss Smarty Pants. And for goodness sakes, get your purse off tha bed. That's bad luck."

I was putting on my lipstick and trying to ignore them, but through the mirror, I watched Fiona roll her eyes. When I turned around, I realized that my room did look pathetic. My Holy Card collection, like baseball cards for saints, was displayed on grim corkboards on every wall.

Some cards had golden rims, some had papery lace, others were plain and simple. Most had prayers on the back. In the Catholic church, at least the old-fashioned Catholic church of my parents, each saint had a following, like a fan club, and people prayed to these saints for various favors. Saint Anthony was the Patron Saint of Lost Causes. So was Saint Jude. There were saints who looked after boys and girls, saints in charge of scholastic achievement, firemen, policemen, even saints for animals, bookbinders and bricklayers. I loved my cards and I enjoyed reading the symbols: lambs meant purity, books meant learning, flowers meant innocence. Each card contained hidden meanings and I sometimes pulled down a favorite saint and read the prayer on the back and even carried others in my purse.

"This place," Fiona said, "should be in a museum."

"Ah," Ma said, "museums 'r good places, they are." Ma smiled as though Fiona had delivered a huge compliment. "And where 'r ya girls off ta today?"

"I'm taking Agnes, I mean *Anne*, to my hairdresser, the one who does all the broadcasters at the station."

"How lovely," said Ma, raising her hand in a blessing. "Bless m'daughters, oh Lord, and may they have a wonderful time at tha hairdresser's a' may they find a parkin' space, and may they 'ave a lovely lunch, which they will receive through Thy bounty, through Christ, 'r Lord. Amen." Ma turned around and left the room.

Or so we thought.

Before we could blink, Ma popped back in. "It wouldn't hurt, Agnes Anne, ta say a prayer ta Mary Magdalene. She's tha Patron Saint a' Hairdressers, ya know." Then she was gone again.

"Agnes," Fiona whispered, "you've got to get out of here. I swear if you don't, you're going to end up as crazy as she is."

"I'm going to leave. Really," I whispered. "I'm saving my money."

"Saving! You've got to have plenty of money by now. What do you spend it on besides Holy Cards and hair clips?"

I winced. I had never shared my entire plan with anyone. But to implement the final piece, I knew I needed an ally. Perhaps it was time to tell someone. I took a deep breath.

"I've been saving for... for... "

"For what?" Fiona prompted. "A marble altar?"

"Stop it. You can't tell anyone."

"Tell them what?"

"No, really." I lowered my voice. "This is a secret."

Fiona nodded and solemnly crossed her heart. "Okay, shoot."

I took a breath and barely whispered, "I'm getting a nose job."

"Oh my freakin' god!" Fiona screamed.

My hand made chopping gestures along my jaw line. "The doctor said he could shave my jaw line and file my chin, too."

"Holy shit!" she yelled.

Ma's voice bellowed from the stairway. "Fiona Marie O'Neil, ya will not use profanity in this house nor take the name 'a tha Lord in vain. That's a Mortal Sin and if ya die with a Mortal Sin on yer soul you'll go straight to Hell."

"Sorry, Ma! Sorry!" Fiona shouted back. She grabbed my arm and pulled me into the bathroom. "Tell me more. Tell me everything," she said. Fiona turned on all the faucets so the sound of the water would mask our voices.

"I don't know exactly when I'm doing it," I said, over the sound of running water. "I have a doctor picked out. I almost have enough money."

"How long have you been planning this?" she whispered. Fiona's face became a mixture of confusion and excitement.

"About a year."

For once I had completely stumped Fiona. I had never seen her at a loss for words. She sank onto the toilet seat. "I can't believe you. You've planned all this out? And never told anyone?"

"Don't tell Ma," I pleaded.

"Oh my god, I swear to you I won't. They'd never let you do it. How long are you going to be out of commission?"

"A couple of weeks. At least. They have a special hotel for people recuperating from plastic surgery. I'm going to stay there."

"No, don't do that. Come to my place."

I smiled, mentally calculating the money I would save. Going to Fiona's would save me a couple thousand dollars. I could book the procedure that much sooner.

"This is so cool!" Fiona stood up and stared at me in the mirror. We were side by side. Fiona was so colorful, so petite.

"Who's the Patron Saint of Noses?"

I laughed and shook my head.

"Saint Blaise?" Fiona said.

"No. He's for throats."

"Maybe it's Cyrano de Bergerac," she said.

I jabbed Fiona with my elbow.

"Bless m'daughters, O Lord," Ma said. She followed us to the doorstep and raised her hand. "And may they receive wonderful beauty treatments like Esther received a' tha hand of Hegai in tha Citadel of Susa."

"Whatever," Fiona said, over her shoulder as she descended the front stairs.

"Keep 'em safe from harm," Ma intoned. "We ask this through Christ, Our Lord. Amen. And may they get a parkin' spot on Union Street at a meter wid time left on it 'n may they... "

I couldn't hear the rest. I busied myself buckling my seatbelt. Sideways glances told me that Ma still stood at the top of the stairs, her lips moving in prayer and blessing. Fiona vroom-vroomed the car and drove us away.

9. The Patron Saint of Hairdressers

FIONA DIDN'T JUST DROP ME OFF at the beauty parlor for this makeover, she actually walked me in and talked to Bonnie the beautician, whose own hair looked like curls of ribbon—some blue *(blue!)*, some white—like something you might see on top of a birthday present. A pang of fear shot through me. *They wouldn't make me look like that, would they?*

The things Fiona and Bonnie discussed were nearly unintelligible, like ordering at Starbucks. Instead of decaf grande half-soy, half-low fat, blah, blah, blah, it was hair lingo. Only somehow it sounded like I was buying stereo equipment, the phrases were full of words like *amplify* and *volumize.* That I didn't know all the buzzwords, made me feel like a goofball. I wanted to interject, *I don't want hair like Bonnie's,* but I didn't want to insult her either.

Bonnie stroked my dull limp hair as though she were testing fabric. I could tell she was getting into this because her breath began to come in fast little gulps. I knew that to her I was no more than a blank canvas. I kept wondering how much this was going to cost. I had my operation to save for and although this hair-do business was necessary for my new career, I didn't want it get out of hand. No one would buy real estate from someone with blue hair.

"Let's get your hair cut," Bonnie said, with forced cheer. "After I've styled it, I'll color it, and then I'll deal with your eyebrows."

My eyebrows? I was afraid to ask what was wrong with them.

"And then I'll do your makeup." Dollar signs were in Bonnie's eyes. I felt like a beauty product pigeon. I wondered if Ritz Charisma was having some sort of employee contest and Bonnie took me for an easy mark. My heart shriveled. Every dollar I spent was one less toward my surgery. It was clear I wouldn't get out of here cheaply.

The shampoo boy, a young Hispanic kid they called Roberto, held my hand and stood me up like he was leading me onto the dance floor. He sashayed me to the shampoo chair, sat me down, leaned me back, and flooded my hair with warm water then squirted on the shampoo. As he went to work, the fragrance of coconuts and apples wafted around me and, as Ma had suggested, I said a short prayer to Saint Mary Magdalene, the Patron Saint of Hairdressers. At home, I had an extra Mary Magdalene holy card. I should have brought it to Roberto. Maybe she could also be the Patron Saint of Shampoo Boys.

While I hung upside down like a bat, Fiona and Bonnie came over and stood above me parsing through color swatches and laying them on my skin. They popped in and out of my vision like this was the morgue and they were identifying a body. The corpse was mine.

"Look Fiona," I said, my voice echoing up from the wash basin. "Don't do anything weird. I want something simple.

Something easy to—"

"Relax, *Anne*," Fiona said, coming into my sight and looking down at me like I was a bug in a jar. "You're going to love it without the ponytail." I heard her say to Bonnie, "My sister's nervous that you're going to make her look like a freak."

Bonnie's laugh sounded demonic.

"Really, she's probably praying right now to the Patron Saint of Hairdressers."

Bonnie came into my vision. "Do hairdressers have a saint?"

I nodded.

"Who's that?"

My voice echoed from the depths of the basin. "Mary Magdalene."

"I thought she was a prostitute," Bonnie gasped.

"Not true. Bad rap."

Bonnie disappeared for a couple of seconds, then popped back into view again. "Actually, I'm not a hairdresser. I'm more of a hair designer. Would that be someone different?"

Roberto flooded my hair with water again; his massage was incredible. I closed my eyes.

"This color looks good." Fiona put a swatch of tickly hair against my skin. "Rose Valentine," she crooned.

My eyes popped open. "I don't want to be a redhead," I said, from the depths of the tub.

"Why? It runs in the family. Only you got Ma's hair." Pity shone in Fiona's eyes.

"If I have to have it colored, I want blonde."

"Blonde?"

"Like Marilyn Monroe."

"Her hair was platinum. No color. Not for you. Look at your sallow skin!"

"I don't care," I said.

Bonnie riffled through the swatches. "How about this one? Blonde with a golden touch."

I felt the tickle of the hair sample against my skin.

Fiona regarded me critically. "That might work," she said.

"It's called Goldilocks," Bonnie said. "Be nice with pink highlights."

"No!" I shouted. "No pink hair, okay? Nothing weird." I could picture Verna going into a total twit if I walked in with pink highlights. I had to speak up. Take charge or else these two would have me looking like a freak. "I want to be blonde," I said. "Blonde like Marilyn Monroe or Madonna or Lady Gaga."

Roberto sat me up. While he dried my hair with the towel, I watched Bonnie and Fiona walk away, crouching together, shaking their heads.

"You know Patron Saint?" Roberto whispered. I nodded. "Who is Patron Saint of sick mother?"

"What's she have?" I said, keeping an eye on Bonnie and Fiona.

He turned around and pointed to his back just below his rib cage.

"Kidney?" I said.

"Yes, yes," he said. "My mother must have dialysis."

"There are quite a few who are known for kidneys. There's Saint Margaret, Saint Benedict, and Saint Marina."

Roberto's face lit up. "So many?"

I reached down for my purse and found a Holy Card for Saint Margaret, one I normally carry because that's my eldest sister's name. I owned plenty of duplicates; I handed it to him. "Give her this."

Roberto thanked me profusely and took me back to Bonnie's station where for the next two hours I was combed, cut, colored and generally tortured with goop, timers, and more washes and rinses than I thought possible or healthy. By the time she was done, my scalp felt like it was on fire and my head ached like I'd been at the dentist all afternoon.

While Bonnie blow-dried my hair with my back to the mirror, I prayed like crazy to the Blessed Virgin Mary for relief and to Saint Mary Magdalene for an end to this torture. But when Bonnie finished and turned me around to face my reflection, I saw waves of golden blonde hair falling around my face and ending below my jaw.

I blinked a few times. The blonde hair framing my face made my eyes look bigger. My skin seemed to have an inner glow and the way Bonnie had outlined my eyes with brown eyeliner and applied makeup across my cheekbones and jaw I looked entirely different. This astonishment must have shown on my face because Bonnie gestured to my head like she was Vanna White and I was a vowel.

"Now, who's the Patron Saint of *that?*"

10. The Perils of Being Blonde

WHEN I WALKED IN THE DOOR, Da didn't look up from his newspaper and can of beer. And Ma, over by the bookcase, was clearing out the magazine rack, a daunting task for sure, as it seemed she had a penchant for saving every magazine she had ever received since she came to San Francisco. In the middle of a toss to her "perhaps-I-should-give-this-away-pile," her body twitched so violently upon seeing me, I thought she might be having an epileptic seizure.

"Ahhh! Ahhh!" she shrieked. "What have ya done to yer beautiful hair?"

My hair had never been beautiful. But if I said that in some sort of retort, it would seem like an insult. After all, Ma had given birth to me, and I have some of her genetic code, specifically, the "dull hair gene." Ma's hair was a lighter brown than mine used to be, its texture thin and now as she turned gray, foggy days made the gray ones stick out as though they had grown from an entirely different head.

"Agnes Anne, 'n tha name a' Jesus, Mary, 'n Joseph, what did ya do ta yer hair?" Ma said, for the third or maybe fourth time.

There was only one way to explain it. I shrugged and blamed Fiona, then ran for the stairs.

"Ha-ha-ha-ha. Wig! 'Tis a wig, Irene! I can spot 'em a mile away. What's got into Agnes these days? First she donna' like 'r job, then she changes 'r name, and now this?" I could hear him shaking his newspaper.

Ma followed me to the bottom of the stairs and yelled up. "'Tis a wig, 'tisn't it, dear? "'Tisn't it?"

I was too ashamed to answer. Blonde? What had I been thinking?

About eight-thirty, I heard Ma praying in the stairway, something she did frequently in front of the icon we called Our Lady of Postpartum Depression. Ma loved this picture and, all through my childhood, visited it to pray nearly every night. Tonight, I heard her voice rising and falling, lilting and lifting as she wound her way through her prayers.

I heard Ma's usual plea to Mary to watch over the household, bless her children and grandchildren, and for Da to drink less. I think Ma should give up praying for Da's abstinence. It was a wish so unobtainable it probably insulted the Virgin's intelligence that she was still asking.

"Bless Margaret, Mathew, Mark, Luke, 'n Baby John-God-rest-his-soul, 'n bless all tha rest 'a tha girls, Darcy, Katie, Agnes, 'n Fiona," she said. I couldn't understand her private mumbles and personal prayers. All I could hear was a word jutting out now and then like a bony elbow. "An' help Agnes Anne, dear Mary," she said, loud enough for the neighbors to hear, "*find herself* 'n stop doin' *bad things* to herself. Let her know tha' she's *perfect* as she is—'r was—'n needs *no improvement!*"

Sitting on my bed listening to this, I crossed my arms tightly in front of my chest and tried to block out the rest of her petitions. Her last one was always a self-deprecating request to make her a better wife, a more perfect mother, and help-mate to her husband, just as Mary was helpmate to Saint Joseph. Ma signed off with a defeated, "Amen."

My brother Luke called these prayers, "Ma's letters to Santa Claus."

After I heard Ma go to bed, I pawed through all the stuff I purchased from Bonnie at Ritz Charisma. Finnegan, the family cat, jumped up on the bed and played with the jingle bell ball. Finnegan loved the sound of crinkling cellophane and the rattle of boxes. After he sniffed through everything, he put his paw straight out and on top of some wrappers and looked at me, but he didn't seem to notice or care that my hair was an entirely different color. Maybe cats were colorblind.

I started to play around with my new makeup, freshening up the base, the cheek color, penciling my newly plucked eyebrows and practicing with the lip liner pencil. Bonnie said I had good skin. I had never thought of that and somehow, since a stranger said it, it made me pay more attention.

I went into the bathroom and got close to the mirror and squinted at my reflection. My skin seemed brighter now that there was lightness all around my face. With my blonde hair bouncing around, I fiddled with it and pulled it behind my ears. I preened and admired myself in the mirror and put on my best Marilyn Monroe gush. The unexpected ring of my phone made me jump.

"I hear your hair makes you look positively sexy," Bruno crooned into the phone.

I wanted to ask him how he knew, but the words wouldn't come. Fiona probably spoke to Katie, who then told Bruno.

"I hear you're blonde. Is it true they have more fun?"

His laugh sickened me. I dreaded that this would spark more creepy attention from Bruno.

"Katie and I can hardly wait to see this new hair-do. Of course, Katie's asleep, but you could come over and I could take a picture of you."

I couldn't speak. I slammed down the receiver and stood trembling and staring at myself in the mirror. I looked like somebody else. My sister Darcy had brown hair and eyes, and Fiona was a redhead, and Katie was a yellow-blonde with pale skin and blue eyes. Who did I look like? Perhaps Da in drag. Suddenly I wanted my dropped ponytail back. My dull hair used to make me inconspicuous. Now, I stood out. A slow panic rose in my chest.

The phone jolted me again from these thoughts and while it rang, I knew from now on, I would have to be stronger. I picked up the phone and with more force than I intended, I shouted, "You leave me alone. I'm not interested in you. Do you hear?"

"Hello? Anne? Is that you? This is Sheldon, Sheldon Goldberg."

My voice stayed trapped in my throat.

"Is this... " Sheldon repeated my telephone number.

"Yes," I managed to say, my breath slowly returning.

"What's goin' on? Are you all right?"

"Um. Nothing. I thought it was someone else. Sorry."

"Wanna' go for a cup of coffee or a drink? Or something?"

"Um. Now?" I glanced around to see a clock. Another call beeped in. I knew who it was. Bruno would start some inane conversation. I wouldn't click over to it. No way.

"What time is it?" I asked.

"It's only about nine o'clock," Sheldon said.

I tried to act sophisticated, like I did this all the time, but truth was, I had never gone out after eight. I read once in a women's magazine that you should refuse last minute invitations because you don't want to seem like you have nothing to do. Even though I was in my nightgown, my makeup was on and certainly my hair was done. It wouldn't take me long to get dressed. But this was a man I had just met yesterday. In a nail salon.

Why was I worrying? He was probably gay!

And it *would* be great to get out of my room tonight. What was stopping me? I forced myself to speak.

"Sure," I gushed, as though I did this all the time. "Where should we meet?"

"Wherever you want. What's close to you?"

"Um. I'm on Church Street," I said. "Near Dolores Park." I didn't know what was close to me. I didn't go out much. Truthfully, I never went out at all.

We agreed on a place and I said I'd meet him there. I knew Fiona did this all the time. "I went out last night," she'd say. I'd ask where. "Just out, you know, for drinks," she'd say. I'd never gotten a clear picture exactly where she went. Yet now I was doing it. I was going out, meeting someone I didn't know, in a place I'd never been.

He might be an axe murder or a sex fiend.

I wouldn't let him take me home. Maybe just walk me part way. *Quit worrying,* I told myself, *he was probably gay.* I already knew he was Jewish, so there could never be anything between us. I could never fall in love with anyone who didn't like the Lord or my precious Virgin Mary as much as I did. I would merely have a drink with him and we would talk and I'd get used to my new blonde hair. I would consider this a practice date.

I held up my head and cocked my chin at an upward angle and glanced at my Marilyn Monroe corner at the side of my bureau. The newly minted Anne O'Neil was going out.

I couldn't help but worry that with my hair this color and with this new haircut, Sheldon might not recognize me. Finnegan did, but he was a cat. Sheldon would probably blink and look past me, tilt his head from side to side because I looked somewhat familiar. But he wouldn't know who I was. I had to be prepared to reintroduce myself. "Hi," I'd have to say. "It's me, Anne. Anne O'Neil, from the nail salon."

"Oh," he'd say. "I didn't recognize you."

Then I'd have to apologize about my hair and then he'd be forced to say something nice about it whether he liked it or not.

I put on a pair of black trousers and a wine-colored sweater Fiona had bought me and grabbed a nice jacket. Before leaving, I leaned down to give my snail a squirt of water, but I didn't see him. Snails are nocturnal and he should be grazing around about now. Taking a closer look, my breath stuck in my throat.

Jude was inside the cat's toy, a ball with a bell inside and holes all over. Finnegan must have dropped the ball when he smelled the cat food I had put on the Baby Tears for Jude. I picked up the ball and shook it. Jude came loose and rattled around with the jingle-bell ball, probably knocking himself silly.

Oh dear God, I probably killed him.

Gently, I tilted the ball. Both Jude and the bell rolled to where there was a hole and I gently shook it, but the snail didn't fall out. I tried again with another hole. And again. With great care, I put the ball back down on the Baby Tears and hoped while I was away, the snail would find his way back through one of the openings. But I didn't have a good feeling about this. Even if he were the Einstein of mollusks, getting out looked nearly impossible.

"Agnes Anne O'Neil, where 'n earth are ya goin' a' this time a' night?" Ma cried out when she saw me in the hallway. She had on a flannel nightgown. Baby kittens in angel costumes danced around her shoulders.

"I'm going ow-oww—" Lapsing back into my old speech

pattern, I got stuck on the "out." I struggled to take a big breath and let the air escape, but my lungs locked up and between thinking of something to say, the embarrassment about being blonde, and trying to engage my speech therapist's techniques, no sound came out at all.

"Where 'n tha world are ya goin'?" she repeated. Her tone suggested I had perhaps become a prostitute.

I didn't want to try the "out" word again, so I whispered, "I'm meeting someone."

"In'na middle a' tha night?"

"It's only a little after nine, Ma."

Like this thought choked her, her hand drifted up the front of her nightgown and clutched at the flannel kittens dancing around her neck.

"Who? Who 'r ya goin' ta meet a' this 'our?" she said, her voice raspy and filled with suspicion.

Her hand didn't seem to belong to her, it seemed to have a life of its own and wandered back and forth below her neck while she waited for me to answer. I wondered if her hand jumped up and started to strangle her, would it be my fault?

"He's just a guy," I said. "His name is Sheldon." I didn't want to tell her his last name. Goldberg would completely freak her out.

"A man, 'tis it? Is tha' wha' all this... this hair 'n this makeup business is about? It's all about a man?" The hand at her throat began to pace back and forth again looking for a place to grab. Perhaps it would clutch her neck and squeeze. Murder was imminent.

I don't know, officer, I would say. *It was her hand that did it. I watched that hand. It had a mind of its own.*

"Agnes, I'm speakin' t'ya. How long have ya known this man?" Ma's hand clutched at her neck and tapped impatiently on an angel kitten's head.

I didn't know what to say. If I revealed I'd just met him yesterday, she might start yelling and maybe wake up Da. Then all hell would break loose.

Ma's eyes crinkled to the size of raisins. I held my breath.

"I donut know what's got inta ya lately, Agnes Anne. Yer just no' behavin' well. I cud understand 'bout tha real estate license. But why did ya change yer name?" She rolled her eyes and crossed herself like she was apologizing to Saint

Agnes. Her hand came back to her throat and grabbed a hunk of nightgown and held on. "Bu'this—this hair a' yers." Her voice scraped like sandpaper. "Bleachin' it blonde like a common—"

"It was Fiona's idea, Ma. I was just looking for a new h-hair style and th-then—" My voice pinched, embarrassment engulfed me like the Red Sea closing in on Pharaoh's chariots.

"Why didn't ya stand up fer yerself? Refuse ta be made inta a harlot?"

"Ma, I'm 28. I need to stretch my legs, er... f-fly... with w-wings." The rest of the metaphor died in my throat.

"A girl's reputation 'tis a precious t'ing, Agnes Anne O'Neil. Goin' out a' 10 o'clock a' night—"

"Ma, I'm not exactly a g-g-girl an-n-ymore. I'm a wo-wo—" *Damn,* I thought. *I am doomed. Sometimes I cannot even get the simplest things out of my mouth.*

Ma's left hand alarmingly crawled back and forth across her chest again as though it was pacing, trying to find a way to strike. Maybe the hand would perform a tracheotomy right in front of me. I pushed the bloody image away.

"Of all ma girls, Agnes, ya 'n Margaret 'ave always been tha *good* ones, devoted ta yer religion. Devoted ta Mary. But now ya—" Utter shock and the threat of scandal seemed to flicker across her face.

What was I supposed to say? That I wasn't good anymore? That because of the changes I'd made, I'd decided to start stripping on Broadway?

"Ma," I said, "people go out late all the time. Fiona says the clubs don't s-start until t-t-ten. An-and it's only n-nine."

She turned away in a huff and marched to her bedroom door and rattled the doorknob. Turning back, she eyed me up and down like she was taking inventory.

"Remember what I said 'bout reputation, Agnes Anne. 'Tis a precious t'ing. Once lost, it canno' be repaired."

Stunned, I watched the hand gripping her throat crawl up behind her neck and latch on.

Just before she shut the door, her head snaked back out and she hissed, "What wud Our Lady say 'bout this business, eh? What wud Mary say? Before ya leave, you'd better say some prayers, Agnes Anne O'Neil, fer yer goin' down tha wrong path."

11. Late Date

I FOUND THE BAR where Sheldon said we'd meet. Trophies and athletic shirts, hockey sticks, baseballs, bats, and autographed pictures of people I didn't recognize seemed to tumble off the rafters and cover every inch of free space. I felt stupid that I didn't know who Number 24 was or Number 16, as their shirts were strewn everywhere. I should have studied the sports pages. A pang of regret swarmed through my middle.

"Hey, Anne," Sheldon said, coming up to me.

"Hey." I liked that word. It was so full of air that I never stumbled over it.

"Wow. New hair," he said. His eyes gave me the once-over. "You've been busy!"

"Yeah." I tried to laugh, but it came out all wrong. I started to put out my hand to give him a handshake, but I immediately stopped. My hand wilted.

"Very nice," he said, still looking at my hair instead of my eyes.

Sheldon looked different, too. Now he had on a plaid flannel shirt, unbuttoned, and I could see his high-necked white undershirt. I felt my face color and didn't know where to put my eyes.

"I have seats at the bar," Sheldon said as he walked me over to them. "What'll ya' have?"

"Umm. Maybe a glass of wine." Then I added in a rush, "I can't stay long," which was pretty silly as I only had church and an open house tomorrow.

Sheldon talked to the bartender about sauvignon vs. chardonnay, dry versus buttery. He turned back to me and nearly knocked me over with his smile. I couldn't help but wonder what he saw in me, why he had asked me here. I noticed his profile. The hook in his nose was bigger than mine. My heart sank. He was a nose freak.

"So what else have you been up to?" he said, taking a sip of some sort of drink in a huge stem glass encrusted with white crystals around the edge. Looked like a gay drink to me.

"Uhhh. Hair. Today was just a hair day. Not very

interesting."

He grinned and waited for me to go on, but I didn't know what to say. To make conversation, the only thing I could think of was to tell him about how my snail was stuck in the cat's toy.

"I have a pet snail," I blurted. *Damn. That was inane.*

"A pet what?" he said. The look on his face was a combination of confusion and disbelief.

"Snail," I said, furious at myself for bringing it up. "You know, what you find in the garden." His eyes widened and I wanted to erase what I had said. Discuss something else. It occurred to me that I could leave, walk out the door and run through the night, back to the safety of my room. Sheldon laughed like this was a joke and then went silent, which made me even more nervous, so I came out with the rest of it.

"The snail is stuck inside my cat's plastic ball." I quickly gulped some wine.

"And so?" He waited for me to say something. When I didn't, he said, "What's the punch line?"

He leaned so close to my head, I could smell his aftershave.

"There's no punch line," I said, raising my voice so he could hear me over the chatter in the bar. "It's not a joke. My snail somehow went inside the cat's toy. You know, like a Wiffle Ball? And he can't get out."

Sheldon's stared at me. I thought he might turn away and hail the bartender for the bill. Say something like, "Check, please. We're done here."

"Well, it got in," Sheldon said, "so logically, it should be able to get out. Right?"

I watched his hand rub his chin and couldn't help staring at the small cleft in it. I hadn't noticed it before, but of course I hadn't been this close to him either.

"I don't think Jude can get out. I tried rolling the ball and getting him over a hole so he'd fall out, but nothing happened." My voice faded. Our eyes met. Jesus, Mary, and Joseph, we were only about four inches apart. I could smell lime on his breath and found myself wishing he would kiss me, but this was a bar. And he was probably gay anyway. And certainly Jewish. I pulled back. Everything was going too fast.

"Give the snail until tomorrow, and, if he doesn't find his

way out, maybe you could saw the ball in half or pry it open."
Sheldon took a leisurely sip of his drink.

"Oh," I said, smiling. "What a good idea. I could cut
through it."

I wondered how a knife could fit inside the holes. They
looked pretty small. Meanwhile, Sheldon beamed and I
realized what my mother said about men was true: Men love
it when you agree with them.

"I've never met a girl with a pet snail." Sheldon's smirk
was playful. "And if you get tired of him, I suppose you could
always eat him."

I shrieked.

We laughed.

He made a joke about cooking escargot.

"I couldn't eat something I named," I said.

"Neither could I." He took my hand. "You're a lot of fun."

My hand perspired and became embarrassingly slippery.
I was afraid to look into his eyes and so I began to form an
undue interest in the tulip shape of my wine glass.

"Tell me about yourself," he said.

I couldn't concentrate. I grappled with breathing. *Don't
be a ninny*, I said to myself. *Breathe out, don't only breathe
in.* I thought of Marilyn. I tried to become Marilyn. I twisted
my legs around each other and sat up taller on the bar stool,
but it didn't work. I nearly lost my balance. Who was I
kidding? I was just Agnes Anne O'Neil and no one else. I
decided to scare him away, give him a real dose of O'Neil. If
he ran, so be it. I took another sip of wine.

"I'm Catholic," I said, holding my head at a foolish angle.
"I come from a long line of bigots. My father's favorite jokes
are about gays, blacks, women, and Jews." To gauge his
reaction, I glanced up at him quickly, then away. Sheldon
was still smiling.

"I believe fervently in the Virgin Mary and pray to her all
the time. I believe she helped me get my real estate license
and find a good speech th-therapist."

*I had to stutter on that word. And why was I telling him
this?*

Anger seethed below the surface, but I had decided to
start this diatribe and so I forged ahead. I took another sip of
wine, then a breath, a bigger one this time, and began to let it

out in that controlled way of Miss Allison's. And Marilyn's.

"I just changed my name from Agnes to Anne. Did you know that? Anne is my middle name."

"You changed your name?" Sheldon seemed surprised. His eyes moved over the bottles above the bar or maybe he had a sudden fascination with hockey sticks. "And..." He paused. "Let me see, you have a pet snail named Jude?" he searched for words. "And a quirky family." He took another sip of his drink.

I knew this meeting was too good to be true. Saddened that whatever had attracted him to me had now evaporated, I told myself it was better for it not to get started in the first place than to be disappointed later. The wine slipped harshly across my tongue.

"And this snail," he said, continuing with a seriousness that made everything I had told him seem absolutely senseless, "lives in your bedroom and is trapped inside a cat's toy."

Feeling increasingly idiotic, I managed to nod. I had the sudden desire to add that I was nearly raped in high school by the guy who married my sister, but I could never say that out loud. I also wanted to say that I had a fight with my mother tonight and that I felt terrible about it. Ma and I used to be so close. I knew that all that garbage might tip the scales and somehow, during this crazy monologue, I had decided I liked this guy and I didn't really want to scare him away. But I had already said too much and it was a minor miracle that he was even still here. It felt like I was sitting in public wearing only my underwear, and it was peppered with holes. This would never have happened to Marilyn.

"Okay," Sheldon said, setting his drink on the bar. "I think you should know a few things about me." His smile nearly knocked me over.

I swallowed hard and nodded.

"I'm Jewish. My grandmother yells at me all the time because I was never bar mitzvah'ed and my mother doesn't really care. My father is dead. So is my childhood dog." Our eyes met. His head came closer and he whispered, "To tell you the truth, I miss the dog more than my father."

"Oh," I gasped. "That's so sad."

"The part about my father or the dog?"

"Uhh, both. *Both.* I'm very, very sorry for your loss. Both losses."

"That's a terrible thing to admit, isn't it?" Sheldon said. He turned away and gazed back to the hockey sticks above the bar.

"Maybe," I said, trying to be helpful, "you knew your dog better than your father."

"That's for sure." A sting of pain flashed across Sheldon's face. His eyes found mine or maybe I found his and we gazed at each other for a few silent seconds.

Oh my God, I thought. *This guy couldn't be gay.*

"I guess it takes a girl who owns a snail to understand these things." His smile was filled with mischief.

I chuckled and so did he. Our giggles swelled into laughter which rolled on too long and probably too loud, but no one at the bar noticed, and even if they had, I don't think we could have stopped ourselves. Deep in my bones I knew this man was a nice person. Someone I could talk to. Someone who could become a friend. But the fact that he was Jewish and I was Catholic felt like a time bomb. I wondered when it would detonate.

I silently let myself in the front door. The smell of what we had for dinner mixed with the cleaning products Ma used created a unique O'Neil house smell: cabbage and Pledge. I closed the door and locked it, then blessed myself at the Holy Water font and felt the cool water graze my forehead as I touched myself forehead to chest, left shoulder to right. Tonight, Mary's eyes seemed kind and almost happy. I found myself smiling up at her.

"I had a wonderful time," I whispered, resting my fingers on the lip of Mary's font. "Do you care if he's not Catholic? Christ was Jewish. You're Jewish."

A voice careened out of the darkness. "Finally, like a bad penny, ya show up."

I jumped and turned around. Ma was sitting on the built-in bench at the bottom of the stairs.

"A' least yer confiding yer sins ta Mary."

"Ma, you scared me." Had she heard what I said?

"I've been prayin' fer ya, Agnes Anne. Worried sick about ya. Out there in'na dark, wanderin' around wid strange men." Her crystal Rosary beads glinted in the semi-light.

"I just went out for a while. You didn't have to stay up." I tried to head for the stairs, but she stood up and followed me.

"I heard voices ou'side. Who were ya talkin' to?"

"Sheldon. He walked me home," I whispered softly. I turned around on the first landing, about four stairs up. I didn't want to wake up Da. He would be like a bear coming out of hibernation.

Ma's lips pursed into a cluster of wrinkles. I watched her gaze down at the flowery rug, worn from years treading feet. Her tongue tisked on the roof of her mouth.

"Ma, I only went out and had a glass of wine with someone. I didn't run off and get married. I wasn't kidnapped. How am I to have a life if I can't go out once in a while?"

"Don't ya be sarcastic wid me, missy. 'Tis eleven-thirty." She tapped on an imaginary wristwatch. "No self-respectin' young woman goes out a' ten o'clock. And now wid tha' blonde mop a' hair—ya—ya look like a—"

"A what, Ma?" I whispered. From upstairs, I heard the distant ring of a phone. My phone. I vowed to disconnect my landline. No one my age had one anymore.

"And tha phone!" she cried out. "It rang every twenty minutes while ya were gone."

It felt like a knife twisted in my gut. I knew who had been calling.

"If it bothered you, you should have answered it," I said, wishing she had. Wondering how Bruno would have covered his tracks if Ma's voice had come on the line.

"Ya should 'ave been home ta answer it, Agnes Anne. Was it tha' young man?"

"How could it have been 'that young man,' if he was out with me?" I turned and walked up to the second landing.

"Then who keeps callin' a' this time a' night? Another man, 'tis it?"

"I don't know, Ma." I turned to take the rest of the stairs two at a time, avoiding a glance at the pinched expressions of the icons on the stairs. "Maybe it's a wrong number."

On the floor in front of my door, I saw Ma's spidery

handwriting on a holy card. I picked it up. It was Saint Anne's card. On the back, Ma had written, *"A reputation, once lost, is forever gone."*

"Ga' night, Agnes," Ma said, under her breath as she walked past me in the hall. "Tell yer caller ta go ta bed. I donut wan'ta hear tha phone all night long."

Before I could even shut my bedroom door, the phone rang again.

"Hello?" I whispered.

"What are you doing?"

Just as I thought. It was Bruno.

"Don't call me anymore, Bruno," I whispered. "All these phone calls are bothering my parents and I don't want to talk to you."

"You sound breathy. Have you been making love?"

I hung up on him.

Ten seconds later, the phone rang again.

"Don't give yourself away, Agnes." Bruno's voice was louder now. "I'm going to be your first real experience. I should have been back then and I will be now. *Do you hear me?* You save yourself for me, goddamnit. You won't get away from me this time. *Agnes? Anne? I love you."*

Stunned and repulsed, I dropped the receiver, then disconnected the cord from the wall. The silence seemed eerie. I wanted to cry, but no tears came. I wanted to pray, but couldn't find the words. I looked into the dish garden and picked up Finnegan's ball and gazed through one of the small holes. Jude the snail was still stuck inside; he looked like a miniature toy next to the giant jingle bell. Everywhere I rolled him, he seemed too big to fall through. Gently, I set the cat's plastic ball back on the green carpet of baby tears covering the soil at Mary's feet and prayed Jude could find his way out.

12. Open House

IT WAS SUNDAY AFTERNOON and Verna Korbel had asked me to hold one of her listings open. Excited, no, *thrilled*—I dressed for success and used all the products Bonnie at Ritz Charisma had sold me, including their signature fragrance, Be My BFF, which wasn't bad if you liked the smell of gardenias and Skittles.

Verna occupied the corner space at O'Neil and Co., a real office with four walls and a door. This was the reward Da gave to the best salesman. Each year, Verna won the contest. Someday, I wanted to be top salesman. Someday, I wanted to be in this office with its view of Twin Peaks. I wanted to buy fancy furniture and surround myself with elegance. In these dreams, I envisioned myself using the latest smartphone and making lots of calls to clients. I'd say things like, "Let's do lunch," and "Catch you later." In these reveries, I never stuttered.

I peeked in at her. Verna glanced up, then down, then up again. "Oh mine gott!" she nearly yelled, throwing herself back in her chair. Then she struggled to stand up while murmuring, "Blonde? Blonde?"

Verna walked around me like she was a general inspecting the troops. "You realize, Aghnez... I mean *Ahne,* zat to be blonde von must be outgoing." She reached out and pinched a piece of my hair and rubbed it back and forth between her fingers. "No blonde zhould be zhy. Remember zat. You musdt liv up to being blonde."

I was beginning to realize that very thing. This morning doors had been opened for me. People who didn't know me smiled. It was weird.

"Vell, let's get to vork. Let me tell you about zee condo on Russian Hill," Verna said, going back around her desk. "It is very cheap unt zhould zell quickly. Any idiot could zell it."

I supposed that meant me, but I didn't care about her backhanded insult. I would be alone at a listing! And in charge! And if I sold it, I would make money!

The condo price was "only" $850,000. It had two

undersize bedrooms, and miniature closets to match. Verna gave me the keys and a long list of what else was for sale "on the hill" as she called it. She wanted me to familiarize myself with the entire list so I could, if this condo didn't fit a client's needs, sell them something else. Verna never, ever missed an opportunity to make a sale. I was her student, so I diligently took mental notes.

At the open house, Verna told me to light vanilla scented candles. I would find the pre-made cookie dough in the freezer and I should bake a few. I was to brew coffee so when people came through the condo, the place would smell like home, even if it was only a home in their Martha Stewart imaginations. Not only was I to open all the drapes and shades, but I was to turn on all the lights and lamps as well.

Oh my God, I'm really an agent, I thought to myself as I went from room to room fluffing the pillows the home stager left, making sure nothing was out of place. I raised shades, flung open the drapes, started the coffee, baked the cookies and lit the vanilla scented candles. Then came the hard part: I had to wait for the customers to come in the door. While I waited, I memorized the list Verna had given me of what else was for sale in the area.

I welcomed the first couple, but they were neighbors in the building and just curious about the unit. I let the looky-loos roam around by themselves, but I knew if Verna were here, she would make me stay at their heels, give them a sales pitch and pump them for information about their friends. "Now iz your chance," she would say, "to chooze your neighborz. Gif me zee names of zeez people you know and I vil contact zem."

That sort of sales technique wasn't for me. I simply couldn't pump people for information. I would stumble all over myself and stutter. Since this was my first day and I was somewhat nervous, I decided to smile a lot and say as little as possible.

An older couple came in and I handed them the sales sheet, a very professional brochure with color photographs printed on thick shiny paper. The woman was probably Ma's age and she told me they were from Cleveland, Ohio. The husband did business in San Francisco and they'd been shopping for a second home in a place without a harsh winter.

The woman never stopped talking and I was glad because then I didn't have to say much. I brought her into the kitchen and seated her near the window to have a cup of coffee. I pointed out what we call in the real estate business a peek-a-boo view, a slice of a grander vista that would be there if it weren't for other buildings blocking it. Nevertheless, she was enamored with this small slice of bay and gazed at the sunlight sparkling across the water and the occasional ship skirting between gaps in the buildings. She chattered about her life in Cleveland. While she talked, her husband paced around the apartment, opened up the fuse box, and stuck his head in the garbage chute.

I offered them the cookies that had just come out of the oven. The lady told me about the deep snow in the Midwest. I was charmed. I told her I'd only been up to the snow at Lake Tahoe, and that it must be thrilling to see an entire urban area blanketed in white. She laughed and patted my hand, then turned to her husband and said, "How do you like this apartment, honey? I could live here." Her husband scowled and asked to see the garage.

Call it beginner's luck, but that afternoon, I wrote a contract for just under full price. It was such a simple sale and the terms were so straightforward that we didn't even have to go back to the office. I knew that if everything went right, my share of the commission, half to Verna because she listed it, half to me as the seller, would be over $8,000. A thrill ran through me. This was serious money. It meant I wouldn't have to wait much longer for my surgery. My secret dream could actually take form! Me. Ugly Agnes could step into the future, a future without a hooked nose and a chin the size of an anvil.

Smiling so broadly my cheeks hurt, I veritably danced through the unit to close it up. I pulled down the decorator shades, turned off the fancy lights, and smugly plumped the froo-froo pillows, this time just for fun. I could hardly wait to tell Verna what I had done on my very first afternoon as a real estate agent. I imagined laying the contract on my father's desk, seeing the surprise grow across his face, his amazement that I made a sale on my first open house. I would smile demurely and take modest credit.

I heard someone else enter the unit and I walked down the hall to welcome them. My heart leapt like I had seen an apparition. Bruno Stark stood in the foyer, his jeans tight and his hands thrust casually in his pockets. But it was the gleam in his eye that alarmed me.

"What are you d-doing here?"

"Waiting to see you, gorgeous. Look at you! *Just look at you!*" Bruno blinked a few times like he was coming awake. In three steps, he was in front of me.

I backed up.

He reached out to touch my hair.

I ducked.

"Wow," he said. "You look fantastic! Blonde! Oh my god, you're giving me a hard-on." Bruno pulled me into a long lingering hug. "Shut up, Anne. Relax. Just let me hold you."

I turned my face away and pushed against his chest. Before I could break free, I felt his lips on my neck, his hand on my rear end, pushing me between his legs.

"You smell fantastic," he said, nestling his head into my neck. "What is that?"

"Panther piss," I said, not wanting to spoil the thought of my new perfume. I pushed him away. "You have to leave, Bruno, I'm closing up."

"Come here," he said. His hand slid down my arm as I tried to pass by him.

"You have to leave," I said, my voice sharp.

"No, I don't." He shook his head. "Not when you smell like that. Not when you look like that." His expression made me back up. "This is the day," he whispered. *"Today."*

"Get out," I said, trying to head for the kitchen. I thought of the pot of hot coffee and how I could toss it in his face. I thought of the location of my phone and how I could dial 911.

He stepped forward and wouldn't let me pass. "Hey. Stop. Don't panic. It's okay."

"Leave. Right now. Get out, Bruno, or I'm calling the police."

"You're always so hostile. Wow," he said, in a watery whisper, "you look sexy."

I glanced over at my cell phone on the counter, the pot of hot coffee behind it.

Instead of grabbing me again, Bruno walked over to the open front door and hit it. The door swung closed. Just before it slammed, it bounced back.

Verna stood in the threshold. "Clozing up already?" she said. "Vel hello, Bruno." She strode into the foyer. "How did you do today, Ah-nne?"

"M-m-made a sale," I said, stuttering my way through the awkward moment. "Nearly full p-price. No contingencies beyond the ordinary." I walked over to her, so happy to see her, I nearly gave her a hug.

"A zale zee firzt day! Goot for you! I told you any idiot could zell zis plaze." She turned back to Bruno, her eyebrows rose and hovered mid-forehead, then she turned back to me, assessing the situation. Bruno in the unit. I was alone with him. I knew she was wondering what was going on.

"Looking for a condo, Bruno? I'd love to zell you one. Zounds like zis von is taken."

My smile remained broad and fake. I hated myself for participating in Bruno's deception.

I watched him make small talk with Verna. I couldn't stand it another second. I retreated into the kitchen and left them to chat while I cleaned up.

Bruno must have been discouraged because he finally left. But I was still worried that he might be waiting for me, so I showed Verna the contract and took a long time about it. I was glad she went through the contract paragraph by paragraph, making sure I had gotten their initials on every page, checked all the right boxes and filled it out correctly. This wasn't hard for me as I had been an escrow assistant for years and was fully aware of every clause in the standard contract but to delay things as long as I could, I asked Verna multiple questions.

When we walked out of the building, darkness had come. Verna went north, my car was parked down the street. I worried that Bruno might be waiting somewhere in the chilly dusk. I quickly climbed behind the wheel and locked my doors, then I touched the Miraculous Medal on my dashboard, giving thanks that I was safe.

I wondered if it would always be this way. If Bruno would figure out what house or condo I was holding open and show up each time to harass me. I wondered how long it would be before I wouldn't be as lucky as I'd been today.

When I got home, I checked on Jude. He hadn't moved much inside the jingle bell ball. Carefully, I picked it up.

"Come on Jude," I pleaded. "Get out of there before you grow too big to fit through one of the holes."

Both he and the bell rolled to the down-side of the ball. As though scalded, Jude withdrew into his shell. No matter which way I turned the ball, which way I rolled him, the shell wouldn't pass through any of the holes. Sheldon was right. I would have to saw the ball open. I remembered that Ma had that knife from TV that cut through metal and brick and frozen meat, so I knew it could easily cut through a cat's toy.

My phone rang and I hoped it might be Sheldon, but it wasn't. All I heard was weeping.

"Hello? Hello?" I called into the receiver.

Listening closely, I recognized the sobs. It was my sister Katie.

"What's wrong?" I asked.

"Bruno's... He's... having an affair. I know it."

My heart dropped.

"He came home tonight with a woman's perfume all over him. It was sweet and sickening. A horrible smell. Nothing I would ever buy. Oh P-U! He couldn't have picked it up from a quick social-type kiss. It was all over him. He must have... must have..." Katie started to blubber again.

Guilt rang me like a church bell. I told her she might be imagining things, but up in heaven, I knew Saint Peter chalked up another sin of mine on his slate and I was mad at myself for lying to her. Why did I have to cover up for Bruno?

But how could I tell her the truth?

"I've been throwing up ever since," she said.

"Oh Katie, I'm sure it was nothing. Why do you do this to yourself?"

"I'm not doing it to myself. I'm sick. I feel so sick all the time. I'm tired of feeling sick and then I have to cope with this? Some woman's perfume?" She started to cry again.

That's when a queer thought bubbled inside my brain. I reflected on all the attention Bruno gained by having a sickly wife—the accolades, the praise, the extra blessings, the way it gave him a special martyr's status within the family. A chill shuddered through me and I again saw the expression of superiority that crossed his face each time he pampered Katie and benevolently kissed her hand. Could Bruno, I wondered, be slowly making Katie sick to get to me?

13. Meet Sheldon Goldberg

WHEN I HEARD THE DOOR BELL, I raced down the stairs to beat my parents to the door. Sheldon stood on the front porch dressed in jeans, a slightly rumpled collared shirt and a wool tweed sports coat. His thick unruly hair drooped slightly across his forehead. I couldn't take my eyes off him.

"Hey," he said.

"Hey," I said.

Da walked up behind me. I felt his body, all 240 pounds of it, lean around me to get a look at the man who had come to pick me up. We were trapped. I had to invite Sheldon in.

As soon as Sheldon crossed the threshold, Da's hand pumped his arm like he was priming for an arm wrestling contest.

"An' yer name?" Da said, when I wasn't quick about making the introduction.

"Sheldon. Sheldon Goldberg."

"Ah," said my father, his hand losing muscular control and suddenly shriveling back to his side. Da's face turned blotchy, his glance towards me, quick as a lizard's tongue. "So I take it yer not... yer nah..."

Sheldon frowned. "Not what, Mr. O'Neil?"

"Goldberg is not a typical Irish name. Yer not in tha club, so ta speak, are ya?" Da's head tilted to one side.

I drowned in mortification.

"Oh," Sheldon said. "No, it's not. And I'd venture to say that O'Neil is not a typical Jewish name either." He laughed lightheartedly. "Would you feel better if I added an O in front of Goldberg?"

Sheldon didn't see me roll my eyes.

This was all my fault. I should have met him somewhere else, but he insisted on coming by to pick me up. I told him it wasn't a good idea, but since we'd been having long conversations each day, he said I didn't have to feel self-conscious about my family. In a weak moment, I had agreed.

Ma stood slightly behind my father and nodded politely, her hands together at the waist, palms cupped as though filled with water. I noticed how skinny her arms were, how her elbows stuck out like bird's wings. My father gave me the hairy eye, then turned his back and disappeared into the kitchen, taking Ma with him. Over his shoulder, I heard him say, almost like a curse, "Don't ferget ta bless yerself, Agnes Anne."

The arms of Our Lady of the Font next to the door seemed to be elevated higher than before. I expected her face to crinkle into a frown. I wanted to bless myself before I went out the door like I always did, but I was embarrassed to do it in front of Sheldon. I don't know why. My faith never embarrassed me before, but somehow, right then, it did.

I tried to be clever and get Sheldon to go out the door first. I hoped that when his back was turned I could sneak a dip into the Holy Water and get a blessing to ensure the safety of this evening. But Sheldon was being polite and held the door open for me.

"You first," I said, trying to maneuver him across the threshold, my smile as perky as I could make it. "I've got Jude in my purse and a knife." I gestured again for him to go first.

"Well," Sheldon said, with a wink, still insisting on me going first, "I have Colonel Mustard and a lead pipe in my pocket."

He made me giggle and I realized he was not going to move. I *did* have to go first. I glanced at Mary's Font and regretted I couldn't sneak a blessing. It must have been the first time ever I hadn't blessed myself as I left the house. A dark unsettling feeling wrapped around my heart.

We got in his car and sped up Market Street. I loved this section of the city, the climb up Twin Peaks, the vista changing at every turn. Sheldon talked incessantly about his parking space. He chatted on and on about how he decided to buy it and what he had to pay for it and how the space was engineered into the side of the hill.

At last a sign reading "Reserved Parking" came into view

and, with obvious pleasure, Sheldon rolled his Fiat into the broad space and came to a flourishing halt. "Ahhhhh," he exhaled. "Isn't this beautiful? All this cement is mine." He turned to me and winked.

The parking pad literally clung to the side of the hill. It felt like we were leaping over Market Street, soaring over the streetlights, flying out to the Ferry Building, stroking the cables on the Bay Bridge. The clock tower was Big Ben, the Bay Bridge, a harp.

"It's beautiful," I exclaimed.

"Better view here than in my condo," he said, getting out and coming around to help me. He paused and looked at the view again. "I wish I lived right here. I should pitch a tent."

We gazed down at the trail of cars on the freeway crawling up to the mouth of the Bay Bridge and at the towering office buildings downtown blazing with light. I felt like Peter Pan and found myself drawn to the edge. As I gazed at the view, the breeze rippled my skirt. I was that gal in Titanic flinging her arms wide open to the endless sea. I was Helen of Troy launching a thousand ships. Then I remembered I was just Agnes Anne O'Neil with a snail in her purse, standing precariously on a cliff.

Sheldon's condo was in one of those cement boxes with stairs like the keys of a xylophone running diagonally up the side of the building. I was used to Victorian bric-a-brac, not rectangular rooms with cottage cheese ceilings. He had decorated with posters of sports cars and a couple photos of rainforests.

In Sheldon's kitchen, we unwrapped the plastic bag and carefully took out the cat's wiffle ball with poor Jude the snail still rolling around inside with the jingle bell. Sheldon held it up to his eyes for a better look and spun it around, trying to roll the snail into the widest part of one of the holes.

"Here," I said, taking the Ginzu knife out of my purse. I felt like we were complicit in some sort of criminal activity. Sheldon fumbled the ball and it bounced into the kitchen sink. He yelped. I shrieked.

"It's okay. It's okay," Sheldon said. Gingerly, he picked up the ball and both of us peered through the small holes of

Jude's prison. My snail had retreated deep inside his shell. Next to him, the jingle bell looked about as big as a wrecking ball.

"Is his shell cracked?" I asked. Heart throbbing, I waited for the fatal news.

Sheldon held the ball awkwardly. "No. It looks all right," he said, letting out a great puff of air. Then he picked up the knife and managed to stick the tip inside one of the holes. It slipped. He placed the knife on top of the ball and because he was left-handed, he cupped it in his right hand. Cautiously, yet with vigor, he began to saw.

The Emergency Room of Davies Medical Center was pleasant and Sheldon's bleeding had slowed to a minor stream, but we had used all the tissue and paper toweling we brought with us, and now the blood dripped on the hospital's vinyl floor tiles. There were forms to fill out, so I helped. I learned all sorts of things about Sheldon Goldberg, like where he worked, who carried his health insurance, that he was born in New York City, and that his mother's maiden name was Coen.

When we came to the question about "How did this accident happen?" we looked at each other and laughed and decided to merely say, "Kitchen knife accident" instead of "Snail Emergency" or "Opening Cat's Toy to Free Captive Pet Mollusk."

It must have been a slow night at the ER because they took us almost right away. When his name was called, Sheldon insisted that I come with him. I carried his jacket, an empty box of tissue, and a plastic bag for the blood-soaked litter. A nurse lead us to a cubicle and Sheldon sat down in a chair that looked like it belonged in a dentist's office.

"Thanks for coming with me," he said, with a shy smile. More blood dripped onto the floor. "I hate needles."

"Here," I said. My eyes found a paper towel dispenser. I pulled a bunch of towels out and handed him some so he could soak up the red still surging from the center of his palm. As I cleaned up the mess on the floor, a voice startled me. Standing up, I found myself nearly nose-to-nose with Dr.

Bruno Stark.

"Agnes! Er- Anne!" he said, fumbling with his clipboard, double checking his paperwork as though he had come into the wrong area. Then he looked from me to Sheldon and back again. "What—what—"

"Th-this is, Sheldon," I stammered. "Sheldon, this is my brother-in-law, Dr. Stark, my sister Katie's husband."

Sheldon reached out his right hand to shake the doctor's, but because of the wound, he stopped half way. Between them, more blood dripped to the floor, the droplets bright red against the gray linoleum.

"What have we here?" Bruno said with interest. "Knife wound?"

"Right." Sheldon retracted his outstretched hand. "Kitchen accident."

"Cooking for my dear sister-in-law?" Bruno's discerning eyes cut through me.

"Something like that," Sheldon said, through an embarrassed wince.

Bruno donned purple gloves and rolled a small table over as well as a stool and began to go to work on the wound.

"I'll wait outside," I said. They both protested, but I didn't want to be quizzed by Bruno and by his expression, I knew he would be demanding answers. Sheldon simply looked miserable. I ignored both of them and headed for the waiting area.

About twenty-five minutes later, I heard my name. A nurse said, "Dr. Stark will see you now," as though I was the one who was sick and needed to see a doctor. She led me through the double doors into a treatment room.

"Hello, Anne," Bruno said, coming in.

I didn't sit. I didn't want to get near him.

"Sit down," he said, motioning me to the treatment chair.

I could see right through his false cheer. "No, thanks. Is Sheldon ready to go?"

"Yes, he'll live. Strange accident. He was awfully dodgy about it, what were you two doing?"

"It happened in the kitchen," I said.

"Sit down. Let's chat." Bruno leaned against the hard patient exam bed; the hygienic tissue covering it crinkled.

"I think we'd better get going," I said. I went over to the

door.

"We? We? So you're dating this guy?"

I didn't know what to say. Was I dating him? We had a drink one night and dinner a few nights later and talked on the phone twice a day. Tonight he helped me with Jude. Do all those qualify as dates?

"I suppose we are," I said.

"Odd choice," he mumbled.

I knew what he meant. Sheldon was Jewish, but I didn't want to talk about it. Not here in the Emergency Room. Especially not to Bruno.

"What does your father say?"

I didn't want to talk about that either, so I shrugged.

"Isn't Malachi upset? He had a difficult time with me, a Kraut as he called me, but at least I was Catholic. God help me if I'd been a Lutheran." He winked and smiled like I might melt and tell him what he wanted to hear.

When I was a teenager, I thought Bruno's teeth were gorgeous. Now they looked wolverine. I repeated my shrug, this time adding a head shake. I opened the door and looked down the hallway to see if I could catch a glimpse of Sheldon. I hoped he might be looking for me.

From behind, Bruno jerked me out of the doorway and closed the door. Fire gleamed behind his eyes. I pushed back from his hug, horrified that Sheldon or a nurse might come in, but Bruno buried his face deep into my new hair. His wet lips kissed me behind my ear, nuzzling along my hairline.

"God, you smell great. Your body is so luscious." He moaned "Why are you wasting your time with that guy?"

I shoved him back and hissed, "Because you're married to my sister and she knows about you. *She knows you're having affairs.*" Wrenching myself away, I grappled with the door and fled down the hall. I knew his eyes were on my back. I longed to be in front of Mary's Font in my hallway so I could properly bless myself and start this horrible evening over.

Sheldon and I stood at the edge of his kitchen like two people returning to a crime scene. The vista truly took my breath away. Dried blood pooled on the countertop, blood speckled the floor, and wads of paper towel were scattered here and there, crunched up and blooming with deep garnet swirls.

"Yuck," Sheldon said. "This is disgusting."

"Where's Jude?" I couldn't believe it. We had forgotten all about him.

"He could be anywhere," Sheldon said, gingerly stepping over a clump of paper towels I had earlier swished across the floor with my foot. "What if he's drinking my blood and is at this moment morphing into a vampire?"

"Oh stop," I giggled. "He has to be here somewhere."

The ball now lay on the countertop, broken open like an egg, the jingle bell beside it. Jude had escaped. Waiting to hear a fatal crunch, I tiptoed around peering into and under things, afraid to even throw out the wadded toweling without parsing through it one more time. It was revolting to see so much blood.

I asked Sheldon where he kept his mop. He pointed to a closet, and I opened it and got out some cleaning supplies. We began to put things back in order. I kept searching for Jude and even fished down in the disposal for him, wondering if he'd fallen in there, but the disposal chamber seemed empty. I couldn't help feel guilty that Sheldon sliced into his palm because of my pet snail; his hand had begun to swell like someone had blown up a rubber glove.

"There he is," Sheldon said, pointing to the coffee maker.

Jude seemed to be gazing at the On/Off switch on the coffee machine. Small feelers standing tall, he looked like he might be having a conversation with it. While we vigorously swabbed the decks and washed Sheldon's blood down the drain, we let Jude continue his exploration of Mr. Coffee.

Every time I squeezed another load of red tinted water out of the sponge, I apologized to Sheldon again. He pretended he had received the Medal of Honor, his acceptance speech magnanimous as he thanked the little people who had helped him come to this low point in his life.

As I gave the mop a last rinse, Sheldon came up behind me, put his arms around my waist, and nuzzled into my neck. Ironically, it was the same place Bruno had nuzzled earlier in the hour. It made me queasy to think of Bruno and Sheldon sharing germs.

My family's big house on Church Street felt like a longed-for slipper after a hard day's work. Tonight I didn't mind that it smelled vaguely of cabbage, fish, and the ever-present touch of Pledge. Closing the front door with care so it wouldn't slam, I turned to the Blessed Mother standing on her china cloud above her font. I slowly blessed myself in the name of the Father, the Son, and the Holy Spirit.

"Oh, Mary," I mumbled, resting my hand on the edge of the china clouds, as I recalled Sheldon's wound and Bruno's horrid advances. "This was not a good night." Then I remembered Sheldon's kiss, the feel of his strong arms around me and I realized that in the midst of the emergency and the revulsion I felt toward my brother-in-law, something wonderful *did* happen tonight.

"Mary, mother of God, help me," I said, looking up into her vacant eyes. "I think I'm falling in love with Sheldon Goldberg."

I smiled up at her self-consciously and blessed myself again. Clutching the snail jar, I took the stairs two at a time and avoided looking at the pinched expression of both the icons of Mary haunting the stairway.

Before I reached the door to my room, I noticed the tip of a piece of paper sticking out from under it. When I opened the door, I could see that it was another holy card. I bent down to pick up a picture of Saint Agnes. On the back, on top of someone's funeral notice, my mother had scrawled, *I'm praying for you to come to your senses.*

14. The Breakfast of Champions

SUNDAY BREAKFAST WAS ALWAYS a grand production. Da liked his "rashers" as he called his thick smoked bacon, and on Sundays he actually pulled out a frying pan and took to cooking them himself. Unfortunately, he always seemed to have the heat too high and ended up burning them or splashing grease all over. Or both. From the scent wafting up the stairs, I could tell Da was nearly finished with his weekly foray into the culinary arts. I wasn't looking forward to going downstairs, and so I spent an inordinate amount of time drying my new hair with my new oversized round brush.

When I finally joined them in the kitchen, the frosty silence was palpable. As though Sheldon was sitting beside me singing a Hanukah song and wearing a yarmulke, the hush in the room made a strange sense of guilt pulse through me.

While Ma loudly rustled the pan with the crusty layer of burned bacon into the sink, Da sat down and cleared his throat. It was one heck of a frog because he "Ahem'ed" over and over. Ma drained the grease into the an empty soup can and opened the windows to let the smoke out.

"I'm gonna make ya a wonderful pancake this mornin', Agnes. I mean, Anne."

"Thanks," I said.

"Old Testament 'r New?"

I thought about Sheldon and how the Jewish bible was the Old Testament. Our bible was both the Old and the New. "Old Testament, Ma."

"So, Agnes Anne," Da said, fiddling around with the bits of bacon left on his plate. "Did ya have a good time las'night?" His voice was up a half-octave and sounded like he was doing a commercial for Lucky Charms.

I decided to tell the truth, not because I lie, but sometimes, I do skirt around things. Before I could get anything out, Da repeated his question. This time, as thought I had suffered a major hearing loss, his voice was even louder.

"So, Agnes Anne, las' night, did ya 'ave a good time?"

"It was okay," I said.

"I heard there was trouble."

I didn't say anything.

"Trouble, there was." Now he sounded like Yoda from Star Wars. I expected him to say, *"Teach you, I will, the ways of a Jedi Knight."*

Fat chance my father would teach me anything.

I nodded and pulled the butter dish and syrup pitcher closer to me, then rooted through the crumbs of bacon cooling on a paper towel in the center of the table and tried to find something edible. I heard Ma squirting the batter onto her skillet and the resulting sizzle.

"I heard Sheldon had a wee accident las'night."

My bacon stopped mid-flight. "You did?"

"Bruno-god-love-him rang in this mornin'. The good doctor told me all about it." I watched him push the last of his eggs onto his fork with his thumb. My heart fell into the burned bacon. "He said there was a knife accident, he did. Sheldon into tha martial arts, is he? Never heard of a sheeny who's inta kung-fu. Ha! That's a good one. Kung Fu Jew."

"Stop it. It was an accident. It happened in his kitchen."

"Ah. So ya went ta tha man's house, did ya?"

"Condo. He lives up on Twin Peaks."

"Ho! Ya hardly know him, Agnes, an' yer traipsin' around his house like Lady Muck?"

"Anne," I said, through my clenched teeth. "My name is Anne. I've changed my na—"

"Yuv changed nothin'!" Da shouted, his temper erupting like a spritz of baking soda and vinegar. "Bruno said tha two a' ya were all lovey-dovey, close as two snappers in a carriage."

I refused to be baited and took a measured bite of bacon and for entertainment, daydreamed about that baby carriage. If Sheldon and I were riding around, we'd be sharing a blanket. I found myself smiling.

"There we go. Almost done," Ma said, from the stove. "'Tis gonna be a good one."

"Are ya paying attention at all, Agnes Anne?" Da shouted. "We're talkin' 'bout a knife wound here. How does a man like tha'—what did ya say he did? He's an accountant, is he? How does a bean counter come for a knife wound? Hummm?" Da's head loomed over the table. "And Dr. Bruno said it was deep! Nearly went through his hand, it did. I'm assuming ya weren't tha one ta stab tha poor bastard, were ya? My very own bottle of water millin' on the green?"

When Da was upset he lapsed into Irish code, rhyming words and expressions that meant something else. Bottle of water was daughter. Milling on the green meant fighting. I didn't want to participate in this stupidity, and I knew anything I might say was going to rile him up. I've learned that when he starts to rant like this, the less said, the better.

"So lem'me get tha lay a' tha land," Da said, like he was

Sherlock Holmes. "Ya go over ta this bloke's place 'n he stabs himself."

I shuffled through the bacon pieces looking for something that wasn't coated with black carbon. I found a piece that was nearly uncooked, like maybe it had been on the edge of the frying pan and barely heated. I picked it up and took a small bite, but I thought I might get trichinosis and put it down. Meanwhile, the silence stretched thin and long and I knew it would be merely seconds until blast-off. I reached for my mental seat belt.

"Want ta tell me tha rest?" Da said. He put both elbows on the table and leaned over his plate. His eyes locked on my face.

Ready...Aim...

I gulped a long swig of milk and looked him straight in his squinty eyes.

"No, not p-particularly."

Fire.

"What kind'a gack do ya t'ink I am?" he shouted. "The man checks inta hospital wid a knife wound 'n my daughter was there wid him 'n ya don't wanna tell yer Da 'bout it?"

"You'll only make fun of him, so why would I want to hear you call him names?"

"Ever since ya went blondie, I swear yuv lost yer senses. There must be somethin' ina bleach that affects tha wits. You used to sit home night after night on your gary glitter pleased as punch wid yourself, but now, suddenly yer out showin' your threepenny bits 'n garglin' in bars late at night. This isn't right, Agnes Anne! This isn't my wee gersha. Yer some'mat else!"

As though I didn't care what my father thought, I raised and lowered my shoulders and dreamt of Jude, saved by Sheldon and now safe and sound, grazing around my dish garden. I thought of Sheldon cutting away at the side of the cat's toy, and purposely avoided remembering the gash of the knife and how I screamed as I yanked it out of his hand. Instead, I chose to recall his steamy kiss and I didn't want to taint the memory of last night by talking about it at the breakfast table. I didn't care if Da thought I stabbed the chief of police. It was none of his business.

"I'm waitin' on ya, Agnes. How did tha' little sheeny come

fer a knife wound? Eh?"

I took another small bite of bacon. The bits of carbon sat bitter on my tongue.

"Here we go," Ma said, presenting me with one of the oblong pancake platters. "What 'tis it?"

"Not now, Irene. This is important." Da's eyes scanned my face. "There'll be wigs on the green, Agnes Anne, if ya don'a come clean and tell me wha' happened last night."

"Well?" Ma said, completely ignoring my father.

I looked down at the pancake. The up and down lines confounded me. There was a circle of squiggles in the center and what looked like perhaps a person standing next to it. I pointed to the squiggles. "Is that the MGM lion?"

"Almost!" she shouted.

"Really? A lion?"

"Who spoke ta lions?" she asked.

"Ferget 'bout tha damn lions 'n tell me wha' happened las' night!" Da shouted.

"Da," I said, with forced patience, "what happened between Sheldon and me is private. We broke no law, we caused no harm, and that's the only story you're going to get. So just stop, okay? I'm 28 years old and I'm entitled to my life."

"Come on, Agg," Ma said. "Yuv almos' got it. Give it another go."

"*Damnit, Agnes. The man was stabbed!*" Da yelled. He pounded his fist on the table.

"Lions against the Christians," I said to Ma.

"Sort of. Try again."

"Come on Agg'. Give yer ol' Da tha scooby doo."

A sense of power welled up inside me and I wiped the cunning smile off my face. I had always felt silence was a sign of weakness, but now I realized there's power in quiet. Look what it was doing to my father. I turned back to the pancake. I didn't have the frame of mind to guess.

"Can't I just eat it today, Ma?"

"No." Ma stamped her foot. "Look a' tha trouble I went ta—"

"Goddamnit, Agnes. The man went ta tha hospital!" Da yelled.

I ignored him and studied the enormous pancake on my

plate. Squiggles, lines, circles. I had no idea what Ma was drawing today.

Da changed his tune and went all pleady. "Come on Agg'. Wha' happened las' night?"

"Why did Bruno call you?" I said, going on the offensive. "Isn't he supposed to keep other peoples' medical information private? Isn't there some sort of law?"

Da pushed back from the table and stood up. "The Holy Water will freeze over before there are secrets in tha O'Neil fam'ly!" He struck a pose that would have been the envy of an emperor. "Bruno-god-love-him, is doin' this family a favor by callin' me. Now that's a man, Agnes, a man who has loyalty." Da's lower lip protruded and once again, he squinted at me and his long bushy eyebrows fanned out over both eyes. "He wants ya t'call him, he does. I bet Bruno's going to give ya an earful about that sheeny. Ha! And it's not up ta you t'give him any cheek. If ya won't listen ta me, maybe you'll listen ta him."

"It's none of Bruno's business whom I choose to date. I don't have to talk to him about *anything*." Appetite ruined, I threw down my napkin across Ma's masterpiece and left the room.

"Agnes!" Ma said, scurrying after me. "Come back 'n eat yer pancake! It's Daniel, i'tis. Daniel inna Lion's Den. Ya were almos' right, luv. Don't feel bad ya couldn't get it! Come back!"

15. Another Open House

SUNDAY AFTERNOON, Verna had me at another one of her listings, a short, squat Victorian located on a steep hill in Pacific Heights, a hill so steep that people park perpendicularly, and the sidewalk is a long flight of stairs. Nervous that Bruno might come by again, I decided to invite Katie over to see the house, then she'd tell Bruno where she was going and he would stay away. But Katie said she didn't feel well and couldn't come.

I entered the empty house filled with trepidation. The house seemed to gape at me like a lonely dragon. I tiptoed through the two and a half baths, three bedrooms, den, dining room, living room and flipped on lights. The only furniture was a dining room table and a folding chair. Verna had said there was cookie dough in the freezer and I popped the cookies in the oven and started a pot of coffee, then laid out the property brochures and made a fan of my new business cards.

About twenty couples came through the house that foggy Sunday afternoon. Driving up in their BMWs and Mercedes, they dutifully wiped their shoes on the welcome mat and trooped through each room, opened closets, turned on water faucets, and planed how to best tear the place apart for a complete remodel. If I lived here, I wouldn't dream of tearing anything out, I'd preserve it and care for it, being careful to keep everything vintage, but I heard the customers talking about granite in the kitchen and travertine shower enclosures. They talked about where the best place might be to add a third bath, and what wall to knock out to expand the master bedroom.

I met a sweet old lady who wanted to find a place with just the right light for her orchids, and another couple trying to find a house big enough for their three children, but the price had to be under $3,000,000 and in the "right" neighborhood. They seemed to be having a difficult time. Then there came an elderly couple looking to downsize, who needed a house within walking distance of shopping. They cringed at the steepness of the hill and wandered back out the front door chattering about condos downtown. Another couple told me they valued a backyard above all things. I escorted the backyard lovers to the property's side yard, the terrace protected by an ancient, well-pruned wisteria, and left them alone to fall in love with the small secret space. About forty-five minutes later, flushed and smiling, they came into the dining room where I was sitting with the property information sheets. We wrote a full-priced offer.

In the course of writing up the contract, I heard an all-too-familiar voice. Bruno's head peered around the corner on the other side of an archway. The couple smiled and deferred to me, figuring this must be my friend.

I greeted Bruno with the barest civility.

"I see you're busy." His smile belied his disappointment. I hoped my stare was icy enough to make him go away. I continued with the offer. Hell or high water wouldn't separate me from the chance to make another sale. Instead of calling me out of the room, he bowed as though to tip an invisible hat and disappeared. I prayed he wouldn't be waiting outside.

After the couple left, I bolted the front door, then I moved cautiously from room to room turning off lights. Wary and guarded, I peered into each room, hoping Bruno wouldn't be hiding somewhere, ready to lunge at me. I half-expected him to be leaning against a wall having a cigarette in one of the upstairs rooms, or to pop out of one of the bathrooms and rip at my clothes. But I was wrong. I was alone.

Out on the pavement, I pulled in the *Open Home* sign from the corner and put it in my trunk. The only voice I heard was the wind blowing through the streets.

There was a note under my windshield. With trembling hands, I retrieved it.

The note said, "You look sexy today."

I ripped it into a thousand pieces and threw it out the window and watched it blow up the hill and scatter. I asked forgiveness for littering.

16. What's Your Secret?

BACK AT THE OFFICE on Monday morning, I showed the offer to Verna and after a few lectures on "The Art of Presenting Offers," and to continue my training, she had me present it to her clients that same afternoon. The "Sale Pending" sign went up on the property. I couldn't believe my luck!

Da, being the office broker, had to approve every deal, and I couldn't help but be filled with pride that he had to initial-off on my *second* contract in my first month.

"Agnes Anne!" Da said, motioning me into his office.

I followed him. He signaled me to take a seat.

"So, ya wrote another contract, did ya?"

"Yes," I said. "Yesterday."

Da took his reading glasses off and eyed me up and down. "And i'twas accepted."

"Yes," I said, again.

He nodded his head and was silent for many seconds. "No one 'as written much of anythin' this month." He snorted and leaned so far back in his leather chair it groaned.

I nodded. The agents complained all the time.

"Or las' month," he said. He looked at me and I saw his eyebrows rise. "Ya know," he said, taking out an accounting sheet, which was not unlike the one he used for tracking Novenas. "Yer commissions, wid tha bump ya get for holdin' open another agent's listin', then tha commission from tha sellin' side, makes yer gross even higher than Verna's. Ya actually lead tha office this month." Wide-eyed, he looked up at me. "I canno' believe it!"

I didn't know what to say.

"I 'ave agents out there who haven't written a contract fer months. They're starvin' out there."

I watched him rock his chair back and forth. "I'm sorry," I said.

"Do'na be sorry! Sorry's fer losers." He leaned over his desk and whispered. "How are ya doin' it?"

I gazed back at him and chewed the inside of my cheek. "I don't know."

"Well ya must be doin' somethin'. Let me hear yer pitch. What are ya sayin' to 'em?"

"I let people walk around pretty much by themselves," I said, trying to think. "I offer them coffee and cookies like Verna told me. And then I ask them what they're looking for."

"Ya mean ya don' try ta *sell* it to'em?" Da looked vexed, as though what I'd been doing wasn't enough. "Ya don't point out all tha good things in tha place and encourage 'em ta make an offer? Then come in fer tha close?"

"No," I said. I didn't want to tell him that because of my stutter, I tried not to talk. I listened more than I spoke.

Da waved his hand like something smelled bad and he needed to move the air. "Dahhhh! Tha' couldn't be all ther' is. Well, it's prob'bly beginner's luck. Don't think this's tha way it's goin' ta be, Agnes Anne. Sales 're difficult. Yuv just been lucky. That's all."

I nodded. "Yes," I repeated, my mind spinning as I tried to count the money that would be coming my way. "Lucky."

"Have ya returned Bruno-god-love-him's call?" he asked.

"No," I said, wondering how he knew Bruno left me a message.

"Why not?" he said.

I didn't want to say that it was a trap, so I looked down at my hands. My fingernails were chipped. I had to go back for another manicure. I wondered if Sheldon and I could go together.

"Ya know," Da said, "he and 'is sister own a rental house in Ashbury Heights. Belonged ta his folks, it did, and now it's vacant so they wanna sell. Ya could get that listin', Agnes Anne." Da gave me his leprechaun smile. "See if ya cud parlay this beginner's luck. If I were you, I'd return 'is call, *Anne.*"

Out in Cubicle City, word spread that I had made my second sale. My neighbors, David and Brent, clapped their hands and congratulated me. They had been the only ones, besides Verna, these last three weeks who had loved what I'd been doing with my hair and noticed my new makeup and clothes. David sometimes reached over to me and propped up my collar and told me to put a scarf with my suit jacket or some other style tidbit. I never knew they were so full of fashion advice.

"Anne," Bruno said, when I finally called him, "how *are* you? Sheldon's boo-boo better?"

"Yes, he's doing fine." I sounded like a total prig. I probably looked like one, too.

"How did you say he stabbed himself?"

"Kitchen accident," I said automatically.

"I didn't want to say anything, the other night but I'm supposed to report any suspicious wounds to the police. Did you know that?"

I had the urge right then to hang up, but I resisted and kept my voice professional. "My father said to c-call you about your p-parents' house."

"What makes you think I'll give that listing to you?"

"Nothing," I replied. "I don't care who you give it to. Da just told me to call you. That's all. Task done. Do whatever you want."

"Listen to you. You're so nasty all of a sudden. Was it the hair? Or the real estate license? Is that what's made you change?"

"I'm supposed to care what you think?"

"Geez, Anne."

Instead of hanging up, I remained on the line. I guess it was the hope that he would give me this listing. I know that greed is one of the Seven Deadly Sins and just the inkling of hope that his listing could be mine and make my money worries go away made me fall right into its clutches.

"So do you want this listing or not? It's a good place. Great neighborhood."

"Of course. Yes, I'd love to sell it."

"Okay then. Meet me for lunch. We'll discuss it."

I didn't want to go to lunch alone with Bruno. I wouldn't mind if we were in a group. Even with one other person. But not alone. Definitely not alone.

"I can't today," I said.

"Tomorrow then."

I wanted to say that I couldn't tomorrow either, but I knew if I wanted the business, I would have to meet with him. I took a deep breath. "Tomorrow," I said, firmly. "I'll bring Verna."

"I don't want to see Verna," Bruno said, his voice a petulant whine. "I want to give this listing to you, not that ball-buster."

I gazed at the row of holy cards on my cubicle wall. In the corner, behind the phone, I spotted my small laminated photo of Marilyn.

"Where should we meet?" I said in a gushy whisper.

"The Bombay Bicycle," Bruno replied. "Do you know it?"

Although I'd never been there, I knew where it was.

"Noon then?" Bruno dropped his voice. "Good. I'll see you tomorrow... *Anne*."

17. Going Indian

THE BOMBAY BICYCLE RESTAURANT smelled piquant and peppery. The hostess showed us to a table not visible from the street. On the long walk to the back of the restaurant, I found myself staring at the tapestries and cloth hangings, paintings of women with six arms, and men with the heads of elephants. I looked around with suspicious eyes, distrustful of the lovely waitress with her flowing sari and plum-colored eyelids.

Before I left the office, I had spoken with Verna to get some direction on how to list a property. She pulled the documents I'd need, the disclosures, booklets on lead paint, earthquake zones as well as the listing contract. After her lecture, I tucked everything inside my aubergine briefcase and vowed to not let Bruno get the upper hand.

"Finally goin' to lunch with Bruno, are you?" Da had said, passing me in the hall. "Good fer you, girl. Knock 'em dead. I can't believe you've had two sales this month. Hah! Luck of the Irish. Sell, sell, sell. Hit that shamrock there fer good luck." He pointed to the shamrock button outside his office. It was right next to another trick button labeled "Panic."

I blinked a couple of times. He had to be kidding.

"Go on, hit it." Da gestured to it again. The green shiny shamrock was about the size of my palm. I knew he had agents hit it for good luck, but I didn't think I needed it. It wasn't as though my meeting was a cold call.

"Go on," he commanded. "'Tis fer luck. Hit tha shamrock."

I had no choice. I pressed the shamrock and heard a wheezing squeak. It sounded like the fart of a puny elf.

The table at the restaurant was a banquette bench for two. Bruno gestured for me to slide in first. I didn't like it that he slid in beside me, not pulling up a chair across from me. He bounced a couple of times and had a goofy smile on his face.

"Hey, I love your hair, but you know that," he said. "This color is fabulous." Bruno reached out and touched it. My scalp shriveled into goose flesh.

"Thanks." I said, again, trying to duck. "How's Katie?" I could tell he didn't like that I brought up her name. As though my hair had ignited into flames, his hand jumped away.

"She's so-so. I wish she'd get over this depression thing. He shook his head as though the miscarriage had been her fault. His eyes tried to find mine, but I looked away. "I don't know how long I can go on like this," he said. "It's a terrible strain."

I flashed back to the last First Friday dinner. Katie's skin, the color of bread dough; Bruno tenderly caring for her while flirting with me. My stomach churned.

The waitress handed us menus and pattered on about the best things to eat. Because of her accent, I had a hard time following her, but it didn't seem to bother Bruno.

When she left, he turned to me again. "Sorry I look like this," he said, rubbing the stubble on his chin. "I've been at the hospital all night. I had to fill in for another doctor, so I've been there two nights. It's been crazy. I've hardly slept."

His eyes said, *Please feel sorry for me.* But I wasn't fooled.

"That's okay," I said. I opened the menu and began to read. Trouble was, I knew nothing about Indian food, and trying to sound out names I not only couldn't pronounce or connect to flavors was futile.

Bruno left his menu closed. "So... how the heck did your friend shove that knife so deep in his palm?"

"Not this again, Bruno." I buried my face in the menu.

"Come on," he said. "What the hell were you two doing?"

"If you think I stabbed Sheldon, why don't you report it?"

My eyes dropped to the basket a busboy delivered to the table. I could detect the scent of fragrant bread. I took one of the pieces. It was flat as one of Ma's pancakes, but smelled oh-so-much better. I ripped off a portion and stuffed it into my mouth. The dough was soft and chewy.

Bruno's face was too close to mine and I was glad to be interrupted by the server. While I became lost in the lady's orange and red sari and tried to figure out how she folded the fabric and pleated it so the material fell gracefully around her, she chatted amiably with Bruno about vegetarian pakoras and chicken masala. He insisted on ordering something called aachar pacharanga and said that we would share. Before she left, I could feel Bruno's arm on the top of the banquette bench behind me. His hand crept down next to my shoulder blades. With the tips of his fingers, he began to stroke my neck.

I immediately tried to shrug him off and he stopped, but then he leaned in so close to my face that if I had tried to look at him, I would have seen double.

"What do you see in this dork you're dating?" he said, softly.

"I like Sheldon. He's nice."

Bruno's voice turned saccharine. "I'm nice."

I threw off his arm and tried to create more distance between us, but it was futile as there wasn't much room on the bench.

"Would you stop that?" I said. "You're married to my s-sister. It's not right for you to be t-t talking like this or behaving like a—a—"

His tone became low and embarrassingly sexy. "A what, Anne? What am I behaving like? Hummm?"

I looked straight at him. "A dirt bag."

He pulled his arm back. "Mind your Ps and Qs," he said, raising his chin. "I have feelings, too." He adjusted himself on the bench. "What if I tell Katie you keep throwing yourself at me? How do you think she'd respond to that?"

"You wouldn't," I gasped. His smile said, *Gotcha.* I needed to attack. "How would you like it if I told my brothers that you're trying to blackmail me?" I lifted my chin and squinted like Clint Eastwood. "How would you like *that?*"

Bruno's eyes darted left and right, then centered on my face. "Well, how would *you* like it if I told *them* their sister was calling me at all hours? They know you've always liked me. You know the tale. I met Katie and threw you over. Who do you think they'd believe? Bruno-god-love-him? *Or you?*"

I swallowed hard. He had a point and it was a risk great enough to make me hesitate. Besides, he was a man and men believe other men.

The waitress placed four dishes down on our table. The steamy tang and mixture of spices made me sneeze.

Bruno leaned in again. "Did you know a sneeze is related to a sexual response?" Bruno's lips were too close to my ear again and his hand had crept back on the nape of my neck. "When we're sexually excited there can be a sort of jump of electricity from the synapses involved with sexual response to the next group of synapses, the ones that involve sneezing."

This spawned a long, uncomfortable silence.

"Do I excite you, Anne?" Bruno murmured. "You excite me."

"No," I snapped. "Curry makes me sneeze." Quickly, I grabbed for one of the serving dishes and pushed some food onto my plate. "Do you want to put your parents' rental on the market right away? Or shall we wait until spring?"

"Right away," he said. He looked down at his plate and nodded, then picked at the fried things. "I think it's time to sell. At first I thought I'd like to move in there, but the place needs a lot of work. My sister wants to sell so I'd have to buy her out, which I suppose I could swing. But I don't have time for a new project and it's obvious Katie can't take on a project right now. Huh—right now, Katie can't do anything."

The tone he used when he said my sister's name made me flinch.

"I brought some comps." I kept my voice professional, grateful that the conversation had finally found its way to real estate. We started talking about values in the area and I managed to keep the conversation on house prices, the length of time to sell a property right now, and how we should get it ready for the market so he could get the best price.

I thought I was doing great until Bruno leaned over and put one arm tightly around my shoulders. His lips touched my ear.

"You want this listing?" he said, through curried breath. "I'll give it to you, if you'll meet me at the little hotel around the corner. Hum? It'll be nice. Just you... and me."

I pulled away. "Stop it."

"Don't tense up like that. God! You're so frigid. For heaven's sake, Anne, it won't be like when we were kids. Just forget what happened to us then. Okay? And I know you're still a virgin, am I right?"

I couldn't look at him. Wouldn't look at him.

"I was a clod when I was nineteen." His hand came back on my shoulder. His fingers stroked my neck. "I've said I'm sorry. You're making me beg for it, aren't you."

I kept my eyes on my plate and stared into the chickpeas and rice, bell peppers and bits of chicken as though they might give me a message.

"I'm groveling now, Agnes. Is that what you've wanted? To see me grovel? I'll grovel at your feet, but then I'll kiss your calves, work my way up to your thighs..."

I forced my face to remain blank, which was something I certainly knew how to do. I've done it since the night of my Junior Prom. I withheld my fall from Grace from my parents, my anger from my sisters, and stuffed my emotions into a tight ball. So tight, I've been able to hide them from everyone. Even from myself.

"Are you even listening to me?" Bruno said. "Can't we have a new start?"

I threw his hand away from my shoulders like it was trash and said under my breath, "Don't touch me." His hand came right back, but this time I grabbed his wrist.

"Don't be so nasty. Come on, Agnes." Bruno twisted his hand free. "You know how I feel about you. Your sister is driving me nuts. Complaining, whining, always depressed. Believe me, it's no life." His voice dropped to a slippery whisper. "But we're adults now. Right? *Consenting adults.*"

If there had been a place to wriggle away, I would have. But the banquette had a side return and I couldn't go anywhere. Like snake venom, my whisper was my only defense and I lashed back with all the poison I could muster. *"You disgust me."*

I glanced around the restaurant, hoping no one was looking our way. There were various couples at tables for two and a family of five in the corner. No one paid any attention to us, but I lowered my voice even more and spoke through clenched teeth. "I'll be happy to sell your property, Bruno, but I will not—"

"You know what I'm going to do? I'm going to caress every part of you, Anne. From your toes to your breasts... and then I'll taste your luscious honey. You're going to beg for me, cry out in ecstasy. Then I'll come into you, slowly... beautifully."

I wish I could say that everything Bruno said repulsed me, but no one had ever said anything like this to me before and, regrettably, his words caused a tingling deep inside the fork of my legs. Even though I longed to run out of there, I also knew a small part of me actually liked hearing this trashy talk. It was weird. Too weird. Against all self-control, I sneezed.

Bruno's satisfaction glowed like embers fanned by a zephyr. "I *do* have an effect on you! Oh Agnes," he said, reaching for my hand, "we'll be great lovers."

While he beamed, I wished I could be sucked into a sink hole. I wished I were being carried out into an ambulance, or better yet, a hearse. But unless Bruno moved, the only way to leave was to slip down under the table and crawl out.

"Oh stop it. Don't be like that. I hate that ice queen expression of yours. It's cold. And rude. And absolutely unnecessary, *Anne.* We're *adults."* He lowered his voice to a conspiratorial whisper. "Consenting adults."

Rage pulsed through me. I had been both tricked and assaulted, only this time Bruno had done it in public.

"Aren't you a little curious about me, Agnes Anne O'Neil? Don't you wonder what it would be like if sex went the way it should? If there were romance and dim lights? Someone loving to... " Under the tablecloth, Bruno found my hand, squeezed it and tried to bring it toward his crotch. "Feel that?" he said. Pride roved across his face.

Repulsed, I jerked my hand away.

"See how you excite me?" His eyes darted hastily around my face, then slowly strayed down to my bust line, and as though he had all the time in the world, his eyes leisurely meandered up my body. A half-grin crept up one side of his creepy face. "And do you know why women like me?"

The churn of foreign food and more emotion than I could handle made my stomach quiver in pain. Vomiting, I realized, might be unavoidable. I tried to form a sentence about the listing that would change the subject, but as quickly as my words formed, the nausea cramped my innards. Words vanished.

"Because I'm good at it," Bruno whispered. "And virgins really excite me."

"Let me out." I glanced around the table, wondering what I could throw up in.

He chuckled like I was playing hard to get. "You'd rather have that skinny Jewish nerd be your first? Anne, it should be me!" His finger lazily traced lines on the nape of my neck. "A doctor. Someone who knows anatomy." His breath came hot on my neck while he whispered, "Someone who knows what every part of a woman is for. What it can do, and what it *will* do."

Across the room, my eyes found a painting of an Indian woman. Her eyes were outlined in kohl black, her hands rested below her face, palms out and peppered with a reddish design. I knew Bruno was still talking, but I wasn't listening to him anymore, I wasn't even feeling his touch. Instead, I gazed into the lady's black eyes and tried to distract myself from the nausea blooming in my midsection. I wondered about her life, what she was doing this very minute. A month could have gone by.

Bruno's face was still too close to me. I pushed him away with one more sharp thrust of an elbow. "Don't you touch me," I rasped. *"Don't you ever, ever touch me."*

"You're trembling, Agnes. You like me. I know you do. Why won't you admit it?"

Venom sprayed from my lips. "The only reason I tolerate you is that you're a part of my family. In truth, I despise everything about you. I'm done. Let me out."

"So sorry. You no play-a the game, you no get-a my listing." His lips twisted into an idiotic smirk.

From the beginning, I knew there was something wrong with this listing coming to me. Of all the agents Bruno knew, with Da and Uncle Jimmy being brokers, and with all the agents in the office, Bruno could have given this listing to a whole host of people far better qualified and with an amazing amount of experience. Instead, he had chosen me.

Of course there had to be a catch.

While a trembling rage fumed inside, my anger was not only directed at Bruno, but at myself and the way I had fallen into the clutches of Greed. Nausea washed over me in pulsing waves.

"Let me out," I said, as calmly as I could. I figured I had thirty seconds before I threw up. Maybe less.

Bruno's face came too close to mine. "You're not leaving until you agree to meet me around the corner."

I swallowed back bile, then collected my papers and threw them back into my beautiful aubergine briefcase. There was no way I would foul it by using it as a basin. I had to get out of here.

Bruno's smug expression made it clear that he was not going to let me out of the banquette bench. The bitter taste of bile stung the back of my throat. I knew there was only one way out and that was to go under the table. I began to relax my muscles and let my bones become jelly. I felt the back of the banquette bench pass my rump, then the small of my back, then my upper back as I slid like a salamander to the floor.

Bruno's eyes widened as I disappeared beneath the linen tablecloth. Once under the table, I crawled out and stood up on the other side, surprising several nearby patrons.

"M-my b-briefcase, p-please?" Stomach churning, esophagus like a racecar revving its engine, I held both hands out to him. Bruno took his time.

"You're being ridiculous about this," he said, casually reaching for my briefcase.

Before I could grab it, a spasm of nausea captured me. My insides twisted. The pain of it made me bend forward. I spied the Tandoori breadbasket. I reached for it and made disgusting noises as I heaved the contents of my stomach between the soft folds of cloth and over the delicious bread.

"Agnes!" Bruno stood and reached for me, his touch far kinder than I expected. "Are you all right? Is it the food?"

"No," I whispered, straightening up, trying to recover my dignity. Then I shoved the stinking breadbasket at him and wiped my mouth on the back of my hand. "It's not the food. It's the company."

18. The Aftermath of Failure

"ZO, HOW VAS LUNCH vis the adorable Bruno Stark?" Verna leaned back in her big executive chair in her private office, the office of my dreams. Da said I had the highest gross last month, but this I knew was only temporary, a strange case of beginner's luck. Who was I kidding? The corner office was a feeble wish, another symptom of my devotion to Greed. I had to rid myself of all of this and vowed that tonight, I would Offer Up my sins and ask the Blessed Virgin to take them away.

"Family trouble," I quickly replied.

"Family trrr-ouble?" Verna said, like dice her Rs, bounced on the granite desktop. "You know, you don't look vell to me, Agg-nez. No, no, no. Zomezing iz wrong,"

In truth, I felt much better now than I did at the restaurant, but I was probably still pale.

"I guess I'm a little upset because Bruno's not ready to sell."

Instantly, I regretted my fib and I said a quick prayer. Yet I was too embarrassed to tell Verna what really happened and so I made my excuses and left her office as quickly as I could.

"Ahnne?" Verna called after me.

I poked my head back through her doorway.

"You need to get your hair done. I am zeeing zee rootz."

Stunned at her bluntness, I nodded. "My hair grows fast. I'm trying to get an appointment." Another lie. I thought I heard Saint Peter up in heaven scratching on his blackboard, scoring another mark in the column under my name entitled Venial Sins.

"Vell, donn't juzt try to get an appointment. Get von," Verna said, with force. "Ze zecret to beauty is constant vigilanze. Nailz unt hair. Hair unt nailz." She slapped the back of her hand into the other palm.

On the way back to my cubicle, I wondered what Da would do if I told him that his favorite son-in-law, Bruno-god-love-him, was dangling the listing in front of me and wouldn't give it to me unless I had sex with him. I also wondered if Da actually contacted Bruno and asked him about it, what Bruno would reply.

Thinking about it gave me a splitting headache. I knew I should Offer It Up, send all the crap to heaven and let Mary and Jesus deal with it and so I began to inwardly chant over and over, *Mary, take this from me. Mary, take this from me. Take this grimy feeling away from me.*

After about ten minutes just sitting in my cubicle and praying, I still felt cheap and dirty. I didn't know what else to do. I phoned my sister Fiona.

"I have to be at the studio in thirty minutes." Fiona snapped. "What's up?"

I tried to be quick, but everything I said came out like I was asking questions.

"B-Bruno took me to lunch? He wanted me to sell his parents' house? I mean, he used to want—"

"Hurry up. I gotta go."

"So we had this lunch?"

"You told me that."

"And all he did was ask me—ask me to—" My throat went on lock-down.

"To what?" she prompted. "I gotta go! Spit it out, Agg."

"T-to have s-sex."

As though I just told her a joke, Fiona laughed. "You've got to be kidding."

"No," I whispered.

"He's your brother-in-law."

I waited for her to process it, feel the same indignation I felt.

"Were you flirting with him? We all know you used to—"

"No!" I shouted. Like specters, four eyes peered over the cubicle wall, then like gophers, Brent and David disappeared. I looked back to my plain desk top, to the holy cards I had tacked to the wall behind the phone. I gazed at Saint Michael and his raised sword, his foot on the monster. How I wanted to shove that sword into Bruno.

"Are you sure you got this right?" Fiona said. The doubt in her voice stung like Ma's iodine on a skinned knee.

"Y-yes, I got it r-right. It was c-crude and em-

embarrassing."

"Agnes—I mean, Anne." Fiona's voice now low and measured. "Bruno would never, never hurt Katie."

"But he leered. He put his arm around me—tried to touch me."

"Bruno always acts like that. He's a touchy-feely kind of guy. I think you're misreading him," she said. "Were you acting all flirty?"

"It was a b-business lunch and he was all over me, asking me to g-go t-to b-bed—" The part about pulling my hand to his crotch never got out of my mouth.

I heard her sigh. "Well, I'm sorry you interpreted it that way, but look, you're in sales now. And you're blonde. Remember? You were the one who wanted to be blonde. It turns guys on. There'll be lots of guys who will hit on you now. Lots of guys who will say stuff you don't want to hear. Take it with a grain of salt, okay? Bruno hugs me all the time and calls me 'The sister who got away.' He's just joking. And you're inexperienced and... well... too rigid. Look, I gotta go."

A zip of static told me Fiona had hung up.

LATER ON IN THE DAY, Da saw me in the hall and I knew I had to face him. He gave me the treatment he reserves for all agents who come in with big listings: a hearty pat on the back and an expansive invitation into his office to share battle stories.

"That's a honey ov'a property, 'is folks' place. Nice that he's givin' ya tha listin' Agnes. Blood's thicker 'n water, eh?" He punched at the air and expected me to follow him into his office. I didn't want to go. No way. But I also knew that to postpone it wouldn't do any good. I might as well get it over with. Head down, I dutifully walked towards the gallows.

"Ya know, Bruno could give tha' listin' ta anyone 'e wants," Da said, over his shoulder as he rounded the corner of his desk. "Ya know tha', don't ya, Agnes?" He sat down and settled himself into his leather chair. "Lemme see tha listin' contract." He put his hand out and made the "gimmie" sign.

I stared at him for a few beats and tried to inhale and control my exhale so I wouldn't stutter. "Bruno wants to sell,

Da... but... um... the price is too high." I hoped he might get my drift.

"Tell him ta come down!" he shouted. "Show him tha comps!" He slammed his fist on the desk. "Ya have ta learn ta control yer client, Agnes. It's part a' tha business. You need ta be more forceful! Yer in a man's world now and yuv got ta learn ta take control." He threw another right hook into the air between us.

"I'm not t-talking about comps." I took a swipe at the perspiration on my upper lip.

Da's forehead wrinkled like a crushed paper fan. I wanted to tell him what really happened, but I didn't know the words. Talking about sex in front of my father was not just difficult, it was impossible. Logically, I knew my parents had sex. After all, they'd had nine kids. I used to think that it meant they'd had sex nine times. Sex was never mentioned in our house. Not one word.

Da tisked and shook his head. "How can I make ya inta a salesman, Agnes Anne? Yuv gotta get in there," he said. He thrust his arm forward, elbow bent and threw me yet another imaginary right hook. "Tell yer client wha' he should do. That's sellin'!"

He flung himself back in his chair and stared at me, as though assessing whether or not I spoke English. Then he whispered, "Ya did give 'im some comps, didn't ya?"

I looked at the papers strewn across his desk. I knew a list of like-properties, sales from the area, was not the problem. The problem was Bruno.

"Good. Good." He nodded. "So when 're we puttin' it in tha paper? What 'n ad campaign we can have with that house! Primo neighborhood. Should sell fer well over three 'n a half million, wouldn't ya say? Might even be bid up."

I tried to nod, but my neck had locked in place. My stomach growled and another wave of nausea tugged at my throat.

"Where's tha listin' agreement?" he asked again.

"In my briefcase," I mumbled. I tried to say, *Unsigned*, but it didn't leave my lips.

"Bring it 'ere!" Da shouted. "Time's a wastin'." When I didn't move, his voice climbed up an octave. "What's wrong, Agnes Anne? Ya look a bit peckish. Don' tell me ya haven't talked 'bout price yet."

"I t-t-told you, n-n-no!"

"I thought ya said ya gave him the comps."

"I *had* comps, but we didn't get that far, Da."

"Wha'da ya mean ya didn't get tha' far? Ya had all lunch hour ta go through it."

In my mind's eye I saw Bruno's leering eyes, smelled the faded scent of tobacco, and could feel the suggestive slimy circles his hand had made on the nape of my neck. Words wouldn't come.

"Agnes." Da leaned forward and spoke slowly like I was dim-witted. *"Did ya get tha listin' er not?"*

"No," I whispered. "Bruno...had some...strings attached."

"Strings? Now just wha' would tha conditions be?" Da leaned back into his chair and crossed his chubby arms over his big stomach and waited.

"Bruno won't give me the listing," I whispered, "unless I meet him at a hotel for sex." There. It was out.

He nearly screamed. "What? You?" Then he collapsed into gales of laughter. "Ha, ha, ha, ha, ha! That's a good one, i'tis. A good one! Agnes, tha man was jokin'! How can ya think tha man was serious? He's married ta yer sister!"

"Bruno withdrew his offer of the listing, Da, when I said I wouldn't do it."

"Ya must'a misunderstood," he whispered.

"W-why don't you phone him yourself? Bruno probably won't admit it to you, but I'd be interested to hear his excuse. Put him on s-s-s-speaker phone. Let's get it over with."

"Yer serious! Ya really think tha's wha' tha bloke meant?"

"I may stutter, but I do understand En-English." My head felt like twenty carpenters were inside pounding nails, the spikes going through my skull at odd angles. There was no use staying in Da's office. I stood up to leave.

"Wait!" he said. "Wha' happened ta tha listin' agreement? Did ya give it ta 'im? Does 'e have it?"

I turned back at the door. "No. I didn't think there was any p-p-point."

"That was yer mistake, Agnes Anne. Ya should'a gotten him ta sign before ya left tha restaurant. He was probably jokin', ya know. Trying ta convince ya ta stop seein' that ridiculous foreigner yer dating. 'Twas all a joke. I told ya this business wasn't fer tha likes of you."

"Right," I said, strangling the doorknob. "Have it your way. I had a lovely lunch with a guy who d-dangled a listing in front of me and w-wanted something in return." I turned to look at him. "Something *you've* always said not to give away."

Da gasped. "Surely ya got it wrong, Agnes."

"My name at the office," I said, over my shoulder, "is *Anne.*"

19. First Friday

THE FIRST FRIDAY IN JANUARY was no exception to all of the others. Hot dishes were wrestled up the front stairs and into the kitchen and the house filled with chatter and children. Bruno and Katie hadn't arrived, which made me feel bad because I should have called Katie and asked her how she felt.

"So little Agnes Anne," my eldest brother Matthew said, swaggering up to me. "How's real estate treatin' ya in this brand new year?"

I told him about my condo sale and also about the big expensive house I had in contract, and he seemed somewhat impressed. Then he said, "So what's this I hear, yer datin' a sheeny? 'Tis it true? Yer datin' a Jew?"

"No one uses that word anymore, Matthew. It's not politically correct." I scrubbed the immaculate countertop with a sponge. My eyes narrowed. "Who told you?"

"Da." Matthew took a swig of beer.

"Figures," I mumbled.

"So when da we get ta meet this gem? I hear he sliced off 'is hand."

I didn't want to go into it. I turned my attention to his little daughter in her sweet blue dress. She showed me her empty glass. "Dara! Aren't you a pretty one today." I knelt down to her level. "Would you like more juice?"

"Next time, bring tha bloke," Matthew said, over my chatter to his daughter. "I'd like ta meet 'im." The hand holding his beer was as big as a rump roast. Introducing him to Sheldon, with his slight build and skinny frame, would be a recipe for disaster. I could see Matthew try to arm wrestle Sheldon though a handshake, pump his arm so he could test his muscles while crimping his hurt hand to smithereens.

I stood up and looked Matthew square in the eye. "If I *did* bring him to First Friday, you'd have to be polite."

He blinked and pulled his chin back a couple of inches. "I'm always polite, never was there a truer gentleman than I." Matthew performed a slight bow. "I would say, 'Hello, Sheldon tha Sheeney, I'm Matthew tha Mick. I do hope yer treatin' me sister with care.'"

When I didn't respond, he raised both arms in astonished surrender. "I'm yer eldest brother, fer godsake. I should be lookin' at who m'baby sister dates."

"Ach! Of all people datin' out tha Faith, I never t'ought it would be our Agnes Anne," Ma said, from over at the sink. She shook her head so hard, her graying hair flopped stiffly against her cheeks.

"We only want tha best fer ya, Agnes," Matthew said. "Why are ya involved with this bloke anyway?"

"I keep prayin' for the Conversion of the Jews." Ma poked a fork in some boiling potatoes as though she was goading them to cook faster. "But it never 'appens. An' now here's our Agnes Anne, out all hours a' tha night."

"Ach, the Jews 're fine tha way they are, Ma," Matthew said. "Who cares if they convert? Let 'em stay in Israel 'n duke it out wid tha A-rabs." He looked back at me. "Bring tha bloke ta First Friday, Aggie. Let him meet tha clan. And if 'e can't stand us, so be it. Send 'im on his way."

Before I could respond, Da leaned in. "D'ya know what this girl did, do ya Matthew? She got all huffy at Bruno tha other day when he offered her tha listin' on his parents' rental house. She misunderstood somethin' he said, stomped out'a tha restaurant 'n stuck him wid tha fare! Imagine tha'."

I held my breath waiting to hear if he knew that wasn't the only thing I stuck Bruno with.

"Made 'im pay? Ahhh, Aggie. Ya shouldn't'a done tha'!" Matthew stared at me like I was an imbecile. "If he was gonna' give ya business, even though yer a girl, you should'a paid. That's tha way things are now. I thought ya knew."

"Ah Matthew, ya wouldn't believe what a prince of a man Bruno is. He's gonna' stay with O'Neil. Imagine tha'! And after wha' Aggie did." Da shook his head as though a miracle had occurred in our midst.

"She's going by *Anne* now," Fiona said, coming over to join the conversation. "I hate the way you guys always put her down. What's with that?"

"We donut do tha'," Da said. "She just donut know how ta conduct business. Agnes Anne's as green as a berry bush."

"She sold two properties this month," Fiona retorted. "Name someone else in the company who did that."

Da's face turned red. The crisscrossing veins popping out on the side of his head began to resemble girders on the Golden Gate Bridge.

"Anne," he said, between clenched teeth, "'as a lot ta learn. She nearly lost tha' listin', Fiona, 'n if it weren't for me smoothin' things over, Bruno might'a gone wid another company. But God-love-him, Bruno understands how naïve yer sister is 'n he didna hold it against 'er. Not even—get this, Fiona—Matthew? 'Re ya listenin'? Not even when yer dear sister threw up a' tha table."

Matthew roared. Fiona shrieked. I went scarlet.

"At the table?" Matthew said, still laughing. "Just like tha ol' days? Ya didn't give him an apple tart as well, did ya?"

Apple tart is Irish for fart. Fiona laughed so hard she had to put down her wine.

"Was it tha food?" Matthew said, as though he had to get to the bottom of things. "Where'd ya say ya were eatin'?"

"They ate at some Indian joint," Da said.

"Ah, well there ya are. I eat Indian and the damn stuff runs through me like shit through a goose."

"You really threw up at the table?" Fiona tugged at my sleeve. "You did? That really happened? You never told me."

"Ah," Da said, shaking his head. "I knew she should'a stayed in the back room. Gah!"

Before I could make a come-back, Ma called out from the oven, "Look a' this blessed lamb." Not one, but two, withered leg bones jutted out, one from each end of the roasting pan. It looked vaguely sexual.

"In the name 'a tha Father, tha Son, 'n tha Holy Spirit," Ma said, in full voice. "I bless this lamb 'n all who will eat it.

ay we accept this nourishment 'n tha name 'a tha Father, tha Son, 'n tha Holy Spirit, as it was 'n tha beginnin', is now and ever shall be world without end."

"Well it was th'end 'a tha world fer tha lamb, wadn't it?" Matthew mumbled.

Da said a quick "Amen," and turned back to me. *"Anne,"* he said, scowling at me as though I was the family dog and had just pooped on the floor. "I spoke ta Bruno 'n he forgave you, vomit 'n all. D'ya hear me? *He's giving ya tha listin' anyway.* Ya' just need ta have 'im sign tha listin' agreement. If they don't come t'night, I suggest ya call him in tha mornin'."

"And fer godsakes, Aggie—" Matthew said, leaning close to whisper, "do it on tha phone so if ya have to, ya can be sittin' in the jacks poppin' apple tarts 'n tha bloke'ill never know."

Fiona shrieked with laughter and slapped me on the back.

20. The Seven Deadly Sins

SATURDAY MORNING, I got up, said my prayers, did my exercises, and decided to call Bruno like Da wanted. Frankly, I wanted to get it over with.

"What do you want?" Bruno said, when he realized it was me.

"Da," I said, with much effort, "said you c-called m-me."

"Oh yeah?"

"He said you s-still want me to s-sell your parents' house."

Silence. Finally, he said, "You know, I didn't appreciate you telling lies about me."

"What lies?" I croaked.

"You know what lies."

So that was the game he would play: say one thing to me and something else to the family.

"I also hear you came by my house to see Katie the other day. I don't want you seeing her when I'm not home."

My heart turned to stone. "What do you mean?"

"I mean you're no longer welcome in my house."

"Bruno," I gasped, "she's my sister."

"You're no longer welcome here, *Anne.*"

I wanted to say, *"Screw you, Bruno,"* but I lost the ability to speak. There was so much silence on the phone it felt like we were stuck in some strange version of freeze tag. The first one to speak would lose.

Finally, I blurted, "So was that why you didn't come to First Friday last night? You're embarrassed that you got caught?"

"Don't be ridiculous. Katie didn't feel well."

I didn't want to argue, I just wanted to make it clear that I was onto him.

"So... I guess I have to give you the listing." Bruno mumbled.

"You don't have to do anything." Knowing that he was trapped made me smile.

"You might as well take it. Any fool will be able to sell that place, but I want a discount on the commission."

"You don't deserve it."

"What's gotten into you?" he snorted. "Ever since you bleached your hair, I swear, you're a bitch."

"I want you to realize that the house probably needs painting inside and if the floors don't shine, they should be refinished," I said.

"Why should I bother?"

"If you want to achieve the best price, then you need to make it a showplace, otherwise it will look like a fixer-upper and the price people are willing to pay will reflect it."

"I don't have time for that. You'll have to supervise any repairs," he said.

"And we should hire a stager," I added. "After the walls are painted and the floors are done, you'll need a decorator to come in and fill it with furniture. It's going to run you probably five grand to start, then a couple of thousand a month, plus the cost of painting and refinishing."

"What other good news do you have for me?" From his tone, I could tell he knew I was right.

"We should go over the comps," I continued, "to see where the price should be. Don't make the mistake of listing it too high, or it will sit on the market too long and when you come down, it will look tired and you may not even get what you now say you won't take."

"I'm going to decide the price, not you," he snapped. "Drop the listing agreement off at the hospital and I'll fill the price in." Without a goodbye, Bruno hung up and I found myself listening to the dial tone.

I wondered if my smile was one of Pride or Greed.

The price Bruno put on the listing contract was probably a half million dollars over what the house would actually sell for. When I told Da Bruno set the price and not me, he practically orbited and used it as the cornerstone in his argument that women didn't belong in the real estate business, especially women named Agnes Anne O'Neil.

There was no use defending myself, so I stayed out of the office as much as I could all that week to meet with painters, floor refinishers, drapery cleaners, plumbers, and gardeners. The house would go on the market the following month and once I got in there and really investigated, I could see it needed far more TLC than I had first thought. Much to my surprise, Bruno was allowing these expenses. He even gave me a budget. I knew this would be the perfect time to have my operation. If I worked quickly to get everything set up, all the work could be done while I was on "my nose and chin" vacation.

I called Katie every day and she kept asking me to come over. Bruno had banned me from their house and I didn't know how to tell her so I avoided the whole thing altogether and invited her out to lunch.

On the way over to pick her up, I fantasized that this would be the day I would tell Katie what happened in high school between me and Bruno. That would put an end the family legend once and for all. I even practiced what I would say. She would cry. Be horrified that Bruno had been such a louse.

I would be supportive. Stoic. And forgiving. Then I would tell her about how he showed up at my listing and tried to kiss me. I would then tell her about our lunch at Bombay Bicycle and the way he used the listing as a lever to get me to have sex with him. In a huff, Katie would leave him.

I imagined how we would get an apartment together, just the two of us, sisters starting our lives over. Of course, she would be sad for being fooled for so long, but I would be patient and get her counseling, someone like Miss Allison, but not a speech therapist. A shrink. A real shrink.

When Katie came to the door, I didn't like what I saw. She was ashen and I felt ashamed that I had practiced my script over and over to myself in the car. How idiotic and stupid I was to think that any words from me would change anything.

We drove to a Chinese restaurant out on Taraval, but Katie had no appetite and didn't want anything. I convinced her to share a bowl of wonton soup. She seemed to admire the soup tureen more than the steaming vegetables inside.

"Don't you like wonton soup?" I said.

She didn't answer.

"Are you okay? I mean, really okay?"

"Yeah, I'm fine," Katie said, shrugging her bony shoulders. Her blonde hair hung limply down the front of her black sweater, reminding me of the long ears of a show dog. A miserable show dog.

"Do you know what's really wrong with you?" I blurted. "I mean, underneath all this bad appetite and crummy feeling. Have you been to see a doctor?"

"I'm married to one." Her gaze told me I was brainless.

"I mean, another doctor. An OB. What's your OB say about this?"

Katie averted her eyes and played with a wonton, moving the Chinese soupspoon like she was sculling an oar. Wordlessly, she hiked her shoulders up and down.

"Maybe you need to see a specialist. Someone who knows about digestion or auto-immune."

"I'm fine," she said. "I just need time. Bruno says it's an emotional reaction to the miscarriage. He says I'm depressed. That's all. He says it'll pass. I'm taking an antidepressant. I feel better than I did before. So I guess it's working."

"Why not come home for a while, have Ma cook for you and have a good rest?"

"Ma? Cook for *me?*"

"She's a good cook." Our eyes met. We both smirked. "You could lounge around and be waited on."

"Oh great, an Irish Spa Treatment: parsley and cabbage baths while listening to the Irish Rovers Greatest Hits. All the while Ma praying over me, showering me with holy cards, making me say the Rosary twice a day." Katie shook her head. "I'd be miserable. Besides, what would Bruno do without me?"

I didn't want to say that Bruno could take care of himself. "You're alone all the time, Katie. He's at the hospital night after night. Why not come home and have, say, two weeks entirely to yourself? There are plenty of bedrooms."

Gazing through me, I thought she actually began to consider it. Then, as though another notion began to crystallize, I watched her eyes refocus and hone in on me.

"So if I did that," she said, slowly, "went to Ma's and flaked out for a while, would this give *you* the chance to insinuate yourself into my house? Be with my husband?"

My breath evaporated. "Don't be silly," I croaked.

"You've always liked him."

"I have not." I watched Katie's expression morph into disdainful pout.

"It was *your* perfume all over him the other night," she said. "He told me. Oh, it was hard getting it out of him, but finally, he told me. It was you." Her eyes bore into me.

"Katie, I didn't—"

"I don't want to hear any excuses. Bruno's always been affectionate, but now that I don't feel well..." She shook her head and fought back tears. "It all piles up."

"Look, Katie. Bruno came to my Open House that afternoon and then he—"

"Don't." She showed me the palm of her hand. "I don't want to know. I just want *you* to know—*that I know.*"

"Bruno had no business coming to my Open House and bothering me. I think you should tell him to stop."

"Oh please."

"Tell him to stay away from me."

"You have the listing for his parents' place. If you felt that way about him, why did you take the listing?"

Unable to form a retort, I shook my head.

Why did I take the listing?

"G-g-g," I said, trying to speak. The word stuck in my throat. "G-g-grra..."

Katie squinted. "Air. You're supposed to speak with more air—like Marilyn. Remember?"

"Greed," I said, in a whispery gush. "One of the Seven Deadly Sins." I sucked in more air, but it wouldn't come back out and I relapsed into the speech pattern I detest. "I w-wanted to m-make m-money. That's w-why I did it. C-c-commissions."

"Greed," she repeated. Katie thought for a few seconds and I watched one eyebrow cock skyward. "Lust is one of the Seven Deadly sins, too. Congratulations. You've got two out of seven."

Now it was my turn for tears to well up. I fought them back. "I do not l-lust for your husband," I said, my lips tight as rubber bands. I wanted to add that I hated him, but she looked so frail, so vulnerable, I couldn't say it.

"Yeah, right," she sneered. I watched her dab at her eyes with a flimsy napkin.

"Just because I dated him in high school doesn't mean that I still l-l-like him."

"Something else has been bothering me," Katie said.

I waited while we listened to the din of the restaurant, the clanking of dishes, the shouting of orders back to the steamy kitchen.

"When... when..." Katie gulped and looked away.

"What?" I said, leaning in. I could tell that whatever she was going to say was going to be a whopper.

"Back then. In high school. I knew you liked him. I couldn't understand what he saw in you. I mean, you were nice and all, but you—"

"Were ugly." That stopped her.

"Let me finish," she snapped. "You weren't ugly, you just weren't in that group. You know, the popular girls, the girls Bruno usually dated."

I nodded. She was right. I was one of the studious ones. The girls who were in the Honor Society and who strove for straight A's. None of us dated much.

I let out a long breath. "Let's talk about something else."

"No. I have to say this. If I don't make it—"

"Don't make what? What are you talking about?"

"You know, if the way I feel leads to something. Some disease we don't know about. I have something I need to... to get off my chest." Katie's voice petered out, her expression an unfathomable mixture of sadness and fear.

Our eyes met. A tear trickled down the side of her nose. She swiped it away.

"Oh my god, Katie. What?" I held my breath.

"Did you know back in high school, we made love... across your bed?"

My chin went back. "Eeuuuu."

Katie rubbed both hands across her temples, as though she fought a headache. "I know... terrible, huh? It gets worse. A lot worse."

I didn't see how it could. Bruno and Katie made it on my bed? My childhood bed? Fiona and I shared a room back then. Katie, older than me by eighteen months, had begged for one of the boys' empty rooms. Darcy had the other. I didn't see how Katie and Bruno could have been alone for that long, but I suppose we all could have been out. *But Ma and Da?* They watched over us like hawks. *Where had they been?*

"Not only did I lose my virginity... but that's when I got pregnant." Her eyes flashed. "Don't look all high and mighty. I heard the rumors about you."

"Rumors?" I said, as if I didn't know.

"That you made it with him in the backseat of his car the night of your prom." Katie saw the horror on my face and added, "Don't worry. I didn't believe it."

"Then why did you say it?" I retorted. A flush of shame ignited across my face.

"Maybe that's why I did it. To one-up you." Her lips parted in a rueful laugh. "And look where it got me. Pregnant and married too young." She shook her head. "I was so stupid. I should have had that baby."

"What do you mean? You miscarried."

She pressed her lips together and her chin became a mass of dimples. Finally, she leaned over her soup dish, head in her hands, and elbows on the table. "Not really," she said into her soup. "Bruno was in pre-med. His father was generous, but we still needed my income. Bruno became more and more upset. Furious that he had been trapped. Everything was my fault."

Tears pooled in her eyes. She choked them back. "He was the one who proposed. He was the one who wanted to run to Reno to marry. He didn't even object when we had that other wedding at Mission Dolores to please Ma. But later, he kept harping and complaining. I told him to leave. We'd get a divorce. I told him I'd raise the baby on my own." Katie's fingers trembled as she rubbed her forehead.

Oh my god, I knew what was coming. I knew it. The clues were there. All the time, the clues were there.

"So you... you... had an... "

She nodded and wouldn't look at me.

The server, probably frustrated that we were taking so much time when the line outside the restaurant was growing, dipped the ladle into the center bowl and gave me more wontons. Katie's soup remained untouched.

"You don't like?" the waitress asked.

"It's fine. Delicious," I replied. The server looked dismayed, but moved on. I leaned over the bowl and whispered, "Did Bruno know?"

"Of course he did," she snapped. "He helped me find the... you know... the place."

My heart stopped in my chest. *If Da knew... I didn't want to think about it.*

"Bruno said he couldn't let a kid stop him from completing medical school. I was frantic. *Frantic!* You have no idea. I could see that he was beginning to hate me. I didn't want to tell Ma what I needed to do. I couldn't."

In a trance, I let my spoon drift to the table.

"Having a baby was my dream. You do understand that. I never really wanted to go to college. I did—half-heartedly— but what I really wanted was to have a family."

I watched Katie choke back sobs. When she found her voice, she whispered, "It was terrible. Humiliating." She shook her head and gazed into her soup bowl. "I regret it so much. You have no idea."

Tears of sympathy began to streak down my face. One fell onto my wontons. "Oh, Katie. I'm so sorry."

For a long time we were frozen, suspended in space. Caught inside a Chinese restaurant where the smell of sizzling vegetables, boiling wontons and pork-fried rice assaulted our nostrils like knives.

"There's more," Katie said, through a gulp.

"More?" I rasped.

"It wasn't my only one. When he was just starting his residency, I got pregnant again. Money was tight. My job at O'Neil & Co. in the back office was our lifeline. At the hospital, they were paying him a stipend, but it wasn't much. His father was sick by then and wasn't helping us anymore. Bruno was furious. He said we had nearly reached our goal. Why had I let it happen? He didn't want to take a loan. Said he wasn't ready for kids."

I held my head, my pounding head, and stared down at the floating wontons in my bowl, transparent doughy sacks holding pink shrimp and diced vegetables. For me, right then, they didn't look like wontons. The pink hue of the shrimp shone through the filmy dough like it wrapped a naked baby. Tiny babies floating in my soup bowl.

"Why?" I finally said, breaking the long silence. "Ma would have been so happy. She would have been your babysitter. They would have helped you with money. We all would have."

"But he insisted. You have no idea how persuasive he can be." Her head rose and she gazed into my eyes. "I think something happened along the way. Something... " Her eyes flicked this way and that, but to nothing in particular. "I wonder if something went wrong inside me. Scar tissue... something. Anyway, I don't think I'll ever hold a pregnancy."

My heart nearly pounded out of my chest. How could she have let Bruno walk all over her? I stared at the dragons running around the soup tureen with their claws raised and tails high as they chased each other around our soup.

"Will God ever forgive me?" Katie whispered. There was a frantic wildness in her eyes.

"Did you go to Confession?"

"Yes. But with a different priest. I couldn't chance that Father Mac would recognize my voice. I was too ashamed. Each time I confessed, I went to Saint Ivan's. Bruno took me. The first time, we both confessed. Then as..." Katie tried to speak between sobs. "Went there the second time, too. But he wouldn't come in with me. He waited in the car. Said it was my fault and my business." She looked up from her untouched soup and bit her lip. "My God, that church was so gloomy. So scary." She stared at me like she saw the furnaces of the underworld and whispered, "Do you think I'll go to Hell?"

I was silent for a long time. I had to say something. Anything. "We're supposed to believe in a forgiving God, remember?" I said, as gently as I could. "If you're truly sorry, God forgives."

She hung her head. "Every time, I did it for him. Because he wanted me to." Katie's mind seemed to drift. "But I can't help but think that if I'd refused... given birth... " A catch in her voice stopped her from going on.

I knew what she was going to say, that if she hadn't ended them, she'd have two kids by now. It was hard to see Katie tormenting herself, the burden of her secrets eating away at her.

"You were barely eighteen the first time," I offered.

She smiled through ashen lips. "I had Bruno and I was in love. Back then, I remember being jealous of you."

"Me?"

"You were so self-contained. Independent. I think Bruno's always... always... " Katie sniveled and shook her head.

"There's nothing between us, Katie. High school is over."

I saw a slight shift in her expression, a relief perhaps only perceptible to me. We were silent again, both of us trying to regain our equilibrium, the noise from the restaurant the only accompaniment to the chaos of our private thoughts. Now I knew what had been bothering her all these years. To top it all off, Katie's had two miscarriages in the last eighteen months. No wonder she's a physical and mental wreck.

"As for Ma's Seven Deadly Sins," Katie said, lifting her hand to count on her fingers. "Greed, Sloth, Lust, Wrath, Envy, Pride. I've done Lust. I've done Envy as well as Pride. Lately I'm a terrible Sloth." Her self-deprecating laugh sounded forced. "So I suppose I'm up to four. I can't think of what the seventh is."

"It's something you'll never be accused of," I said, looking down at her untouched soup.

"What's that?"

"Gluttony."

21. Operation Vacation

EARLY SUNDAY AFTERNOON, in preparation for my big surgery day, I packed a suitcase with lounge clothes and a lot of books. All along, I had said vaguely to my parents that I was heading north on my vacation and they assumed—I don't know how they got this idea—that I was going to the wine country to sit in a hot tub, perhaps have a mud bath and a massage. Every time the subject came up, I cringed and let the misinformation stand.

I told Ma that she could reach me on my cell phone and that I didn't know exactly where I would be staying. In my head, I parsed through this lie and convinced myself that I didn't know exactly where I'd be staying because it might be on the day bed in Fiona's alcove or on the couch in her living room. Anyway, both locations were north of Noe Valley.

Da yammered on about the Napa Valley. "The wine country's a fine place. A fine place, indeed," Da said, checking out the ham sandwich in front of him. "Perhaps yer Ma and I will retire up there. Eh, Irene? We'll have a cottage midst the grapes."

"'Tis a nice place," my mother said. "I hope ya hav'a wonderful time, Agnes Anne. I hope yer not goin' ta be sick up there too. Yer okay, aren't you? You look a bit peckish."

"I'm fine, Ma."

"Is it tha' yer worried about bein' alone? Is that what's botherin' ya?" Ma's face was kind and earnest. "Why don't ya take a girl friend?"

"I'm bringing books, Ma. I'm going to read and rest." I did my best to feign a smile.

"Oh, that's good. You do need a rest. Yer not lookin' right." She raised her hand toward me in blessing.

"Bless m'daughter O Lord 'n keep her safe from harm. Bless tha mud baths 'n tha water that comes up from tha center a' Yer earth. May she find comfort as tha children a' Anah played 'n tha hot springs 'n tha desert."

"Amen," I said, loudly, so she would stop. Unfortunately, it didn't work.

"And may tha pools be tha right temper'ture, O Lord, and tha—"

"Thanks, Ma. I gotta' go."

"Wait! I'm no'finished," Ma said, opening her eyes. She cleared her throat and began her prayer again. "'N when she's lyin' 'n tha hot water, which has come from tha center of Yer earth, O Lord, 'n she's lookin' up at' Yer stars, may she see tha error of 'er ways 'n decide ta leave tha' Jew she's datin' 'n find a nice young Catholic man. We ask this through Christ, 'r Lord 'n Mary, Blessed Virgin, Mother a' God. Amen."

I was so angry, my throat closed.

"Can't ya say Amen, Agnes Anne?"

I wouldn't say it.

"Too much tension," Da said. "Agnes Anne's never done well wit' tha tension, Irene. Real estate 'tis a stressful, nerve-rackin', nail-bitin' business." He shook his head. "Ya can quit anytime ya want, Agnes Anne." He patted the enormous sandwich Ma had set in front of him and squished the layers of meat, tomato, lettuce and bacon together and lifted it to his mouth.

I ran for the door.

"What the hell?" Fiona said, letting me into her apartment. Her frown seemed chiseled into her brow. "You're not bringing your snail collection into my apartment."

"It's not a collection. There's only one little snail and he's just adorable. Really." Fiona squinted. "Jude will stay in the dish. I swear. You won't even see him." I set my little garden on her coffee table and rolled my suitcase over to the wall.

"No way," she said. "No snail. No how." Her chin backed up so far, I thought she might break her neck.

"What do you want me to do?" I whispered, looking from the dish garden to her and back. It was too late to return home and drop it off. My parents thought I was half way to the wine country.

"Set it free," she said.

"No. He's become like a little mascot. And he's happy in

the garden."

"Have Ma take care of it."

"I might not be home for two weeks, you know that. She'd kill it with cleansers."

"Release it into the wild," Fiona said, motioning to the outside. "The Marina District's loaded with snails. He'll find friends."

While I wrestled with this dilemma, Fiona tugged my suitcase over to a small alcove in her living room.

I couldn't help it, tears came to my eyes. My distress was not really, I suppose, about the snail. The day had merely gotten away from me. I had deceived my parents. And now I carried Katie's terrible secret. I couldn't share it with Fiona. Tomorrow someone would slice up my face! Not being able to keep my dish garden was a petty thing, but I couldn't deal with it right then.

"I'm sorry," Fiona said, coming over to give me a hug. "It's just that..." We both looked down at the dish garden. Jude was nowhere to be seen, but I wasn't worried. I knew he would be somewhere hiding underneath the baby tears, the miniature shiffileria, or maybe clinging to the underside of the wandering Jew.

"Maybe I could call Sheldon," I murmured.

Fiona's face brightened. "Good idea. Do it now."

I found the cell phone in my purse and called him. I must have awakened him because he said, "What?" about three times.

"I'm at my sister's," I said, "over in the Marina and I'm having...you know... that procedure I told you about... anyway, it's tomorrow."

"Right. Right."

"And I brought my dish garden with me."

"Don't tell me. Jude got the jitters and bolted. He's half way to Spokane."

"No," I said. "He's here. That's the problem. My sister doesn't want a snail in her apartment and I was wondering if you could keep the dish garden for a few days."

"Snail sit?" he said, through a guffaw. "You want me to *snail sit?*"

I could imagine him bolting upright on his couch, some sort of sports game flickering on the TV.

"Could you? I'd really appreciate it, Sheldon. He won't go anywhere. He'll just stay in the garden—"

"—and climb into things. Then I perform the rescue and end up in the hospital again and the next thing you know, I have to explain to everyone in my office what happened."

"No jingle bell balls. What could he possibly do?"

"I'm giving you a hard time, Anne," Sheldon said. "Sure, I'll snail sit. When do you want me to pick him up?"

Fiona hailed me with a flapping dish towel.

"My sister says to come for dinner."

22. Under the Knife

MEMORIES OF A TWILIGHT STATE where I heard, but could not see; dreamed, but could not talk, swirled around me like water foaming up from within a deep green lake. Yes, I was swimming in drugged contentment. Even so, I sensed something was wrong. The doctor had bent down and stared into my swollen eyes. He told me I should spend the night at the hospital.

Who was I to refuse?

In my floating state, Dr. O'Malley could have made me sign the *Communist Manifesto* or join Al Qaeda. All he had to do was put my fingers around the pen and show me the line. He told me something about excess bleeding and asked me if I've been taking aspirin, which I didn't think I had. Had I? Maybe after Katie told me about losing her virginity on my bed and what happened after, I took some for the raging headache it gave me. I couldn't remember. And frankly, I didn't care.

Dr. O'Malley told me not to worry and, while he gently held my hand, he took my pulse. "This is purely precautionary, Miss O'Neil," he said.

I had no memory of being wheeled to a hospital room. Nor did I remember eating anything. I didn't remember getting up to go to the bathroom, or talking to anyone. But I did remember drinking water through a straw threaded through the tight gauze slit between my nose and my chin. I also remembered waking up hearing Da gasping and choking above me, squalling like a baby, yelling at me, asking if I had been wearing my seat belt.

I thought he was part of a nightmare or maybe something I was watching on TV. I even searched around for the remote so I could shut him off.

Ma squeezed my hand as though I had become a kite and might fly away. She slapped at my wrist and massaged my fingers and told me not worry. She prayed out loud to Saint Anne, then she beseeched the Virgin Mary to come to my aide, and called on Saint Patrick and Saint Christopher, Saint Teresa of Avila, Saint Agnes, Saint Margaret and I don't know who else. In this surreal nightmare, Matthew and Mark stood at the foot of the bed. I had never had such a vivid dream, but then again, I had never taken so much medication.

Later, I found out that Katie had been rushed to the emergency room after collapsing downtown. She had an emergency number on her phone. Someone called it and Ma answered. She called Da. He called Bruno, but he was in surgery. Then he called the boys. And then everyone, except Luke and Darcy, descended on the hospital.

At the front desk, Da asked for O'Neil. He must have been out of his mind. He should have asked for Stark, Katie's married name. The receptionist gave him my room number and so they all marched in, a great Irish parade, my dad's chest probably heaving at the thought of harm coming to his fair-haired Katie. I suppose when he saw my new golden blonde hair lying across the pillow, he figured out I wasn't Katie. The horror of this discovery must have knocked him on his knickers.

"Agnes Anne!" he cried. Literally. I mean that. Tears tumbled down my father's face as though someone had turned on a faucet. "Dint ya wear yer seatbelt? Where's Katie? Where's Katie? Were ya together? Did she go ta tha wine country, too? God in heaven, losin' two daughters in one day!" He screamed, "Lord help me! Help me!"

I was so drugged I couldn't help but tell the truth. "It wasn't an accident. I fixed my nose, Da," I said, still confused and wondering if Da and the boys were really there, embarrassed that if all this happened to be a dream, it would mean I was talking out loud to the fairies. But Ma's grip was like a vice.

Of course this was real.

"Fix it? What fer? There's nothin' wrong wid' it," Da said, tightening his grip on my other hand, holding me fast to earth.

"Yes, there was," I said, the truth about the O'Neil nose out on the table, so to speak.

"Yer nose? 'Tis a noble nose! And yer chin? They did som'at awful ta ya there, as well?" He bent over over me.

"Took the witch out of it, Da." I swear I spoke with a brogue. That's what drugs will do to you, make you revert to the old days and imitate the people around you. I hadn't spoken this way since I was nine or ten.

I peered out at him through the slits in my swollen eyes. Da's face had become the color of a sun-baked tomato. "'Tis tha mark'a nobility!" he screamed. "Ya had no right ta become God 'n dash it ta pieces against tha rocks!"

I had to admit, at that moment, that's exactly what my nose felt like—dashed against the rocks and pounding with pain.

"But Katie!" Ma said, sawing my other hand back and forth to get my attention. "Where's she, Agnes?" No one paid any attention to her, the men went on talking about my nose.

"It's 'er nose, Da," Mark said, gesturing with two hands toward me, "Why shouldn'a she change it? Fer Christ's sake, 'er nose looked like tha prow of a ship!"

I don't know why, perhaps it was the drugs, but instead of crying at this insult, I began to laugh. Yes, my nose *was* like the prow of a ship. Thank you. Someone said it. Good old ship's prow Agnes, a face that could literally launch a thousand ships—every one of the sailors rushing to get away from the giant prow Da now had dubbed my Noble Nose.

"But Katie!" Ma said, yelling over the din. "Where *is* she? Wher's she gone?" Ma dropped my hand. "Boys, stay here. I'll go find Katie."

"Good fer you, Aggie," Matthew said, ignoring Ma. He grabbed my toes and gave them a couple of quick tugs.

Da was not so easily assuaged. He screamed at Matt, "Ya t'ink yer skin 'n blister should put tha fix on her garden hose?"

I started to laugh again. Skin and blister meant sister. Garden hose was nose. It was all too stupid. Like Alice in

Wonderland chasing a white rabbit down a hole, here I was again with these absurd people speaking in rhymes.

"'Tis not funny, Agnes Anne, my little lyin' bottle of water." He turned to the boys, "She told us she was goin' ta tha wine. Up ta tha hot baths! Now look at 'er!"

"She looks like she mixed it up on the green, all right," said either Matthew or Mark.

"Who did this ta ya?" Da yelled. "Who was the son-of-a-bitch doctor who defiled yer beautiful nose?"

Before I could stop myself, protect the doctor whose skill I used to free myself from a life of ugliness and sure spinsterhood, I found myself muttering, "Dr. O'Malley."

"O'Malley, did ya say? And you trusted an *Irishman with a knife?*"

Then Da railed on and on about his Irish Heritage, and how we were descended from Kings and Queens ascending and descending from all manner of Celtic nobility, who all had, if you were to listen to him, Great Big Gorgeous Royal Proboscises, which was the first time I had ever heard this story. Then he stopped and stared down at my bandages and found the spiraling pupils of my swollen eyes and yelled, *"And there ya are, Agnes Anne, pretendin' ta be sick, lyin' on your gary glitter, when yer sister Katie's near death! Do ya hear me in there, Agnes Anne? Ya ungrateful little liar? Ya hear me? Near death!"*

I bolted to an upright position, which was difficult, because the bag holding the pink fluid draining from my chin as well as my nose flopped around.

"Katie?" I screeched, probably sounding like a banshee with a head cold. "What's wrong with her?"

"Yer poor, poor sister," Da sobbed. "'N then I come in 'ere ta find this! Me own daughter goin' under tha surgeon's knife out a some sick desire ta become what yer not!"

Da morphed into the color of cooked crab and his own nose seemed sharp as a claw. I feared it might loosen itself from his face and come over to pinch me, but that was the drugs talking. I fell back to my pillows in surrender. If I died right here, right now, I would deserve it, and one hundred completed First Friday Novenas would not change where God would put me.

My sinuses were so full they felt like they were about to explode and while my throbbing chin bulged, the juices from it flowed like a disgusting river into the bag pinned to my chest. Through my swollen eyes, I found my brothers and managed to croak, "What's wrong with Katie?"

"Katie," one of them said, "was brought in by ambulance this afternoon. We t'ought this was 'er room."

I started to cry. Da began sobbing so loud the nurse came in. Then he began to berate the nurse, whom he called White Stockings, for accepting me as a patient. Squinting to find the poor lady in all this hubbub, I tried to apologize, but my brothers were shouting for Da to put a cork in it.

He yelled back at them to mind their own business. Beyond all of them, Sheldon Goldberg stood in the doorway, as sparkling as a mirage, and half hidden by an enormous bouquet of red roses.

23. Red Roses for a New Lady

I'LL SAY ONE THING, Sheldon was a conversation stopper. The entire cacophony—Da berating the poor ambushed nurse, my brothers trying to tell him to stuff his gob because Nurse White Stockings had nothing to do with it, and Da yelling back that he wanted to take Doc O'Malley out to the green—halted.

"Hello, Mr. O'Neil," Sheldon said, entering the room. I don't think he could figure out where to put the huge bouquet so he could shake Da's hand. Sheldon juggled the vase to his left arm and reached around it with his right, which, by the way, no longer had a bandage. But he bobbled the vase and had to revert to the two-handed flower grab.

"*Youuu,*" Da said, dragging out the word like he was pulling a red scarf out of a magic hat. "*Youuu* made 'er do this!"

Sheldon blinked and backed up a step. "Oh, no," he said, his calmness admirable under the circumstances. "I love Anne the way she is. She was the one—"

Love? Did Sheldon say love? Under my goalie mask of bandages, I blushed.

My mother returned, rescued the flowers and set them on

the wide windowsill.

"Katie's on a different floor," she reported. I couldn't tell if anyone was listening.

Sheldon, who had obviously come from his office, looked wonderful in his suit and tie. My brothers, on the other hand, wore dirty jeans and t-shirts and had just stepped off someone's roof. Matthew and Mark eyed Sheldon as one might inspect a new pallet of shingles. I wondered if they would walk around him a couple of times, maybe even give him a kick to see what he was made of.

"Hello," Sheldon said, oblivious to the danger. "Sheldon Goldberg" He stuck out his hand.

Matthew shook it.

Sheldon winced. That was the hand with the wound.

Then Mark had a go.

Another wince.

Da remained apoplectic and gripped me as though I were a three-year-old and just might get lost in the crowd. Ma nodded like she was at a double funeral.

"So, what do ya do?" Matthew blurted out, as though Sheldon was here to apply for a job.

"I'm a CPA," he said, casually. Both hands were now deep in his pants pockets. I wondered if he was hiding them so they wouldn't make another attempt at a squeeze.

"Oh," my brothers said, as though this news was something to ponder instead of accept. The way Matthew kept nodding, I started to worry that he was going to say something about being Jewish.

"Jewish?" Matthew said.

Under my gauze mask, I silently screamed.

"Yes. Yes, I am." Sheldon looked pleased to announce this and then shrugged as if to say, *There it is. What can I do?*

Mark shook his head like it was a sad, sad thing to behold.

Matthew turned around and gave me a *Look at the mess yer in* stare.

Da began to cry again, but I didn't know if it was for Katie, for me, my face, or because the man who had just brought me flowers was Jewish. There were too many things going on, and as I've said before, I was on drugs.

"Gees, Da," Matthew said, "can ya put a cork in it?"

"Me own bottle of water, look at her! Lying on her gary glitter." His chin trembled and tears fell at the sides of his big hooked nose. The nose I used to have.

Sheldon seemed confused. "What's a gary glitter?"

Matthew coughed, then said out of the side of his mouth, "Rhymes with shitter. Sort of a cockney thing tha' Irish people sometimes do. Talk in rhymes, ya know. Da Jews do tha'?"

Sheldon's brown eyes darted back and forth. I wondered if he would flee.

Da began whining again. "Me own bottle of water doing this ta 'erself..."

"Would you like some water, Mr. O'Neil?" Sheldon asked. He looked ready to leave the room and fetch it.

"Nah, nah, he donut mean—" Matthew said, not wanting to explain what Da meant.

"Dry yer arse, Da," snapped Mark.

"I'll do as I need!" Da shouted back at him. "Look at her—ruined. Mutilated!"

"Jaysus, she's not dead," Mark shouted. "Aggie's just bobbed 'er nose, and more power to 'er."

"A nose she shoulda'a left well alone!" Da said, letting my hand go and raising a finger to the ceiling. "A noble nose, fine 'n strong. An intelligent nose, fair 'n smooth as tha best oak a' tha finest tree."

As though Da stood in the center of a Greek theatre, he waxed on like that, a regular soliloquy entitled *Ode to the Nose* and delivered by a man cursed with the same unfriendly hook that was just removed from my craggy face. Down in the orchestra pit, my brothers made snide comments, which included words like beak, ugly muzzle, and horned snout.

Somewhere in the middle of this sideshow, Fiona came in. Delighted to see Sheldon, she kissed him, hugged Matthew and Mark, kissed Ma, and settled Da down.

Nurse White Stockings, eyes flashing with both pity and the kind of fear reserved for the mentally insane, made her escape. I wondered if we were now going to hear one of those coded announcements on the intercom, *"Dr. Armstrong to the fifth floor nurses' station. Dr. Armstrong? Fifth floor nurses' station."* Soon, a SWAT team would swarm the room and remove Da.

Fiona sent the gathered O'Neils to Katie's room, and before I could start blubbering about Katie, she explained that Katie was dehydrated and needed fluids and would be all right. She pointed out the near overflow condition of my drizzle bag to a nurse, then someone else came, changed out the bloody fluids flowing from my face, and shot a hypodermic needle into a valve protruding from the tangle of clear plastic tubes above my head. I wanted to smile at Sheldon for surviving his first O'Neil crisis, but as I went blurry, I felt his lips on my forehead and his warm gentle squeeze on my hand.

"Hey, Anne," Sheldon said, his voice soft and cheerful. "The worst is over. You take care, now." And then he vanished.

I managed to mumble, "Thanks for the roses."

How long I was alone, I don't know, but when I next opened my eyes, Bruno Stark was leaning over me.

"Well, well," he said, in his doctor's voice. "What do we have here?"

Alarm bells clanged in my head. I blinked and madly tried to focus.

"Whatever you did, you sure set your father on fire," Bruno said through a chuckle. "So, here lies little Agnes Anne," Bruno said, "trying to find beauty in an ugly world."

I didn't speak.

He leaned down and whispered, "I'd take this body of yours any day of the week. No need to go to all this trouble, *Anne.*" The way he said it, it felt like he had stabbed my heart with a sliver of glass.

"Get out of here," I said, thickly. I fumbled for the nurses' call button.

Bruno took it out of my hand and dangled it above my face.

"Will going to all this trouble make sex any better? Is that what you think?" he whispered. "Oh, but of course, how would you know? You haven't had any yet. Have you, Anne, the perfect little virgin. You've been saving yourself for me."

Like a drunken cat taking clumsy swipes at a ball of yarn, I tried to grab back the call button.

Bruno laughed and let it swing in a large lazy arc above my head. "Maybe now your self-image will be better and you'll like me a little more. Eh?" He ran his other hand expertly down my chest, and with the ease of someone who is used to feeling bodies, squeezed my right breast like it was a bicycle horn. "Did you do any breast-work? Not that you're lacking in that department."

I cringed, grabbed for the blankets, and tried to cover myself.

"Just checking."

Where had my brothers gone? Sheldon had left, but Da must be here somewhere. I prayed he would walk in on us now. Bruno braced his arm on the top of the headboard and leaned over me.

"So you're doing all of this for Sheldon the hand stabber? Is that it?"

I closed my eyes against Bruno's revolting smile.

"I swear, I'll still be your first. Do you hear me in there, Anne? Open your eyes. Listen to me. I'm going to be your first." He lowered his lips to my ear. "You'll be mine before the bruises heal." He let his hand graze my breast, twirl lazily around one nipple and sink under the covers to find my crotch.

"Get out of here," I croaked, batting him away with clumsy hands.

He leaned closer, his hand still in my privates swirling and dipping into me.

"Stop." I thrashed and squirmed.

"No. I won't stop. Do you like it? I bet you like it as much as I like virgins," he whispered. "Am I right, Anne?"

"No. Stop."

Ma's voice called out from the doorway. "How is she, Doctor?"

Bruno straightened my blankets and clipped the call button to my sheets as though this is what he had been doing all along.

"Oh, she'll live, Irene," he said, over his shoulder. "Rhinoplasty is a simple procedure these days. Looks like she had some excess bleeding, so they kept her overnight, that's all. I wouldn't worry about it."

"If it were only her nose," Ma said, coming into my view,

"then why is 'er whole face wrapped up?" She peered down at me like I might be a ticking time bomb.

"Apparently, our little Agnes Anne decided to have some mentoplasty, too."

"Menta—what?" Ma's confusion made her look old and sad, like maybe she'd come down with Alzheimer's and in the near future, wouldn't remember my name.

"She's bobbed her chin, Irene," Bruno said. He reached out to touch my chin and changed the direction of my gaze. "From the look of it, I'd say, they shaved off quite a bit of bone."

"Oh no, Agnes!" Ma gasped.

Bruno's cell phone rang and after he read the screen, he left the room. This wasn't his hospital, so I hoped it meant he had to leave.

"Tell me, Agnes," Ma said, gently. "Does this face business hurt?"

My eyes darted around, trying to find Bruno. I heaved a sigh of relief when I didn't see him.

Ma leaned over me again. "Do ya hate yerself, Agnes? Is tha' it? Da ya hate yerself so much that ya consented ta this mutilation? Is tha why ya did this harm to yerself as well as ta us? Lie and connive? And all fer wha'? Pride." Her finger wagged in my face. "One of tha Seven Deadly Sins."

Tears spilled out of my swollen eyes and were absorbed by the gauze around my face. I had no idea I did anything to harm my parents, and my voice burbled out from the split between the ace bandage around my chin and the tape over my nose.

"I did it for me, Ma." My breath came in short gasps. All I could think of was the way Bruno violated me, the way he put his hands all over me. I wondered if he would come back when they were gone. I didn't know how he would do it, but after what just happened, I knew he might. What if he raped me right here in the hospital? *I had to tell Ma.*

"Ma," I said, grabbing for her hand, "you've got to help me." My heart crashed into my chest, nearly breaking the skin with its violent beating. I tried to catch my breath. How could I explain this to her? How could I go back twelve years and tell her everything?

"Mary Mother of God, Agnes, yer shakin' like a wet dog. What's wrong wid ya?"

"Bruno," I whispered, clutching her as though I needed to wring the words from her instead of from me. "Where is he?"

"Bruno?" Ma turned around and looked towards the hall. "He might'a left. Or gone back ta see Katie. Goodness sakes, you've made us worry. You've created an uproar like this family 'as never seen." She glared at me like I had robbed a bank or slain children in the park and she couldn't understand why I'd gone over to the Dark Side.

All this time, while Bruno had dangled the call button above my head, I'd forgotten about Katie, poor Katie lying somewhere sick in this hospital. While her husband groped my body and told me he would have sex with me, my sister needed my help.

"Ma," I said, trying to spit it out. "He's not good. He's not what you think."

"Who isn't what, Agnes? Whad're ya talkin' about?"

"Bruno—he's coming," I said through a ragged breath. "He's coming after me. And he's going to—"

"Yer shakin' again. Come on, dear, ya poor wretched girl. Why did ya do this to yerself?" Ma adjusted the sheets around me and tucked me in. "I canno' figure out what's gone wrong wid ya."

"He attacked me, Ma... the night... the night of... and now he's coming after me."

"That's nonsense. Bruno didn't attack you. He just stopped inta see ya."

"No. Yes. Yes, he did. In high school. And just now. He put his hands all over me." I gulped tears.

"Yer all riled up, child. Calm down. Please calm down. Let's pray together ta tha Blessed Mother."

Ma went over to the sink and found a cloth, wet it, and came back and began cleaning around my mouth, daubing at my runny nose, which caused great red splotches to bloom on the cloth. She discarded it and found another.

The drugs pulsing though my system gave me a placid courage, or at least a lack of will to hold it all in. While a deep sadness within me still bubbled, the same force that loosened by tongue made me tremble with new intent. I had to tell Ma what happened that dreadful night. But I wouldn't tell her

Katie's terrible secret. God, no. I would take that to my grave.

"What're ya mumblin' about, Agnes Anne?" Ma bent over and again daubed at my eyes, this time with a tissue. "Mary, mother 'a God, I canno understand a t'ing yer sayin'. Let's do some Hail Marys. Ready? *Hail Mary, full 'a grace...*"

24. The Unwrapping

BACK AT FIONA'S, I settled into the alcove and turned on the television. I couldn't forget what Bruno had said about dropping by. The first thing I did when Fiona left for work was put the deadbolt on. I even practiced looking through the peephole.

Whenever I took one of Dr. O'Malley's pills, I fell into a zombie-like sleep. When I managed to be awake, I still snoozed on Fiona's couch and alternately watched movies and dozed, then played back the parts I thought I'd missed.

If Bruno came over and rang the bell during these drug-induced sleeps, I never heard it. But it didn't stop me from worrying about it. In fact, I became almost paranoid. Every time I got up to use the bathroom, I peeked out the window and scanned the street for his car.

When I felt a little better, I called the home stager in charge of Bruno's listing. She was an unctuously sophisticated woman with an English accent. She seemed to know how to work within Bruno's budget and was making forward progress. She told me the painters had left and the floor finishers were sanding and would be spreading the stain and final coat soon. The draperies, the ones that they could use, were coming back from the cleaners. The last step was placing the rental furniture in the main rooms on the ground floor.

"Ven are you coming back?" Verna said, when I answered the phone.

"A week from Monday."

"Unt you vil hav a new face?"

"Sort of," I said.

"Of course you vil, and it vil be goot, Agnez. You are very schmart unt brave to do zis. I myzelf did it long ago..."

"You did?" I was completely stunned, but listened eagerly to the tales of Verna's operation and tried to picture her with a larger nose. It was a nice way to pass the time.

Another ring of my phone. I heard Bruno's voice, low and sexy. "Hello, Anne. Swelling going down?"

"I'm fine," I said. "You're not coming over, Bruno, if that's what you think."

"Who said I was coming over? I'm calling to find out if you've spoken to the stagers lately."

"Yes, I have. Today as a matter of fact. They're on schedule. Everything should be fine."

"Good. And we're set to put the house on the market the week after next?"

"Yes," I said, curtly.

"Did rhinoplasty also make you bitchy?"

I made no reply.

"I'm not after you, okay?" I could hear the contempt in his voice. "I don't know what you told your mother about your night in the hospital, but whatever it was, I don't appreciate the innuendos. She came at me with all sorts of questions the other day."

I could feel my face flush and was glad he couldn't see it. I was also glad to hear him squirm.

"You were really out of your mind that night. You tripped out on drugs. I didn't say or do *anything*. No one is after you. Agnes Anne. Especially not me. Is that clear?"

When I didn't speak, he said, "Now be a good girl and take your pain pill and crawl back into your cave and go back to la-la land."

He clicked off. I sat in the silence of Fiona's apartment. I thought back to that afternoon in the hospital. I remembered him teasing me, his hands all over me. Now I was doubting myself. Had it really happened?

On Wednesday night, Sheldon came over, but I had taken a pain pill and all I remember is seeing him waving at me as I lay dazed and stupefied on the Hollywood bed in Fiona's alcove. He told me that Jude had grown and I riffed off on how snails grew and I could picture Jude pushing his shell bigger, stretching it out like elastic. I knew that couldn't be biologically correct. I had taken a lot of science in high school and college, and I should have been able to remember how snails grew, but I was brain dead.

The next day, I called Ma, who at first would hardly talk to me, but then gave a mighty sigh and said that she supposed I was old enough to "defile my body" and launched into a lecture about the Sin of Pride and how it brought down "many a man 'n country." She made it sound like I was a turncoat or a spy. Frankly, I stopped listening to her and her list of "consequences" both here and in the afterlife. I figured it was too late anyway, and if God or the Blessed Virgin were ticked off that I had messed around with my face, I'd just have to deal with it post mortem.

A few days later, I had my follow-up visit with the doctor. I wasn't supposed to drive, so Fiona arranged for Ma to take me. Ma sat in the waiting room perched on her chair like a bird waiting to devour its prey, asking each person what they had done to themselves. There was a burn victim who had skin grafts, which to Ma was an acceptable use of plastic surgery. A child who had an ugly birthmark removed from his face—also acceptable. But when she learned that another woman like me had "vanity surgery," she clucked like an old hen.

I elbowed Ma, my eyes imploring her to knock it off. When my name was called, relief washed over me. Then when Ma saw that Dr. O'Malley was of African descent, I thought she'd deliver twin foals.

Dr. O'Malley treated Ma with good humor and a chuckle of amusement. She questioned him about his entire family tree, trying to figure out how an Irish name could have possibly come to him. Dr. O'Malley said something about southern slave owners. Ma remained speechless throughout the rest of the appointment.

When Dr. O'Malley unwrapped the bandages and I stared at myself in the mirror, I saw a swollen, bruised, but different face. There I was without my anvil chin and hooked nose. My face was, if I didn't consider the swelling, more oval. Turning sideways, I could see that my nose was straight. Wow. No hook.

"The swelling will continue to go down," Dr. O'Malley said. "In a month, you'll never guess it happened."

I couldn't stop smiling. Ma couldn't stop harrumphing. The doctor said I needed to go back for the removal of the stiches and said that I could, if I were careful, have a shower. But he admonished me not to stay in the shower too long.

On the way back from the doctor's, Ma never stopped talking about my ugly bruises. She gave me a lecture entitled Defiling My Face, then I listened to a diatribe about the Consequences of Vanity. I completely tuned out. She wouldn't let me leave her car by myself, but walked me up to Fiona's door. I didn't want her to follow me in, so I thanked her for the ride and gave her a kiss. Ma didn't read the clue that our time together was over.

She barged through the door before me, marched over to where I had been sleeping, made my bed over, and when I sat on the bed and reclined, she began to recite the prayers for the sick.

"Ma, I'm fine."

"Yer not fine. Yer foolin' yerself," she snapped. And then, in her reciting voice, she said, "Bless poor Agnes Anne, Lord. May she heal quickly. As she rests, dear Blessed Mother, let 'er t'ink about wha' she's done ta herself." As Ma waxed on, there was only one thing to do: feign sleep.

Finally, Ma bent down and gave me a peck on the top of my head and left. I could hear her muttering about Our Lady's tears all the way to Fiona's front door.

After a nap, I decided to clean Fiona's apartment. That was the least I could do for horning in on her. When I opened the medicine cabinet to put something away, the sight of men's deodorant, shave cream, and a collection of razors stunned me. Had all that "man stuff" been here the whole time?

I stared at it so long, I found my legs crumpling under me. I sat down on the lid of the toilet and gazed into space. I had never thought about my sister's sex life. Since I didn't have one, I guess I never thought of Fiona as having one either. But now that I saw razors and styptic pencils next to her blusher and eyeliner, my mind iced up, then thawed, then froze again.

I stepped into the shower and let warm water cascade over my head and neck. Not too much water, but not too little either. While I washed my hair, I contemplated the thought that Fiona was not a virgin. Had she been living with this guy? Or was it an occasional weekend? Did it only happen on Saturday nights? But then why would all his toiletries be here? I couldn't believe it. But I couldn't *not* believe it either.

25. Fighting Back

THE RING OF THE PHONE jolted me from my daydream. It was Katie, crying so much I couldn't understand her. "Slow down," I kept saying. "Tell me what's wrong."

"My hair. My hair," Katie said, coughing and choking.

"What's wrong with it?" It wasn't like Katie to cry over a bad hair day.

Through great sobbing gulps, she managed to rasp, "It's falling out."

"Oh my God!" I mumbled. "It's okay. It's okay, Katie. I'm coming."

I scooped up my car keys and was galloping to my car when I remembered I wasn't supposed to go to their house alone.

The hell with Bruno.

And I wasn't supposed to drive.

The hell with the doctor's advice.

I was on my way.

I knew Katie couldn't answer the doorbell, so I went around back and let myself in using the key she always kept under the loose brick. I found her in the upstairs master bathroom crying. I frankly couldn't see that she had lost any hair. Her hair never had much body anyway, and hung down like baby hair, silken and soft.

She showed me her brush. It was clogged with huge clumps of blonde hair.

I winced. She cried. Then I cried, too.

Next thing I knew, I heard Bruno rushing up the stairs calling her name.

Only wearing underwear, Katie stood up and fell sobbing into his arms. I watched him as he held her and rocked her. It embarrassed me to be there, not only because he told me never to come over when he's out, but the underwear-thing was awkward and frankly, weird. I searched for Katie's nightgown, or for a long shift. Anything to cover her. While I searched, I felt like I was a voyeur, peeking through the slats in a fence, their intimacy sweet. I found a long cotton T-shirt and stood behind Katie and handed it to him.

Bruno draped it over her head and pulled it down to cover her thin body, the bones on her spine like pale blue stones marking a line down her back. He glanced at me without being sour, his face winsome and worried. Silently, I helped him get her to bed.

Katie could control herself now, her sobs diminished to hiccups and feathery burps and she spoke without tearing up. She looked up at Bruno, then at me, and whispered, "Am I dying?"

I looked at him. He was the doctor. He should know.

"No, of course not. You've got to eat more, Katie. I think the hair loss is nutrition-related. You've got to eat that special pudding and protein powder. It has vitamins and minerals." He looked up at me for confirmation. "Right? Doesn't she have to eat more?"

I remembered our lunch together, the way Katie hardly touched her soup. Wholeheartedly, I agreed.

"Bring me that bag over there," Bruno said.

My eyes followed his. A leather case stood in the corner. I knew what he was going to do. He was going to give Katie a shot.

Downstairs, Bruno paced around, nervous and upset. I wanted to leave, but I also wanted to ask him a few questions about Katie so I watched him walk in circles around the kitchen, raking his hand across his blond hair.

"What's wrong with her?" I whispered.

He took a sideways glance at me. I thought he'd answer me, but he didn't. Since he wasn't going to talk, I headed for the back door, the same way I came in, but Bruno grabbed my hand and pulled me back.

"Thanks," he said, holding onto my fingers with both of his hands. "Thanks for coming."

"She was afraid," I stammered. "Hysterical."

He dropped his eyes. "I know."

I watched him shake his head and run his hand through his hair again. I saw that it was thinning on top. I wondered if this was what surfers looked like as they aged, resembling young boys playing middle-aged men. Eager to get out of there, I stepped again toward the back door. A cry escaped Bruno's lips, a yowl that might have come from a dog, except Bruno and Katie owned no pets.

Startled, I swung around.

Bruno grabbed both my shoulders and brought me roughly into him. I could feel the warmth of his body pulsing through his shirt. We rocked back and forth as though we were once again in high school and dancing to a slow grinding beat, our shoes stacked against the wall at the side of the gym in a jumble of laces and squat heels.

"Katie!" he cried through a hoarse whisper. "My Katie! She's so—so—"

"What's wrong with her?" I whispered. He clung to me so hard, I had to speak to the back of his neck and waited through his convulsive sobs, performed like an underwater waltz, totally in silence.

I had to know Katie's illness. He had to tell me what it was. She was my sister, and no matter how terrible the news might be, I would face it with her. Pushing him away, I walked to the kitchen door, the one that connected to the hallway, which connected to the stairs and if we weren't careful, would act like a megaphone and announce the unthinkable to the patient in the bed above.

Katie must not know. At least not today.

Closing the door silently, I turned around to face him. "What's wrong with her?" I repeated.

Bruno wiped the tears from his eyes and shook his head. "I don't know exactly." He sobbed a couple more times before he regained control. "I just don't know."

He walked around the kitchen, gazing at the linoleum floor as though he could read a message in the green and black pattern. "It could be anorexia. It could be—" He shook his head again. "Some sort of intestinal problem. Ileitis. Crohn's disease," he said, his face a mosaic of dread and confusion. "At first, I thought it was depression. I've taken her to a specialist. We're looking... we're looking...."

"Good. I hope you—or they—find it right away. I can't stand seeing her in so much pain."

As he nodded, another tear slipped out of each eye. I had never seen Bruno cry before, never seen him weak, never seen him less than in complete control. I didn't want to go to him and give him any comfort. After that hospital scene, I didn't trust him, so I thought it best to leave and opened the back door to head down the stairs.

Swiftly, he came up behind me and yanked me back into the house. I cried out. I wiggled and reached for the knob so I could pull myself away from him, but he spun me around and clasped me to him in a giant and dangerous bear hug.

"Agnes Anne," he said, his voice scraping like a rusty hinge. "Stay with me. Don't leave me now. I'm so afraid. Stay."

I didn't know what he meant. Did he mean *Stay with me now because I'm freaked out about Katie?* Or *Stay with me because my wife is out of commission and I need another woman?*

"Don't leave," he said, again, releasing me from the bear hug. He took my hand and pulled me back into the kitchen. I don't know why I let him. I suppose I was so shocked, so much had happened that day, I had let my guard down. When my bum pushed against the kitchen door, slamming it shut, my heart tumbled to my knees. He had a hand on each of my shoulders, pinning me against the door. Like a cornered dog, I stared into his eyes. They were filled with mayhem.

Deliberately and slowly, he leaned his hips into mine. Through my clothes, I felt his arousal.

"Stop it," I said. With both hands, I pushed him away.

He paid no attention to my force and rocked his hips into mine again, one hand straying to my breast and moving suggestively back and forth as I tried to wriggle and writhe away from him.

"Bruno," I said, sharply, trying to squirm loose. Ten seconds ago he was crying about his wife and now—

"Your nipples, Anne," he whispered, "they're erect."

"Stop it," I spat. His breath poured hot on my face.

"You want me. Tell me you want me." His lips covered mine in a slimy and painful caress.

I pushed him back and twisted my head away to break his lip-lock, which squished my sore nose against his face. Pain shot through me. I cried out.

His erection now big as a broom handle, his voice became throaty and terrifying. "Anne, this is our chance. Come on. Come on." He yanked at my slacks and fumbled for the zipper. "We should have done this before."

"Knock it off!" I yelled, giving him an elbow to the solar plexus. I'd been duped again, duped back into this house, and duped into silence. I didn't care if Katie found out. She had to know what an animal she had married. Maybe this would make her leave him.

"Shhh," he said, clapping a hand over my mouth. "Don't talk."

My chin smarted and I opened my lips against the pain and tried to bite his fingers. "Stop it!" I said, swatting at him now, round-housing at his head. Going into high gear, I whacked and bashed, hitting him with my fists. He forgot I was raised with three burly brothers, and if I'd learned anything as an O'Neil, it's how to physically fight. I landed a good punch directly on his ear.

Stunned, he stepped back and covered his ear, then looked at his hand. I saw blood. He looked at me with shock and astonishment. Then he swore under his breath.

Before he could lunge at me, I tore out the back door and ran to my car.

With trembling hands, I put the key into the ignition and started the car. My face was so sore, tears of pain ran down my cheeks. I found myself automatically offering up the pain, calling upon Mary to help me. But all I wanted to do was open the window and spit the tast of Bruno out of my mouth.

26. Ye Lyin' Bottle of Water

FOR THE SECOND TIME THAT DAY, I climbed into the shower. I knew I wasn't supposed to overly drench my wounds, but I couldn't help myself. I stepped into the flow of clean water, soaped up my face and neck and let the slimy odor of Bruno's aftershave pool at my feet and disappear down the drain.

While I changed into a velvet warm-up suit and donned thick socks, the facial pain of the altercation with Bruno still throbbed with every heartbeat. I went in search of the painkillers and curled up on the couch with a soft afghan. Next thing I knew, the phone was incessantly ringing and the apartment was dark.

"Hello? Hello?" Fiona's voice seemed mixed with a rabble of other voices.

"Fiona?" I said, still confused.

"Listen, dear, I'm not coming home tonight."

Dear? Since when did Fiona call me dear?

"Stop!" she said to someone. I heard a giggle. "It's so noisy in here," she said. Her laugh sounded like tinkling bells.

"Fiona, I–"

"What? I can't hear you."

"Go outside," I yelled into the phone. *"I have to tell you something."*

"What? What?" Fiona said.

There was no way to segue into this, so I yelled, "Bruno attacked me!"

"Isn't it a great game? We're watching it here too."

"No! Katie is losing her hair. I went over—"

"What? Katie? I'll give her a call. Ma wanted me to bring a carrot salad for First Friday. You know how it's always better if you do it a day ahead. I was going to do it tonight,

but something's come up. I won't be home. Thanks, hon. I'll see you tomorrow. Call me if you need me. Bye-bye."

Hon? Was my sister on crack? She'd never talked this way. Perhaps I shouldn't complain if she was loaded because

I'd just spent the afternoon in a painkiller stupor while riffing on how much I missed my pet snail. Who was I to criticize?

It crossed my mind that I could call Sheldon and tell him what happened to me today, but I didn't want to involve him in my family's soap opera. Dejected, and with much drama, I sniveled through fixing scrambled eggs and toast, and slathered lots of jelly across the warm bread. Then, as though I might be committing suicide, I clutched at the bottle of pain pills and took another. Then took one more and swore under my breath that if this didn't knock me out, I would take a third.

Lying down, I tried not to think of Fiona sleeping in someone's bed. I thought she said his name was Paul. I tried to picture what he looked like, how they might lie together and make love. What would it feel like to want someone inside you? I flashed on the force of Bruno's arms, the power of his body, his determination to compel me to have sex with him. Revolted and filled with self-contempt, I thought I might throw up, so I walked aimlessly around the apartment waiting for something to happen. In my daze of discontent, the Blessed Mother kept me company, and after I lay myself back down, I spoke to Mary as though she sat at my bedside.

The phone rang at 6:30 a.m. It wasn't even light out.

"Are you going to mass this morning?" Fiona said.

I fumbled for an answer.

"You should go."

She's telling me I should go to mass?

When I didn't reply, I heard her say, "Are you alright?"

"Yeah."

"Are your stitches out? How's your face look?"

"Swollen, but good—I guess."

"You sound woozy. Have another cup of coffee. I'll come by and pick you up in fifteen minutes."

I remembered Bruno. His face on mine. His erection pressing into me and the way I slugged him in the ear. I didn't want to see him this morning. "No," I said. "I'm not going to mass."

"Not going to mass on a First Friday? That's not like you."

"Well, I'm not like me anymore."

"Okay," Fiona said, cautiously. "I'll see you tonight then. You *will* go to First Friday tonight, right?"

"Right. I'll try the cover-up stuff you bought me."

"Did you make the carrot salad?"

"No, but I will. I'll make it right now."

Grating carrots became my penance for not going to mass. So did cleaning the apartment. By the time the clock had ticked its way to dusk, the place reeked with pine and lemon. Even the molding next to the floor looked bright white and every corner gleamed like pearl jewelry.

I had decided not to take any more pills. Now the slight discomfort of my face seemed to keep me awake and sharp. I stared out the window, waiting for Fiona.

"Hi," Fiona said, running in the door and dropping an overnight bag.

I nearly gasped. My sister had an overnight bag!

All along, she had planned to spend the night with Paul.

Fiona noticed my stare. "You don't have to go all holier-than-thou on me," she snapped.

"I'm not—"

"Yes, you are." Fiona picked up her bag and hurled it into the bedroom with so much force, her hair came loose. When she finished readjusting her hair clip, she turned to me and yelled, "Quit staring!"

"I'm not—"

"Yes, you are!"

I looked away and watched the television. Bombs were dropping over the Middle East destroying innocent lives. It was not lost on me that bombs were also dropping here. Right in this room.

"I'm tired of your condescending, judgmental, priggish opinions!" Fiona shouted.

Wow. Three modifiers. I listened to her screaming at me; all the while taking small swiping glances at her like she had become some ghastly phantom that just swirled in the door and would soon fly back out.

"I didn't say anything, Fiona," I finally said. "You're the one doing all the talking."

"You should see your face," she said, planting her arms on her hips. "You don't have to say a thing. Disdain is peeling off of you like old paint."

I wondered if I had mental telepathy or something. How was I communicating and yet not speaking a word? I hadn't had a pain pill since this morning, so it couldn't be an hallucination. No, this was really happening. My sister's personality was unraveling before me.

"I'm sick of it, Agnes. Sick of it. And if that's the way you feel, then I think you should go back home." The click of her chunky healed pumps rattled into the bedroom.

"Fine," I whispered. My chest tightened. I wondered if I was being kicked out because I stared at Fiona's overnight case. I guess I had. There was no way to take it back.

"Da knows about your operation," she called from the bedroom, "so there's nothing to hide anymore. Right? The reason for you to stay here no longer exists. So it's time for you to go back home."

"Fine!" I said again. My petulant irritation probably made me sound the way I did when we were kids and argued over little things. With a sense of exaggerated urgency, I began to pitch, lob and stuff clothes into my suitcase.

On the way over to First Friday, I wanted to tell Fiona about Bruno and what had happened, but the whole time we were in the car together, Fiona chattered on her cell phone like a magpie. First she chattered to Paul, then gossiped to a girlfriend. Next she spoke to someone at work about an interview she was doing the next day. She even stayed on the phone while she parked the car, and giggled with someone else while helping me remove my suitcase.

Fiona and I were just dipping into Mary's Font by the door for our blessing when Da passed through the entryway. I had to reach low into the bowl to find the Holy Water. Today, the bottom was barely covered.

"Oh, no," Da said, eying my baggage like I had joined the IRA and was toting a suitcase bomb. "Oh, no, ya don't!"

Fiona acted haughty. "Don't what?"

"Agnes Anne can't come back here. Tha little liar left, remember?"

"Da! That's a terrible thing to say!" Fiona's eyes rolled from Da to me and back. Her expression told me how badly she wanted me out of her apartment. The worry on her face that I would be coming back home with her made me want to cry. Was I unwelcome everywhere?

"She said she was goin' to tha wine and look wha' she did." Da gestured to my head. "Look at'er mince pies. They've gone blueberry."

I thought the makeup Fiona gave me hid the bruises pretty well.

"Euah! And her Gregory Peck!" he said.

My neck. Maybe the makeup wasn't that good.

"No," I said, stammering like a thief caught with his hand in the till. "You *assumed* I was going to the wine country. I only told you I was spending my vacation north."

Da's eyebrows first went up, then scrunched into a squint. I was getting the hairy eye again. Big time.

"Fiona's is north," I said, my argument for this point well rehearsed. "The Marina's north of Noe Valley, isn't it?"

My brother Mark, now in the entryway, howled with laughter. He loved it when something dodgy could be pulled off.

"Out, ye damn bottle 'a water!" Da shouted.

Ma came in from the kitchen, wringing her hands. "Mal, leave the angel alone."

"Angel? Angel, she's not! Before she nipped her garden hose, she shoulda' used 'er Uncle Ned. And—" His finger pointed right at me. "This daughter a' mine can come home when tha Holy Water freezes over."

Matthew came up the stairs with his wife and two daughters. I stepped out of the way so he could reach into Mary's Font. Both girls begged for a hike-up so they too could have a blessing.

"I didn't get any!" Dara complained, trying to reach.

"There isn't much Holy Water, luv," he said, lifting his other daughter, Colleen, so she could bless herself. "Ma," Matthew yelled over his shoulder, "Mary's 'bout a quart low!"

Jennifer seemed shocked to see my swollen and bruised face. I guess Matthew hadn't told her. As I was explaining what I had done, Da stomped off and Ma became so flustered, she followed him. I didn't know if I should move my suitcase upstairs, or have it ready so I could quickly flee back to Fiona's.

Fiona picked up my bag, and lumped it up the stairs. Halfway, Da reappeared, holding a full glass of whiskey and ice and yelled, "If that's Agnes Anne's bag, put it back in your jam jar, Fiona!"

I was surprised when my brothers both voiced objections.

"Of fer chissakes, let her stay, Da," Matthew yelled.

"It's none a' yer business," Da yelled back, which caused another round of yelling and cursing.

My brothers' wives, Susan and Jennifer, quickly disappeared into the safety of the kitchen. I imagined them cowering behind the roasting pans or hiding in the larder. Meanwhile, my brothers were practically duking it out with Da. Every O'Neil in the entryway, except for Ma, who was busy crossing herself, got into the argument.

While the hubbub grew, I became strangely detached. Like cold air descending the stairs, it came over me that I was not like these people. Even though I knew I must be one of them—for I have—*at least had*—Da's nose and Ma's chin, in another way, I was an orphan, adrift on my own private iceberg.

Darcy headed up the front stairs. She had a figure like Marilyn Monroe, her breasts pointed forward like the cones of high-beam headlights. Domenic carried the hot dish. Four kids in designer clothes trailed behind. All of them ignored Mary's Font and marched straight to the back parlor where the television perpetually blared.

"What's going on?" Darcy said. She looked at Fiona holding onto the banister with one hand, holding my suitcase in the other, and shouting down at Da. Then Darcy looked over at Matthew and Mark, who were both red-faced and bellowing, then her eyes found me.

"You look fabulous!" Darcy squealed. She came over to me and kissed my cheek. "Fabulous. Oh, Agnes, I mean, Anne! I heard about the surgery. This is wonderful." She grabbed my shoulders and turned me from side to side like she was admiring a new sweater.

"She looks like a brasser!" Da screamed.

"Stop it, Da," Darcy said. Her face reddened and her eyes narrowed to pin pricks. "You try to make every one of us feel bad about ourselves. Don't you dare work your muck on Agnes. Don't you *dare*. She has a right to improve herself. Look how pretty she is! Look how big it makes her eyes."

"Well, yer right there. Those 're tha biggest shiners I've ever seen," Da said.

"Why do you always put everyone down?" Darcy yelled.

"I do nothin' a' tha sort!" Da screamed. "It's a sin of Vanity we're talkin' about! This one," he said, pointing at me as though I no longer had a name, "is so vain she wud risk 'er precious life so she cud change tha looks God saw fit ta give 'er."

I noticed a police car in the driveway and shuddered to think that the neighbors had resorted to calling 911. It was my brother Luke who climbed out of the cruiser. He took the stairs two at a time and when Domenic saw him coming he pressed himself against the open door to let Luke pass.

"Jaysus Christ, can you people hold it down?" Luke yelled. "I can hear you clear out on the street." He sounded angry enough to arrest every one of us. My handsome police officer brother, who curiously didn't speak with a brogue, glanced around at the scene, then reached over to touch Mary's Font, but only grazed the rim of the bowl. His Sign of the Cross was haphazard at best.

Luke scrutinized the arguing O'Neils, now fallen silent. His eyes stopped when he saw me.

"Wow." He stared at my nose, then my chin. "Wow," he said again, pushing his hat up. "You're awfully bruised, but it's going to look good. Really good."

"Well," said Da, "I'm glad tha Police Department approves a' lyin' 'n self-mutilation."

"Dear Saint Joseph," Ma said putting her arms out and

closing her eyes, "we entreat ya ta send us yer calm. Help us, Saint Joseph, ta love one another as ya loved Jesus, 'n your lovely wife, Mary. Keep us from hurlin' insults at each other, keep us safe from—"

"Later, Ma," Luke said. To my amazement, Ma opened her eyes and stopped praying.

Katie and Bruno walked up the stairs next. Bruno looked around the crowded foyer, at still Fiona standing on the stairs, Ma in her praying pose.

"What's going on?" he asked.

Pale as a marble statue, Katie jostled the dish of her famous cheddar scalloped potatoes. I wondered if she would drop it, but Ma came to the rescue and Katie used her newly freed hand to dip into Mary's Font and bless herself. Everyone started asking Katie how she was and I was relieved the attention switched to her.

After the crowd in the foyer dispersed, I looked up at Fiona, still on the stairway, my bag on the step below her feet.

"*Anne,*" Fiona growled, "do you really want to live here?"

Tears welled up in my eyes. I've lived nowhere else and I knew someday I would leave home, after all, this had been my goal, the reason for all my self-improvement. But right now, my emotions overwhelmed me.

"You'd better come back to my place."

I heard the resignation in her voice. If I came back with her, she would wear her sacrifice like a hair shirt.

"Why not stay with us?" Bruno said.

"No, that's—"

"How perfectly wonderful!" Fiona squealed. "Oh, Bruno, that's a great idea! Then Aggie can take care of Katie during the day."

She had to be kidding.

"No," I said, with some force behind it. "I just don't feel up to it right now. I couldn't."

Fiona's expression went from joy to concern. "You and Katie can sleep in and you're well enough to fix meals. You could help Katie get better." Her nod was vigorous and far too exuberant. I could almost see the inner workings of Fiona's brain, see her thinking of her future nights of connubial bliss without her sister's carcass on the day bed in the alcove.

Katie, probably wondering where we were, peeked out from the kitchen. When she realized we were talking about my potential arrival at her house, her smile matched Fiona's.

As though we had suddenly become a team, Katie's healing team, Bruno slipped his arm around my shoulders. When Fiona began to struggle back down the stairs with my suitcase, Bruno left my side to meet her halfway and whisked my case out the front door so he could load it into his car.

Panic welled up within me. Things weren't falling my way and I knew I didn't have much time.

"Fiona—re—re—" I tried to say "remember," my thought, to recount what happened yesterday at Katie's house and what I had tried to tell her over the din of the crowd in the bar last night. Words were swirling around me like leaves in a cyclone. I didn't know which ones to pick out and which ones to skip over, and whether or not Katie should know about this right now.

Katie still stood in the threshold of the kitchen and I had the urge to protect her from hearing what I needed to say, so I came up close to Fiona and grabbed her elbow and moved her toward the living room. "Bruno—yesterday—he—I'm telling you—"

"It's going to be fine," Fiona said, patting me on the back as though I were the retarded sister. "I'll help you shop for an apartment. Think of it! You won't have Da yelling at you or Ma praying for you in the stairway. This is a wonderful solution. Besides," she said, lowering her voice, "Katie needs you. She really does."

I came around to face Fiona so Katie couldn't read my lips. I half-whispered, half-mouthed, "But you don't know what happened yesterday!"

"I do, too. I called Katie last night," she whispered. "*I told you I would.* Bruno said you had a problem. Aggie, you're so naïve that—" Fiona shook her head. "He told me all about it." She put a hand on my shoulder and looked at me with both compassion and sadness. "I think you overreacted."

"I did not!" I hissed back. Then without whispering, I mouthed the words, "He kissed me and—"

Katie's bony hand slipped around my shoulder. "Oh

Agnes," Katie said, "I mean, Anne. Thank you, thank you, thank you for coming home with me. I need you so much. And I'm such a crab. I'm sorry I've been so awful. I've been overly sensitive and—" She enveloped me in a bony hug and whispered in my ear, "Don't tell anyone about my hair. This is a wig."

I pushed her back and looked into her worried eyes. "Of course not."

I could hear Bruno coming back up the front stairs two at a time. He knew how sisters talk and he quickly walked up to us and enveloped all of us in a stomach-turning imitation of a group hug. "We'll take good care of Anne. Won't we, Katie?" Bruno's voice dripped with fakery and I was sure Fiona would spot it.

"I know you will," Fiona said, practically flirting with him. "And Anne can help get Katie back on the right track. Feed her all the right things." Fiona gave me a nauseating wink.

If I had drawn Fiona's face, it would have been a smiley button. If I had drawn my own, I would have been puking on her feet. So they wouldn't see the tears in my eyes, I turned away and stomped into the kitchen to find the bar. Luke was already there, filling his glass with ice.

"This family," he muttered. "I swear, this family…" He heard me sniff. "What? You're not letting them get to you, are you?" He bent down so he could see my eyes. "Hey, hey, hey," he chided.

Damn it. I picked up a cocktail napkin that said, "Hail, Hail, the Gang's All Here," and swiped at my tender eyes so hard I nearly yelped.

Luke set down his glass and grabbed me by both shoulders. "Ag—I mean, *Anne*. You absolutely did the right thing! If Da had known that you were going to have an operation, he would *never* have let you do it. You're going to look fabulous! You *do* look fabulous."

Luke's sincerity calmed me. I smiled up into his handsome face. Luke received the chiseled part of Da's countenance as well as Ma's high cheekbones, but somehow the beak and the turned-up chin passed him by. The night I was conceived there must have been some pissed-off saint who made me bear this curse. *It wasn't fair.*

"By the time you heal," Luke said, "you're going to have to swat the guys away."

I wished he hadn't said that.

"Luke?" I blurted. "Can I stay with you?"

"Me? Why would want to do that? Katie needs you."

I leaned close to him, so only he could hear. "I don't like Bruno. I don't... want to be... there."

"Oh, that," he said.

I realized he was referring to the old family legend about me and Bruno. Would it follow me forever?

"Bruno keeps—"

"Hey, I only have a one bedroom apartment. Don't tell Ma and Da—" He leaned close to my ear and whispered, "Sometimes I have a roommate."

27. The Visit of the Virgin

UNCLE JIMMY ARRIVED wearing a brown and green tweed sports coat. Auntie Lucy wore a similar tweed dress. It looked like they had taken down someone's drapes and hired a seamstress to make matching outfits. Da was at the piano in the other room. Trying to show how much we all want Katie to feel better, Da sang *K-K-K-Katie*, one of his standards. Uncle Jimmy's voice soared above all the rest, a true Irish tenor, occasionally a quarter tone off-key.

"K-K-K-Katie, dear little Katie, You're tha only g-g-g-girl that I adore. When tha m-m-moon shines over the c-c-c-cow shed, I'll be waitin' at tha k-k-k-kitchen door." I've always thought it strange that a song glorified stuttering. Funny thing was, I never stuttered when I sang.

Uncle Jimmy insisted Katie come into the living room. Like he was guiding a car into a tight parking spot, he gestured in long straight motions. Finally, Luke walked Katie to the piano. Katie looked ashen and washed-out. I felt guilty that I was resisting taking care of her.

Mary, Mother of God, help me become less self-serving.

In the kitchen, I could hear Ma blessing the roasts, and took it as a cue to get in there and help.

"Bless this lovely cow," Ma said, flinging pepper on the roast. "'N bless this grand pig," she said, turning to the second roast. "'Tis a lovely t'ing too. Let's give t'anks ta Saint Francis fer givin' us these animals."

"Oh, fer godsakes, Ma," Matthew said, sharpening a knife. "Saint Francis 'ad nothing ta do wid it."

"Oh, but I think a' Saint Francis when I see all this animal flesh. I feel bad sometimes that we're eating 'em."

"We're omnivores, Ma. See these pointy eyeteeth?" Matthew bared his teeth like a vicious canine. "They're fer chewin'." Matthew stabbed the carving knife and fork into the rump roast and moved the meat to the cutting board. Then he moved the pork roast to a different cutting board. While he did this, Ma began to heat the pan to make gravy. The women started to carry the side dishes and salads into the dining room and corral the children to the table.

I was helping out in the dining room when I heard Ma scream. "Oh, my Lord!"

All of us dropped our dishes on the table and rushed into the kitchen. Ma stood over the gravy pan and peered down into it.

"Look!" she said, making the Sign of the Cross. "'Tis tha Virgin Mary! Oh, my God!" Over and over, she made the Sign of the Cross and repeated, "Blessed Mary, Mother of God, pray fer us sinners."

"Give it a stir, Ma," Matthew said. "It'll go away."

"No!" she yelped. "Don' touch it! It's Mary, I tell ya. She's come t'us! Right here 'n my kitchen! Why? Why? Wha' does tha Blessed Mother want? Wha' does it mean? Malachi!" she screamed. Da was still pounding the piano in the other room.

Darcy and I squeezed in next to Ma. "I see it," Darcy said. "Look at her! Look at it. It *is* the Virgin Mary."

I tried to see the Blessed Mother's image in the gravy pan, but no mater how I squinted, I couldn't make it out.

Mark came around the counter and stuck his head over Ma's shoulder. "Nah. That's not tha Virgin Mary. It's tha Zig Zag Man."

Matthew snickered and continued carving the roast.

"Who?" Ma said, looking up. "Who's tha Zig-Zag man?" Ma's hands clasped together in prayer and her voice lowered. "Why's she visitin' us? Why's she here?" Over and over, Ma made the Sign of the Cross.

"What's goin' on?" Da said, lumbering into the kitchen with Uncle Jimmy.

"Tha Virgin Mary," Ma said. Her breath came in shallow gasps. "Look—look—" She gestured to the gravy pan.

Everyone stepped back so Da could see. "Well, I'll be..."

Auntie Lucy came over and muscled her way in. "Oh, my Lord! I see it! Should we call someone? Call a priest?"

"Not unless you want ta invite him t'dinner," Matthew said, continuing to expertly slice the meat.

"Yer all crazy if you think that's tha Virgin Mary," Mark said, after he had another look. "Who's ta say it's not a Muslim woman? Or someone wearin' one a them hijabs?"

"No," Auntie Lucy said. "'Tis tha Virgin. Look at her!" The two of them fell silent, held hands and moved their lips in silent prayer.

There was a sudden pushing and wiggling as everyone gathered around, lifted the children up one by one and stared deep down into the gravy pan. As much as I loved the Virgin Mary, to me it just looked like a swirl. Finally, Matthew took the whisk and gave the gravy a good stir.

"Why'd ya do tha'?" Ma shrieked. "Tha Blessed Mother was right here'n our midst an' look what ya did!"

"Tha food's gettin' cold, Ma, 'n who wants ta eat cold gravy? Heat it up again, will ya? Give it a boil an' a stir. If yer lucky, maybe she'll come back."

Ma was too busy to scold him for swearing. With trembling hands, she reheated the gravy and when bubbles appeared all around the edges of the pan, she took it off the heat, stirred it up and poured the warm brown sauce into the gravy boat. Darcy, Katie, Fiona, Susan, Jennifer, Auntie Lucy, and I gathered around and watched carefully to see if the Blessed Virgin would reappear. She didn't, but everyone talked about it anyway.

"Did you hear about that lady whose piece of toast had her image?" Jennifer said.

"I saw the Virgin once in a rust stain in the shower," Auntie Lucy said, having another sip of her whiskey and soda.

"The stain was there fer years," Uncle Jimmy said, "but then a clever cleanin' lady used Zud on it and poof! The Virgin Mary went down the drain."

"Ahhhh!" Ma screeched. "There i'tis again!" This time she pointed to the pork roast pan. "A'tha bottom! Look!"

We all scrambled to gaze down into the greasy pork drippings.

"Nah," Da drawled. "You women are so emotional. That's no'tha Virgin Mary. It looks more like a harbor seal."

From across the room, I heard Bruno's snickery laugh.

"Dear Lord," Da said, stretching out his arms to say grace, "we are gathered here ta share in Thy bounty. If that was yer dear mother in tha gravy, we thank you fer showin' us 'er image. We also thank ya, Lord, fer this First Friday 'n pray fer the health a' our daughter Katie, 'n give thanks fer her wonderful carin' husband, Bruno."

Da stopped and looked at him. "God-love-ya, Bruno, yer tha best." Then he closed his eyes and carried on. "Watch ov'r him, Lord, 'n help 'is healin' ways tend 'r precious Katie Marie 'n bring back 'er lovely energy. 'N God bless 'r four gospels, Matthew, Mark, Luke 'n baby John, God rest 'is precious little soul."

I watched Ma make the sign of the cross. Baby John may not have made it through infancy, but he was still alive at this table. And if you believed my parents, he was the best of all of us and if Baby John had made it into adulthood, he probably would be able to walk on water.

"We ask, Lord, tha'ya forgive Agnes Anne fer maimin' 'er face and succumbin' ta tha clutches of Vanity 'n Self-mutilation. We pray tha' she recovers 'er good sense 'n turns away from a life dominated by pride 'n airs."

"Oh, Da," Fiona and Darcy said, one right after the other.

While I blushed, Uncle Jimmy and Auntie Lucy stared at me as though they didn't know me anymore. "Agnes Anne," Auntie Lucy whispered, "yer so bruised. Wha' were ya thinkin'?"

From across the table, Bruno winked.

"'N may Agnes Anne turn away from tha man she's been runnin' around wit' 'n find a nice *Irishman* 'r if she can't find 'n Irishman, maybe a German like Bruno, 'r even an I-talian like Domenic. Lord we wud be grateful fer anythin' at this moment. Even a cigar-smokin' Cuban. We implore you, Lord, ta send someone to Agnes Anne more like herself."

"Wha'? Some shy bloke who stutters?" Mark said, under his breath.

His wife, Susan, jabbed him with her elbow and giggled. Immediately, she suppressed it and forced her face to go limp.

When Da said his final Amen, Matthew, Mark and Luke shouted their usual, "God is a Gael!" and we all sat down.

Da reached behind and pulled his Novena Book off the sideboard and while we served ourselves from the platters and plates strewn across the table, he took out his Saint Margaret Holy Card and turned it over and cleared his throat. "Lest anyone ferget why we observe First Friday—"

"Da," Matthew cried. "Don' do it t'us again! Yuv read this ev'ry freekin' month fer m'whole life! Fer once, skip tha commercial. *Please.*"

Da didn't pay any attention to his eldest son. "Number one," Da read. *"I will give them all tha graces necessary fer their state a' life.* Two. *I will establish peace 'n their families..."*

While he read through the twelve benefits of practicing First Friday, we glanced at each other, rolled our eyes and made enormous grimaces. Mark took the top of his hair and plucked at it so it stood up the way Da's sometimes does and moved his lips and head in unison to Da's speech. Fiona started to laugh.

Finally Da was at number twelve. *"The all-powerful luv a' my heart will grant ta'all those who shall receive Communion on tha first Friday a' nine consecutive months, tha grace a' final repentance; they shall not die under my displeasure,"* we broke out into applause. Domenic whistled like he was at a ball game. The kids' table joyously cheered along with us.

"Now," Da said, absently daubing the lead of the pencil on his tongue, "I saw Fiona, Katie, 'n Bruno this mornin' a' Mission Dolores, 'n of course, Ma." We watched him put checks on all the appropriate lines in his Novena Notebook. "Ah, yes, then there was Jimmy 'n Lucy." Next, he looked over at Matthew and Mark. "Boys?"

"Went ta Saint Brendan's," Matthew said, after a long

beat of hesitation. "All a' us."

"Mark 'n the girls, too?"

Matthew nodded. I noticed Susan's blush and the way her eyes fell to her napkin. Jennifer hung her head.

"If ya were up at'Saint Brendan's, why didn't ya just flip down tha hill an' join us a' Mission Dolores? That would'a been easy."

"Had ta drop the kids. We were awfully late, Da. Didn't wanna make it any worse."

"Ah," Da said. He made the proper checks on their lines. "Oh, look a' this," Da said. "Matthew 'n Jennifer, 'n Mark and Susan 'ave nine in a row. Congrat'lations!" Da happily drew two lines to separate this achievement from the rest of the checks to come, then flipped the crinkly pages to the back of the book where the Novena's Received pages were located and made strokes on each of their lines.

"Ah, that's grand. You'll be 'n heaven before tha devil knows yer dead." He turned to Luke.

"'Fraid I didn't go, Da," Luke said, his voice soft and apologetic.

"Oh, Luke, yuv missed tha last two months."

Luke nodded regretfully. "Had to work. Couldn't help it."

After a long sigh, Da looked up. "Darcy 'n Domenic?"

"Saint Bart's," Darcy replied. Domenic, I noticed, paid no attention to Da's bookkeeping and continued to eat. I knew he was doing this for Darcy. I thought it touching that Domenic loved Darcy so much that every month he would sit through this pageant. I wanted a man like that. Someone who would love me so much, he would even put up with First Friday. I thought about Sheldon. He was Jewish, but a good man and a patient person. Would he ever put up with all this?

"Good, good," Da said. "Agnes Anne?"

"I didn't go," I whispered. Shame colored my face. "I overslept." That was a slight lie. I didn't want to go and bump into Bruno.

"Agnes! Ya were at eight! You 'ad only one Friday ta go ta get yer Novena! Now you'll hav'ta start all over. Oh, no. Oh, no." Da shook his head sadly. "You 'n Luke 're pullin' up tha rear."

"Aggie," Luke said, giving me a wink, "the two of us will be outside heaven's door, our noses pressed to the screen. I wonder if we'll be able to see the others in there having a good time."

"Why no' find a mass tonight?" Da said. "Don' let this opportunity get away! Agnes Anne, 'tis a Novena! T'would be a shame ta start all over."

I felt the stab of loss pass over my heart and knew it would be next year before I could get another First Friday Novena. I had plenty of others, but somehow it felt like salt on a wound.

"There aren't any masses this time a' night on a Friday," Ma said. She leaned forward and looked down the table. "Do ya know of any, Jimmy?"

Uncle Jimmy stopped buttering his roll. "Might be one up a' University a' San Francisco."

"Agnes," Ma said, the disgust in her voice thick as piecrust. "Just a' tha time ya need tha Lord most of all, just a' tha time yer datin' out'a tha faith 'n are maimin' yourself wid needless medical procedures, ya miss mass. What's goin' on wid ya? Don' ya have an alarm clock?"

"Oh, for goodness sakes," Fiona interrupted. "She didn't feel well. Can't she get dispensation because she was sick?"

"Why couldn't ya wake 'er up? Fix 'er a cup a' tea?" Ma asked.

Fiona glanced sideways at me, her eyes pleaded not to reveal that she hadn't slept at home last night.

"There's nah dispensation when tha cause a' tha sickness is vanity surgery," Da snapped. He heaved another sigh, slipped his Saint Margaret Holy Card back into his Novena Book and tossed it on the shelf behind him. Over his shoulder, the statue we had dubbed Our Lady of Dyspepsia, held her arms out in what was supposed to indicate surrender to the Holy Spirit, but right now looked like unbridled defeat.

"Oh, my Lord," Auntie Lucy said. "Look a' this!" She held up her cocktail glass, now mostly ice. "Look! Tha Virgin! Inside m'ice cube."

Uncle Jimmy leaned over and took the ice cube out with a spoon. "I'll be darned. It does look like tha Virgin."

"Lemme see," Da said.

Uncle Jimmy returned the ice cube to the glass and passed it on. When Bruno got it, he took a long look, smirked, and handed it on. Then Katie, Susan, Mark, Jennifer and Matthew each took a look as it passed by.

Ma stood up and came over to Da and both of them peered down into the pale amber liquid. I caught Katie's eye. "Did you see it?" I whispered.

She rolled her eyes and shrugged.

While everyone debated whether the ice cube had the image of the Blessed Mother or not, Bruno looked down at his plate. "Look!" he cried. "I see the Virgin in my mashed potatoes."

28. Kitchen Suds

AFTER DINNER, the children escaped to the TV room, the women wrestled dirty dishes into the kitchen, and the men remained at the table to smoke and tell stories. No one questioned or complained about this division of labor, as I think all the women enjoyed, under the sympathetic eye of Our Lady of the Scullery, the chance to tell stories of our own in the privacy of our kitchen clubhouse.

"I t'ink we should say some prayers ta tha Blessed Mother, girls," Ma said to us as she washed the dishes that couldn't be put in the dishwasher. Steam curled up from the suds like incense. "We need ta figure out why she came. What does she want? Why tonight? Is she here ta warn us?"

"Warn us of what?" Darcy asked.

No one had any explanations.

"I think she came," Ma said, rattling silverware into her plastic dishpan, "because of Agnes Anne. Because she's datin' outside tha faith 'n because a' what she's done t'her face."

"Oh, for godsakes, Ma," Darcy said. She dried a platter and handed it off to Katie to put away. "Lots of people bob their noses and fix their chins."

"She's also datin' a Jew!" Ma said, over her shoulder. Then Ma turned her back and dug into the suds like she was wrestling a gremlin and had him in a choke hold.

"What's he like?" Katie asked.

"He's... a little taller than me," I said. "Brown hair. Curly. He's an accountant. His name is Sheldon." I looked from one sister to the other and gulped, then forced out his last name. "Goldberg."

"Goldberg," Darcy repeated. "So he really is Jewish."

I set a dried glass on the counter, invoked Marilyn's gushy voice so I wouldn't stutter, and said, "Yes. He's Jewish."

My sisters-in-law looked like birds on a fence. Their heads spun between Ma at the sink and me at the counter.

"You've got to be kidding," Darcy said.

"No, I'm not kidding."

"You're sure."

"Of course I'm sure."

"It just doesn't seem right, Agnes. You of all people dating someone like that."

I tried to make comeback, but no sound came out.

"The most important decision of your life and you're—"

"Leave her alone, Darcy. She's just dating him," Fiona said, coming to my defense.

"Well, since she's dating him, she apparently decided *something*."

"Who says she's marrying him?" Fiona said.

"Then why date him?" Darcy threw up her hands; the dishtowel flapped like a flag.

"He's nice," I said, through a gush of air. "We have a good time. He makes me laugh. He's kind. I've never met anyone like him."

"Well there you go," Darcy snapped. "You *have* made up your mind."

"Geez, Dar," Fiona whined. "It's not illegal to date someone who isn't Catholic."

"It is in this household."

"Look, Darcy," I said, my temper bursting, "you don't even live in this household anymore."

"From what Da said tonight, you don't either." The thought hit me like a slap. Fighting back tears, I ran out of the kitchen.

Once inside my room, I turned on the light and looked around. Would this be the last time I would be here? I walked over to one of my bulletin boards crammed with holy cards and fingered a card with a portrait of Saint Francis, dear Saint Francis, so content to leave behind the glamour of life that he vowed perpetual poverty. I'd done the opposite. I'd buried myself in the back office at the company, hidden from everything, but now *I wanted back in. I wanted the glamour of life.*

"Here's where yuv gone," Ma said, sticking her head through the doorway. "Are ya'll right?" Ma walked over to me and reached up to sweep my hair from my face. "Agnes Anne, you donut hav'ta leave. Da wudn't really t'row ya out. He's just in a temp'ary state a'... well, ya know 'ow he gets."

A lump the size of a hardboiled egg grew in my throat. I nodded.

"I donut wan'ya ta go, Agnes, but I know Katie needs ya fer sure. But—" Ma put a hand on my shoulder. She seemed smaller tonight, bird-like, yet strong. "Ya will come back won't ya? I'd never t'row ya out. No matter what yuv done— maimed yer face, defied yer looks, died yer hair this shameful blonde, 'n lied ta me, *lied to us*—yer still m'daughter."

I watched tears tremble in her brooding eyes.

"No, Ma. I might come back for a time, but I need to get out on my own."

I watched two tears slide down her cheeks, straying into the deep wrinkles on each side of her freckled nose.

"I know you thought I'd stay here forever, Ma," I said, sitting on the side of the bed. "That I'd be the one to take care of you and Da in your old age—"

"Who said tha'?" Ma sat beside me. Both of us stared at my collection of holy cards. They took up the length of the wall.

"I overheard you say that one night."

Ma sniffed and wiped her face with a cotton handkerchief she pulled out from her sleeve. "There ya go again, Agnes. I have no idea what yer talkin' 'bout." She blew her nose. The honk of it, startling.

"Last year, Ma, as I was coming up the stairs to go to bed, I heard you say to Da, 'Agnes Anne will be a blessing to us in our old age.' That's what you said. I know you expect me to be here forever, but—"

"Well, I might 'a said tha', but it didn't mean ya have ta stay here ta the bitter end. I'm not dead yet. Malachi 'n I will make it on our own." She sniffled. "Ya needn't stay here an' wait fer us ta die. Ye can ignore yer family duties."

"There you go, Ma. You just said it again."

"Wha'? Wha'? I said ya donut hav' ta stay."

"As soon as I can, Ma, I'm going to rent an apartment."

"Oh, Aggie," she said, in a small voice. "And live alone? All alone? Why not move in wid Fiona?"

"I want my own place." I swallowed hard. I knew the reason I would never move in with Fiona.

"It's Da, ind't it? He's so—"

"It's not Da," I said, quickly. "I have to have my own life, Ma. I'm twenty-eight. I need to have my own life."

"But Agnes, yer goin' off tha path. How will ya handle it? Look wha' yuv done ta yerself. Yer a mess 'a bruises. Yer linkin' up wid tha wrong people. I donut know wha' ta do wid ya." She leaned sideways and hugged me tightly.

"Ma, what I've done to my face is an improvement. You'll see."

"No one can ever improve 'n God's work. That's why Mary came tonight," she said, through a sniffle. "Mary knows I've failed as a mum. That's why Mary came t'night—ta rebuke me." She choked back a sob. "T'alert me that m'girls need ta get back 'n tha straight n' narrow."

"Ma," I said, putting my arm around her. "I never saw Mary in the gravy boat, or the pork roast pan, or the ice cube. Mary didn't visit us tonight."

"Yes, she did," Ma said, firmly. "Mary was here because yuv chopped yer face all up 'n yer datin' a Jew. She wants ya ta come ta yer senses, Agnes Anne. She even came t'Auntie Lucy's ice cube!"

"Ma, Auntie Lucy had too much to drink. I couldn't see the Blessed Mother in that ice cube of hers. And Bruno was just having fun with us. He was laughing at all of us when he said the Virgin was in his mashed potatoes."

Ma shook her head. "No, I saw her. Plain as day. Twice 'n tha gravy, once 'n the pork roast pan, then in Lucy's ice cube. It's true I never got ta see tha mashed potatoes, but Bruno-god-love-him saw it, so it must b'true. Over 'n over Mary has visited us tonight." Her voice dropped to a whisper. "I t'ink she wants ta warn us, Agnes Anne."

"Maybe it's not about me, Ma. Maybe it's about Katie."

"Katie," Ma repeated. She began to pace around the room. "Tha' could be. Tha' *could* be it. Katie's as thin as a starvin' cat come in from tha field, all skin 'n bones, no flesh a'tall. Oh, I'm glad yer going ta help her, Agnes Anne. Each mornin', I wan' ya ta cook 'er some oatmeal. She needs ta eat it wid heavy cream so she'll gain weight. Make 'er eggs and thick bacon. I'll give ya some soup bones. I want ya ta start a big pot 'a barley soup first ting in tha mornin'. Make it wid lots 'a veget'bles 'n legumes. Are ya listenin' ta me?"

The thought of going to Bruno and Katie's made me feel like vomiting. All through dinner Bruno kept smiling at me. It was a wicked smile. He was going to try something. Try something tonight. If not tonight, tomorrow.

"Let's bring Katie here, Ma," I said. "She could have my bed. I'll get out the cot. Or I could stay down the hall in the boys' old room."

"Ach, I've tried, love, ta bring her here. Bruno won't hear of it, but he's tha doctor 'n he takes such good care 'a our Katie... we hav'ta listen t'him."

"I don't want to go to their house, Ma. Remember when I was in the hospital? What I told you about Bruno?"

Ma stopped pacing. "Lovey, ya were so out 'a yer head tha' night. I spoke ta Bruno. He didn't know either."

"Of course he didn't! He will never admit anything!" I said through clenched teeth. *"I will not go to their house. I don't trust him. I won't go."*

"What are ya talkn' 'bout? He's yer sister's husband."

"He attacked me, Ma. Why won't you believe me?"

"Agnes Anne, how c'n ya say tha'? Against yer own family!"

"He's not my family!"

Ma came over to me and lifted my chin with her bony finger. Staring into my eyes, she said, "Don't make Mary cry, Agnes Anne. Won't ya take care 'a yer sister 'n 'er hour 'a need?"

I thought of Katie's skinny frame, her pale face. Katie did need me. The guilt of refusing Ma's request rang me like a church bell. But I was adamant. I would not go to their house. I would go to a hotel tonight and then see Katie in the morning.

"Oh, m'good Lord! Look!" Ma said, staring at something over my shoulder. "The Virgin! Why, her image—it's as sparkly as diamonds!" Ma walked over to my desk as though she were in a trance and gazed down to the area where Jude's dish garden had been.

Outlined by Jude's silvery tracks, the image of the Blessed Virgin seemed to glisten like mica. I could make out her headscarf, her eyebrows, eyes, nose and chin. It was the Mona Lisa smile that took my breath away. "Oh my God," I whispered. "It does look like her."

"Malachi! Malachi!" Ma screamed. "Come up here!" She dropped to her knees and beat a clenched fist against her heart three times. *"Mary, mother 'a God, pray fer us sinners. Mary, mother 'a God, pray fer us sinners. Mary, mother 'a God, receive 'r prayers."*

I gazed at the crazy pattern of Jude's snail tracks across my desktop and tried to prove to myself that it was a trick of the eye. But no matter how I looked at Jude's shimmering trails, a portrait of the Blessed Mother shone back at me.

My knees turned to jelly. I sunk down beside Ma.

"She's blessing ya, Agnes Anne." Ma whispered, over and over.

Da, Bruno and Katie trooped up the stairs to see what Ma was screaming about. When Da saw my desktop, he crossed himself over and over while mumbling, "I'll be damned."

Jude's tracks were plain as a photograph. The Blessed Mother's picture was on my desk. *My desk!* Had she come because she was angry about my face? Or was she offering me protection at Bruno and Katie's? Or did it have nothing to do with me at all?

Da lowered himself to the floor. I followed. The family scrambled through the door. Some gazed at it. Some kneeled. We said a few prayers. Bruno paced back and forth in the hallway. I heard him mutter, "Clever little mollusk."

29. Settling in at Bruno's

MA DIDN'T LISTEN to Bruno's protests not to assemble food for Katie. She began to load bags with soup bones and tonight's leftovers. She bagged oatmeal, barley, a bunch of carrots and a head of celery for the soup. I turned away, hunched over and called a taxi.

"What are you doing?" Bruno snapped. He took the phone from my hands and disconnected me. Katie came up behind him.

"I'm not staying at your house," I said, grabbing it back. "I'll drop by in the morning."

"Of course you're coming with us," Bruno said, loud enough for the whole house to hear.

Everyone floated over to the vestibule and gathered around me. I was a fish in an aquarium. Eyes everywhere.

"I- I- I- don't w-w-want to st-st-st-stay with th-them."

Matthew and Mark rolled their eyes. Susan and Jennifer seemed sympathetic. Fiona had her hands on her hips.

"Aggie, suck it up," she said. "Katie needs you."

"Ya need ta watch yer sister!" Da yelled, elbowing forward. "Blood's thicker than water. Simple as tha'."

Ma stood in front me. Her bony hands gently cradled my bruised jaw. "Take care of yer sister, Agnes Anne. What about the Virgin? Are ya really goin' to refuse her?"

Tears came to my eyes. Katie linked her arm in mine and whispered, "Thanks, Aggie. Thank you so much."

When Bruno saw the grocery bags Ma had thrust in my hands, he went ballistic.

"This will only make Katie worse. Do you understand?" The grocery bags landed on top of my suitcase. "She needs to eat a bland diet. Don't cook any of this crap from your mother. Do you hear me, Agnes? I have Katie on a special diet."

"I'll make the beef barley soup very bland. The broth will be good for her."

"No, it won't. Don't cook any of it. I've told your mother a thousand times that Katie needs rest and recuperation. But does she listen to me? No. She's too busy seeing the Virgin Mary in the soapsuds." He slammed the trunk. "I'm the doctor here."

"Of course you are, honey," Katie crooned. She reached out and touched the back of Bruno's head, the way one might pet a child. I saw him flinch.

"Get in the car, Katie. You too, Agnes. This family of yours. I tell you, I'm sick of them. If I see one more Virgin Mary on the wall, in a pan of drippings or in the succotash, I'll lose my effing mind."

"Oh sweetie," Katie said. "They mean well."

"And then there's your Aunt Lucy, completely looped and seeing things in her whiskey glass." Bruno climbed in the car.

"Ma says she drinks because she never had any children," Katie said, adjusting her seatbelt.

"Most people drink because they *have* children." Bruno continued his tirade, but I wasn't listening. I was planning how I could block the door of my room tonight and keep safe. While Bruno ranted about how the BVM has ruined our family, it calmed me somewhat to know that tonight scribbled across my desktop I had a sure sign of her protection.

Fog shrouded the Sunset District in a mist so thick Bruno turned on the windshield wipers. I couldn't help but gaze out the window and look for the Virgin Mary in the cloudy haze shrouding the city.

When we pulled into the driveway and alighted from the car, water droplets swirled around us and clung to our coats, making all of us slightly iridescent. It made me think of Jude's snail tracks. Katie insisted we hang our coats up in the laundry room to dry. While we did this, Bruno hovered around both of us, helping with our coats and finding hangers.

"Why don't we give Agnes," he said, as he worked, "sorry,

I mean *Anne*, some privacy and let her sleep down here?" He pointed to a small room off the kitchen; undoubtedly in the 1930s it served as a maid's room. Now it was a small TV room. I knew the couch hid a bed.

My mind whirled with worrisome scenarios. I would rather be closer to Katie in case I needed to yell for help.

"Maybe," I said, my voice just as helpful as his and equally fake, "I should be closer to Katie in case she needs me one night while you're working. I couldn't hear her from down here."

Disappointment flickered like firelight in Bruno's eyes. We were playing a game.

"Oh yes," Katie said, beckoning me down the hall. Her thin fingers pointed up the stairs. "How about the middle bedroom? My sewing machine is in there, but there's also a bed and a TV."

"Sounds wonderful," I said. I quickly rushed over to my suitcase and practically sprinted up the stairs behind her.

Scratching the back of his head, Bruno followed. I knew he was irritated.

Katie was exhausted and needed to get to bed, so the household settled down fairly quickly. I didn't know whether to unpack or to keep my suitcase pretty much intact, so I set it inside the closet on the floor and only took out what I actually needed. I called Sheldon on my cell and told him where I was. Since he didn't know how I felt about Bruno, Sheldon's voice was cheerful and we made a date for tomorrow night. Knowing that I'd see him the next day made me feel better.

The date was a goal, an anchor. Yes, I told myself, I would make it through this night.

I heard Bruno and Katie talking in the room next to mine. I couldn't help myself. I listened, but I couldn't understand anything they said. Just when I was getting comfortable and the cold sheets were warming up, I heard a faint knock at my door. The locks in this old house were the skeleton key type, but they worked and I had been sure to turn the key and try the door myself to make sure it was locked. I watched the doorknob turn back and forth. Bruno wanted in.

Quickly, I turned off the light, sat in the darkness and hugged my knees.

"Mary, mother of God," I whispered over and over, "protect me."

He tried the doorknob a few more times.

"Very clever, *Anne*," he said, softly.

I heard his evil chuckle.

"Round one."

30. Houseguest

LIGHT WAS SEEPING UNDER the shade and I knew the night was over. Somewhere in the house, a shower was running. I figured it must be Bruno getting ready for work. Their bathroom was attached to their room. My bathroom was in the hall. Opening my door, I quickly ran across the hall and used it, hoping that when I flushed, Bruno's shower would go cold. Or maybe all hot and scald him. Such a stupidly miniscule revenge, but nonetheless, it made me feel powerful to do it.

After I scampered back across the hall, I resolutely locked my bedroom door and listened for his footsteps. I knew sleep was over for me, so I dressed and switched on the television to the news and turned the volume way down. About twenty minutes later, I heard Bruno's car pull out of the driveway. Only then did I make my way downstairs for a cup of coffee.

While it brewed, I filled a big pot with water and looked around for the bags Ma had sent. Where were the soup bones? I found them outside in the garbage can. No harm done. I pulled out the grocery bags and riffled through them and began to boil the beef bones for the barley soup.

There wasn't much to eat in the refrigerator, but I found milk and a bowl of vanilla pudding and a tin of protein powder. There were no leftovers, but the vegetable bin was filled with lettuce, albeit wilting, and tomatoes, onions and a few potatoes. The egg bin had a half dozen eggs, the freezer was filled with frozen dinners. I wondered what Katie ate for breakfast and lunch and who had been cooking dinner for the two of them. When I threw something away, I noticed take-out food containers in the trash. That was it. Bruno brought in take-out, at least for himself.

About nine o'clock, I peeked in on Katie. She was just coming around. I ran downstairs to brew a cup of tea and make a small bowl of oatmeal.

"Here's some oatmeal," I said, presenting a perky breakfast tray with a camellia I had plucked from their yard.

"Where's my pudding? I need the protein powder," she whined.

"Let's forget that today, Katie, and—"

"I need it! No, you give it to me. Bruno warned me you'd do this, Agnes, and I want my usual breakfast. Nothing from Ma."

I sighed and tried to be patient, but it was hard. "What if the pudding isn't agreeing with you? What if that's your problem?"

"Don't be ridiculous." Katie turned her head away and closed her eyes.

I brought the tray back to the kitchen and stirred up her usual pudding cup with the protein powder. I didn't want to try it myself. The last time I did, I had the runs for two days.

"What do you want to do today?" I asked, as she finished breakfast. I opened the draperies and lifted the shades. Weak sunlight trickled across the light blue carpet. I went over to the mirror and turned to the right and left, admiring my new profile.

Katie pushed herself into a sitting position and absently ran a hand through her hair. I turned back to the mirror and stared at my yellowing neck. An agonizing animal cry rose from the bed behind me.

Katie's fist held another clump of hair.

I ran to her and held her frail, sobbing body and took the clump from her. I told her everything was all right, that it would grow back. I told her she would get well again. I told her things I didn't believe.

"I think I'm dying," she sobbed. "And I don't want to die." Gulping for air, she choked out, "Am... am I dying?"

I looked down into her watery eyes. I didn't know what to say. "Let's leave," I whispered. "Let me take you back to Ma's."

"Will I go to Hell because of the... of the..."

I didn't want her to say the word. "Of course not. You confessed, didn't you?"

Gulping like a gold fish, she nodded.

"You had Absolution, right?"

She nodded again.

"Look at all the Novenas—the First Fridays you've said through the years. You won't go to Hell, Katie. Let's get out of here. Get you some treatment. Try new doctors."

"I'm under treatment!" she shrieked.

"Then why aren't you better?"

"Don't be mean." She sobbed into a corner of the top sheet.

"I'm not being mean."

"Yes, you are." Katie sunk down into the folds of the blankets. Watery bloodshot eyes peered over the crumple of sheets. "What if I go to Hell?"

I grabbed for her hands. They were sweaty and cold. "You won't go to Hell."

I couldn't say the same for Bruno.

That afternoon as Katie slept, I took a walk and mulled things over. The way Bruno insisted she eat that stupid protein powder and vanilla pudding seemed more and more suspicious to me. I vowed to take a sample of it and have it analyzed. I didn't know how to do that, but maybe the Internet could help. Another idea occurred to me: what if I went to the Main Library and did some research? I could take the N Judah down there and research symptoms and the P word. Yes, face it. I'd be researching poison. Poison with a capital P.

This whole concept left me with shaking and sweaty hands. It meant that I thought Bruno was capable of harming my sister. Which would mean that I thought he was capable of murder. My heart pounded in my temples. I ran back to their house, checked on Katie, who was sleeping soundly, thank heavens, and grabbed my purse and coat.

I approached the library like it was a live grenade. I hadn't done any research since college and I didn't know how to even frame the question. Was there a section in the Dewey Decimal System entitled Poisons? Things poisonous. Things sort of poisonous. Things a husband could give a wife to make her feel unwell so he could ingratiate himself to his in-laws? What if there were a silent poison that no one could detect? *The untraceable poison.* I needed guidance. I knew librarians know a lot about everything, but I didn't want to reveal my actual intent. So, God forgive me, I decided to concoct a lie.

"Excuse me," I said, sitting down on a grey stool in front of the librarian's metal desk. I waited for her to turn around. Oh my goodness, this gal had more studs in her nose and ears than Ma's pin cushion. "I'm writing a story. A children's story. No, it's a s-s-story for adults. And... um... Definitely not for children." I tried laughing at my gaffe, but it came out fake. I felt my face grow warm. "I don't know what made me say for children! Ha, ha, ha."

"Poisons in a children's book?" the librarian mused. I tried not to focus on her nose ring and diamond stud, her red and purple-tinged hair and sparkly eye shadow. "It might be a magic potion." She ticked her chin thoughtfully with her long lime-green nails. "You could make it up. What does the potion need to do?"

"It has to be something... you know, something a character could slip another character that would make them feel sick, you know... sort of..."

"Something Agatha Christie-like?"

"Yes!" I exclaimed. "Like that." I tried not to count the studs going up her left ear.

"Something like the way Livia poisoned Caesar Augustus?"

"Oh," I said, my brow furrowing. "She painted the figs with arsenic, right?"

"I think so." My librarian was getting into it now. She popped up and beckoned me to follow her. We walked deep into the stacks. "By the way," she said, over her shoulder, "my name's Gloria. What's yours?"

I introduced myself to her back. She turned around and stared at my neck.

"I think your bruises are cool." She wrinkled her eyes into an enormous squint. "Car accident?"

"Surgery," I whispered. "I had my nose fixed and my chin reduced."

"Far out. Such great colors. Purple. Yellow. Blue." Her head bobbed around me for a closer inspection.

"I should have—makeup—forgot, I guess."

That afternoon I had a tour of poisons, potions, suicide drugs, herbs, and authors who murdered people with common household items, elaborate concoctions, and just plain strychnine. Gloria kept coming back to my table and espoused idea after idea. She brought me a book on symptoms, on how to poison people, on poisons used in World Wars I and II, poisons used in the Cold War, recent poisonings in Russia. How to mix your own poisons out of what one might find under the sink and how to make hemlock soup.

Every fifteen minutes, Gloria would leap out of the stacks. "Remember Ella Zielinsky in *The Mirror Crack'd from Side to Side?*"

I shook my head.

'The poison was in the nasal spray." Gloria grinned and I could see her tongue stud. "There was another book, I forget which one, but it was overdoses of nicotine." Gloria absently twirled her diamond nose pin. Goose bumps ran down my arm. "How about foxglove?" she offered.

"I remember that one," I said. "Digitalis. Foxglove in the salad. Hard to prove the lady was murdered because the lady already took digitalis pills for heart problems. Right?"

"Right," Gloria said, through an exhale. "So cool."

Within a half-hour, not only did I have some new ideas, I realized I was probably wrong about Bruno. How could he be poisoning Katie? What in the world would he use? Where would he get it? I guess he could get it at the hospital. But don't they have elaborate systems so drugs aren't overused or leaked out of the hospital? Maybe I was over-wrought. Still tired from my face surgery, still angry that Bruno had tried to attack me in the hospital. Or maybe he hadn't and I had hallucinated the whole thing. In that case, maybe I was the nut.

I glanced at my watch. I had to get back to Katie before

she woke up, so I decided to check out a few of the books Gloria had pulled for me and read them at night. But I knew I'd have to hide them. I didn't want Bruno to be tipped off, even if he wasn't doing what I thought he might be doing, which I now didn't think he was. *But he could be.* But if I tipped him off that I thought he was doing it, he might hide things from me and I needed to take a sample of that pudding and protein powder.

I returned to Katie and Bruno's with *The Poisons and Antidotes Sourcebook; Deadly Doses: A writer's guide to poisons;* and for recreational reading, a couple of Agatha Christie mysteries.

"Call me anytime," Gloria said. "I love this sort of stuff. Good luck with your writing."

I thanked her and vowed to never, ever eat lunch with that woman.

31. Finding an Apartment

IT WAS TUESDAY and Bruno was off duty. He wouldn't be on call at the hospital until Friday, which meant he would be hanging around the house. When he was home, I constantly listened for his footsteps on the stairs, always aware of his position in the house. I regretted I hadn't moved faster on finding an apartment of my own.

Verna told me about an apartment building she listed for sale that had a vacant unit and I made an appointment to see it. Sheldon said he'd come with me. The apartment was in Cow Hollow, a great neighborhood just down from Pacific Heights and not quite as far as the Marina. The building was modern by San Francisco standards. Probably built in the 1970s, so most of the charm had been extracted; still, there was a peek-a-boo view of the bay. When Sheldon and I got there, Verna was waiting. She looked at me with great curiosity.

"Vell, vell, vell," she said, looking me up and down like I was a piece of meat. "Zings are getting better for you, eh Agnez? You two zhould move in here togezzer."

I nearly died of embarrassment. Sheldon and I had only kissed, and since my operation, only barely, because it hurt to have any pressure on my lips. My face burst into flames.

Sheldon did the man-thing: pacing around the empty apartment, sticking his head into the bathroom, the bedroom, and the linen closet, the electrical panel, as well as the trash chute. He nodded solemnly. "Good deal, Anne. You should take it. Jude could live over there." He pointed to a niche in the kitchen.

"No pets in zis building," Verna said.

"It's not a pet," I said. "It's a... moving sculpture sort of a thing."

Verna squinted. "A bird?"

"No, um..." My mind flew. I resisted saying the S word.

"No von vants to hear a noisy bird. No parrotz. I could ask if a little bird, a parakeet, perhaps, vould be akzeptable."

Sheldon laughed. "Jude is her pet snail."

Verna turned and regarded me as though I had transformed into a banana slug.

"Rully, Ahg-nes. You could do better zan zat for a pet. A fish vould be better than zat. A turtle. A little bird. Anyzing. But a schnail?"

She said snail like she was saying schnitzel.

"A schnail? Rully? You own a schnail. Von of zose zings in zee garden zat has a house on its back? Unt zat is your *pet?*"

I nodded and gave her my best perky smile. Then Sheldon and I looked at each other and laughed.

When Sheldon dropped me back at Katie's, it was late. I could hear the television in the living room. It was tuned to some sort of sporting event, so I knew where Bruno was in the house. I didn't want him to know I was home, so I sneaked up the stairs and slipped into my room. When I started to lock the door, my heart did a flip-flop—the key, that skeleton key I used each night to lock my bedroom door—had disappeared.

I turned on the light and searched for it on the floor. On the other side of the door. On the floor of the hallway. Inside.

Outside. It wasn't there. And I knew why.

Bruno had taken it. This would be the night Bruno would come after me.

My heart beat fast, but I knew I had to stay calm, stay calm and think. There would be a way through this. *Mary, mother of God, show me the way.*

I remembered that in my parents' house, some of the skeleton keys fit multiple locks, I took my shoes off and skittered down the hall, going silently in and out of the other rooms, finding door knobs, and checking for keys. Katie's door was closed and I didn't want to disturb her. My heart pounded in my temples. I had to figure out a way to barricade my door. To my great relief, I found a skeleton key in a bedroom closet door lock. I ran back down the hallway, slipped into my room, and tried the key. I was in luck. It worked.

I gathered up my toiletries and slipped into the bathroom, washed my face without running much water, brushed my teeth the same way, and then, when I was all set to sprint back across the hallway, and only then, did I flush the toilet.

Now Bruno knew I was home.

It only took him a minute to come up the stairs. Sitting ram-rod straight on top of the bed, I hugged my knees to my chest and watched the door knob move back and forth, a gentle try, a secret try, to open my door. But I had fooled him.

Bruno rattled the doorknob and knocked loudly. It was a solid, impatient knock, thunderous enough to cause my heart to jump and the hair on the back of my neck to rise.

I wanted to yell out that his actions were performed in the wrong order. I wanted to shout that a polite person, a normal person, would knock first, then try the knob, then rattle the door if they found it locked. But Bruno had revealed himself. He had tried the door first, without knocking, and only knocked when he couldn't get in.

"Anne?" Bruno roared.

It made me almost smile to surprise him in this way, to make it impossible for him to come in. I inhaled and waited.

"Anne?" he said, more calm this time, but loud. I worried that he would wake Katie.

"Anne!" he shouted.

Why did he yell? Had he drugged Katie with a strong tranquilizer and knew there was no danger of waking her up? Did this mean she would be unable to help me if I screamed? I swallowed hard.

"W-what?" I finally said, my voice so thin, I had to say it twice.

"Open the door."

My reply was firm. "No."

"I need to talk to you," he said, his tone changing. Now he sounded almost parental.

"I'm too tired, Bruno. Talk to me tomorrow."

"Anne," he said. "Open up this door." He banged his fist against the wood.

"Why?"

He rattled the door again like a small angry boy and kicked the bottom plank. "Open it right now. Do you hear me?"

Where was Katie? Why hadn't this awakened her?

"If you don't open this door, Anne, I'm going to call your brother. And you know what I'm going to say?"

I knew what he'd say. That I've been coming on to him.

"Good." I said. "Call them all. And call my parents, too. Let's have this out, Bruno. I'll tell them everything. About the way you attacked me the night of my prom. About what you did to me in the hospital. Are you ready for them to know everything? *Are you?*"

His voice became low and guttural. "You little bitch. If you ever, *ever* say anything, I'll—"

I thought I heard metal on the other side of the door. It was a curious noise. Was he trying to insert the key he had taken? But I knew these old skeleton key locks. There can only be one key in the chamber at a time. My key was inserted on this side, so he wouldn't be able to insert one from the other side. I was safe.

"Go away, Bruno. Your key won't work."

"If you won't open up, I'll break this damn door down, *Anne.*" He pounded it again. With a heavy foot, Bruno kicked twice at the door, the sound violent and startling.

"Open this door, goddamnit. Let me in right now. I'm finished with your bullshit. Open this goddamned door." He kicked the door again.

I watched with horror as each kick caused the door to bulge. It sounded like a wrecking crew was taking the whole house down.

"Stop it!" I screamed. "Katie! Katie! Help! Help!" I ran to the wall separating our two rooms and banged on it, pounding with my fist. *Why wasn't she waking up?*

Bruno started kicking higher on the door, in the place where the wood became recessed in rectangular insets and was thinner. With every kick, I watched the wood throb. It wouldn't be long before the door broke apart.

A splinter dropped on my side of the door and I screamed and dug around in my purse for my cell phone and punched in 911. The conversation was brief. I told them who I was. Where I was. And cried for help.

In an astonishing crunch of split wood, I saw Bruno's hand come through the center panel below the doorknob. I watched him reach upward toward the lock. He was trying to find the key so he could unlock the door. Or maybe his plan was to take the key out, bring it to his side so he could open it.

I lunged for my key and before he could touch it, I snatched it from the lock.

When he found the keyway empty, he was livid. "Goddamnit, Agnes," he yelled.

He withdrew his hand and I heard the sound of a key being inserted from the other side, the key he had stolen. Before he could insert it, I shoved my key back into the lock on my side.

Mary, mother of God, help me.

Bruno's temper got the best of him and the kicking began again. Splinters of wood flew onto the floor at my feet and I glimpsed his trousers through the missing wood.

Hands shaking, I kept my key in the lock, but the door began to break apart. Splinters flew. Wrenching wood. But I still clutched my cell phone. I called Sheldon.

"Hello?" he said.

"Sheldon. Sheldon—" My breath shallow and rapid, my throat closed. I couldn't speak.

"Anne? Is that you?"

"Sheldon," I screamed. "Come back!" Bruno's foot knocked out another piece of the door and I screamed again.

I was sure the door would now give way and Bruno would appear before me, a specter so terrible I wondered if I might die of fright.

"What's wrong?" Sheldon shouted. He had dropped me off less than a half an hour ago.

"Please come back," I cried.

Bruno kept yelling and kicking, but the old door was stronger than I expected; the bottom inset was in shambles and the panel next to the doorknob had a chunk missing, but the door still stood. I watched Bruno's hand come through and search for the lock, trying again to snatch the key from my side. I ran to my suitcase, found a high-heeled shoe and used it to pummel his hand with the pointy end. I regretted I didn't own stilettos. Fiona was right, every woman should own a pair. I landed a direct hit below his knuckles and he took his hand back. A string of swear words bit the air.

I dialed 911 again, but the noise of sirens and blinking lights in front of the house made me close my phone and run to the window. Flashing lights played off the neighbors' houses. The ping of the doorbell chime made Bruno curse. I glanced from the blue and red lights reflecting onto the bedroom walls and over to the fractured door. I wondered when I could safely get out.

I could hear Bruno pacing the hall and mumbling, "Oh Jesus, Agnes Anne, look what you made me do. Look what you made me do."

The ringing of the doorbell downstairs changed into heavy knocking.

"You'll be sorry you ever did this," Bruno rasped. "Do you hear me?" His fist struck the door. More splinters fell on the floor. "You'll be sorry, goddamnit. *You'll be sorry.*" He kicked the bottom panel again, the way an obstinate child might show his displeasure at having lost a game.

"Where's Katie?" I screamed through the door. *"Where is she? Where's my sister? I'm going to make her leave you. You're a monster!"*

The doorbell rang, followed by knocks, then pounding.

I thought I heard Bruno go downstairs.

This was my chance. I grabbed for my suitcase, snatched my Holy Cards off the bureau and shoved them in my pocket. With trembling fingers, I used the key to open what was left of the door. There were so many splinters on the floor, I had to clear them away before the door could open wide enough to let me pass.

At the front door, Bruno spoke calmly to several officers. I didn't know what they were saying, but I knew his tone was soft and professional. Inside my head, I was screaming *Faker! You creepy faker!*

"I was the one who called," I managed to breathlessly say. I didn't want to talk about Bruno in his house. I wanted to be outside so I walked past Bruno and the two policemen at the door and dragged my suitcase onto the lawn then looked up and down the street for Sheldon. Surely he would be here any minute.

The officers parted to let me through. One of them followed me. "What's going on?" he asked.

"He-he-he was going to aat- att-" I stopped, out of breath. *Mary Mother of God, help me.* I seized another breath and let it out in a rush. "Attack me." There. It was out. Their faces were patient and urged me to go on. "I couldn't lock my door. He took the key! I found another and when he couldn't get in, he began to beat the door down."

"Calm down. Calm down," the officer said. "It's okay now. We're here."

Another officer came over. "He said he was worried about you, miss. He wanted to tell you that your sister is in the hospital. Did you know that?"

"Katie? In the hospital? No."

"He was worried that you might harm yourself. That's why he tried to get to you. He says he wanted to save you."

So, that was Bruno's game. Dr. Bruno Stark was going to convince them I was a nutcase.

"He never told me. H-He never said that. He just tried to kick in my bedroom door. That's all he did. Kick and kick and kick. He was going to come in and at-at-at—" I switched tactics. "Come with me. Come up and see what he did."

No one moved.

"Calm down, Anne." Bruno's voice oozed fake compassion. He had come over to my circle. All eyes bore into me. I looked around the group of firemen and medics. No one else seemed to hear the insincerity but me. I saw pity in their eyes. I also saw how they respected him.

I forgot about my Marilyn Monroe speech tactic and stuttered miserably. "You d-don't underst-stand. H-he w-was g-going to at-attack m-me."

"There, there, Anne," Bruno said, putting his arm around my shoulder so he could bring me close. Out of the corner of my eye, I saw him shake his head from side to side as though I was nuts and everyone should humor me. "Officers, I suggest you go up there and see what Anne did to her bedroom door."

"Y-you did that," I countered, shoving him away. "Y-you k-kicked it in. You took the key so I couldn't lock m-my door."

"I was so worried about you, Anne. I thought with the strain of Katie being back in the hospital, you'd take too many pills again. You'd use the knife you took from my desk—oh, I know you have it. I thought you'd use in on yourself." He looked at the officers and shrugged. "She has a self-hate thing. Just had some facial surgery and," he said, as a professional sadness pinched his eyes. "I'm afraid she expected the surgery to solve all her problems. Sadly..." He shook his head.

The hate I had for this man swamped me. Couldn't they see he how he lied?

"That's not true and you know it. You know it! *You are a liar! A LIAR!*" The relief I gained by pitching my voice into the damp night air exhilarated me. Words came out in a torrent. I screamed at Bruno for being smug. I shouted that I wanted to bash in his arrogant mouth, shatter the conceited tilt of his head and knock out every tooth in his egotistical smile.

His expression, however, remained a mask of composure. As though I saw him in slow motion, he turned to the officers, and made an expression that said, *Look at her, see what I mean? She's lost it, poor thing. She's come undone.*

"Miss?" said one of the men standing on Bruno's lawn. "I think you should come with us and have an evaluation."

"I am not crazy!" I screamed at him. "Nor am I suicidal! This man kicked down the door to try to get to me. He's been after me for years. He was coming through the door to rape me. Don't you understand? *He was going to rape me! And he put his wife in the hospital in order to be alone with me!"*

Another officer moved Bruno away from me and toward the house. We became two groups again, each of us championing our side to those trained to professionally listen.

"You're safe now," the officer with me said. I wondered if he learned this voice at the police academy. "Let's get you some help tonight," he continued. "Wouldn't you like to get to a safer place?"

"Yes. Yes," I quickly agreed. I continued to tell the officer about Bruno, about him propositioning me at the coffee shop, his remarks about marrying the wrong sister, about the way he attacked me in the kitchen the other day, and the more I spoke, the more I noticed the policeman's detached expression. I shouldn't have yelled. A bad feeling began to settle over me. This was not going in the right direction.

"Go upstairs," I pleaded. "Look at the way he kicked in the door! The splinters go in, not out. I was *inside*. He was *outside*. Please. Please look. He just said I kicked the door, but *he* kicked it in. He was trying to get at me. He was going to rape me, not save me. He's a liar. My brother-in-law lies!"

I glanced sideways at Bruno's group and back to the two officers standing with me. Bruno's group was larger. I could hear strains of his slick voice. He was characterizing me as the bruised up, self-mutilating sister-in-law.

We did go upstairs and the entire troop followed, both sides filed inside. It was pathetic the way the door had been kicked. I pointed out the splinters, the lock, and the key I had used to stop him from unlocking the door. Bruno's face was a mask of calm.

"I was rescuing you, Anne," he said in his slippery voice. "Rescuing *you*."

I couldn't stand it another second. "You were coming in to get me," I shrieked. "Don't you see?" I shouted at the policemen. Their waxen faces told me the answer.

I'd had enough. I ran down the stairs, tying to hold back my emotions and hoping Sheldon had arrived and I could get out of this house forever. But Sheldon wasn't there. I saw Luke drive up, parking his car at a haphazard angle in the street, red and blue lights flashing against the houses. I don't know how he found out. Maybe he recognized the address on his police radio or a buddy called him. Releasing frustration and pent up fear, I burst into tears. Luke held me while I cried, the phone and curly cord attached to his shoulder, lumpy against my sore face.

"Luke, he's telling them I tried to commit suicide. It's not true." I sobbed into his shoulder. "Really. You know that. Bruno... Bruno..." Damn it, I couldn't stop blubbering. I wanted to hide. I needed to pee. And then I felt a telltale sting. At first I thought I had been bitten by an insect. But then the world wobbled and my muscles relaxed. Sheldon's face appeared above me through a foggy haze. I knew what they had done.

I had been tranquilized.

32. Vacation at Hotel Loony

A NURSE WEARING A LIGHT BLUE SHIRT and matching surgical pants wheeled me into a room and waited by my side, ostensibly to help me unpack. But all she did was take away my belts, my razor, and everything in my cosmetic bag. She also took away my shoes. I asked her for my antibiotic pills. I still needed to finish the last three. She refused and said a doctor would have to prescribe it.

"It's already been prescribed," I said.

"Sorry."

While I sat on the side of the bed, groggy as all get out, Nurse Hijack continued her foraging through every pants pocket and every elastic pouch in my suitcase. Not having much gumption, I suppose because of the tranquilizer, I waited passively and watched this ransacking of my possessions as though it was happening to someone else.

When she found my library books, her eyes went from the titles to my face and back.

"I'm doing some research," I mumbled, in defense of the poison theme.

"I see."

"You won't be needing these," she said, as she slipped the books on poisons into the blue plastic garbage bag. Nurse

Hijack paused when she held my Agatha Christie books, but turned and put them on my nightstand. Next, she held up my Rosary. An electric shock scampered up my spine.

"That's my Rosary!"

"I'm sorry," Nurse Hijack said. Pity flickered in her eyes, but only momentarily. I watched the beads slither into the blue plastic bag.

"But you can't—it's my Rosary," I said, wondering if I should call her Nurse Pickpocket instead of Hijack.

"Some things," the nurse said, "are deemed not safe. We'll return them later."

"Not safe? Like…" I paused, trying to make my mind work, wishing for some adrenalin or some coffee. "You mean you think I would… harm myself? With my Rosary beads?"

Her eyes gave me the answer.

"Who would kill himself with a Rosary?" I said this half belligerently, half with humor. I tried to imagine if suicide would even be possible with a Rosary. The wires holding the beads together aren't very strong. I figured to kill myself, I'd have to swallow the cross and hope to choke. It was absurd.

"I'll ask the doctor," Nurse Hijack said, with a smidgen of sympathy.

I thought of the scrutiny and the medical evaluation those beads would have to undergo. If they were deemed safe, would they then be administered by prescription only?

Rx: one Rosary to be taken each night, as needed.

33. Shrink Day

IN THIS PLACE, this institution for the crazy, which they were quick to tell me was a private institution, not the county loony bin, breakfast could be had on a tray or be taken in a small dining room. They asked me which I preferred. I opted to go to the dining room. Even though it embarrassed me to be one of them, I wanted to see my shipmates. Maybe I wanted to see how crazy they looked so I could get a comparison.

A staff member stood in the middle of the dining area, clapped her hands with gusto and shouted to get our attention. She invited some of us to a group meeting after breakfast. Some of us, she said, had our psychiatric appointments. I was invited to meet my shrink.

I walked up to this person and asked if I had time enough to have a shower first. She told me I could only shower when the doctor ordered it.

"A shower has to be... p-prescribed?" My eyes roved from one staff member to the other. They turned away from me. I had my answer. Cleanliness, like Rosary beads, must have a prescription.

Just contemplating talking to a psychiatrist made me nearly die of embarrassment. No one in our family ever went to a psychiatrist. Only crazy people went to shrinks. And now I was supposed to tell shrinky-dink stranger everything?

Dr. Helfer tried to make small talk. He told me he retired years ago, but still came back to this institution because he enjoys the work. I wondered if he relished feeling sorry for the people in here.

"Tell me, Agnes, how do you feel today?"

"I use my middle name," I said, unable to help myself from correcting him. "I don't like the name Agnes anymore." I had to tell him because I didn't want to go through this—whatever it was—and have to hear my old name.

"Ahhh." He made a note on the paper in front of him and I liked that. It signaled to me that Dr. Helfer would listen to me. But another thought occurred to me. What if he now thought I was schizophrenic? The two faces of Agnes.

They'd never let me out.

"I'm not a schizo," I said, perhaps too defensively. "It's just that I never liked the name Agnes. Now I go by my middle name, which is Anne, with an E."

His head tilted to one side like he was a dog trying to understand a complicated human principle, something beyond *out* or *fetch.*

"I connect Agnes with the word ugly," I said, trying to be helpful. "So about a year ago, I decided I needed to plan a way out."

"A way out?" he said, perking up.

"No, no," I said quickly. "Nothing bad like—I just wanted to change my life, Dr. Helfer. Leave my parents' house. I needed a way to reach my potential, that's what I meant. Not—" I couldn't say the word suicide.

"That's fair." Dr. Helfer's nod reassured me.

"I hated my job as an escrow secretary. It was fun for the first few years, especially when my sister Katie worked at O'Neil & Co. with me, but when she quit I was lonely and the job wasn't very challenging. I was at a dead end and when I heard my parents tell each other how glad they were that I would live at home forever, I knew I had to do something. I didn't know what to do or how to change, so I prayed. I prayed a lot. We're Catholic, so I prayed to the Virgin Mary." I smiled at him with, I must admit, a bit of pride. "I have a Special Devotion," I said, softly. Usually, this is met with admiration.

"What's that?" Dr. Helfer said.

"A Special Devotion?" I couldn't believe he didn't know.

The doctor nodded.

"It means Mary is a very important part of my life. I pray to her. I honor her and she helps me." I stopped. I didn't want to tell him more.

"So, this Mary-worshiping. It's sort of a cult?"

"No. Lots of people have a Special Devotion to Mary."

He frowned and thought for a few seconds. "Fair enough. Go on."

"Well, Mary helped me develop my plan."

"Your plan," he said, changing positions in the big chair behind the desk. "Tell me about this plan."

"Well, it had five points." I tried smiling at Dr. Helfer, but it didn't seem to gain me anything, so I decided not to bother.

"Ahh, I see," he said. "And the Virgin Mary helped you make this plan?"

"Yes." The thought of Mary made a warm feeling of relief flood through me. I knew she was here helping me. She wouldn't let me down.

Dr. Helfer leaned forward. "Does Mary appear to you?" He whispered this as though one of the patients wandering the hallways might hear and think I was more nuts than they were.

"No," I said, "not like she appeared to the children at Fatima or Lourdes, but she's real enough."

This sort of stumped him. I wondered if he's even heard of these places.

"Go on," he said. I noticed his tone had become cautious and his interest in me, absolute.

"With her help, I developed a plan to set myself free."

He made a doctorly noise, sort of an approving, "Ahem."

"She was with me when I—sort of—sort of—"

"Take your time," he said.

I took a deep breath. "I prayed to her the night I knew I had to change my life. That's what I'm talking about. Changing my life."

"I see. That's fair. You made a plan. Good." Dr. Helfer nodded. "Tell me about this plan."

I launched into my plan, the whole of it. I told him about my makeover, my stutter, my real estate license and my surgery.

The doctor looked both interested as well as pleased. "That's an ambitious plan, Anne. How did you do?"

"Good. I guess I've done it all. The operation was the last thing. Can you see the bruising?"

The doctor nodded. Of course he could see the bruising. Today I had no access to makeup. Only that librarian appreciated my purple and yellow blotches.

"I've completed everything, and as soon as the bruises go away and my face stops swelling, I guess I'm done. This is the new me." I smiled and had the urge to say, "Tah da!" but he might think was crazy, and if I were crazy, he wouldn't let me out. And I had to get out of here, so I forced my eyes to stare into his and hoped I looked normal.

Dr. Helfer's head quivered. "So you were unhappy with the results of the facial surgery?"

"No. Not at all. This is what I've always wanted."

"You're sad that it didn't change your life?"

"How could I be sad? I'm just getting started with my new life. I even have a boyfriend."

He leaned back in his chair, so far back the chair yelped like someone had pinched it. I watched Dr. Helfer frown at the ceiling.

"So, Agnes, I mean Anne, we need to figure out why you are in denial."

Anger churned inside me like I was a pot on slow boil. "I'm not in d-denial," I said. "I didn't try to commit suicide. What did Bruno, I mean Dr. Stark, tell you?"

Dr. Helfer brought the chair back to a sitting position and held a file with both hands. "I haven't spoken to Dr. Stark. But it says here, Anne, that you tried to commit suicide."

"But I didn't."

I rambled on about Bruno, about last night, about the police. Dr. Helpfer listened, but he didn't say anything, he read my file. I stretched my neck and tried to read sideways. I could see my name. These papers might have been the notes from the police or the brief interview last night when I came in. I wanted to grab them and read them myself. I watched as the doctor read a page, flipped it over, and read the next, the rustle of the paper the only sound in the room.

My God, I thought, *I have a file! This file might follow me. Other people will know.* "Anne," *they'll say.* "We can't deal with you. You have a file."

34. Analyze This

LATE IN THE AFTERNOON, I thought I heard Fiona's voice. I ran out into the hall and up to the front desk. Fiona wasn't there. A few minutes later, a staff member called my name and took me to a room behind the nurses' station where Fiona stood, her raincoat still wet from the weather outside. I had no idea it was raining. I didn't care about the water running off her slicker; I hugged her and hugged her. I asked her about Katie.

"Katie's fine," Fiona said, holding both my hands. "They gave her an infusion of fluids and sent her home this morning. Ma's worried about you." Her voice dropped to a whisper and she came in close. "Ma wanted to come, but she was raving about all of the images of the Virgin Mary. Especially the one on your desktop. You know—the one your snail made. Wasn't that freaky? Anyway, I told her not to come. No use giving the impression you're from a nutty family." She winked.

I nodded and watched her take off her slicker and hang it on a coat rack. There was a table in this room and we went over to it and sat down.

"Listen, Fiona," I said, "I've got to tell you what happened at Bruno's—"

The staff lady, the one who walked around with a clipboard, came into the room and interrupted. "Since he was at the scene last night, I'd like to have your brother, Luke, here before we begin," she said. "So refrain from talking about the issue." Her smile was both meager and fake.

I ignored her and turned back to Fiona. "You should have seen what Bruno did. He was a maniac!"

"I'd like to wait until your brother Luke gets here," Clipboard Lady repeated. The irritation in her voice was one notch down from nasty.

"Luke's always late," I mumbled, suddenly ashamed I was in my pajamas and robe and everyone else was dressed.

"We can chat about other things," Clipboard said. Her smile, as well as her know-it-all attitude, grated on me. I hated the way her short brown hair stuck to her scalp like a swimming cap.

Fiona and Clipboard talked about the rain and how long it was supposed to last, which I didn't participate in because I didn't care about the weather. Rain or shine, I simply wanted to get out and never see Bruno Stark again.

Finally, Luke showed up, his police uniform dark blue and somehow too formal for this place.

"Good," Miss Clipboard said, when my brother was seated. She began to riffle through the papers. "You're Luke O'Neil, and you're Fiona O'Neil? Do I have this right? Brother and sister of Agnes Anne?"

Even though Fiona had been there the whole time, Clipboard acted like she had never seen Fiona before. Suddenly it felt like this was a play and I was in it. Trouble was, I didn't know my lines.

"What I'd like to discuss today is the history leading up to last night," Clipboard said.

My God, only last night? It felt like days ago.

"This whole thing has taken us completely by surprise," Fiona said. I could detect a tremble in her voice. "I feel terrible about it. If Anne needs help, we want to do everything we can to help her."

"I think I'm well right now," I interjected. "I don't need to be here."

Luke addressed Clipboard. "What happened last night was totally out of character. Totally."

"So, you didn't see Anne's depression?"

They shook their heads.

"That's because I'm not depressed." I tried to smile at Miss Know-it-all Clipboard to show her she didn't scare me, but mid-smile, my lips twitched.

Clipboard flashed me a *You'd-better-be-quiet-because-this-is-none-of-your-business* look. Then she said in her clinical voice, "Describe her relationship with Dr. Stark."

Here it comes again.

"She's known Bruno Stark since high school," Fiona said. "They used to date."

There it was. And Clipboard's reaction flashed like a strobe light. "Ah," she said, turning to me. "Has it been difficult seeing your sister with your old boyfriend?"

"Tell me," I said, looking first to Fiona, then to Luke, "do you think after all I've done for myself that I would ever, ever, *ever* commit suicide?"

Luke met my eyes. Slowly, almost with reluctance, he shook his head. It was the kind of shake that was not one hundred percent positive. At best, it was a maybe. Nonetheless, it was the answer Clipboard needed to see.

I looked to Fiona, my eyes implored her to answer the same question.

She shook her head the same way, not vigorously, but agreeably. Two down.

"So, what did Bruno say about last night?" I asked. "I bet he came to you this morning and gave you his version."

They didn't reply, but their faces revealed that I was right.

"Tell me what he told you," I demanded.

My siblings sat in front of me, birds on a fence, and eyed me with great sadness. I wondered if they would fly away.

"Well?" My eyes flew back and forth from one to the other, then I sneaked a quick glance at Clipboard. I turned to her and said with all the politeness I could muster. "I have the right to know what he said to them."

"Dr. Stark said you were carrying on," Clipboard said. "You were screaming and crying in your room. Threatening to harm yourself. Threatening to commit suicide if he didn't divorce your sister."

"What?" I screeched. "That's crap! I was screaming because he was kicking in the door. He keeps telling me that he's going to have sex with me." I felt my face flush.

Clipboard, like nature abhorring a vacuum, didn't like all the silence, didn't like the way Luke and Fiona were staring at each other in their own private communication.

"Anne," Clipboard said, "you're telling us that you weren't going to harm yourself, yet I have other information. We need to get to the bottom of this or we can't release you. We want you to be safe. This is for your protection. Do you understand?"

I looked at her. "Ok," I said softly.

"Have you always been jealous of your sister?" Clipboard asked.

What kind of a question was that?

"No," I said. "Katie's always sick. She's married to a creepy guy who is trying to cheat on her. I only have pity for her. And now she's trapped. And everyone in my family always falls all over Bruno, thanks him for taking care of Katie. Meanwhile, she just sinks lower and lower and we don't know why."

From the other side of the table, Fiona and Luke continued to stare.

"How do we know Bruno's *not* the one making her sick?" I said, my voice too shrill. "He keeps giving her this vanilla pudding and p-p-protein powder stuff. I had some with her and, afterwards, I had diarrhea myself. What if that's what's making her sick? What if he does this to get attention?" I stopped my rant and gazed at the tabletop. "I'm reading *The Pale Horse*. It's an Agatha Christie. The main thrust is about unexplained deaths. Then a character is made sick. She was poisoned with thallium... "

I immediately regretted that I had spoken about this. It sounded so silly. "What if he's not in love with her anymore and wants her out of his life?"

Fiona's frown went from her hairline practically to her chin. I'd never seen Luke's eyes so big.

Clipboard's nods were large and all-knowing. "So that's why you have those books on poison."

"Poison?" Fiona frowned. "What are you talking about?"

I sighed. "What if Bruno is—doing something—to Katie?"

"But, look how he's stood beside her," Luke said. "Bruno-God-love-him, wouldn't do anything to hurt his own wife."

"Wanna' make a bet?" The moment those words flew out of my mouth, those hateful words, I realized I had gone one step too far. Now I looked like a nut job.

Clipboard adjusted herself in her chair. "You have to take responsibility for a few things, Anne."

We were all silent. Three O'Neils sat and stared at a stranger who had been inserted into our lives.

"Explain why you had a knife," Clipboard whispered.

"What knife?"

"The knife you were trying to use on yourself. Last night."

"I didn't have a knife."

"Come, come. You even have a Holy Card with Saint Michael and his raised sword. His knife is not unlike your knife, smaller of course." She tossed the card and Saint Michael spun toward me.

I glanced at the card and appreciated that Saint Michael's foot was on the devil, his sword poised above it's head.

"I don't own a knife," I said.

Silence.

"Bruno told you this? B-Bruno said I had a knife?"

Clipboard didn't speak. She didn't have to, as her expression filled with grave misfortune, I knew she had a trump card up her lab coat sleeve. I prayed I wasn't in for a reenactment of *One Flew Over the Cuckoo's Nest*.

Clipboard brought out a manila envelope. We watched as she shook out an object. It was a fairly small knife, like one might buy in a touristy gift shop, an imitation dagger.

"That's Bruno's letter opener," I said. "I think they bought it on their honeymoon."

"Don't you think it's a bit of a coincidence that it looks like the knife on your holy card? Saint Michael's sword?"

I stared at the card and then glanced at the knife.

"Dr. Stark said you were trying to kill yourself, Anne. Trying to kill yourself because he would never leave his wife and you've always been in love with him." She folded her hands on top of my file.

"Dr. Stark is full of crap, Miss Clipboard." Again, I regretted this outburst. It was crude. The drugs must have loosened my tongue and let words that I would never normally say, fly out of my mouth. I felt a blush creep across my face and wondered if I was appearing unbalanced.

"My name is Dr. Crisp." She slipped the letter opener back into the envelope. "So, you are going to maintain that you were not trying to harm yourself last night?"

"That's right," I said, the anger in my voice undisguised. "And it's a good thing I didn't have that knife or I might have used it. *On him.*"

I watched as she wrote something down in my file. Next thing I knew, she threw down one of my laminated photos of Marilyn Monroe.

"Is this yours?" Clipboard asked.

I nodded.

"Do you admire her?"

"Very much."

"Didn't she," Clipboard said, softly, "commit suicide?"

35. Terror and Consequences

AT THE ENTRANCE to my room, I had an enormous urge to slam my door. But there was nothing to slam. The lack of a door pointed once again to my alleged craziness. Only sane people get doors. Crazy people get open space.

In a few minutes, a nurse came in with a tiny paper cup and some water. "Take this," she said.

"What is it?" I asked.

"Dr. Crisp prescribed it. It's a tranquilizer."

"Dr. Crisp can go stand on her head," I said. I crossed my arms in front of my chest.

The nurse's lips curled into a sly smile. I had a feeling she agreed with me. However, this didn't dissuade her from continuing to hold out the pill. Finally, I put it in my mouth and swallowed some water, then lay down on my bed. I decided to say a Rosary on my fingers. I closed my eyes, made the Sign of the Cross, said the Apostle's creed, one Our Father, three Hail Mary's, one Glory Be and then got into the rhythm of the Rosary.

"Agnes Anne? Agnes Anne!" The voice near me pierced my exhaustion, brought me back.

Electrified that Bruno might be looking down at me, my

eyes popped open like hot kernels of corn on a griddle. I found myself staring up at Father Mac. Floundering under the bed sheet and blankets, mortified that I lay before him in a bed, I tried to sit up.

"Just lay there, child. Don't get up." Father slid a chair next to me. "Tisk, tisk," he said, regarding the bruises on my face. "What happened here?"

"Oh that," I said, noticing the way his eyes swept back and forth across my face. "I had my nose done, Father. My chin, too."

"You—you did, did you?" He seemed perplexed. I was probably the first cosmetic surgery case he's ever seen and now I was in a psych ward. I wondered if he thought one followed the other.

He tisk-tisked again like I'd been a bad girl. "You know, Agnes, God loves us no matter what our shape and size."

"I know that, Father. I was just unhappy about my face and decided that I had the means to fix it."

"There's no need of that," Father said. "God, my dear, made you perfect. He never makes mistakes."

I thought of Fiona's spectacular looks, of Katie's angelic face, of Darcy's movie star beauty. "Yes, Father. I know that. But I think you'll agree that some of us are more perfect than others."

"Oh, Agnes," he sighed as though my face was my biggest problem. "God doesn't need us to improve on His creation."

I have always hated this kind of logic. Crossing my arms in front of my chest, I stared at the ceiling. "I heard you had a heart operation."

"Yes, yes," Father readily admitted. "I did."

"Why?"

"My aorta had a defective valve. Bicuspid aorta they said. Most people have three leaflets in their valve I only had two. They replaced it. It's amazing what they can do these days."

"Wasn't that improving on God's creation? He created you a certain way, didn't He? Maybe He liked you that way. Maybe God thought your heart didn't have a defect, that two leaflets instead of three were perfect." I lost the nerve to go any further. I could tell by the way Father Mac coughed, he saw my point.

"Your parents are very worried about you Agnes Anne. Fiona didn't want them to come here, so I suppose that's why they sent me. Tell me what's going on. Why has it come to this?"

I stared at the ceiling as though I might see a sign that said One Way, or Yield, or Cuckoo Birds Walk This Way. But the ceiling was made of white cottage cheese and I could detect no advice. I would not lie to Father Mac.

"My brother-in-law Bruno tried to attack me," I blurted. "I called 911, Father. Now Bruno's angry with me. He said I would regret it. But I don't."

"I heard the word suicide," Father Mac said. The gravity in his voice reminded me of the preachy way he spoke from the pulpit, the word *suicide* quivered with Terror and Consequences.

"I heard it too, Father," I said, smiling at him. "But Bruno's lying."

Father Mac leaned forward so his elbows were on his knees. "Agnes Anne," he whispered, "if what you say is true, this is very serious, very serious indeed."

"Yes. This is very serious, Father. I didn't try to kill myself. Why would I? I have a new career ahead of me, a boyfriend, and a new $20,000 face. Why would I want to end my life when I have worked so hard to make a new beginning?"

He frowned and nodded his head. "Will you give me your confession, Agnes Anne?"

"Of course. But one thing, Father."

"What's that?"

"Ask Bruno for his."

The next morning, I had another session with Dr. Helfer. Today he looked like a child masquerading as an old man. His neck seemed to have shrunk, or maybe his oversized collar grew.

I checked for dandruff. It was there again, great dunes of it, poor man. He must not be married. No wife would allow such dandruff. Sitting in the eye of his own dander vortex, I could feel only compassion toward old Dr. Helfer. I knew what it was like to be humiliated. He didn't know it, but in this strange way, we were kin.

"How are you today, Anne?" Dr. Hefler said, as though we had been friends for years.

"Fine. I need to leave, Dr. Helfer. I'm missing work." I thought of Bruno's listing. The painting and repairs must be done by now or nearly done. I had to kick things into high gear to get it on the market. I wondered if the painters had left, if the stager had moved in her props, set the glassware and china on the dining room table with color-coordinated napkins and vases of flowers and other things stagers do.

I could hardly wait to see it and this urgency to leave stabbed at me. I had so many things to do: write ad copy, schedule a photographer for the brochure. There was printing and a dozen other things I needed to do. Then I thought of how I might bump into Bruno out at the house and I broke out into a chilling sweat. I didn't want to see him. I didn't want to see him ever again.

I wondered what I could do when it happened. It crossed my mind that maybe I should give the listing up. Let Verna have it. Stay away from Bruno at all costs. But five percent of over a million dollars, even though it would be divided with the selling agent, was a staggering amount of money to leave on the table. Greed, one of the Seven Deadly Sins, toyed with me. God forgive me, but I knew I would walk over hot coals to get that money.

"These things take time," Dr. Helfer said.

I felt rage building again inside me. Hatred toward Bruno fumed through my veins. I didn't know how long I could control myself.

"Why does it take so much time to get out of here?" I asked.

"The State does not allow people who have tried to commit suicide to leave until we feel they are safe to be on their own. You know this is a wonderful institution. It's not the county facility. This is a private hospital, but we still need to evaluate you and convince the court that you are not a danger to yourself. Otherwise, Anne, it wouldn't be right to release you."

It sounded like he was talking about a fish. Catch and release.

36. Leaping from the Looney Bin

THE NEXT MORNING, the most incredible thing happened. The same woman who took all my stuff the day I came in, gave me back the plastic bag with everything in it and told me I could leave.

Just like that.

She also said someone from my family would be here to pick me up.

Just like that.

I pulled my suitcase out of the closet, pulled out the contents of the plastic bag, which had contained the "dangerous" items they took from me that night, and repacked them. It was wonderful to shower without an attendant and change into real clothes. Could Luke be the one to pick me up? Most likely, it would be Fiona. I hoped it wouldn't be Ma. I didn't need all that drama right now.

I had extra time to spend on my hair and makeup. My bruises had faded a little more and now foundation covered the remaining traces fairly easily. The bridge of my nose, however, still was still puffy. I enjoyed tracing the even straight line from between my eyes, down the center of my nose to the tip. I applied mascara to my slightly swollen eyes, put on eyeliner, used eyebrow pencil, lipstick, and had enough time to blow my hair dry until it was positively feathery.

Even I was impressed. A sideways glance showed that the hook was gone! My ungainly chin had been nipped into a less severe angle and my face appeared more oval. Add to that my new golden blonde hair and a thrill ran through me. Today I would walk out the door, forget about this stupid bump in the road, and get on with my life.

Dr. Clipboard and an assistant were waiting for me in the room behind the nurses' station. I liked hearing the click, click, click of my high heels as I walked in. It made me feel powerful to be dressed in office clothes.

Both of them seemed surprised and complimented me on the way I looked. This made me smile and I flung out my arms and spontaneously cried out, "This is the new me! Why would I want to end it all? See? This is what I've been working for!"

Their faces remained blank and I felt silly that I had misread their expressions. I shouldn't have said anything at all.

"You're not out of the woods, Anne," Dr. Clipboard said. "I'll be honest with you. We're crowded and we need to release patients whom we believe are not a threat to society or to themselves." Before I could make a pleasing noise or form a thank you for this confidence, she added, "Your mother's here to take you home."

"M-my m-mother?" I didn't feel like seeing Ma right now. The vows I had just made to myself about cooperating lay in shambles. I tried taking a deep breath.

"My phone isn't charged. Can you call me a cab? Please?"

"You know, Anne, you're very lucky to have a relative pick you up."

I thought of the Stockholm Syndrome, where prisoners sympathize and agree with their captors in order to survive. I wondered if I had become a victim of it, for I suddenly felt so grateful to Clipboard, I nearly genuflected.

"The court has mandated two visits with a psychiatrist a week. Will you do this?" She turned her clipboard toward me and thrust out a pen. "You don't even have to pay for it. The state pays."

"Okay," I said, taking the pen and signing. "I'd be happy to see Dr. Helfer whenever he wants and I... um... and... I'm so... um... so very grateful that a relative is picking me up."

"You don't' have to be sarcastic, Anne," Clipboard said. We can hold people for 72 hours. Longer if we feel they are a danger to themselves. You know that, don't you?"

I didn't like the threatening tone veiled in her voice, but she didn't worry me. I knew I had passed some sort of test. That Helfer had written a favorable report. I was being released!

I smiled at Clipboard and felt sorry for her that she was stuck here with these psychos. To leave this place, I would do whatever they said. I vowed to sign up for the Stockholm Syndrome and fall in love with Dr. Dandruff.

Ma greeted me like I had just escaped a burning building, her hug so hard and heavy, I thought she might break my neck. Together, we wheeled my suitcase out the door and around to the parking lot.

My heart froze.

Bruno stood beside his car, smoking a cigarette. I stopped and stared. Time passed. It was like the shootout at the O.K. Corral.

"I'm not riding with him."

"Agnes, don'be rude," Ma said. "This's tha person who saved ya."

"He most certainly did not."

"Can'ya not be civil?"

"No. I can't. And I won't."

Bruno's smirk slithered up the side of his face, but his eyes were leery. I glanced towards the street. There were buses nearby. I could also grab a cab. My gaze turned to Ma's worried eyes.

"Bruno is a creep and a liar, Ma, and I won't go anywhere with him. I'll catch a cab."

I turned my suitcase around and started to roll it to the edge of the parking lot.

"No, you won't," Bruno said, coming after me. He ripped the suitcase handle from my hand. "You will climb in this car, Agnes Anne, and I will drive you home."

"That's right, dear," Ma said, running after me. "Please?" She grabbed my hand. "We'll ride tagether."

"Ma, this creep would sell his soul to the devil if he thought he could get what he wanted. He's fooled you all into thinking that he saved me. He didn't. He was breaking into my room to rape me. Get it?"

"Agnes Anne O'Neil, apologize ta Bruno right this minute."

"Apologize?" I turned my back and continued to walk. Bruno could keep my suitcase.

Out on the street, I saw a cab almost immediately, hailed

it and hopped in. Bruno and Ma followed in his car. Ma kept rolling her window down and trying to talk to me.

"Hey, lady," the cabbie said. "You know those people?"

"Unfortunately, I do." I turned away from them and slouched lower.

The cabbie rolled his window down and shouted over at them when we hit the next light.

"Hey! Hey! What's your beef?"

Kill me right here, Lord, I thought to myself.

"What? What?" the cabbie shouted out the window. He stepped on the gas the second the light turned green. "I think that lady said the Virgin Mary is crying for you. That make sense?"

"She always says that."

"That your mother?"

"Yep." I turned back to check on them. Bruno got stuck behind a car making a left turn.

"What'd you do? Elope?"

"It's too long a story for a short cab ride."

"Yeah, yeah. Everyone's got a story. I hear 'em all day."

I wondered who might be in the office at noon. A few agents were talking on phones, hunched down in cubicles. When they saw me, their expressions fluctuated between welcome, fear, sympathy, and embarrassment. Then, after they looked away, they looked back, this time with intense curiosity.

That's when I knew they knew where I'd been.

I was the returning refugee from plastic surgery, the nutcase who had to be tranquilized and sent to the psych ward. Maybe they thought I'd go postal, pull out a gun and mow them all down. I wondered if I made a sudden move, if they'd duck and cover.

Uncle Jimmy spotted me and ran over. Today his sport coat was the green and red plaid. His bow tie was emerald. His shirt, blue. I wanted to burst out laughing, for if Uncle Jimmy were unlucky enough to be brought into the psych ward, he would look crazy. But we knew him here at O'Neil & Co., so Uncle Jimmy to us, looked normal. That's when I realized that mental health was like the first rule of real estate: *Location, location, location.*

"Darlin', darlin'," Uncle Jimmy said, giving me an enormous hug. "I t'ought you were—" He pushed my shoulders away from himself so he could look at me.

That's when I realized Uncle Jimmy probably told everyone about me by first saying, *"Don' tell anyone this, but did ya hear 'bout poor Agnes Anne? Nuthouse, I'm afraid."*

"I'm fine, Uncle Jimmy. Really, I am." I tried to move on, but now his arm was draped around my shoulders and I was trapped.

"You shouldn't be here," he said. "You should be restin'."

I extricated myself from his arm and said over my shoulder, "I gave rest up for Lent."

Of course, I didn't. It was just a funny line I learned from Uncle Jimmy himself. Maybe that's why he didn't laugh.

"Oooooooo" Brent and David began to squeal as they came up the hallway. "Your face." They drew out the word so it lasted several seconds. "So cuuuuuute."

"You think?" I smiled.

"Oh my god, oh my god, oh-oh-oh!" David hopped around like he was doing an imitation of Peter Rabbit, which again, if I had performed that little dance where I'd just been, they might have kept me another seventy-two hours.

While we were celebrating my nose and chin job, Uncle Jimmy shifted from one foot to the other, as though he was unsure of what to say.

Behind me, I heard a whacking noise and the clatter of wheels. Bruno, his face a peculiar shade of purple, forced my suitcase through the door, his blond hair mussed and flopping around with the effort.

"Here," he said, rolling the suitcase to the side of the reception desk. His stare, pure cold fury. "Good luck, Agnes Anne."

We watched him turn around and stride out the door.

"Uh oh," David said. "I'd say someone has their panties in a bunch."

My hands trembled, but I was fascinated that David, who didn't know Bruno, saw his anger and reacted to it with humor. I wanted to be able to do that some day, but right now I was filled with so much anxiety, it would be easier to climb Everest.

"Agnes Anne," Uncle Jimmy said, his thumb pointing to Bruno's departure. "Wha's goin' on here? What did ya do ta make 'im so angry?" He looked from Bruno's retreating figure, to my suitcase, and back to me.

"Bruno just has his panties in a bunch." I walked over to my suitcase and started to wheel it to my cubicle.

"I can't get over the difference in you!" Brent said. He took hold of my suitcase and wheeled it for me.

"Let's celebrate your new face!" said David. "It's Mardi Gras! Let's do lunch."

Grateful for their enthusiasm and relieved that I didn't have to be alone, I let them whisk me off to a neighborhood bistro.

37. Looking for Stockholm

AFTER LUNCH, I wanted to call Sheldon. I hadn't spoken to him since our date last Saturday night. I wanted to tell him what I've been through, but I couldn't get up the nerve. I didn't want him to reject me. Instead I called Fiona to let her know I was out of the—I didn't know what to call it—loony bin wasn't politically correct. Sanitarium? Nuthouse? Something in me couldn't say the words Psychiatric Hospital.

I logged onto my computer, checked my emails, and sent most of them to the trash. Time passed. A shadow crossed my shoulder. I turned around. Da stood above me. I found myself staring into the famous down-turned, squinty, eyebrow covered eye.

"Agnes Anne?" Da said, his voice firm and almost solemn.

"Hi, Da." Years of training made me stand up. But like we were magnets of the same polarity, we resisted each other and did not hug.

"Come wid me, lass," he said.

I heard Brent and David inhale. I couldn't look over at them.

"Anne?" David called after me.

I turned around.

Like identical prairie dogs, David and Brent had popped up above the cubicle wall and were watching me.

"Are you going to be all right?" David said.

"Want us to come with you?" Brent offered.

Somehow, it validated my own feelings to see the anguish in their faces. I shook my head and tried to give them a reassuring smile, and followed my father through the cubicles to his office. When I crossed in front of Pansy, I swear she looked like she had choked on her gum. I tried to review the Heimlich Maneuver.

I stepped inside Da's office.

He shut the door.

I sat.

He paced.

"This's serious business, Agnes," he muttered.

"My name is Anne," flew out of my mouth so quickly it even shocked *me*. Immediately, I regretted it. Da looked beyond irritation. I would feel awful if this small act of defiance gave him a heart attack. Did I remember how to perform chest compressions?

"First ya go under tha knife," Da said, shaking his finger in the air. "Then... God, Agnes Anne! Ya use a knife on yerself!" Tears glistened in my father's eyes.

"No, I didn't, Da. Bruno said I did, but I didn't."

"Taking yer life's a sin, girl," he said, his whisper hoarse. "A Mortal Sin! *A sin 'a no redemption.*" As though he stood in front of the ovens of Hell, he broke out into a profuse sweat. "Do ya understand wha' tha' means? *Eternal damnation!*"

"That's why I would never do it, Da. Don't you know me better than that?"

He paced back and forth, one hand in his pocket, then both hands behind him, then both hands in his pockets. My eyes followed him around the room.

"How could ya do this ta yer mother?"

"I didn't—" His look of reproach took my breath way.

Da shook his head. "She's been prayin' fer ya, Agnes Anne. Prayin' an' prayin'."

"I know."

"How cud'ya do this?"

I didn't answer.

"Ya hav'ta get o'er him, Aggie. I know tha' lovin' someone who doesn't luv ya back is difficult. I had girlfriend, at least I wanted 'er ta be a girlfriend, but she wud'no 'ave me. I loved her s'much. I would'a given tha moon 'n tha stars fer her ta like me." He looked down at me and whispered, "I know how tha' hurts, Agnes Anne. I do. *I truly do.*"

"Before you met Ma?" I said, in complete wonderment. "You loved someone else?"

"Ya," he said. Da plunked himself into his desk chair and sighed. "Before I met yer mother, there'as someone else."

I contemplated this odd bit of information. I had never thought of my parents having a life before they met each other.

"It's hard ta see her so often," he went on. "Ta remember what ya had together, or thought ya had—ta know things could 'a been different."

Was he talking about another woman? Was he comparing this other relationship to Bruno?

"Every night I t'ink'a her. I remember her in my prayers 'n I bless her."

"Even now? You think of her still?"

With turned down lips, I watched him nod.

"But you love Ma, don't you?"

"Course I do. God gives us choices, Agnes, but he also gives us challenges. Bruno's yer challenge just like Lucy's mine."

"Auntie Lucy? She was the one?"

"That was a long time ago, Agnes Anne. Ya must ne'er tell anyone. I'm sharin' this with ya because I t'ink it'll help. But it's our secret."

Da and Auntie Lucy?

"Is that why she drinks?" I blurted.

Da shrugged. "She never 'ad children. Perhaps that's why. And if I'd married her, I wouldn't a' had all of you. It would'a been a different life."

"Does Ma know?"

"Goodness, no. 'T'wud be a burden. I love yer ma. She's a good woman 'n she's raised all 'a ya well. I'm only sharin' this wid ya, Agnes, 'cause I wan'ya ta know that yer not tha only person in'a world who's been rejected."

"I don't love Bruno, Da. I hate him."

Da shook his head. He didn't believe me.

"Bruno saved ya, Agnes Anne," he said, softly. "Saved ya from Eternal Damnation."

"No, he didn't. He was coming after me, Da."

Da's head shook like a metronome.

"He's not who you think he is," I whispered. "He lies."

"Have ya seen Father Mac 'n made a good confession?"

"Yes. But I didn't confess to something I didn't do."

"In order to get past it," Da yelled, "ya hav'ta *admit it*, Agnes Anne." The slam of his hand on the desktop sounded like a gunshot. "Ya 'ave no idea how worried Bruno-god-love-him was about ya. Face it, he married yer sister 'n ya've ne'er gotten o'er it!"

"That's not true!" I shouted back.

"Bruno came ta us in tears. He told us everythin', Agnes Anne. How he saved ya, how he took tha knife from yer hand. *Ya need to t'ank him. Not deny wha' happened.* Then, lass, ya need ta move on wid yer life."

Somewhere in this monologue, tears began to stream down my cheeks.

"I took tha listing away from ya, girl. I had ta. Verna's handlin' it. You'll get a fair cut, but Bruno's listin' isn't yers anymore, understand?" He shook his head like I was a gonner and whispered, "Right now, you need ta rest. I'm sorry ta say that I can't rely on ya."

My father's words hit me hard. I'd always been reliable. He used to call me Reliable Aggie.

I had to admit there was a part of me that was oddly relieved that the listing would no longer be mine. I wouldn't have to see Bruno alone in that house. I wouldn't have to talk to him. Perhaps it was all for the best.

Or maybe, this was "Hello Stockholm."

38. New Digs

MOVING INTO MY NEW APARTMENT was one of the most exhilarating things I'd ever done. It was my Big Step, the final demonstration that I had become the New Me.

Ma came over in her khaki pants rolled up mid-calf and arms full of disinfectant, scrubbing compounds, rolls of shelf paper, sponges and rags. While I made up my bed and unpacked my clothes, she first scrubbed the kitchen, then headed for the bathroom. She was a scrubbing freight train bound for glory.

"Agnes Anne," Ma said, her head so low it was nearly inside the toilet. "I hate ta see ya go from home, but I s'ppose it's time."

I had unwrapped a new shower curtain and was pinning it up. The pattern was a checkerboard made of roses. I knew it was corny, but I liked it.

"I didn't want it to be so sudden, Ma, but this apartment came up." I glanced at her sideways, afraid she would confront me and ruin this glorious moment of independence.

"I wish you'n Fiona wud move in tagether," Ma said. "Get a larger place. Tagether."

I knew that would never work, but I didn't want to tell Ma why.

"Rents'r too high now, Agnes. Yer waistin' yer money."

"This was pretty reasonable," I countered.

"I don't approve of girls movin' out 'n their own," Ma said, sprinkling cleanser all over the toilet and taking her brush to it for the second time. "The first night I spent away from home 'as with yer father 'n I think that's how it should be."

"That was the olden days back in Ireland, Ma. It's different now."

She flushed the toilet and stood up. "I want ya ta behave yerself, Agnes Anne."

"Of course, Ma," I said, quickly.

She sprinkled more cleanser into the toilet and began to scrub it all over again. "I regret tha' you 'nd yer father 'ad words tha night he turned ya out. He's a good man, but—"

I stopped attaching hooks to the shower curtain and wondered what she would say next.

"I t'ink i'twas tha Arthur Guinness talkin'," she mumbled. "If it were up ta me, Agnes Anne, I'd hav'ya around ferever, ya know tha'."

"Don't be sad, Ma. I'm not leaving San Francisco." I figured this was as good a time as any to address the suicide issue. "You know, Ma, what happened that night at Bruno's..."

"Ach! Tha' ter'ble, ter'ble night 'n Bruno-god-love-him—"

"Listen to me, Ma." I took her arm and tried to turn her toward me. "I never tried to commit—"

"Donut say it!" Ma yelled. She raised the dripping toilet brush like it was a sword. "Tis a ter'ble word. And tha visitation of tha Virgin tha' night. The way she came to us over 'n over. That's wha' gave ya protection, Agnes Anne. Mary sent Bruno in ta save yer life."

"No, Ma. That's not what happened."

"I donut want ta hear it," she said. "I donut want ta talk about it."

"But you do know, Ma, I would never commit—"

"Hush. Not a word more. Yer're safe 'n that's all tha' counts." Ma returned to her scrubbing. Any hope I had in changing her mind and setting the suicide story right had passed.

Before she left, Ma gave me a hug, then said she had something for me. She took a roll of newspapers out of her cloth sack and began to tear through it. One of her many Virgin Marys emerged. This one was the traditional blue-gowned Queen of Heaven. Mary stood on a star-studded earth and looked up to the sky in rapture. It was beautiful and over and over, I thanked her for it.

Since I had my cell phone and didn't need a land line, we put Mary in the unused telephone nook in the entryway. She just fit.

Ma kissed me good-bye at the top of the apartment's outside stairs. It was unfortunate that, as she left, Sheldon was coming up. He had a takeout food bag in one hand and balanced my dish garden in the other. They politely greeted each other, then Ma turned around and shot me her famous "Mind your P's and Q's" look.

After dinner, Sheldon helped me hang a few pictures. We put the dish garden in the kitchen where there was good light, but not direct sun. A few of the plants didn't look healthy. We looked around in there for Jude and found him sunken into his shell and hiding under the African violet. No doubt about it, my snail had grown bigger.

When it started to get late, Sheldon and I sat on the couch and watched the news. During the weather report, somewhere between New York and Chicago, he kissed me. I kissed him back.

I had never felt so bold and yet so helpless. His kisses were warm and soft. Then he began to explore my mouth with his tongue. I explored his. Thoughts of good and evil, virtue and sin clanged around inside my head.

Mary? I thought. *Are you with me?*

Sheldon's hand slipped across my stomach, mine slid onto his chest. I loved the smell of him and soared with the pleasure of his touch. Each new sensation made me fly higher.

Oh Mary, this is wonderful.

His hand rose to just under my breast, the warmth of his hand radiated up. I froze in anticipation, and melted with the feel of his fingers stroking me.

Mary mother of God, is this what making love is like?

While his kisses deepened, new sensations took me to a place I had never been, but yet I had—*long ago, I'd been there with Bruno.* Even though I was twelve years downstream from that hideous night, and even though I kept telling myself this was different, the urge to hit and kick and fight Sheldon off became a whirling panic boiling inside me. I couldn't control my rage.

"*Stop,*" I said, gasping for air.

"What?" What?" Sheldon said, as though he was coming out of a deep dreamy sleep.

"*I can't—*" My arms stiffened and pushed against his chest.

He stopped. Our eyes met.

I hadn't realized we had reclined.

"What's wrong?" he whispered.

I was breathing hard, but not out of passion, out irrepressible panic. I struggled to sit up; my breath came in short gasps.

I stared at the coffee table and knew I could never explain what was going on in my head. I looked around for Mary and could see her in my mind's eye patiently waiting by the front door, her blue gown crisp and pure.

"You have to go," I said, nearly wheezing, unable to look at him, wishing he wasn't looking at me. If I'd had a bag, I would have slipped it over my head.

Sheldon's voice was gentle. "Are you all right?"

I stood up, wanting to flee. But to where? I lived here. But I wanted to be alone. *I had to be alone.*

"I'm sorry," I said. "I'm tired. You should leave."

Sheldon stood up and looked down at me. "Was it something I said? Something I did?"

"I can't talk about it. I can't..."

"That's all right." He tried to give me a hug, then walked toward the door. Before he opened it, he turned around. "Are you okay?"

"Yes, I'm fine," I said, quickly. "I think I'm just tired."

"You're trembling," Sheldon said, coming back to me.

"No, I'm fine. Don't touch me."

"Anne? What's wrong?"

"Nothing. Go. Just go. I'll be fine. I am... fine."

I could tell he was confused and maybe hurt. But I couldn't help it. Everything was sliding in on me again. When the front door closed, I was angry at myself for not being able to push Bruno out of my mind.

Angry that I still heard his voice in my head.

Angry that I couldn't seem to move past my prom night.

Angry that in some strange and hideous way Bruno continued to ruin everything.

39. Showing Bruno's Listing

VERNA STOOD IN THE DOORWAY of Bruno's parents' place with a stack of glossy information sheets. I couldn't deny that it made me feel bad I wasn't the one handing out the brochures and greeting agents. I looked at the sheet and the price of the house. Verna was right. It was way too high. She never succeeded in getting Bruno to lower it. I swallowed my smirk. Bruno was even too strong for Verna.

Today I brought a potential client, an older woman named Mrs. Einsford I had met when I held open one of Verna's listings. I strolled through the house with her and I marveled at what the stagers had done: The dining room with the Asian paintings, the pineapple lamps on a gorgeous walnut credenza, the celadon green plates on the dining room table. All of it brought the house alive.

When I showed Ms. Einsford the sunroom, she was pretty impressed. I could see her imagining her orchid shelves against the wall, calculating the angle of the incoming light. In the midst of all this eye-candy and staged furniture, Bruno stepped out of a hallway. His voice shattered my calm.

"Hello, Anne," he said, crossing his arms in front of his chest, as though to block my path.

I hadn't seen him since he shoved my suitcase through the door last week at O'Neil & Co.

Face to face, I stared into his eyes. It took me a few seconds before I found my voice. "This is Ms. Einsford," I said, turning to my client and bringing her forward. When I glanced at him, I didn't like the snooty look on his face.

"Hello," Ms. Einsford said, with unmistakable cheer.

"This is Dr. Bruno Stark. He grew up here," I said, trying to make conversation.

"Oh you did, did you? What a wonderful house."

"Yes, thank you." Bruno made a curt almost formal bow. His eyes strayed to me again as though to assess my face as well as my clothes. Ms. Einsford began chattering about the eastern exposure and the grandeur of old homes. I had never heard her so chatty. I could tell Bruno didn't want to make small talk, so just to irritate him, I made small talk with her.

Ms. Einsford stayed a long time at the house. So long, that Vera winked at me and gave me the keys to lock up whenever we were through.

"Take your time, Ahnne," she whispered. "Make your client feel zat zis iz her home. I know you can do it."

I nodded and took a deep breath. It would be so cool to sell Bruno's listing, I could practically taste success. I pictured myself handing Vera the sales agreement. Meeting Da in his office. Seeing his expression of disbelief. I would cloak my face in a Mona Lisa I-told-you-so-smile.

Ms. Einsford and I dawdled in the house. She liked the back part of the house because of all the light. She chose a room for her orchids. Showed me where she could put in a laboratory-type sink. I couldn't imagine living in a big house like this by myself. I was having trouble being alone in a one-bedroom apartment. When I took Ms. E. back to Russian Hill, she turned to me as she left the car and said that she would seriously think about making an offer on the house, but at that price was too high and so she would be low-balling it. Just knowing I had a chance at a sale made my heart fly to the clouds. Imaginary money fluttered down around me like snowflakes. Or maybe it was like Dr. Helfer's dandruff.

When I came into the office the next morning, there was a strange tension, an electricity I couldn't understand. People were gathered in groups, chatting, their voices louder than usual. All eyes turned toward me. I couldn't figure out who they were looking at, so I glanced behind. There was no one there.

They were looking at me.

"W-what?" I managed to stammer. "What's wrong?"

"Your listing," someone said. "Verna's listing. It burned down last night."

"Oh no!" I whispered.

"It looks like arson," someone said.

"Major damage," said someone else.

Everyone began to chatter. No one knew the real facts, but everyone shared what they did know, then talked about other fires, other times. Stories I didn't want to know.

I made my way to my cubicle and sat down. My hands were shaking. I heard Da's voice asking about me. Asking Pansy if I was in the office yet.

"Your father wants to see you," David said, hanging his head over the cubicle wall.

I looked over at my Holy Cards, at the Blessed Virgin, Saint Michael the Archangel slaying the devil, Saint Francis with a bird on his finger, and all the rest I had pinned in a long row. I glanced at the photo of Marilyn Monroe down at the end and reminded myself to breathe. I stood up and walked over to Da's office.

"I su'pose ya heard?" Da said, pacing around.

Uncle Jimmy stuck in his head in for a listen.

"Yes," I said. "I heard Bruno's place burned—"

"Ta tha nubs, it did. Ta tha very earth." Da's hair was already messed up and standing straight up from the back of his head, making him look somewhat deranged.

"Bruno's fit ta be tied, he is," Uncle Jimmy said, coming in. His sport coat today was a gray and green plaid. It looked like a horse blanket. Did Auntie Lucy dress him this way on purpose? I pushed away the vision of Da pining over Auntie Lucy. I couldn't let my mind wander. Not now.

"Ya were in tha' house yesterday, weren't ya?" Da said. One eyebrow hovered like a fury moth while underneath his brow, his pupil shrank to a decimal point.

"Yes. I was the last one out." I looked from Da to Uncle Jimmy and back. "Can't it be repaired?"

"God no," Uncle Jimmy said, his brogue strong. "I drove by. There's not a t'ing there. Not a bloody t'ing. Only smoke an' rubble."

Trying to picture that particular lot without that particular house, I sank to the nearest chair.

"'Tis indeed," said Da. "Agnes Anne, did ya see anythin' odd at tha Stark place?"

I shook my head.

"A door open? An oven on?"

"No."

"Did ya lock tha door, Agnes?"

"Of course I locked up. I'm always careful about locking up."

Da looked at his desk calendar and shook his head. "Ya must ha' let it open, girl. Someone must'a gotten in."

"Oh no, Da. I locked the door. I remember locking it." Self-doubt engulfed me. I watched Uncle Jimmy float off down the hall. Da still stared at me without blinking.

A nebulous wave of guilt swelled in my center.

Had the fire been my fault?

Later, Verna appeared at my cubicle. Her hat, a fuzzy blue Frank Sinatra affair, and cocked to one side, exposed her shiny patent leather hair. I watcher her plant her left arm astride my cubicle door, the other stayed on her narrow hip. "Vat dit you do?" she barked.

"Nothing. I locked up. Ms. Einsford can—"

"I knew I zhould hav stayed," Verna said, her eyes in fiery slits. "I zhouldn't hav left you alone. I vil not be blamed for zis. You did zis to get back at Bruno because you hate him." Her finger waggled in the air for a couple of seconds like she might, under different circumstances, enjoy salsa dancing. She spun around and stomped back to her office.

I heard Brent mumble to David, "Seriously, that lady needs to get laid." Anyone within earshot started to laugh. But I couldn't because it made me crazy to have people think I might have left the door unlocked.

I dialed Ms. Einsford. She was shocked to hear about the property. "Not meant to be," she said, philosophically. I asked her about locking up.

"Remember? You dropped the keys on the mat and we both bent down to pick them up."

"Yes," I said, glad for the reinforcement. I did remember. Certainly, I locked the door. And even tried the doorknob to be sure. I felt like shouting a cheer. Next thing I knew, my phone rang.

"Well," Bruno said, drawing out the word. His voice made my flesh crawl with spiders. "I see you've added arson to your list of antisocial behavior. Your file is getting longer, Miss Anne."

"I didn't—"

"You were the last person in there, weren't you, *Anne*? You did this to get back at me, didn't you. Fire is the symbol of sex. Naughty, naughty."

I heard my name being paged. My father, Verna, and a man in a sport coat were waiting for me in the conference room. All eyes riveted to my face.

Introductions were made. The man, an arson inspector, wrote my name in his notebook. I told him my entry time. Exit time. How Ms. Einsford remembered me dropping the keys, picking them up, and how I had locked the door. Then he asked me the most bizarre thing: "What shoes did you wear yesterday?"

I thought for a moment and recited my outfit. "These shoes. I guess. Yes," I said, with faltering confidence. "I wore these shoes."

He asked for them. *Asked for my shoes.*

Was this a joke? Or maybe he was a pervert, had a shoe fetish. I've heard about people like that, but he was saying this right in front of my father and sweaty Verna, whom I could tell no longer liked me and right now looked like she wished that last month I had succeeded in killing myself.

Bending down, I produced one shoe and brought it up to the table. I wanted to make a joke about Prince Charming, but knew it would fall flat.

"I need both shoes," the inspector said.

He had to be kidding.

"And I'd like to see your car," he added.

I was proud of my new car, my new used car, pre-owned as they say. But getting there was awkward. He had my shoes. He asked me if I had others.

"Yes," I said, "in my car."

With obvious reluctance, he gave me back my shoes and walked me to my car, which was parked across the street. David and Brent were watching me from the front window. David was moving up and down like he had to pee.

The inspector walked around my car and bent to look under it like he was checking the brakes. I opened my trunk and foraged around for my gym bag and took out my tennis shoes and put them on. Then I handed my high heels over to him like I was Dorothy surrendering the Ruby Red Slippers to some creature from Oz.

He pulled a kit from his briefcase and he began to examine my car like it was evidence. While I stood awkwardly to the side, he swabbed little pieces of cloth here and there, made a phone call on his cell phone, then turned to me and said he'd like to have my car towed for examination. If I wasn't willing, he said he would produce a warrant.

I thought he was kidding. I looked around. Where was Da? Did I have to face this by myself?

It was right then I knew what had happened: Bruno had called the police and pointed his finger at me. I was arson suspect number one, the former inmate at the local psych ward. Self-destructive and filled with hate. Maybe it was anger or maybe it was fear, but my breath came in short gasps. I thought I might faint.

David and Brent appeared behind me and introduced themselves. I could tell the inspector didn't like them, but they wouldn't leave. They stood protectively beside me. David even grabbed my hand and held it. They were my new gay parents.

40. Boyfriends at First Friday

THE HORRIBLE DAY OF THE FIRE also happened to be First Friday. Over the past two weeks I'd been rushing around so much, collecting things from my sisters for my new apartment, that the exhaustion of moving, painting my apartment, hanging new drapes and shades, as well as sneaking over to see Katie, caused me to oversleep. I missed mass. I knew Da would be disappointed. He would remind me that I had foiled my attempt to begin my Novena.

Fiona called me at the office to remind me to bring Sheldon to First Friday tonight. I reminded her to bring Paul, a plan we had concocted a couple of weeks ago. Anyway, contemplating our boyfriends meeting the family was a lot more fun than talking about the smoldering rubble at

Bruno's parents' house.

"Don't' forget to do your hair," Fiona reminded me.

My stomach soured. I needed to get to Ritz Charisma. My roots were showing. My hair seemed to be so heavy, instead of swinging, it flopped around. Not even the hair goo and volumizers Bonnie sold me made a difference. My nail polish was also chipped, and lately I'd become slip-shod in applying makeup each day. Sadly, I knew I was reverting to my old ways, my shy old introverted ways. I wondered if I was on a slippery slope, sliding on the trappings of hair salons and makeup experts, and soon I would be caught in an avalanche, tumble head over heels and land a jumble of chic debris.

Sheldon and I stood on the O'Neil front porch, me holding a hot dish and Sheldon holding a bottle of wine. Da's singing could be heard from outside. He was in his cups, as Ma would say. Cups indeed. Da was stinking drunk and it was only six o'clock in the evening. I could also hear the dulcet tones of Uncle Jimmy's off-tune tenor voice loudly crooning the end of an old Irish ballad. Uncle Jimmy couldn't be far behind in the race to the last whiskey.

With a piano flourish, they switched to a fast song. I heard the familiar strain. "... *old mother Leary put the lantern in the shed. The cow kicked it over and this was what she said, Ther'll be a hot time in the old town tonight. Fire! Fire! Fire!"*

The song about fire was not lost on me, or for that matter, Sheldon. The front door was locked. I hadn't brought my key so, like strangers, we had to ring the bell.

"Hi, Ma," I said, pecking her on the cheek. I gave her the hot dish I'd covered with foil and swaddled in dish towels to keep warm. I glanced at Mary's Font, her cape seemed more blue than I remembered. I snatched a quick blessing, crossing myself with speed and hoped Sheldon wouldn't see and think I was superstitious.

"Hello Sheldon," Ma said, with stiff hospitality. The hot dish prevented a handshake.

"Good evening, Mrs. O'Neil," Sheldon said. He presented her with his bottle of wine. It was dressed up in a gold and green sack. "I thought you might be able to use this," he said.

I hoped Sheldon didn't catch Ma's eye-roll. I knew what she was thinking: This family has already had enough alcohol tonight.

Before I could move through the foyer and follow Ma back into the kitchen, my brother Matthew came up the stairs. "Horse is out of tha barn, buddy," he said, giving Sheldon's ribs a tickle.

Sheldon jumped, his hands involuntarily covered his crotch with the bottle of wine. While Ma headed to the kitchen, Sheldon tried to zip, but there was nothing to zip. It was one of Matthew's stupid tricks. A flush warmed my face.

"Ha, ha, ha, ha. Had you goin', buddy, didn't I? Didn't I?" Matthew hopped around like he was chasing a soccer ball. "Hi, I'm Matt. Met ya at tha hospital, remember?"

I scowled at him, but before I could actually loosen my throat to verbalize, Matthew's wife Jennifer and four children came streaming in. Jennifer held a potato salad the size of a television. These were the days of Lent. This First Friday would be meatless and for a family who loved its beef, its lamb, its turkey, and chicken, these Fridays were dark days.

Da and Jimmy's voices clashed in bad harmony. "*Late one night when we were all in bed...* "

"Can ya hold it down in there, Da? Yer wakin' tha banshees," Matthew yelled into the living room.

"*Did ye leave the door open, Agnes Anne? Let in the fire bug?*" Da shouted, as he pounded the piano.

I pretended not to hear. All of us, as though passing through the eye of a needle, began to file back into the kitchen. Matthew lifted his youngest daughter, Colleen, up to Mary's Font so she could bless herself.

"Ma!" Matthew shouted, "Mary's still 'bout a quart low!"

I wanted to apologize to Sheldon for my brother's stupid zipper joke, but Matthew's other kids, Mitchell, Dara, and Jamie, began running around out of control. Little Colleen followed. Neither Matthew's wife, Jennifer, furtively searching for a spot to set down her potato salad, nor Matthew, who was now busy at the bar, paid any attention to their noisy children. After chasing each other around the kitchen island, the kids followed the music and ran into the front room.

I felt a pang of guilt that I wasn't here earlier to help Ma with the dinner. I moved other pans, dishes, and mixing bowls out of the way and make room for the dishes that would be coming in the door.

"What can I do to help, Ma?" I mumbled, noticing the enormous pile of fish on the counter.

"Baked cod tanight," Ma said. "I'll bread it and pop it into the oven."

"Ah, cod," Matthew said, with a thoughtful nod. "Gah, I hate Lent."

"Better than it used ta be," Ma said. "Back then, we used ta fast 'n tha Fridays of lent. We only had meatless soup."

"A drink, Sheldon?" I said, trying to walk him over to the corner of the kitchen where all the booze stood ready for consumption. The colorful bottles looked exotic, and for me, held the promise of courage.

"That would be nice," he said. His tone was amiable, but after that scene in the foyer, he seemed guarded. I thought he must be miserable, and I stopped the urge to give him an elbow and say, *I told you so.*

"We have gin, vodka, bourbon, and scotch," I said. "Also beer and wine."

Sheldon decided on scotch on the rocks. I fixed it for him and tried to ignore the singing in the next room, which wasn't easy. The tune was now "Mother McCree," one of Da's sappy Irish standards usually reserved for the end of the evening when we sometimes gathered around the piano to sing the chorus to Ma. But he was singing it now. Sheldon had no idea what a bad sign this was. If Da began to sing "Goodnight Irene," it would signal the end of Da's appearance this evening.

"Good grief, Ma," Matthew said. "How long 'as Da been 'n his cups?"

"Came home wid yer Uncle Jimmy a' four." she said. "They've been drownin' themselves ever since. Ter'ible sad about Bruno's parents' 'ouse." Turning to the sink, I heard her mumble, "God-love-him."

"'Tis terrible," Matthew said. "Heard it's gone. Tee-totally gone."

"Tis," Ma said, as she crushed stale bread with a rolling pin to make crumbs for the fish.

I handed Sheldon his drink. Then concentrated on fixing my own. I decided on gin and tonic. Darcy and Domenic arrived, their kids already running around like little wild dogs, barking and roughhousing with their cousins.

When I had my drink, we toasted and our eyes met, as though to say, *The worst is over*. How were we to know it was only the beginning?

Silently, I prayed Bruno wouldn't show up tonight. I had spoken to Katie late this afternoon. She wasn't feeling well again. Chances were, I told myself, they'd stay home. I tried not to remember the way my car looked heading backwards up 24th Street. I wondered where it was now and could picture it draped with yellow police tape like on *CSI*.

Little Colleen came into the kitchen. A strange look crossed her face. I thought she was beginning to cry. I leaned down to ask what was wrong, but I couldn't understand her. Before I could introduce her to Sheldon, a stream of vomit as straight as a bullet came at me. I tried to step sideways so it might miss me and flow like the spurt of a lawn sprinkler right between me and Sheldon. When I jerked sideways, little Colleen slipped on the trail of her own vomit, a backward retraction of fluid tracing a line from the cabinets to her mouth. It was all in slow motion, and if I were a dispassionate observer, the physics of it were truly amazing.

As though she were a baseball player and I second base, she made a great slide, the heels of her black Mary Jane's slammed into my instep, catching me off balance. My feet slid out from under me as though all along, I had been standing on ice.

My legs slammed into Sheldon's. He lost his balance. I grabbed for him. He grabbed for me. Tumbling like clumsy horses, we slipped, slid and struggled to defy gravity. Our heads bashed against the cabinets, our elbows banged against cupboard doors. My rear end landed hard, my drink flew up in the air and splashed mostly on Sheldon, his scotch flew up and landed mostly on me, Colleen's vomit was now smeared underneath us and mingling with our spilled drinks.

All the while, Colleen never stopped screaming and in one more cataclysmic wretch, she spewed another stream of vomit so straight she could have knocked an apple off a kid's head at eight paces. Thankfully, it went forty-five degrees off center and missed us.

The piano playing stopped. I heard Da howl from the other room. *"Wha's tha' racket?"*

Matthew hollered back, "Jus' bowlin' fer Jews, Da."

I watched the gin and tonic roll off Sheldon's shirt. An ice chip defied gravity and clung to his necktie. Sheldon's scotch dripped on my skirt and the smell of Colleen's stomach juices nauseated me. Her mother, Jennifer, stood above us, apologizing and stooping to pick up her squalling, dripping, dribbling offspring. With an amazing one-armed grab, Jennifer led Colleen to the back bathroom.

Ma found a mop. Mark's wife, Susan, appeared wielding an entire roll of paper towels and began blotting everything and everyone while apologizing profusely to Sheldon, whom she really hadn't even met and it was too late now for formal introductions. Stunned and humiliated, tears were backing up behind my eyes.

Matthew reached out to help Sheldon stand up, ripped off a long length of the toweling and wiped him down like Sheldon might be a lathered-up horse. It was at this moment, Fiona blithely came in with her boyfriend, Paul. She set down a pink bakery box, and surveyed the kitchen crew, who were now obsessed with wiping up the floor. I was doing my best to wipe off my blouse and skirt and tend to Sheldon. We looked like an advertisement for Bounty.

"What happened to you?" she said, as I tottered to my feet. Side stepping the heaps of paper toweling, Fiona said, "Hello Sheldon. Nice tie, but the feng shui is all wrong for you. You should wear red for power, green for energy. There's too much brown here." Her hand fluttered back and forth like she was erasing him. "This tie is so depressing." Rolling her eyes dramatically, Fiona craned her neck to have a closer look. "Why is there ice on it?"

It seemed like hours before I got a fresh cocktail and when I did, I tilted my gin and tonic back and had several swallows. Sheldon asked me if I was all right.

I didn't know the correct answer. I had a responsibility to my guest, whom my family had teased, knocked down and insulted, yet through it all Sheldon had remained composed and kind. Suddenly, I realized that I didn't care that our religions didn't match. Sheldon Goldberg was a nice person. *A good person.* Certainly better behaved than any O'Neil who showed up for First Friday.

Next thing I knew, Katie and Bruno strolled into the kitchen.

"Bruno-god-love-ya! Yer 'ere!" Matthew called out. To me, his cheer sounded like a personal betrayal. *Didn't he know Bruno practically had me committed? And now he's trying to blame me for setting a fire?*

Katie and Bruno brought take-out boxes. "Chinese vegetables. Meatless," Katie said, setting the white bag down on the counter. Fiona began introducing Paul around.

Mark's wife, Susan, unwrapped two dozen stuffed hard boiled eggs and passed the platter. The odor wafting up from all those eggs reminded me of Colleen's sickening performance. I declined Susan's offer. I didn't want the next Projectile Vomiting Event to be mine.

"Time ta fix th'tartar sauce," Ma called out. Someone mixed the mayonnaise with sweet pickle relish and found an appropriate bowl.

"Girls! Get tha side dishes out," Ma commanded.

Food was heaped onto serving dishes, the kitchen a vortex of activity. Away from the bustle and commotion, Bruno and the guys stood talking in groups.

"We're ready! Everyone out!" Ma called.

All O'Neils were on deck. The men found the chairs. The women brought out the food and seated the little ones at the two corner card tables.

Da and Uncle Jimmy and a few of the kids were still at the piano. Da was pounding away at *It's a Long Way to Tipperary.* Colleen, cleaned up and looking just fine, thank you very much, sang and clapped like she had never vomited all over me, never dragged me down, never caused my legs to careen into Sheldon and set him off balance. It was amazing. I had to try hard to resist the urge to trip her.

Ma hushed the singers gathered around the piano and when they looked up and saw the platters of fish and steaming bowls go by, they followed the scent like stray dogs and took their places at the dining room table.

Da stood at the head of the table, his arms outstretched like he was quieting the fish. "Bless us O Lord 'nd these thy gifts tha' we receive from Thy bounty. Bless O Lord, all who dwell here."

I wondered why he was saying this. No one but he and Ma dwelt here now.

"......'nd bless all m'children 'n their spouses 'n their children... 'n 'specially bless..."

Da waxed on with a blessing for this and that. The longer he spoke, the more my brother Matthew silently laughed and rolled his eyes. He looked at Sheldon and then me and then mimicked a big nose, pointed to me, pointed to Sheldon, then mimed a baby in his arms, and put the big nose on our baby.

I was beyond humiliation. My shame turned to fury. A hot potato flew across the table. Fiona had seen his parody and retaliated. At the same time Matthew caught the potato, a roll flew from Darcy's direction and bounced off Matthew's chest. The potato must have been hot because Matthew juggled it and set it down on his plate, then shook his hand like his wrist was loose.

I hoped he was in pain.

"...'n may Fiona," Da intoned, "tha' gorgeous red headed lass, get married 'nd 'ave a passel a' kids of her own."

"Geez, Da," Fiona said, under her breath. "Get on with it. It's supposed to be a blessing not the State of Union Address." I noticed that Paul hunched his shoulders like he was trying to shrink himself.

"Bless Katie 'n bring back 'er apple cheeks 'n vibrant youth. Lord willin', may she get pregnant 'n bring forth a son fer Bruno-god-love-him."

I heard Katie make a sucking noise.

"…'n bless Bruno-god-love-him, tha best, most loyal 'n understandin' husband, tha healer husband who stands by our Katie in 'er time of need."

I watched Bruno pick up Katie's hand and kiss it.

"… 'n who stood by Agnes Anne when she 'as in tha depths 'a her depression."

"I was not depressed," I said, under my breath. Sheldon squeezed my hand.

"…'n fergive dear Agnes Anne, Lord, fer goin' under tha knife 'n ruinin' her noble nose 'n chin. May she see 'er inner beauty 'n turn away from tha glamour of evil."

"Da!" Darcy snapped. "Give us a break."

"…'n fergive Agnes Anne, dear Lord, fer datin' out 'a her race—"

"Put a cork in it Da," Mark blurted. "Tha guy's white, ya should a' least be glad 'a tha'." Mark shot an apologetic look our way then helplessly shrugged. He was right. None of us could control our father. Like a storm, we could only ride it out.

While blood pounded in my head, I noticed Sheldon's blush. Fiona's date, Paul, looked round the table, probably hoping he wouldn't be next.

"…'n dear Lord, bless Bruno fer savin' 'r dear Agnes Anne from self-mutilation 'n pos'ible death 'n may it not be true tha' Agnes left tha door open 'n caused tha' fire in Bruno's parents' place. Ter'ible t'ing it 'tis, too. 'N if she did, may she find tha courage t'admit wha' she's done 'n… after a good confession, Offer It Up fer yer great glory 'n tha' 'a yer mother, Blessed Mary, ever Virgin."

"I did not leave the door open." The words exploded from my lips. "And another thing—" I said. *I did not try to commit suicide. Bruno made that up.*

"Now Anne," Bruno said, his tone friendly as a razor blade, "I *saved* you."

"Baloney! I shouted. You were trying to come in."

"Don'a bring it up," Matthew barked. "Yer gonna' cause a—"

"Anne's right," Fiona said, her voice surprisingly loud. "Bruno has some explaining to do."

As though the whole family had been straining to release their own frustrations, everyone began talking at once. Darcy

pleaded with Da to wrap it up. Ma started in with how we
shouldn't talk about what happened at Bruno's, then Darcy
criticized Da for passing judgment on us. Of all the voices,
Mark's was the loudest.

"Da," he shouted, "end tha grace, will ya? Tha fish's
gettin' cold 'n tha troops are in revolt!"

There was no way to stop Da now, for I don't think he
heard us. He still had his eyes closed and his hands were still
stretched out in front of him. Da was a runaway cable car
careening down the Hyde Street hill, breaks gone and
skidding to the bottom.

Eyes still shut, he began to blather about his
grandchildren. About my brother's wives, who were
beginning to look stricken, waiting for the back-handed
insult. I suspected that Mark's near-divorce last year might
be the next subject. He knew it too because he grabbed for
Susan's hand and held it. Matthew's wife was already
grimacing and looking from side to side, as though preparing
herself for a comment about her housekeeping or the way she
lets their kids run wild.

"Boys, help yer father." Ma gave both Matthew and Mark
a quick jerk of the head.

"May Mary, Mother of God," Da intoned, his body now
swaying in a circular motion, "bless this 'ouse 'n all who
blessedly dwell wit'in it. 'Tis through yer blessed intercession
tha' blesses 'r lives... 'n we bless this wonderful food ya'ave
blessedly set before us."

It seemed all his blessedly-blesses had led him back to
the beginning, for he started the grace all over again. "Bless
this food 'n these Thy gifts... "

The O'Neil clan knew what Ma meant. It was time to get
the hook and walk Da off the stage or grace would go on until
the fish became cold as yesterday's soup and we had deserted
the table.

I leaned forward to check on Uncle Jimmy and I could
see he would be no help. He was red as a beet and had
whiskey in his water glass.

As though we were in church, Auntie Lucy stood straight
as the spine of a book, eyes closed and head bent. I wondered
if she might be sleepwalking.

Matthew came up on one side of Da, Mark on the other. Da's hands were still extended in prayer, his head down like he might fall forward onto the table, or worse, fall sideways into Ma. The domino effect would be spectacular and make Colleen's kitchen shenanigans look like a puppet show.

Matt, now at Da's elbow, said softly into his ear, "Let's go, Da."

Da opened his eyes, but didn't seem to see. "Is tha movie over?"

"Fer sure i'tis," Mark said. Then he began to sing, *"It's a long way ta Tipperary, a long way from home."*

Da picked up the tune and the three of them raised their voices and sang loudly and off key. Like some Irish cliché, they toddled out of the dining room, Da in the middle, Mark and Matthew supporting him on either side like they were dragging an old friend home from the pub, which in a way, I suppose they were.

"I'm so sorry, Sheldon and Paul, that you had to see this," Ma said. Her face reflected keen shame. Most of the clan both grumbled and apologized and swore to our two guests that this sort of thing has never happened before. I noticed the ones left unscathed by Da's monologue crossed themselves not once, but twice.

"No problem, no problem, Mrs. O'Neil," Sheldon said, with gentle ease. "I understand completely." He smiled and then added, "My people sing show tunes."

41. God Is a Gael

IN CHILLY SILENCE, we passed the food around the table. Everyone took at least a polite taste of each dish, the only sound the clink and scrape of utensils. When Matthew and Mark returned to their places, Da's seat at the head of the table, instead of gapping like a missing front tooth, had a new occupant: Ma.

"Well done, boys," she mumbled under her breath. "We'll tend ta tha Novena notebook later."

"I'll do it," Matthew said. He grinned like a fat cat with a mouse, stepped over to the sideboard and picked up Da's Novena book. "I'll mark down tha' we all went, eh? Didn't we all go ta church t'day?" He didn't bother to poll anyone or even look around the table. "Of course we did."

"The Indulgence doesn't work, Matthew, unless ya go," Ma said, coldly. "Ya can't fool tha Lord."

"No one does this anymore, Ma," Mark said, in his brother's defense. "All this Novena business—it's like praying ta tha dinosaurs. We're in tha New Millennium. It's 2012! I'll bet we're tha only family in'a world still doing novenas." He gazed around at all of us. "Am I right?"

Matthew turned back to the crinkly pages of Da's Novena book, found the right spot, licked his pencil and made a bunch of checks down the last column.

"Matthew," Ma warned, "that's no' right. You *know* that's no' right."

"Sure i'tis," he said, slamming the book shut and tossing it back on the sideboard. He smiled like the Cheshire cat.

Matthew and Mark clinked glasses. "God is a Gael!" they both shouted before they guzzled another draft of beer.

"God is a what?" Sheldon asked, his voice soft and polite. "Wind? God is wind?"

"Nah, nah wind. Gael! God's an Irishman! Did'nah ya know?" Matthew winked.

"Oh," Sheldon said, amiably. "He probably is."

Someone passed Sheldon the fish platter and he slid a golden brown piece of cod onto his plate.

Uncle Jimmy looked around and then his head drooped forward as though he might still be in prayer, but we all knew he was drifting off to sleep. Judging from the looks of Auntie Lucy, her own tabletop slumber wouldn't be far behind. I vowed that if either one rested a head on the dinner table, I would march Sheldon right out of the house.

It was Susan, Mark's wife, an ex-flight attendant with a knack for hospitality, who managed to start up a conversation. "So, tell me," she said to Sheldon, "how did you two meet?"

I wasn't sure how to answer. Sheldon, however, had no such hesitation.

"We met at a nail salon," he said, his voice casual. He took a bite of cod and began to chew.

The rattle of knives and forks halted, the abrupt silence of so many people, astonishing.

"Beg your pardon?" Susan said.

Everyone waited for Sheldon to swallow. "At Pretty Nail Town on Twenty-fourth."

"Who'as gettin' ther nails done?" Matthew said. His watery blue eyes, Da's eyes exactly, scrutinized Sheldon as though he had just revealed a prison record.

"I get a pedicure every couple of weeks." Sheldon's voice was nonchalant, as though he might be announcing a dental appointment or a trip to the Laundromat. He had no idea of the bombshell he'd just dropped. I glanced once again at Our Lady of Dyspepsia and silently cried for help.

"Yer feet?" Matthew said. The furrow on his brow deepened. "Ya go ta one of them women's places ta get yer feet done?" Matthew's eyes bounced from one family member to the other, as though he searched for a quorum.

"Bunions," Sheldon said. "Frequent pedicures really save me."

"I never knew a man cud go inta one a' them places," Mark said. "Wha' tha hell do they do ta ya?" Mark ignored the bowl of green beans his wife was trying to hand him and stared at Sheldon with intense curiosity.

Bruno laughed out loud, then looked at me with mock pity, as though he were saying, *And you refused me for him?*

Katie didn't seem to be paying attention to any of us. There was a bluish pallor growing across her upper lip and I could see pain in her eyes. I wondered if she might bolt from the table and head for the bathroom.

"What color do you usually have your toenails painted?" Bruno asked.

"I don't go in for polish," Sheldon said, through a good-natured laugh.

"'Tis it a man er a woman who does this ta ya?" Matthew asked. Neither of my brothers had taken a bite of food since this discussion started and the progression of platters and bowls around the table had become a logjam at each of their places.

"A woman. Usually two. It's a hot soak, then a foot massage, then a pedicure."

"A woman!" Matthew said. A bubble of laugher erupted from his mouth like he was blowing up a balloon. "Tha' cud be good. And they rub yer feet, do they?"

Ma's brow knit together so tightly that two parallel lines ran from her hairline to the bridge of her nose. "May I remind you, Matthew 'n Mark, tha' Jesus had his feet washed by tha Magdalene."

"Oh that's a good one, Ma, i'tis," Matthew said. "Jesus Christ 'ad tha first pedicure."

"—an' it's in'a Bible!" said Mark, his laugher high and jolly. Finally Mark took the dish from his wife, "Is all this foot business a Jewish t'ing er somethin'?"

On the sideboard, Our Lady of Dyspepsia, downcast and pale, arms poised in surrender, seemed to be warning me. *Never show your brothers any weakness*. I kept my expression calm and refused to partake in this discussion.

It was at that moment that Da's snoring in the next room became so loud I was sure someone passing on the sidewalk outside could have heard it and wondered if we were using power tools. Susan started to giggle, then Matt, then the rest of us began laughing. Through all of this, Uncle Jimmy, head still bowed, chin resting on the top of his plaid bow tie, never woke up. Auntie Lucy fluttered her eyes every two or three minutes and looked around like she was trying to prove that she had never fallen asleep.

The food bowls and platters began to circulate again and eating resumed, but Sheldon's presence at the table was regarded as comic relief and I knew I could look forward to hours of gibes and teasing. I was not only dating a Jew, but a man whose gender was suspect. My right hand found Sheldon's left, and with the backdrop of Da's rasping snores, I gave his hand two short squeezes. Sheldon returned the signal. We were united like spies in the enemy's camp.

After dinner, the women became a retreating army and cleared the table. The men stayed behind and I feared for Sheldon, but at least he had Paul, Fiona's date. I glanced at my brothers, trying to telepathically insist that they knock it off, but they were oblivious. If Sheldon was worried, he didn't seem to show it.

Every few minutes, Da's snore changed. Punctuated by a few short warning blasts and what seemed like a minute of silence, he seemed to down-shift into a lower gear, then the snore would start up again. Uncle Jimmy and Aunt Lucy quietly left for home and the children headed for the television.

The Mary in the kitchen, the old oil cloth tableau above the sink, rolled her eyes upward to heaven and looked like she might be sarcastically commenting on the messy scene below. We were a merry group, as we tackled each chore, my fellow kitchen mates. Katie wanted to help, but we could see how tired she was so we had her sit on a kitchen stool at the island. We rubbed our sponges over the bar area, snagged stray glasses and wiped down countertops and rewashed the corner of the floor where Sheldon and I had our vomit slip n' slide. A crash of crystal made everyone gasp.

Several wine glasses had tumbled to the floor, then as though she was supple as a silk scarf, Katie slid quietly from her perch. I heard a thud and watched in horror as the top of her head seemed to come off. It was her new blonde wig.

I lifted Katie's heavy head and slipped her wig back on, trying desperately to spare her the humiliation of revealing her patchy pink scalp. Although the wig was back in place in a blink, I didn't like the way Katie's neck was limp, her head floppy and as lifeless as the codfish we had just shared.

Susan and Jennifer were coming in from the larder holding the fish-baking pan and when they saw Katie sprawled across the linoleum, they dropped the pan and rushed over. Fiona squatted down beside me. Ma shouted for Da, then for Bruno. Darcy was already at the phone calling 911.

"Malachi! Malachi!" Ma screamed. "Oh m'God, what's goin' on? Katie! Katie! Are ya all right?"

Luke, probably on a break, had sauntered in the back door with his partner just then, ready to have a bite of leftovers or a taste of coffee and dessert.

The kitchen filled with people. Bruno knelt beside me and felt Katie's pulse. He tried to lift her up, but she was so limp it was difficult to get a grip on her. I could hear Luke use his police radio.

Ma began to pray aloud. *"Hail Holy Queen, 'r life, 'r sweetness, 'r hope. Ta thee we cry, poor banished children of Eve..."*

"Let's move her into the living room," Luke commanded. Luke, his partner and Bruno nested their hands and moved her. Small particles of glass fell out of Katie's wig, making a sparkling path behind, reminiscent of Jude's silvery trail. I flashed on the shining drawing of Mary on my desktop.

They set Katie on the rug in the living room. Bruno started CPR. Luke paced in front of the house, talking into his radio again. Da came awake and asked what was going on. He crawled on the floor with the rest of them, talking to Katie, patting her leg while Bruno straddled her torso and pumped viciously on her chest, then bent to put puffs of air into her mouth. Somehow, it looked slightly obscene and I turned away so I wouldn't be caught staring.

"Wha' hap'ened?" Da said. His eyes, like moths, darted from person to person. "Wha's wrong wid 'r?"

"Dunno'" Matthew said. "She fell."

Darcy explained how she was sitting at the counter drying glasses and then slid off the chair.

"Maybe she hit 'r head," Mark offered. "Maybe she's knocked out cold."

"Open yer eyes, Katie darlin'," Da said, patting her leg. "Open yer eyes. Open yer eyes, pet."

Ma was at Katie's other foot, touching her and praying out loud.

"Turn then, most gracious advocate, thine eyes 'a mercy toward us..."

I couldn't listen. I couldn't join in. Even though Bruno was breathing for her, Katie's lips were turning a peculiar shade of popsicle blue. Over and over, we watched Bruno's mouth cover hers and force his breath into her lungs, then with two hands, he compressed her chest one, two, three. Somehow it wasn't enough. Katie's lips darkened to pale indigo.

My heart stopped. From behind, I felt Sheldon's arms slip around me, surrounding my waist, his warmth covering my back.

I heard the sirens. Luke was out in front shouting to the fire department. They came in with a stretcher and equipment and the family stepped back. Only Ma remained hunched on the floor, deep in prayer, seemingly oblivious to the crowd in the room. *"Hail Mary, full 'a grace, blessed art thou amongst women..."*

The medics gave Katie oxygen, started an IV. One of them opened a suitcase with some electronics in it and placed paddles on her. The medic counted. In unison, they lifted their hands and moved leaned back. Bruno was standing now, pacing, stopping, watching.

Drifts of snow might have covered the living room, the way Ma trembled. Darcy and I put our arms around Ma's shoulders. Again I noticed the blood dripping down her shin.

"Pray ta tha Blessed Mother, girls. Pray fer Katie. M'daughter. M'baby," she whispered. "Dear Lord, please don't take Katie from us."

We bowed our heads. One family member reached for the other's hand until we had formed a circle and said an Our Father, then a Hail Mary. The next prayer died in my throat. I watched Katie's head, the blonde hair of the wig tied back by the strings of the oxygen mask, disappear down the front stairs.

We rushed outside. Bruno climbed into the ambulance and we stood, stupefied, as we watched it roll away, the keening yowl of the siren fading as it found its way into the foggy night.

"Please, Mary, watch after m' Katie," Ma said over and over while constantly crossing herself. She ran back into the house and went over to Mary's Font and looked up at the china figure and prayed some more. The rest of us started grabbing coats, purses, and car keys.

"Bless yerself before ya leave," Da screamed at us. "No one leaves without a blessin'. D'ya hear me?"

I blessed myself, then turned to Sheldon and did a blessing for him. He looked startled to feel my wet fingers tracing the Sign of the Cross from his forehead to his solar plexus and from one shoulder to the other, but he didn't object.

The hospital made all the O'Neils unusually quiet. The children lolled on stiff chairs, leaned heads on parents' knees, and knew something dreadful had gone wrong. They looked too frightened to fuss.

Fiona reached for my hand, as well as for Paul's. My heart clanged in my temples and thumped in my forehead while my eyes roved around the room, past my silent brothers, past my sisters-in-law clinging to their children, and rested on Ma. She sat next to Da and rocked, holding her elbows, whispering her prayers. Face blotchy, eyes watery, I wondered if she would be the next to pass out.

Bruno came out of the double doors, surveyed the room and with heels clicking like the tick of a clock, walked over to Ma and Da.

"They're trying," he said, softly, "but she's not responding." Before anyone could ask a question, he spun around and disappeared back into the labyrinth of hospital corridors.

Ma and Da, straight-backed and prim, sat like a new version of American Gothic. Father Mac had arrived and, after greeting us, went into the Emergency Room. When he returned, he walked over to them, his prayer book clasped tightly to his chest. We gathered around. I figured he would lead us in a family prayer. Instead, he leaned down and held one of Ma's hands, shook his head, and gently told Ma he had administered Last Rites. Our Katie now sang with the angels.

From that moment, something inside me froze. Fiona and I locked eyes. They were little girl's eyes, the eyes I had seen every day of my childhood. As though someone had wrinkled up a piece of paper, I watched Fiona's face crumple.

"Why?" she wailed. "What the hell happened?"

My face began to contort, but I kept my emotions in check. I gazed over Fiona's shoulder to watch Ma weep into Da's chest. Da stroked her hair. His face fought to regain control and then, for a second or two, would lose its composure and give in to the awful truth that his daughter, his fair-haired Katie, was dead.

Darcy wept into Domenic's shoulder. Matthew fell forward, hands covering his face while he rocked back and forth. His wife patted his back like she was burping an infant.

Susan and Jennifer began to organize us and conducted the children back to the house. My brother Mark stomped out of the waiting room like he was going to see someone in charge and make a complaint, maybe give God a piece of his mind. I could almost hear the string of expletives running through his head, but I knew God would not be moved. What had happened was as solid as a brick wall and the O'Neil clan had merely slammed into it. Heaven would make no adjustments. Not even for us. Not even if God were a Gael.

42. Fall from Grace

MY PHONE RANG early Saturday morning. Grateful to remove myself from the swirling grief I felt over Katie, I eagerly flipped open my cell phone and croaked, "Hello?"

It was Ma telling me I had to be strong. I felt bad that I wasn't the one telling her to be strong. We were having lunch at Bruno's today. She told me there was work to do and that God helps those who help themselves—whatever that meant. She assigned me a grocery list. It gave me purpose to have a mission.

"Should I invite Sheldon?" I asked.

"Wha'ver ya want, Agnes Anne. Honoring tha dead knows no religion." Abruptly, she hung up. Ma had more calls to make and when she was organizing, Ma was glorious.

Fully awake, I turned around and looked down at Sheldon, asleep in my bed, curled up like a little boy. He took a long inhale, and stretched out. His feet bumped the leg board, his arms hit the bedstead.

"You okay?" he asked, his voice full of sleep. He turned toward me and touched my shoulder.

"Yeah," I said. I clutched my nightgown around me and flopped back on my pillow, too tired to be embarrassed, but not tired enough to forget what happened last night. A gong clanged inside my head, the sound of it made me wince.

Bong: There is a man in my bed.

Bong: There is a MAN in my BED!

Last night, after they allowed the family to see Katie, Katie with the tubes up her nose and shunt down her throat, Katie with the blue paper shower cap covering her balding head, we said so many prayers over her that the staff asked us to leave because they needed the public area for the families of Friday night casualties.

We all came back to Ma's and cried. The only one missing was Bruno. Finally, Sheldon took me home to my place.

I moved like a metal creature with robot feet as Sheldon helped me fit the key into the lock and open the front door of my new apartment. Sheldon asked me if I was all right, a question he had repeated every few minutes. He slipped his arms around me; I cried into the crook of his neck.

I pounded on his chest, I wept and wailed. I blamed myself for letting Katie sit so high on that stool. I blamed Bruno for bringing her tonight when she obviously was too sick to leave her bed. I cursed God for not hearing our prayers when the emergency crews came. And I wondered aloud why Mary wasn't with me, why she had let us down. Before I knew it, I had collapsed and Sheldon carried me to my bed.

He slipped off my shoes. Took off my jacket. Unbuttoned my blouse. Found a flannel nightgown and put it over me. Hiccupping, I stood and slipped off my skirt and my pantyhose. Gently, yet with a comforting firmness, he pushed me back onto the bed, covered me up with my new down comforter, and climbed in beside me. We slept like spoons.

I woke to feel Sheldon's warmth beside me. I turned toward him and even though he was sleeping, I don't know why, I began to kiss him. Over and over, I kissed his face, his lips. Then with my tongue, I parted his lips so I could explore his mouth, while my hands, as though they had a mind of their own, explored his body.

I wanted him. I wanted to feel every part of him. I wanted him to know me completely. Even though a voice in my head told me it was a sin, I ignored the voice. I threw my judgment away. And when thoughts of Bruno's attack intruded, I pushed those thoughts out of my mind.

Bruno doesn't own my mind.

Right then, in the middle of the night, I had no shame, no common sense, only a furtive sensation of pleasure, a throbbing desire so strong it lessened the ache in my heart.

Sheldon was a gentle lover, and I a clumsy one. His hands melted into my back, thawed my trembling thighs, and stroked my nervous breasts. I had never wanted a man in my bed, not really. But now one was here. I rejoiced at the smoothness of his skin, the feel of his chest hair against my nipples. My head said, *No, no!* Then, my head said, *Yes!*

That!

This is what I want.

Yes! No! No, I don't want that.

But I did.

It's too much!

I can't!

And then...and then...I did.

I brought him inside me. Sweetly. Strongly. Pushing, pushing until something inside of me snapped and broke in two.

I thought it was my heart that had broken, but there was a rush between my legs and we were rocking, soaring, flying while a deep sound of pleasure hummed in my throat and Sheldon said over and over and over, "I love you, Anne O'Neil. I love you."

43. Casseroles and Confusion

THE O'NEIL CASSEROLE MILITIA, whose weapons against falling apart were meat, hot dishes and cold cuts, liquor and prayers, marched into Bruno and Katie's house on Saturday afternoon. There were bakery boxes, plastic platters of cheeses, trays of shrimp, an entire pre-cooked and pre-sliced roast beef brought in from the delicatessen along with loaves of bread in need of slicing, jars of condiments requiring decanting to small bowls. There were things cold and things cooked, things sweet and things savory. Bruno, eyes sunken and clearly not wanting us around, stared at us like we were poltergeists, intruders from another land.

I watched Bruno bite back his resentment of the invading O'Neils. But he had no choice. He was helplessly outnumbered. I couldn't help but wonder if after Katie's funeral, we would ever see him again. I hoped it would be a precursor to complete severance of all connection to him. After all, they had no children, so why would he choose to hang around at the O'Neil's now that Katie was gone? It made me feel worse to think I had to lose Katie to be liberated from Bruno, but there it was, a strange benefit from this dreadful tragedy.

People began dropping by the house to pay their respects. Ma set me to making pizza from scratch. She prayed over the oven. She prayed over the dough, the cheese, and the salami. She prayed over the cleanser in the sink. She blessed the dishes people brought as well as the people who brought them. Making your own pizza was stupid. I knew this. My sisters rolled their eyes. But I didn't care. Hands in the dough and squeezing it, the act of preparing food felt like therapy.

Darcy began to get antsy about the funeral plans, and asked where Katie was now and if we could visit her. When Bruno couldn't answer her questions, Darcy called several funeral homes to inquire about funerals, wakes, and vigils. Then she called Holy Cross Cemetery about gravesites.

Bruno came in and heard the chatter, then drew himself up to his full height. He said he would take care of everything. His tone said it was none of our business.

Perhaps it wasn't our business. Katie is—or was—his wife. We were merely her family, but behind Bruno's back, I watched Darcy roll her eyes.

Ma walked over to him and blocked his way. "So, Bruno dear, when is tha wake?"

"I don't know," Bruno replied. "There's an autopsy first, Irene, which will delay things. Unless, that is, I can get a doctor to sign off."

"Sign off?" Ma and I said, at the same time.

The new phrase rolled over in my mind like a rockslide. Ma's hand fussed with her white lace collar, then she stroked her stiff gray page boy, which today looked to be made of silver wire.

Sign off, I thought. Is this what death is? You have to get a doctor to agree how death occurred and *sign off* on the death certificate? I thought of the pudding and protein powder that I had taken from their house. It was somewhere in my car. My car was still in Impound.

I watched Bruno's face stiffen. His chin seemed more pointed than I had ever noticed. He rocked back and forth from heel to toes and back.

"I'd rather not have her cut up," he said, without meeting our eyes.

Everyone flinched. Would our sister really be sliced and diced by strangers? Had it already happened? I had a quick vision of Katie lying in some laboratory, pieces of her scattered here and there. Her brain on a scale. Her face rolled back and resting across her neck like a rumpled scarf. Gagging, I clutched the side of the sink and held on, hoping the wave of nausea would pass.

"How long wud all this take?" Ma whispered.

"A day or so. Maybe longer."

I turned around and watched as Bruno moved to the side to walk by her, but Ma parried and blocked his way.

"'Twas it tha fall? Is tha' what killed her?" Ma said.

"Or was it a heart attack?" Darcy asked, coming forward to be on Ma's right. Fiona and I stepped to the other side, then Jennifer and Susan moved in behind him. Now the O'Neil women were a gauntlet to be reckoned with.

Bruno shoved his hands in his pockets. He studied the floor. "Maybe the fall. Concussion. Aneurysm. Stroke. Heart attack..."

The visions of last night held us in hushed spell. Ma stepped aside and let Bruno pass. We watched him drift out of the kitchen like a glassy-eyed specter.

"So when da we see 'er?" Ma whispered. "When's tha Rosary? Who's tha undertaker?"

Ma's voice traveled up an octave. "'N where's Katie now? Is she still 'n hospital? Or is she some'ere else?"

Baffled, we could only stare at each other and like little girls playing house, we aimlessly fiddled around in Katie's kitchen. We found her kettle and boiled water for tea. Fumbled one more time with the coffee maker, gave up again and went back to the instant. Found her sugar bowl and creamer. Filled them. Found the ice bucket and filled it. Found a tub for the sodas Sheldon and Paul brought back from the store and dragged the bin out to the dining room.

I couldn't look at Sheldon. I was too embarrassed about last night. No one knew he had spent the night at my place, but I wondered if they could tell anyway.

Through all of the hubbub, the voice that was missing was Da's. He sat in Bruno and Katie's living room and did not speak. He did not cry. When he did speak, his voice came out in a hoarse whisper. All he wanted to do was sit alone and stare into space. He didn't seem to listen, or care, what anyone said.

He didn't even want a whiskey. He only asked for his coffee. Fiona, Darcy and I, took turns waiting on him. He refused all offers of sandwiches, casseroles, cold cuts or fresh pizza. Nor was he interested in biscuits, cookies, cake or pie.

Back in the kitchen, we whispered about Da and wondered what to do.

We rinsed plates and put them in the dishwasher. Cleaned something. Washed something. Heated food on the stove. Served guests. Repeated the story of last night. Comforted and took comfort from others. The purpose created a rhythm, gave us a reason to go on and not retreat to our beds, pull up the covers and shut off the lights. We were awake and working. We were sisters all. We were family.

44. P.T.V.S.S.

IT WAS LATE IN THE AFTERNOON when Sheldon and I arrived back at my apartment, the silence between us almost palpable. Sheldon had things to do. I had things to do, and he awkwardly left, wanting to give me a hug and a kiss, but I didn't want that. I wanted to be alone.

As soon as the door shut, silence and loneliness engulfed me. And, because of what happened last night between me and Sheldon, I felt estranged from God. Distant from Mary. I wanted to pray, but I couldn't calm my mind long enough to concentrate. I longed to talk to the Blessed Virgin, but I was too ashamed.

Could I have prevented Katie's death?

I shouldn't have let Katie sit on that high stool. If I hadn't, maybe she would be alive right now. Why did I lose my virginity last night? What had I been thinking?

Guilty, guilty, guilty.

In the kitchen, I peered into my tiny Eden, inhabited by Jude the Miniature Mollusk. I couldn't find him. I watered the garden, plucked out the dead leaves and fluffed up the stray branches, encouraging them to stand tall. Finally, I took out the small statue of the Blessed Mother and gave it a rinse. Jude was on her back, clinging to her skirts. Gently, I set him on the baby tears and put Mary in her place under the schefflera.

"Mary?" I whispered, "I'm a terrible person." Tears came into my eyes, but I resisted the urge to give in to them.

I waited for her to speak, which was pretty silly because, after all, she was a plaster statue, and a tiny one at that. I vowed not to tell any of this to Dr. Helfer.

"Do you hate me?" I said. I don't know how long I stared at Mary in my little dish garden. It was probably only a few minutes, but as I worked my way through the jumble of emotions crowding my head, time became irrelevant.

What could I have done to save Katie?

Why did I let Sheldon into my bed?

Why did I start kissing him?

If Katie hadn't died, none of it would have happened.

Did Bruno have anything to do with her collapse?

I had fallen from Grace.

I was no longer a virgin.

What if I became pregnant?

What if I got a disease?

If I were pregnant, how would I tell my parents?

Shame encircled me. Croaking and sobbing, I slapped along the wall and tried to find the bedroom. I struck something. It crashed to the floor. I fumbled for the light switch. The Mary Ma had given me landed in pieces on the hardwood planks.

Now I had killed Mary.

I gazed down at the porcelain pieces, horrified to see Mary's head lolling crazily to one side, her arms separated from her body and at odd angles. I moved away from the mess and found my bed, climbed in and covered up.

The phone kept ringing. My clumsy paw kept swiping at the noise. Fiona's voice seemed to emanate from my hand and I fumbled the receiver to my ear. She sounded like she had a cold.

"Have you been crying?" she asked me.

I nodded.

"Are you all right?" she said.

Am I? I asked myself. *Am I all right?*

"Anne? Are you there?"

"I don't know," I said finally. I sat up and turned on the light. The bed was messy. The sheets still had blood on them. The blood from last night. My blood. Virginal blood. I started to cry.

"Fiona," I said, coughing and hiccupping. "Sheldon and I...after we came back here...we..."

Fiona's voice was calm and soothing. "It's all right. I'm coming over. I'll be right there."

Twenty minutes later, dressed in a snappy jogging suit and out of breath, Fiona appeared at my door.

"I know what you're going through," she said. "I know all about it."

I watched her push a handful of red hair off her face and struggle to catch her breath. When she finally spoke, her voice was filled with authority.

"You have P.T.V.S.S."

"P.T.V.—what?" I whispered through a trembling shudder. "What's that?"

"*Post Traumatic Virginal Stress Syndrome.* I made it up myself. Believe me, it's real."

Engulfed in shame and weighed down with remorse, I could only weep and blubber excuses. Excuses for my lack of self-control, my skid into the blurry world of immorality. Fiona wouldn't hear any of it. She pushed me into a hot bath laced with Epsom salts. While I wept endless apologies and worried about the condition of my soul, wailed about Katie and asked a dozen times why she died, Fiona began to piece my life back together.

I don't know how she did it, but within an hour, my bed was made with clean sheets and Mary was off the floor. Shards, body parts and Mary's head fanned out on a cookie sheet on the kitchen table. Fiona pledged that someday we would have a glue-fest and Mary would emerge from the broken bits and chunks, good as new. Ma would never know.

Soon, the television pulsed with the old movie, *Breakfast at Tiffany's,* the statue pieces were moved to the coffee table and the fragrance of buttered popcorn filled the air. We snuggled together under an old afghan Darcy had given me and stuffed greasy salty puffs of popped corn into our mouths. We watched Holly Golightly blithely stride across the screen blowing smoke into the air from her long cigarette holder.

The ache in my center over Katie's death slowly became more bearable because now it was divided between Fiona and me. As for what happened with Sheldon, I could not speak to Fiona of the wanton abandon of my senses, my irrational ravaging of his body or his entry into mine. The sounds in my head were as nonsensical as static and Fiona, as though she knew my inner conflicts, made me listen to another station.

"You'll be all right," she murmured, putting her arm around me. "The first time is always a bummer, and not very romantic either."

"Why is it," I said, "that we were both raised in the same house and yet you...don't care...no, that's not right. I mean, how come it doesn't bother you if...if you...you..."

"Make love?" Fiona said. As usual, she was blunt as a brick. I watched one eyebrow cock back. "I rejected all that superstitious Catholic crap ages ago." She stuffed a handful of popcorn into her mouth and spoke while chewing. Small bits of fluffy corn flew out at every S and Th sound. The word superstitious nearly covered me.

"I love the church. I go to mass, but I don't think there's a trap door that sends you to hell if you make love. Look at some of the saints. Saint Augustine for instance. He was a lothario and he still went to heaven. They made him a saint for godsakes."

"Are you comparing yourself to Saint Augustine? He was a philosopher and invented a school of thought."

"Yeah, yeah, yeah," Fiona said, grabbing more popcorn.

I took another handful myself. There was never a way to win an argument with Fiona.

"It was you and Katie who bought into the whole Catholic thing, including the fluttering Cherubim and Seraphim flying in a little circles up in heaven singing 'Holy, holy, holy.'"

"Okay!" I said, loudly. I hated being mocked.

"You even played nun as a kid, remember?" Fiona said, wiping her hands on a napkin.

When I became older and learned about Margaret's life, I knew I didn't want to become a nun. Then I felt guilty because I didn't have a vocation. I would have been so easy if I had had one; I would have had a direction, a mission, a clear path to my life.

Fiona laughed, but not at me; she laughed at Holly Golightly. We knew the dialogue in this part of the movie and said it together.

"The blues are because you're getting fat and maybe it's been raining too long, you're just sad that's all. The mean reds are horrible. Suddenly you're afraid and you don't know what you're afraid of. Do you ever get that feeling?"

Did I ever! Fiona put her arm around me again and we ate more popcorn and said the lines we knew, crying when we wanted to, whether or not it was about the movie or because Katie wasn't here with us.

"At least you bought some furniture and gave the snail a name," Fiona said, giving me an elbow. We both howled with laughter comparing Holly Golightly's apartment and her nameless cat to my apartment and my snail. We cried because this movie was a favorite of Katie's.

When the movie ended, we put on *Sabrina*. We even brought the shards of the Blessed Mother over to the coffee table and began to glue Mary back together and I let Jude have a slow romp around the table.

"He's actually kind of cute," Fiona said, as she settled herself on the other side of the coffee table and picked up an arm and a what appeared to be a shoulder.

I smiled at her. "I know," I said, softly. "He's me, really. I'm that snail, moving slow, having a big shell on my back."

"Look at those little feelers," Fiona said, leaning over to take a closer look. "Hey, guy, go for it!"

Jude continued to cruise along the table's edge, his head high and his feelers tall. I was glad Fiona appreciated my little pet.

Just as we were gluing Mary's head back on, amazed that it fit and that the mend didn't show, I couldn't stand holding back my suspicions about Bruno. "Fiona? What if Bruno did something to Katie to cause her..." My throat locked up and I couldn't say the last word.

"What do you mean?" Fiona stopped gluing.

"What if he made her sick? On purpose."

"Bruno wouldn't—" She handed me another piece of the statue, which was made up of several other pieces she had glued together. I fiddled around and tried to find the place where it fit.

"I don't think he would do anything like that."

"I'm not so sure."

"I know he has problems. Ego problems. I believed you when you said he was kicking in the door that night. But you have to admit you were over-the-top emotional. Now you're asking me to jump to the conclusion that he would hurt his own wife."

I couldn't look at her because she was right. I *was* asking her to believe Bruno was evil enough to commit murder.

"You've always been a pessimist."

Fiona was also right about that.

My cell phone rang. When I didn't pick it up, Fiona did it for me. It was Sheldon, but right then I was too embarrassed to talk to him. Fiona walked the phone into the other room and I could hear her whispering, but I couldn't understand what she said. Then she came back and she shoved the phone in my face. "It's for you."

45. Meet You at the Statue

SUNDAY MORNING, we gathered like wounded soldiers in front of Our Lady of the Belgian Waffle at the side of the cemetery at Mission Dolores. I looked up at Blessed Mary ever virgin, Blessed Mary mother of God, this Mary with the waffle on her head, this Mary with hands like a cowgirl who looked like she could jump down and sweep the streets as well as bless the poor and, judging from the mitt on her right hand, maybe even play first base. Even though I was ashamed and felt clogged with sin, I loved this Mary more than ever.

But was she so disappointed in me that she no longer could love me?

We brought flowers this time, flowers that had been sent for Katie, and placed a dozen roses at Mary's feet. No one was late for mass at the Basilica this time. Nor was anyone absent. Except for Bruno. Solemnly, we walked into the basilica together.

I didn't care what Fiona had said yesterday. Because of what I'd done with Sheldon, I knew I was not entitled to receive Holy Communion without first taking the sacrament of Reconciliation, which meant a confession to a priest. But if I didn't go up to the altar, I knew it would upset Da and Ma. They would want to know why I wasn't receiving Communion. Da might even think the reason I wasn't going was that I had set fire to Bruno's parents' place. Or that Sheldon had spent the night. I didn't know which one was worse.

Fiona sensed my conflict and stayed close beside me. During the mass, Fiona brought her head close to mine and whispered, "Sex is an affirmation of life, Anne."

I had no idea what that meant, but I nodded anyway.

Through the readings and Gospel, my mind tumbled and pitched. Tears seemed inevitable, and in a frantic bid to compose myself, I tried to say a few decades of the Rosary. I decided to say the Glorious Mysteries. The first decade was for the Resurrection of Jesus. The second, for his Ascension into Heaven.

While saying the Hail Marys, I tried to imagine Jesus rising in a golden light, floating up to the sky. Instead, I saw Katie. Her long blonde hair had been restored and was flowing down her back, which was good. Certainly better than seeing patches of bare scalp. But then I noticed the way her shoulder blades stuck out through her dress. She was the thinnest of all the angels, which I took as a personal rebuke. I should have gotten her to eat more. If I had, maybe she wouldn't be dead. If she hadn't died, I wouldn't have collapsed. If I hadn't collapsed, Sheldon wouldn't have spent the night. I'd still be a virgin.

In the middle of the next decade of the Rosary, my emotions ambushed me. My tears were not only for Katie, but for myself. Why hadn't I stayed away from Sheldon? Why had I let him put me to bed? It was my fault we had made love. *My fault. My most grievous fault.*

Floundering in a sea of shame, a dark whirling current began to suck me down.

"Wha's wrong wid 'er?" Ma said, leaning forward to get a better look at me. "Agnes," Ma said, loud enough for the three pews forward and behind to hear, "hold yerself tagether. It's tha Elevation of tha Host."

"Leave her alone, Ma," Darcy said. I saw pity flash in Darcy's eyes. Had Fiona spoken to her?

Did she know?

"Come on girl," Mark mumbled from the pew in front of me. He turned his head slightly, and spoke out of the side of his mouth. "Don't start now, Aggie, you'll 'ave us all crashin'."

I tightened my trembling chin and sniffed back my tears.

Mark's wife, turned and said, "Why didn't you bring Sheldon?"

"Shhh!" Ma hissed.

Susan rolled her eyes and turned around. Facing away from Ma, Susan leaned back and whispered, "It's a shame you didn't bring Sheldon."

Mark poked her with his elbow. "He's a Jew fer Christ's sake. Why wud he want ta come ta mass? Anyway, Aggie can do better than tha'."

Words of defense teetered on my tongue.

"Yer not bonkin' this bloke are ya?" Mark whispered.

I couldn't stop the blush traversing my guilty face.

While his eyebrows reached to his hairline, Mark's finger pointed at me and then out into space and back to me again. "You 'n 'im?" he whispered. "You 'n 'im. Fer real?"

Was my fall from Grace so obvious?

Fiona cuffed Mark on the head. "Don't be ridiculous."

Ma reached out over Da's lap and used her song sheet as a weapon. Slapping at Mark's shoulder, the paper made noises as it missed him and hit the back of the pew.

"Shh! This is tha most important part a' mass. It's the Consecration 'a tha Wine! Quiet!" Then she sighed. "Ah, Agnes Anne, yer a mess."

Ma was right. Nose running and makeup washing down my cheeks, indeed, I was a wreck.

The sound of kneelers hitting the back of pews rattled through the Basilica. It was time for Communion. I wasn't entitled to receive the host. But I also knew if that I didn't, Da would think I had a Big Sin on my chest. People were filing out of the pews and walking up the center aisle. It was our turn. My feet were lead. I couldn't move.

"Agnes Anne," Da whispered. "Get goin'."

My feet seemed nailed to the ground. Fiona grabbed my hand and tugged. We became little girls again going up to the altar rail in our fairy white dresses and veils. We were sisters united in a strange solidarity of birth order, Catholicism, and O'Neil lore. But it didn't make me any more worthy of Communion. I looked up and saw the Host. Guilt rained over me.

"Body of Christ," Father Mac said, holding the wafer of bread in front of my eyes.

Forgive me, Lord. I'm not worthy to receive You.

I began to cross my hands over my chest, a signal I was here for a blessing, not communion.

"Body of Christ," he repeated, louder this time, as though I might have a hearing deficiency. Behind me, I could hear Da say, "What tha heck's wrong wid Aggie?"

Fiona hit me hard in the small of the back, my mouth opened and Father plunked the host onto my tongue instead of into my palms. I tasted the simple wheat host and felt guilt wash through me. It was done: Communion without Absolution. The weight of a new sin singed my heart.

Back at the house, the knock on the door after dinner made little impression. After all, the doorbell had been ringing all day. I figured it was another neighbor. We had adjourned to the living room and were enjoying a cake someone brought over. Before anyone could answer the door, Bruno let himself in.

Under a two-day growth of beard, his face seemed relaxed and his bloodshot eyes almost jubilant, but his body twitched this way and that and wouldn't stay still. Bruno told us Katie's Rosary would be at the funeral home on Tuesday night. Her mass, Wednesday morning at Saint Ivan's.

"Saint Ivan's!" Ma gasped. "Why there? Why not Mission Dolores?"

"Katie liked Saint Ive's." Bruno cocked his chin upward with a Napoleonic flare.

My stomach twisted into a knot. I knew the significance of Saint Ivan's. That was the church where Katie had asked for forgiveness for her abortions. I glanced at Fiona. She shrugged, which meant she didn't know.

"The autopsy was not needed, by the way," Bruno said. A slight smile tilted at the corners of his mouth. He jammed his hands into the pockets of his windbreaker and turned to walk a few paces, then came back. "I got a doctor to sign the death certificate."

I didn't miss the slight head-down smile he gave to the rug. I wondered if anyone else thought it odd.

"What's tha cause 'a death?" Matthew asked, lowering his cake-filled fork.

Da looked up at Bruno from his easy chair, his face expectant. For the first time in my life, my father looked old.

"Cardiac infarction," Bruno replied.

All of us continued to stare.

"Otherwise known as heart failure," Bruno said, filling in the silence.

The only sound came from the dining room where a few kids were still eating and talking. More O'Neils were coming into the living room.

"Heart failure? Why wud Katie 'ave 'eart failure?" Ma asked.

Bruno leveled his gaze. "An-or-ex-i-a," he said, each syllable pronounced individually as if it were a separate word and anyone named O'Neil was too stupid to understand.

Ma shook her head like she had a surprise dip in a cold lake.

"It's an eating disorder, Irene," Bruno said, with exaggerated patience.

We all knew Katie had constant diarrhea and didn't eat. We all knew she had cramps and sometimes threw up. We also knew she was depressed about her miscarriage. A shameful blush crept over my face. Since she was married to a doctor, we had all stepped back and let the doctor in the family lead us. But I knew Bruno had led us astray.

"Maybe it was the pudding and p-protein powder," I said, trying for a hearty Marilyn gush. "M-maybe that had something to do it."

"I have no idea what you mean." Bruno's eyes sliced through me.

"Sure you do." I threw down my napkin and stood. "You had something to do with her death, Bruno. I *know* you did."

Bruno's mouth gaped open. He took a step toward me. Then halted.

"Whatever, Agnes Anne. Let your delusions lead where they may. You're crazy—certifiably crazy—and so is this entire family."

We watched Bruno spin on his heel and march out of the house. Before he slammed the front door, he nearly said something. But he must have thought better of it and turned away. The second the front door closed, everyone was all over me with questions.

Some believed me when I told them that the pudding and protein powder made me cramp and feel sick. Others said that Bruno-god-love-him couldn't have—wouldn't have—done anything to hurt Katie. Fiona was on my side. Darcy was doubtful and my brothers just squinted and shook their heads, as though in deep wonderment.

It was Luke who really popped my bubble.

"If that's true," he said, softly, leaning into my ear. "If Bruno *did* do something, and you took a sample of it, then you've ruined the chain of custody."

"What chain? What?"

Luke sighed. "It's only your word against his. You'll say that's where you got the protein powder. He'll scoff and say it's yours. Who's to say you didn't plant it?"

I swallowed hard.

"Anyway, where is this stuff now?"

"The pudding and protein powder are in my trunk."

Luke bit his lip.

"Is that bad?" I whispered.

46. The Rosary

TUESDAY NIGHT AT THE FUNERAL HOME, the pungent smell of flowers could have made an asthma sufferer drop dead. Flowers lined the back wall, stood on easels, and sprayed out of large vases on the floor. Grief seemed to emanate from the heavy drapes and dark walls. It didn't help my self-control that the organ music coming from the speakers was maudlin.

I wondered if all of the other mourners who had ever said good-bye to a loved one in this room had each left a trace of their sorrow behind. Death and misfortune seemed to drop from the ceiling and peel off the walls like old paint. Steeling myself to gaze into my sister's face for the last time, I was surprised to find that her casket hadn't arrived.

Ma looked nice, dressed in her best dark suit. She had placed a swirl of black tulle on top of her head and a velvet bow held her hair in place, tying it up nicely at the back. She looked like a schoolgirl with an old face. Together, we walked up to the brace of flowers and began to read the cards attached to the floral sprays. The messages were sweet and heartfelt.

"Has Da cried yet?" I asked Ma, as we read a tag from one of Katie's high school friends.

"No," Ma whispered back. "I talked ta Father Mac. He says sometimes people don' cry. It's so much emotion, tha person shuts down."

We moved to the next spray of flowers. It was so big, they had put it on a high easel. It was from Darcy, Fiona, and me. We had all chipped in. It was a magnificent arrangement and it made my heart nearly break to behold it. In the enormous white expanse of flowers shaped into a heart, miniature pink roses spelled out, "Sisters Forever." I took a tissue from my purse and wiped my eyes.

"Ahh, that's luv'ly, Agnes Anne," Ma whispered.

Next, we stood in front of a mammoth spray of dark pink roses. They were just opening, and deep inside, they were white. Pure white. I opened the card. It was from Sheldon.

Da peered over our shoulders. "This one's from Sheldon, Mal," Ma said. "Look a'tha beauty of it. 'Tis a lovely t'ing."

"From tha Jew boy? I'll be damned."

"Da," I said, my tears abruptly drying and my whisper barely controllable, "that's not very nice."

"Agnes Anne," he said, between his teeth, "I always call a spade a spade, a mick a mick, and a Jew a Jew." Before I could make a comeback, he looked around and said, "Where's Katie? When are they bringin'er out? I always said she's be late ta'er own funeral."

Bruno had come up behind us.

"Where's Katie?" Da repeated, turning directly to him.

"Oh," Bruno said, fingering the area above his brow while dropping his gaze. "I...um. We're umm...we're not having a body present. Katie wanted to be cremated."

"What are ya talkin' about?" Da said, his voice louder than I'd heard it since the night Katie died.

Bruno faced him and I noticed how much shorter he was than Da. "There will be no body displayed," he said, his voice sharp as a knife's edge.

"Have ya gone daft? Off yer nut? We're all here ta see Katie! Ta say our goodbyes. Fer godsakes, bring 'er out."

Bruno's eyes drifted to the floor.

"Bruno-God-love-ya, I want ta see Katie!" Da bent down so he could look up into Bruno's face. "Where the hell is she?"

Darcy and Domenic had arrived and so had Fiona with Paul. They joined us up at the front while friends were filing into the pews. I saw so many people I knew—former teachers, childhood friends, that it was difficult to concentrate. Then Da yelled, *"Where is she?"*

My brothers came up to see what was going on. I noticed the funeral director had entered the room and stood discretely at the side.

Matthew said, "How can ther' be a proper Ros'ry if there's no body?" He looked from priest to the funeral director and back. "If me sister's not 'ere, then where tha hell is she? What tha heck did'ya do wid her?"

The funeral guy approached and mumbled something about wishes but obviously didn't want to get involved, especially with the likes of my brothers.

Father Mac took charge and said we could all say the Rosary without a body, but Da ignored him.

"Listen, you," he said, pointing a stout finger at Bruno's chest. "I've 'ad 'bout enough a' this. Ya had no right ta cremate m'daughter. Katie wud'a never wan'a tha'. Never."

"I beg to differ," Bruno said, raising his chin and talking directly up into Da's face. "We had long talks about it. This *is* what she wanted."

"Long talks about it!" Da screamed. "She didna' mull over death! Whay wud she? She was a young woman! No decent O'Neil would want ta be burned. That's bullberry, Bruno!"

Da was becoming so agitated I thought he might punch him square on the nose. Bruno took a step back.

"I must remind you," the funeral director said, coming up to them, his voice melodious and gentle, "that this a place of worship and reflection. If you have something to discuss, I suggest you take it outside."

"You'd better believe I'll step outside," my brother Mark said. "And Bruno Stark, yer goin' ta step out wid me."

The boys didn't merely go into the anteroom, they walked out to the parking lot. I followed. Joke was on us. Bruno stayed inside.

It was cold out there, the wind and fog had pushed in from the ocean and I had left my coat in one of the pews. Shivering, I wrapped my arms around myself and listened to my brothers complain.

A police car pulled into the lot. It was Luke. He threw his hat on the seat before he slammed the door and came over to us. "What's going on?"

Matthew and Mark stopped shouting long enough to explain the dilemma to Luke.

Another car swung into the lot. It was Sheldon's. I walked out to meet him. He noticed my brothers standing in a huddle, talking in loud voices. "What's going on?" he asked.

"Katie's body isn't here." From Sheldon's expression, I could tell he didn't know the significance of this information.

"Should it be?" he asked as we walked toward the group.

"Yeah," I said, through a shiver.

"I thought this was a memorial service before the memorial service."

"No. It's a wake before the funeral and she's supposed to be here."

"What's a wake?"

"It's when you sit with the body of your loved one for a while and then say the Rosary and have a small service. Actually, it's now called a vigil."

"Oh, shiva." Sheldon said.

"What's that?" I asked.

"It's when you mourn and people come to visit."

"I guess it's the same thing, then. Years ago in Ireland, they would sit with the loved one all night long and never leave the body alone. People had drinks and told stories. I think it probably was to make sure the person was really dead, but now... but we c-can't." My face crinkled as the lead weight in my chest expanded. I stopped walking.

We were close to my brothers. Sheldon put his arms around my back and hugged me. "So if Katie's not here," he whispered, "where is she?"

I blubbered into his shoulder. "I don't know. I don't know where she is."

At the Vigil, the Rosary was said not with glory, but with vengeance. Bruno's discomfort showed plainly as he rocked from one knee to the other. I was sure he could hardly wait for this to be over.

When you say the Rosary with a group, the leader says the first two sentences of the Hail Mary and the congregation says the last sentence. Father Mac led us. After the Apostles Creed, the Our Father and three Hail Marys, we got into the meat and potatoes of the Rosary, five decades made up of one Our Father, ten Hail Marys, and a Glory Be, thrown in for good measure. We were saying the Glorious Mysteries.

"Dearly Beloved," Father Mac said, "We think of Christ's glorious triumph, when on the third day after His death, He arose from the tomb and for forty days appeared to His Blessed Mother and to His Disciples." Father Mac lowered the prayer book, turned around, bowed his head and said an Our Father. The people joined in. Then he said, *"Hail Mary, full of grace, the Lord is with thee. Blessed art thou amongst women and blessed is the fruit of thy womb, Jesus."*

Those gathered, at least the ones who were Catholic, said the rest of the prayer, *"Holy Mary, mother of God, pray for us sinners, now and at the hour of our death. Amen."*

On the second Hail Mary, my brothers began to emphasize the words, *Pray for us SINNERS*. The rest of the mourners were rightfully confused as each time my brothers said it, it sounded like a declaration of war.

The litany of Hail Marys went on, prayer after prayer, the shouts intensifying and the words of the Hail Mary changing to "Pray for THAT sinner."

Somewhere in the third decade, which was dedicated to the memory of the descent of the Holy Spirit onto Mary and the Apostles, someone, maybe Matthew, threw a hymnal at Bruno and hit him square in the back of his head while my brothers said, "Pray for THAT sinner."

The shot was magnificent. Bruno grabbed his head and spun around.

Matthew said under his breath, "Ye feckin' arse hole, burning m'sister."

A few Hail Marys downstream, it was Da who grumbled, "I hope ya burn n'hell, ya German heathen."

Fiona and I tried to say our Hail Marys louder so we might drown out the voices of the men in our family, but it was a losing battle. Pretty soon, the boys stopped saying the Rosary altogether. Still on their knees, they propped their rear ends against the pew benches and spoke to each other, completely ignoring the Rosary.

They continued commenting about Bruno, about his

soul, and how he'd burn in Hell just like he was burning Katie. Then the kids started asking questions and the mothers tried to shush them. My brothers told the kids that Uncle Bruno was burning up Auntie Katie's precious body and how wrong it was for an O'Neil to be cremated. I could tell the kids were shocked. The older ones looked like they were staring into a flaming abyss and then with frightened eyes, regarded their Uncle Bruno with new-found terror.

The chatter from the O'Neils became so disruptive that Father Mac turned around and halted the Rosary altogether.

"I would ask the family of Katie O'Neil Stark to please respect the Rosary," he said. "Let us all entreat Our Holy Mother to look after our dearly departed." He gave Da the fish-eye.

"When the Holy Water freezes over, will my Katie be cremated!" Da shouted. He stood and walked back down the center aisle and slammed open the double doors. We were left hearing the flap, flap, flap as the doors settled into place.

47. Trouble with the Holy Water

WE TROOPED BACK TO THE HOUSE like a defeated army. The kids, because of the hour and because they had been cooped up so long, were whiney. Colleen begged her Uncle Mark to lift her up to the font so she could bless herself at Our Lady of the Font. Once one kid got a dip and a blessing, the others lined up clamoring, "Me, too."

Mark began to lift them one after the other up to the font. Little Dara complained that she couldn't find the Holy Water and had to be lifted even higher so her arm would go over the china lip and her wee fingers would find a touch of liquid. To help Mark out, Matthew tossed a glass of ice cubes into the font and cleverly raised the water level.

Da trudged up the front stairs and came across the threshold like he had seventy pounds of rocks on his back. I watched him put his coat in the closet, stow his hat on the upper shelf, and then stop in front of Mary's Font. His hand gripped the edge of the gilt cloud, as though he had to brace himself lest he fall over from grief and exhaustion. Bowing his head, he said a silent prayer, then reached into the font for a blessing.

Who knew that on tonight of all nights, his two fingers would swipe across ice?

A stifled scream escaped Da's lips. Half the children yelled for their mothers, the other half ran away.

"Wha'?" Mark said, running back to the entryway. "What's wrong?"

Da didn't move. His fingers were still poised in the air. Mouth ajar, he looked like a small child trying to take a deep breath before crying out in pain. Red spread across his face, then deepened, while the onslaught of this mysterious spasm intensified.

I knew he was trying to speak, but he couldn't get his words out, his breath had fixed itself somewhere between his lungs and throat. I watched a vein swell like a balloon under the skin of his neck. It looked like a prelude to a stroke.

"It froze overrrrrrrrrrr!" he yelled. His inhale bleated like a backwards screech. When he finally had his breath, he bellowed, *"Tha Holy Water! Mary's water! 'Tis frozen! Oh God! It froze over!"*

He jerked his body away, paced around in a circle, then returned to the font as though he had worked up the nerve to try again. He looked down into the font, but his hand seemed paralyzed.

"God help us!" he screamed again. "It's frozen! *That means Katie's goin' ta be cremated! D'you understand, boys? Tha Holy Water froze! Our Katie will be burned a'tha stake like some heathen durin' the Inquisition."* He turned away and walked again in a circle. *"My Katie! My Katie! It means God damned Bruno is goin' ta burn up yer sisterrrrr!"*

No amount of logic satisfied him. No number of excuses convinced Da that the freezing of the Holy Water wasn't divinely ordained. Da babbled on about fire and ice, miracles and retribution, and the protection of our Blessed Mother and the promises he had made through the years if this or that didn't happen, the Holy Water would freeze over. Now here it was.

Da began to sob and, like he was a broken vessel, all of his pent-up grief and heartache, anguish and misery poured out of him.

I knew this staggering display of emotion was for the best, that no parent should have to bury a child and that sorrow should be released and shared. But the sight of Da crying and jerking uncontrollably around the foyer, the sobs wracking out of him as though he were trying to dispel the Devil himself, chilled me to the marrow.

Ma began weeping, then my brothers. The kids became so distressed that a couple of the little ones wet their pants. Susan and Jennifer were the only ones who acted rationally, drying tears, changing clothes, and taking charge of the sobbing and wailing O'Neils in the entryway.

"Come on, Da," Matthew said, opening his arms. He grabbed Da in a bear hug and the two of them wobbled. I thought they'd both fall over.

"Katie! Mi Katie!" Da screamed her name over and over. *"Tha' damn Bruno is goin' to burn my daughter! Me own bottle a' water! That goddamned bastard! I'll kill him fer this!"*

"Come on, Da" Mark said, his eyes full of tears. He reached out and put his arms around them both. "Let's go upstairs. Come on... come on now, Da."

"Tha Holy Water froze over! Don't ya know what that means, boys? Look fer yerself! It means there's no hope! She's a gonner. Katie'll be burned sure as tha sun rises."

"Listen, Da," Matthew said. "I t'rew in some ice cubes ta raise tha water so Mark wouldn't hav'ta lift tha kids so high. It's only tha'. It's not a sign, Da. Are ya listenin'? *The Holy Water didn't freeze over.*"

"No, no. It's not in cubes," Da said. "The t'ing's frozen solid, I tell ya. Frozen like a lake in winter. It's a solid sheet, I tell ya. The Holy Water froze over! *It means we'll never see Katie again!*"

Da's sobs became a deep keening wail, the sound so painful that Ma leaned against the stair rail. I thought she might collapse. I ran over and walked her to the bench at the side of the stairway. We hugged and huddled and passed the tissue box back and forth while we listened to Matthew and Mark walking Da upstairs.

When we heard the sound of the master bedroom door close, Ma took a few minutes more to regain her composure before she said she needed to help with the kids.

Sheldon sat down beside me on the bench—I had almost forgotten that he was still there—but my eyes were locked on Mary of the Font. I was sure she regarded me with disappointment. Could my wickedness have caused the Holy Water to freeze? Impossible. I saw Matthew toss ice cubes in the font. Why did Da say it was slick?

"I'm so sorry, Anne," Sheldon said, putting his arm around me and pulling me toward him.

I pushed him away, stood up, and went over to the font and dipped my first two fingers into the bowl to see for myself. *I nearly screamed.*

It was true. Mary's Font was cold and slick.

"What is it?" Sheldon said, coming over.

"The Holy Water—Da's right. It's frozen solid!"

Sheldon was tall enough to look in and peer over the side. "It's just ice," he said, rocking it back and forth to loosen it from the sides of the fountain bowl.

"But why isn't it lumpy? How could it be totally frozen?"

Sheldon managed to tilt the ice and pick it up. "Maybe someone put something in it to make it freeze this way."

"Like what? No science class I ever had did something like that."

Sheldon cleared his throat, then hemmed and hawed. "I know what you mean. I don't get it, but there has to be a logical explanation."

The frozen piece of ice Sheldon held up looked like a miniature ice rink, flat and thick. With a small splash, he dropped it back into the font. We stared at each other, our thoughts interrupted by the phone. Automatically, I walked over to answer it.

"That was a terrible display tonight, Agnes." Bruno's voice cut through me like a knife.

I wanted to sass him back. Ask why Katie's body wasn't at the wake and hear his paltry excuses, but my throat wouldn't work. Not even a stammer escaped.

"Are you there?" he demanded. "Hello?"

"What did you do to her?" I said, in a gushy whisper. "What poison did you use? Strychnine? Arsenic?"

"What did I do to her? I tried to save her! Are you people all freaking nuts?"

I tried to respond, to find a come-back, but everything began swirling in my head and I couldn't think of anything but the frozen Holy Water. The ice seemed beyond the laws of physics. Turning around, I glanced over at Mary, but her face refused to reveal the slightest clue as to what was happening and why. Crazy me. Mary was a statue. What did I expect from her? Maybe Dr. Helfer was right. I spent my time talking to imaginary people.

"Agnes?" Bruno yelled. *"Are you listening to me?"*

As though I was not standing in this foyer at the side of the stairway, as though I didn't give a fig about Bruno and his repulsive voice, as though the water in Mary's Font was normal, a surreal calm descended over me and I had an uncontrollable desire to irritate him. I took a long deep breath, and whispered in my best Marilyn voice.

"Anne," I said. "My name is Anne."

"Don't you give me any crap, Agnes. You tell your hooligan brothers and your pig-headed father that I am going to have my *colleagues* at the funeral tomorrow. Do you hear me, Agnes? *My colleagues!* I will not have a duplication of that scene tonight. Do you understand? Katie and I had discussed cremation and that's what she wanted. Are you listening to me, ANNE? Are you?"

He was screaming so loud I had to hold the phone away from my ear. Even Sheldon, still at the font playing with the smooth elongated piece of ice, heard him. I didn't bother to say good-bye. I just I hung up, then sat down so I could contemplate the Holy Water, frozen solid as an ice rink for elves.

48. Where's Katie?

THE MORNING OF KATIE'S FUNERAL MASS, we all met again at the house. To my great surprise, Da was not thundering around cursing Bruno. In fact, he was nowhere to be seen. Ma kept pacing around the kitchen in her black high-heeled pumps, her legs swinging awkwardly from her hips as if she had ridden a horse all night.

"Malachi wonut move," Ma said, twisting her hands as though she was washing them under imaginary water. "He jus' stares a'tha ceiling 'n wonut talk. Once'n a while he mumbles somethin' 'bout tha Holy Water. But I canno' get 'im ta budge."

"Oh, let him be, Ma. He had a scare last night," Mark said, while rooting around an enormous pink bakery box. He plucked out a glazed donut the size of a squirrel.

"'N I haven't? She's m'daughter, too. Tha way eve'yone goes on 'bout it, you'd t'ink Katie jus' dropped down tha chimney 'n didn't 'ave a ma a'tall."

"Come on, Ma." Mark's voice was kind, but I could sense his exasperation. I had a feeling this conversation had been going on for some time. Mark's eyes were puffy and he looked like he'd been crying most of the night.

"Well, who takes tha brunt 'a things?" Ma shouted. "Me. Who's 'ad ta argue wid Bruno-God-love him? He wonut even 'ave a funeral a'Mission Dolores. Lord knows why we're goin' clear over ta Saint Ivan's today."

My stomach churned with acid. I knew why. I could picture Katie at Saint Ive's crying through her confession to some anonymous priest. Someone she didn't know.

Ma went on, still washing her hands under invisible water. "I donut even know if we're goin' ta tha cemetery, er what cemetery that might be. It should be Holy Cross, you know, but after this Saint Ivan's business, who knows? We might be goin' ta Mars."

"Saint Ive's is a nice place," Matthew said. He poured himself a mug of coffee and turned around to lean against the counter, coffee in one hand, donut in the other. Mark drifted off to the parlor to watch television.

"You've been there?" Fiona asked Matthew, filling her cup.

"Mark and I went to mass there this morning just to check it out."

"I've no idea why Bruno chose tha' place..." Ma's voice trailed off. "We 'ave no connection there 'n I never heard Katie speak of it. Or Bruno fer that matter." Ma extended her fingers and counted on them. "First Communion a'Mission Dolores. Confirmation, Mission Dolores. Marriage, Mission Dolores. An' now? The most important event of all, her entrance inta Heaven? We're all going off t'a place we've never been? What's on tha' man's mind?"

"Calm down, Ma. I t'ink it will be all right," Matthew said, licking the sugar off his fingers.

"You t'ink. You t'ink! Ye have no idea what I've been goin' through. And look a'yer brother, never takin' his eyes off tha' telly. Is basketball as important as his poor dead sister's funeral?"

"Ma—" Mark whined, turning away from the TV set. "It's March Madness."

"It was all I cud do ta get Bruno and Father Stanovich or whatever his name is, t'agree that tha O'Neils will take part in tha funeral mass. Otherwise, we'd just be observers! We'd be sending Katie off fer all eternity and not participating in a t'ing!"

Ma was truly losing it, her brogue had become so strong I had to struggle to understand her. I watched her face wrinkle and tears begin to streak down her cheeks. I went over to give her a hug.

Domenic, Darcy's husband, who'd been standing quietly in the doorway holding a mug of coffee, said, "I called Bruno about the grave marker. My Dad would make her a wonderful one, but Bruno wouldn't talk about it..." His voice trailed off and he hung his head.

"What about the casket?" Darcy asked, sharing the doorway with her husband. "We'll be able to see Katie today, won't we?" She looked from one to the other. "Surely, she's attending her own funeral. Isn't she?"

"I donut know," Ma said, through a sniffle. "I donut know about tha'. I told Bruno wha' we wanted, but..." She waved her tissue in the air, then had a good blow, the honk as loud as a blast from an eighteen wheeler.

"Ach! The bastard." Matthew turned away from everyone and licked the sugar glaze off his thumb and forefinger. I watched him stare down into the pink bakery box, eyeing the pastries like a hungry jackal.

"And yer father!" Ma began again, the fever pitch in her voice still keen. "He wonut get out'a bed. Bruno-god-love-him is killin'm sure's placin' a knife n'his heart."

"Bruno-god-love-him," Mark said, abandoning the TV and coming back to the kitchen. "Bruno-goddamnit is more like it." He joined Matthew at the bakery box, first lifting a cruller, then a scone, and finally choosing a bear claw.

"Agnes," Ma said, pointing to me. "Go up t'yer Da. See if ya can talk some sense n'him. Get 'im out a' bed. We've got ta leave, ya know. I don' want ta go ta tha funeral alone. But I will! I swear ta ya, I'll go by m'self if he wonut get out'a bed."

"Grandma?" little Aula said, tugging on her skirt. "Are you going to make picture pancakes? I want Mini Mouse."

"No, luv," Ma said, gazing down at her. "We donut 'ave time fer picture pancakes this mornin'."

Ma poured a mug of coffee, stirred in two spoons of sugar, and handed it to me. "Here. Convince yer father ta get out of bed."

With reluctance, I took the coffee and mounted the stairs.

My knock on the bedroom door was timid at best. Da didn't tell me to either come in or go away, so I opened the door and took a peek. "Da?" I whispered. "Are you awake?"

He lay face-up, staring at the ceiling. His cheeks were ashen and his eyes looked like they were hiding behind puffy flesh-colored pillows.

"Have some coffee, Da." I tiptoed over to his side of the bed and didn't want to stare, so I glanced up to the black velvet paintings my parents had collected through the years. Our Lady of Guadalupe glowed at me from the middle of an orange and yellow spray of fiery leaves. Next to her, the Blessed Mother held her baby, and over near the bathroom, President Kennedy stared out at the room. Then I noticed a mess of crumpled paper on the floor at the side of the bed.

"Da," I gasped, gazing from the floor to his face and back, "what happened?" I recognized them. They were pages from the bible and they were scattered everywhere.

"Gaaa!" he growled, twisting from one side to the other. "I was lookin' fer some consolation this mornin'. So I went ta The Book a' Wisdom. Totally pissed me off. Couldn't find a drop a' wisdom. Not a bleedin' drop."

I bent down and began to gather up the ripped and wrinkled pages. "I'll iron them, Da. Put them back for you. Katie's funeral is in an hour," I said, still collecting them, straightening them out. "You've got to get ready."

Tears trickled down the sides of his face and disappeared into his gray sideburns.

"Wha's tha point?" Da croaked. "I don' t'ink Katie'll be there. She's lost. We'll never see 'er again, Agnes. When we left her inna hospital, how's I ta know tha' was tha last glance?"

"Even if Katie's body isn't there today, she'll still be with us."

"I donut understan' why God makes us suffer." He brought a corner of the sheet up to his eyes and took a swipe.

I didn't know what to say. If Da didn't know why God made us suffer, surely I didn't either.

"Why did He take Katie? Why her?" he sobbed into the sheet.

My heart sunk. I should have been the one to die. I glanced over at my mother's side of the bed, over to the lamp made out of a plaster statue of Mary. Katie had nicknamed it Our Lady of the Lampshade. This Mary's arms were outstretched, palms up. She looked like a willing target.

"I'm so filled wid mem'ries a' raisin' you kids. I cano' get tha images out a'my mind. Margaret 'as always tha spiritual one. Perfect tha' she became a nun. Darcy tha dark beauty, high-strung 'n hard to handle'n now those four kids—what pistols they are. Fiona's 'r bright spot, her flamin' hair like a beacon 'a joy. 'N you, Agnes Anne, ya were always tha steadfast reli'ble one, faith rigid as a stone wall."

I'd never heard myself described as a stone wall before. I've always known I was shy, and I always had faith, but stone walls were inflexible, stiff, and unyielding. I couldn't help but ask, "Da? Am I that rigid?"

"Hah! Like tha Sphinx itself," he said. "Yer tha only one in tha lot who'as a Special Devotion t'Our Lady."

I did have a Special Devotion to Mary, but I wondered if Da could sense I wasn't a virgin anymore. I wondered if something on the outside of me, something I couldn't control, announced my Fall from Grace.

"T'bad ya ruined yerself," he mumbled.

I gulped. A sob escaped my lips. "I'm sorry, Da," I whispered.

"Vanity surgery," he spat. "Wha' n' tha hell were ya t'inkin'?" His eyes regarded me with distaste.

Vanity surgery? He wasn't talking about—

"We can't d'anythin' 'bout tha past, now can we?" he said. "But'r Katie, she was tha fairest 'a tha whole lot, that long blonde hair... those bonnie blue eyes. She'as..." He gulped back tears. "M'little Gaelic princess... gone..."

In my mind's eye, I saw Katie's wig come off her head, and glimpsed her patchy pink scalp. Da didn't know about that, nor should he ever.

"Da?" I said, as though I needed to gently wake him. "You've got to get ready now." I wondered if he would ever sit up. I wondered if I told him that I broke up with Sheldon last night, if that would make him feel better. Then I decided he'd rather hear about Mary's Font. "I wanted to tell you, Da, you were right. Mary's Font did freeze over last night. I saw it myself."

Like marbles on a roulette wheel, Da's eyes ricocheted around his sunken sockets and finally focused on my face.

"Tha boys tol' me they t'rew in ice cubes," he said, "but if they did, then why did tha font freeze solid? It should'a been lumpy, like ice melting' in a whiskey glass, not smooth."

"Exactly," I said, lowering my voice to a whisper. "Maybe it's a miracle."

His mouth turned up into a near-smile and he pushed himself up on one elbow. "Ya saw it yerself then, did ya? Ya saw it."

"Yes, Da. A solid sheet of ice at the bottom of the font. So slick and smooth, elves could have danced on it. Sheldon picked it up and turned it over and over. It confounded him too."

"Well, 'e would be confounded, he's Jewish," he said,

throwing his weight back against the pillows. "Is tha ice there now?" Da's eyes grew worried. "'Tis it frozen still?" He shimmied up into a sitting position, his hair, what was left of it on top, stuck up here and there in wild clumps.

"No. I checked. The water's awfully cold, but the ice is gone."

"'Tis my fault. I always swear too much." He crossed his arms on his chest. "I shouldna'. Goddamnit—I mean, gaaaa!" He jerked around like he'd been stung by a bee "It's all m'fault! I'as tha one who said tha' so-and-so wouldn't happen unless tha Holy Water froze over. I shouldn'ta said it. That's a type 'a curse, Agnes Anne. It's wrong." After a pause, he whispered, "But God help me, I didna' want it ta mean that he'd burn her up. That we'd never see Katie again." His chin trembled. Tears were filling his eyes.

"Maybe Bruno will change his mind, Da, and the casket will be there today." I picked up the coffee cup, waiting for a chance to hand it to him.

"And Bruno's crematin' her!" he yelled. "My little Gaelic princess... burned!" Da's chin filled with tiny dimples and I thought he would start to cry again. "Maybe Bruno did this," he gulped, "because a' tha house."

"What house?"

"Tha fire," he whispered. "He's pissed because 'a tha' fire."

It felt like a dagger pierced my heart. "Da, about the fire, I didn't start it—"

Da gave me his famous hairy eye. "I never said ya did." He reached out and snatched the mug of coffee from me. "I said ya left tha *door* open."

"But I didn't do that either! Maybe Bruno did it."

"Burn down 'is own house?"

"For the insurance money. Bruno told me he insured it for more than the sale price."

Da slurped down his coffee in four gulps.

"Well tha' cheeky bastard, that scorchin' liar!" he said, smacking his lips. "I'll not give Bruno the pleasure of m'absence t'day! *Last night the Holy Water froze o'er fer godsakes!* For good 'r bad, surely it's a sign. *Our Lady was here last night, Agnes!*"

He shoved the empty cup back into my hands and I stood up to get out of his way.

"There's miracles all around us!" he shouted. Da hauled himself out of bed like a great rumbling beast, thundered into the bathroom, and slammed the door.

"He may be burnin' one O'Neil," I heard him say, "but tha' German heathen won't take us all down! We're O'Neils, goddamnit!" He opened the door and stuck his huge head back out. *"Remember, Agnes, t'day God is a Gael!"*

"Da's out of bed, Ma," I said, catching my breath. "He's getting ready."

Ma crossed herself twice and raised her eyes to Our Lady of the Scullery, that the old catechism tableau above the kitchen sink. The boys over by the bakery box raised their coffee cups to each other and clinked.

"Ha! Knew he would!" Mark said.

"Can't keep an O'Neil down," agreed Matthew.

While I watched them, a special expression telegraphed between Matthew and Mark. Fiona saw it, too.

"Wait a second," Fiona said, under her breath. "What are you guys planning?"

"Nothin'. Nothin'," Matthew said. He sat down and began to eye the sugar bowl. I watched his tongue roam aimlessly around his mouth, pushing his cheek out here and there. Something was going on.

"I don't care how much you hate Bruno," Fiona said. "You can't let it ruin our memories of Katie's service. This mass is for Katie, you guys, but it's also for us. We need to say good-bye to her. Not throw prayer books or take Bruno out to the parking lot and work him over. Okay?"

Matthew and Mark looked here and there, pursing and straightening their lips. Definitely suspicious.

"This m-mass is for K-Katie," I repeated.

"Is tha' right?" Da said, standing in the doorway. He looked imposing in his black suit. His eyes were doleful, yet razor-sharp. "Well 'f this mass is fer Katie, she should be there, dressed in nice clothes 'n properly laid out in'er casket. Di'ya call tha Father a' Saint Ivan's, Irene?"

"Yes, dear. We worked out a few t'ings 'bout tha service."

"But wha' about tha body?" Da bellowed. "Has Bruno found our Katie yet er is she still lost in outer space? Perhaps traveling in one of those nice funeral cars—a hearse. Yes, that's it! Instead of attendin' her own funeral, Katie's ridin' around inna big black hearse. If she's not there t'day, that's what I'll pretend... She's out there ridin' 'round San Francisco tryin' to find Saint Ivan's. *Because, damnit, I donut t'ink she's ever been there 'n her life!"*

"Malachi O'Neil, yer not ta speak ta Bruno," Ma said. "Yer not 'ta speak ta Father Stanovich either. D'ya hear me? I forbid it." As she said this, Ma had her finger in Da's face.

"Woooooooo," everyone in the kitchen said at once. Never had we seen Ma this riled up. Da was so shocked, he lost his voice.

Uncle Jimmy and Aunt Lucy came in the back door. Uncle Jimmy was wearing a green blazer with tiny white stripes running up and down. Today his bow tie was black. So was his bowler hat. As usual, Uncle Jimmy looked like an advertisement for whiskey.

The rest of us were in dreary black or navy. The kids were milling about, their hair bows beginning to slip, shirts beginning to untuck. I could see the kids were cranky from the late nights and that they were on a short fuse. The scent of disaster hung in the air like foul smoke.

Ma walked over to the stove and grasped the corners and bowed her head over the burners like she was praying at an altar, perhaps to Saint Martha, the patron saint of cooking. But I suspected her petitions were probably to Jesus and Mary. Ma was wearing the same tulle hat she wore last night, only this time all of her steel gray hair was combed tight and pulled severely back into a bun. Ma turned around to face us and cleared her throat.

"Listen ever'one. Listen," Ma said, clapping her hands like we were her catechism class and she was about to give us assignments.

The kitchen chatter twittered to a halt.

"I know we don' like wha' Bruno's done, bu' this mass is fer Katie. Do'ya hear me, boys? Fer *Katie*. I'll not be havin' ya ruinin' it like ya did las' night a' the Vigil. I was disgusted with yer behavior. Are ya listenin' to me? It's a matter of respect fer yer sister and fer the Lord. D'ya hear me, boys?"

Matthew and Mark didn't look up. Fiona and I raised and lowered our eyebrows at the same time. Something was definitely up with those two.

Luke came in the back door dressed in a dark suit. Handsome and tall, he looked more like Ma than I had ever noticed. He surveyed the scene. "What's wrong now?" he said.

"No shenanigans, Luke. This mass is fer Katie," Ma said, pointing a finger at him.

He raised his arms like he'd just been arrested. "Don't look at *me*, Ma."

Fiona and I turned back to Matthew and Mark. Both of them looked as innocent as Michelangelo's cherubs.

"I've spoken ta Bruno about tha mass," Ma said. "He agrees that the first readin' 'ill be said by Matthew, the oldest boy." Ma handed my brother a sheet. "A copy 'a this'll be on tha lectern. Second reading will be by Darcy, oldest girl... that is...tha oldest girl *here*." Ma handed Darcy a sheet and looked like she was about to cry. "I haven't...haven't called Margaret in Ireland..." Ma shook her head and made an effort to control herself.

I wanted to go to Ma and give her a hug, but felt if I did, she might break down, then I'd break down, and we'd all dissolve. We didn't have time.

"Well it's nice ta see tha' you n' Bruno are all lovey-dovey again," Da said, striding into the center of the kitchen to inspect the donut box. "Since yer so close ta tha good doctor, Irene, why can't ya get him ta put off burnin' Katie at the stake?"

"Where's Mitchell?" Ma said, looking around. "He's one 'a tha altar boys. The other one is from Saint Ive's."

"Right," Matthew said. "Mitchie's outside."

"I 'ope 'e's not getting' dirty," Ma warned.

Jennifer headed for the back door. I could hear her calling to him.

"Where's Sheldon?" Fiona asked.

It felt like a spring snapped inside. "I t-told him not to come... I... uh... we..."

Matthew and Mark leaned forward. "Ya broke up wid tha'

bloke? Well, I was waitin' fer tha'," Matthew said, slamming down his empty cup.

"Just's well," said Mark. "Any man 'ho paints 'is toenails—"

Fiona's grip on my forearm felt like an eagle's claw, her whisper hoarse and directly into my ear. "You didn't break up, did you?"

Tears came to my eyes. I wouldn't look at her. Couldn't look at her. I wanted to talk to Katie. *She would understand.*

"Why? Why did you do that?" Fiona growled.

"Just 's well," Matthew said. "He's Jewish. Never woulda' worked, Aggie. The Jewish faith is a whole different ball game. Latin wouldn't do ya any good over there." I couldn't listen to his hollow laugh.

"Yeah," added Mark. "They talk Yiddish or somethin' and the men wear little round beanies like they're all bishops."

"What were you thinking?" Fiona whispered. "He's one of the nicest guys I've ever met."

My mouth moved like a fish out of water. How could I tell her? How could I express my confusion, my guilt... the cold blanket of remorse that clung to me? And then the ice in Mary's font...

"Stop it, Aggie." Her lips again came close to my ear. "It's Just more P.T.V.S.S., that's all. Call him up and tell him you're sorry."

Ma clapped her hands to get our attention. There was a big discussion about cars and who would ride with whom. The kids wanted to ride together, but there wasn't enough room. With much squalling and shifting around, just like in the poem, *Kits, cats, sacks and wives, the O'Neils headed to Saint Ive's.*

49. Girl on Fire

DA AND I ENTERED SAINT IVAN'S blinking in the semi-dark. From above, the organist played various minor chords, then launched into a complicated fugue. It felt as though we had entered a haunted house. Abruptly, the music paused, then deep whistle blasts of air poured through the base octaves of the organ pipes, which sounded like the hollow blast of a cruise ship leaving the dock. The farewell vibration rattled through me. Katie was sailing away on the Titanic.

The altar, a huge rococo affair carved out of rose-colored marble, held a gilded crucifix and the most enormous candlesticks I had ever seen. I looked for Katie's casket, hoping that during the night, Bruno had relented and called off the cremation, at least until after the funeral.

One thing I liked and I could tell Da did, too, was a large icon of Mary in a small side chapel. As though pulled by a magnet, we both walked over to take a closer look. The painting on wood was surrounded by a jewel-encrusted frame twice the size of the oil painting itself. Mary seemed to squint at Da and me. The Christ Child she held looked more like a miniature man than a baby.

"A Black Madonna!" Da said, through a gasp. "Lovely, just lovely." Transfixed, he gazed at the icon, then with the awkwardness of a horse, Da lowered himself to the old kneeler in front of the painting. "They say, Agnes Anne,"he said, over his shoulder, "whenever ya pray t'a real Black Madonna, if yer sincere, she'll grant yer request. I'm goin' ta pray that Katie shows up today."

My heart pounded as I thought of Sheldon, sex, and the freezing of the Holy Water. Was Mary pleased that I had told Sheldon I couldn't see him anymore? I was so mixed up, I dropped to my knees beside Da, hunched over, and began to pray. I don't know how much time passed, as I had entered a bubble of my own, but I remember Da struggling to stand up, me helping him, and the two of us gazing with longing at the BVM.

Back outside where everyone was gathering before the

service, the intense light blinded me and my eyes were forced shut. When they adjusted, I could see old friends, acquaintances from high school, and chums from elementary school days as well as a couple of nuns from Mission Dolores.

The whole of O'Neil & Co. showed up, including Pansy the receptionist, her nails a respectable shade of pale lavender, and her gum, if she had any, parked somewhere deep in her mouth. Verna stood beside David and Brent, her wide-brimmed hat black and tilted at a nice angle. I wondered who was watching the office. I suppose they closed it today. No harm in that.

David and Brent came up and gave me a big hug, as did Verna. She made no comment about the condition of my hair. I tried to do it this morning the way Ritz Charisma taught me, but my hands were shaking so much, I couldn't run the dryer correctly. I had to revert to my old standard, the dropped ponytail set in a black bow to hide the rubber band.

There was a slam of car doors and I saw Sheldon heading up the front stairs with Dr. Helfer. *Sheldon! What was he doing here?*

The two of them were chatting as though they knew each other. What was even more strange, Sheldon walked right up to me as if last night had never happened and I had never broken up with him. With great ease, he began to introduce me to Dr. Helfer.

"We know each other," Dr. Helfer said, through a smile. I could see compassion in his eyes. I must have looked confused because he continued, "I've known Sheldon since he was a little boy."

Practically staggering, I couldn't help but wonder if he also knew that we had sex, then I realized if Sheldon's mother and Dr. Helfer were friends, Sheldon might be talking to him on a regular basis. *Oh, my God!*

Why was Dr. Helfer even here? I was his patient and I hadn't visited him since Katie died so how did he know about the funeral? Then I remembered that Bruno and Dr. Helfer knew each other and the doctor was probably here to support his friend.

This made my mind race. Did he know my sister, too? How much did Bruno talk to Helfer? Did Helfer discuss me with Sheldon? It all seemed so wrong.

And why was Sheldon here? Last night when he dropped me off at my place, I had told him we couldn't date anymore. I never said it was because the Holy Water froze over. I didn't give him a reason. He just stared at me and walked me to my door.

Sheldon took my hand. "How are you today, Anne?" His voice was kind and gentle.

"Why are you h-h-here?" I asked, not trusting myself to raise my eyes.

"I thought you needed support," he murmured. He brought my hand to his lips and kissed it.

The guilt of seeing him, the strange relief that he had come, then the immediate fury that he was here and he hadn't *listened* to me, made a peculiar mixture of rage and longing boil within me. The enormity of these fast-paced emotions made me nauseous and I had to will myself not to run to the curb and retch.

Over Sheldon's shoulder, I saw Bruno walking toward us. He stopped and crooked his finger to call me over. My cement legs hardened to the ground. I didn't let go of Sheldon's hand. Bruno's flinty eyes bored into me.

Bruno stomped over to me and kissed the air next to my ear. "I don't want a repeat of last night," he whispered. "Did you talk to your brothers?" He pulled away and stared into my eyes. They were filled with daggers, these eyes of his. I turned away.

"Is that clear?" Bruno repeated, tightening his grip on my forearm.

Words didn't come. And then something reminded me of Marilyn and I found my breathy voice and gushed, "Go tell Matthew or Mark yourself."

"You know what I mean, Agnes," he said, squeezing down on my arm even more. "Did you tell those hooligans what I said last night?" Suddenly, he noticed Dr. Helfer. Bruno's manner instantly became friendly and I was shocked when no one seemed to mind its pure fakery. Perhaps Dr. Helfer didn't know him well enough to see through it.

Bile returned. I swallowed it back. Too much was going

on. I felt weightless and fuzzy-headed. I watched Verna come up to Bruno and fawn all over him. I glimpsed the new role he would play: the sad and long-suffering widower, grateful to bask in sympathy.

Sheldon took my hand. "Are you all right?" he asked. He slid his arm around my waist and began to walk me slowly toward the front doors of Saint Ivan's.

I wanted to shake him off, but I couldn't, for in my swooning dizziness I literally needed Sheldon for support. Nonetheless, I wished he would go away and leave me alone, but the feel of his warm arm across my waist awakened something within me. A strange quivering involuntarily wound its way through me, melting the anger and hardness in my heart. I had the sudden desire to fall into his arms. Immediately, I countered this reckless craving, this yearning for him, by telling myself this walk together would soon be over. Soon he would stop touching me. I wanted to run from the church, flee from my desires. I wanted never to see him again. I wanted him to make love to me on the church pew.

That's not true, another voice within me said. I argued with myself as we walked together through the huge front doors of Saint Ivan's, our legs in perfect step.

"Stop it," I hissed at him. I tried to walk faster so I could distance myself from Sheldon, but my legs were unsteady and I stumbled.

"Take it easy," he whispered. "Let me help you."

I was losing Katie today and a part of me didn't want this interruption. Nor did I want to be reminded of my sins. I slid into the pew where my sisters were, but Sheldon not only kept up with me, he slid in beside me.

"What did Bruno say to you?" Fiona asked.

"He doesn't want a repeat of last night," I whispered. My hand found my throbbing forehead and rubbed it. "That's…" I paused, then forgot what I was going to say because Sheldon came so close to me, I could smell his aftershave as well as feel the warmth of his body. It was like Fiona and Sheldon were the bread and I was the meat inside a guilt sandwich.

Darcy and Domenic, sitting farther down the pew, leaned toward me and wanted me to repeat what Bruno had said. Then Ma and Da turned around from the pew in front and wanted to hear it as well. Bruno's request for good behavior rippled through our side of the church. The rustle of whispers sounded like kindling beginning to burn, a prelude to a bonfire.

50. Where There's Smoke...

THE ORGAN PIPES SHOUTED to the stained glass windows and the base notes vibrated my innards, crying out to all in the church that Katie O'Neil was dead. Those of us who knew the song sang it as best we could, pulling and dragging along our reluctant and fumbling church mates, helping them to diligently plod with us through the verses.

After the opening blessing, the priest stopped and cleared his throat. "Normally in a Catholic Funeral Mass, the body is present," he said. "The second best might be, if the person has chosen cremation, we would display the ashes of the deceased in a suitable urn and have them here with us at mass. Unfortunately, today I see that we have neither body nor ashes." He looked at the front pew where Bruno sat with his sister and her husband. "I understand the family's angst over this issue" Father Stanovich turned toward the O'Neil side of the church. "And I also understand that this has caused great heartache in the family. Nevertheless, it apparently was the wish of the deceased..."

Da said under his breath, "Like hell it was."

"...and thus we will proceed and pray for the soul of..." The priest halted at this point so he could refer to his notes, which awkwardly appeared from the folds of his vestments. He read, "Katie O'Neil Stark," as though he were announcing a name during college graduation.

My heart wore a tight girdle. I hated this church. I hated that we didn't belong here. Was this the priest Katie had confessed to? Or had it been someone else? Maybe it was good that he didn't know her. She had been anonymous. There was some comfort in that.

One of the altar boys, the one we didn't know, stepped down two stairs and walked over to the priest, turned his back to us, and presented the mass book he had been carrying. The priest opened it, flipped to the page he needed and began to say the first prayer. Before he had finished, I heard a great hiss coming from the tabernacle, much like the hiss of a snake.

No one seemed to pay any attention to this hissing. I thought it might be the sizzle of an old radiator. Looking up above the tabernacle, I noticed a wisp of smoke coming over the marble wall above the crucifix. It descended like a filmy curtain, rippling past Christ on the cross, flowing like a veil all the way to the ground. The misty drape began creeping across the floor and flowed silently under the priest's robe and out the other side toward us.

"Is there a fire?" Darcy gasped.

"Fire!" someone shouted.

I watched spellbound as the smoke continued to curl along the floor drop to the first step, then the second, and slither out between the break in the altar rail. More kneelers were knocked back into place, more scuffling as people moved toward the doors.

"Fire!" more voices called out.

I turned to see the front doors open and people push out into the bright light.

"We've got to save the Holy Mother!" Da yelled. He scrambled out of the pew, over to the side chapel, and went right for the icon of Mary.

"'Tis not fire," Matthew shouted, looking back to the departing swarm. "Hold yer horses everyone. We're not on fire!"

The priest spun around. The force of his swirling robes made the smoke curl around him in a hazy vortex. He bent down to sniff at it and then walked out of the sanctuary with both haste and purpose. I figured he needed to pull the fire alarm.

"'Tis tha Holy Spirit! I think it's after ya, Bruno," Matthew said, his voice unmistakably gleeful. "Look a'it! It wants ta talk to ya! Maybe Katie's in tha mist, eh, Bruno? Wann'a talk to her? Explain why ya burned 'er up?"

Sure enough, the smoke seemed baffled by the rug and started to form a hump right at Bruno's front pew. Bruno seemed shocked beyond speech. He turned to watch people flee, looked back to the altar and up at the smoke, which was now so thick it flowed over the wall above the crucifix like Niagara Falls.

Over in Mary's small alcove, Da still tried to shake the icon loose. I heard a ripping sound and suddenly the frame around Mary came off in Da's hands, but the icon remained pinned to the wall. He turned and shouted to the mourners, "Help me save Mary! She's wooden! She'll burn!"

Ma dropped her purse and missal and scrambled out of the pew. She tried to shake the icon loose from the wall. "She wo'nut budge, Mal."

Da turned to keep an eye on the thick, smoky fog pouring down through the altar rail and out into the pews.

"What 'ave we here?" Da asked no one in particular. "I smell nah smoke. 'Tis it a miracle?" Like a sleep walker, Da moved toward the mist still holding the icon's frame in his hands, his steps short and halting.

"'As Katie come ta see us?" he whispered. "Are ya there, Katie?" He stared into the mist like it might be a television and perhaps he could tune it in and get a glimpse of this daughter.

Bruno, still as a statue, clenched his jaw so tight his head trembled. He spoke through his teeth. "Stop this charade, O'Neil!"

The fog had indeed stopped at Bruno's pew, which I found so startling, I dropped to my knees, as did Darcy, then Jennifer and Susan. I half-expected to see a vision of Katie in the mist. Fiona, though, kept standing and leaned forward over the pew to take pictures with her cell phone. Sheldon joined her.

First it was the sauce pan, then the ice cube, then Jude's snail tracks, I thought. *The Holy Water froze the night she died. Could this be another miracle?*

"What is this stuff?" the priest said, looking this way and that. It was now up to his waist. He parted it with his arms.

Someone said it didn't smell like smoke. I heard more commotion behind us, more people leaving, and in the distance, the unmistakable sound of sirens.

"Maybe Katie's come fer retribution, eh Bruno?" Mark growled. "She did'na wan' cremation, eh? Maybe she's back, eh? Maybe she's here ta give ya a piece 'a her mind, eh? What d'ya think a tha' ye corpse burner?"

The mist arched its back, rose to Bruno's eye level, and began to envelope him. He cast his arms back and forth trying to force it away, then he turned to helplessly watch as his colleagues fled through the ancient church doors. Bruno's lips curled into a snarl and his legs crumpled under him. The sound of Bruno's head striking the wooden rail echoed throughout the cavernous church.

I heard the rumble of fire trucks and soon beefy firefighters poured through the double doors wearing their thick black and yellow jackets. They told us to evacuate. Da still stood in front of the entrance to the small side chapel, protectively holding the frame of the icon, the mist now enveloping both him and Ma. Axes in hand, other firefighters boldly ran up to the altar and disappeared into the smoke. Another fireman ministered to Bruno, now sitting up and surrounded by a couple of his stalwart colleagues, the ones who hadn't fled the imminent flames.

"What's this?" Father Stanovich shouted as he spotted Da with the icon's frame. He ran to the side chapel, sending the mist swirling into the air. "What are you doing with our icon?"

"We have ta save Mary!" Da shouted.

The firefighters watched Bruno bleed into his handkerchief. Bruno started to swear under his breath, accusing the O'Neils, damning Da as well as my brothers. A couple of Bruno's colleagues announced to the firefighters that they were doctors.

All the O'Neils were again told to evacuate. But I didn't feel threatened. The smoke was thick, but breathable. We ignored the request. Fiona, Sheldon, and I left the pew to stand protectively in front of Mary's tiny alcove.

"What are you doing with that frame? Put it down," Father Stanovich yelled.

"H-h-he thought the p-place was on fire," I said, shocked that Da could be accused of anything but the best of intentions. "He has a special D-Devotion to Mary. He would never—"

Father Stanovich turned to me and narrowed his eyes. "He just destroyed a three-hundred-year-old icon!"

"He's rescuin' Our Lady from tha fire!" Ma countered.

A firefighter came up to us. "Father?" the man said. "It's a smoke machine. Basically dry ice and a fan. You're not on fire."

"Dry ice and a fan." Father Stannovitch regarded Da with newfound contempt. "Dry ice and a fan and you try to steal our most precious—"

"Hold on now, Father," Da said. "Mary's precious ta me. I thought there was a fire, for goodness sakes. Fire wouldn't hurt one a' these stone statues, but Mary here. I wouldn't let anythin' bad happen ta Our Lady. 'Tis a Black Madonna!"

"You've gone too far, O'Neil," Bruno said, staggering out of the pew while he still blotted the cut and bump on his forehead. "You and your trashy family have gone too far."

"Don't ya be callin' my family names, ya corpse burner." Da took a step toward Bruno. Bruno's friends moved in-between. Sheldon and I each held one of Da's arms, but he stepped forward anyway and, as he did, we heard a nauseating crunch. Everyone looked down.

Through the dissipating mist at Da's feet, a red stone lay cracked and smashed like a bug on the marble floor.

"Oh, my good Lord!" the priest said. "You've stepped on a jewel! Stop it! Put that frame down or we'll lose every precious stone in it. Do you hear me? *Put that frame down!*"

"Oh! I'm sorry," Da said, taking a sudden step back. "I'll replace it. I'll get all a' this fixed."

"I don't want you to touch a thing, Mr. O'Neil. Do you hear me? We have experts to fix this. And believe me, you *will* get a bill. *You will get a bill for all of this.*"

When the smoke began disappearing, people started to come back into the church. One of the firemen asked Bruno if he wanted a ride to the hospital, which of course he didn't because half the ER doctors were right here.

Bruno turned his back to us and spoke in whispers to his colleagues while his sister daubed at his temple like Bruno's droplets of blood were as precious as the Blood of Christ.

Da surrendered Mary's frame and we all looked for stones that might have fallen out. Sheldon found one and handed it to Father Stanovich. The frame was taken to the sacristy at the side of the altar. Turning around, I saw Dr. Helfer. He gazed at me sadly, his eyes heavy with both misfortune and sympathy. There was enough fodder in this funeral to last for a month of psyche sessions.

Because the Black Madonna was no longer overshadowed by the enormous jeweled frame, the actual painting of Mary seemed bigger now than it had before. I tried to pray to her, but I couldn't. My head seemed to be in a worse jumble than before and in my mind's eye, I kept seeing Bruno sink to his seat, then fall forward and hit his head. I'd never seen Bruno helpless before and the picture of it filled me with perverse delight, which I'm sure was another sin.

Straight as a stick, Ma stood before the icon. "Terrible 'bout 'er frame," she said, softly. "Yer right, Malachi. If tha place were ta go up in flames, someone 'ad ta save Our Lady. I donut care what tha' priest said. Frames can be replaced. The icon 'a Mary can't. I'm proud 'a ya, dear. Proud 'a ya. Ya did the right t'ing."

Da nodded, blew his nose, and soon we all returned to our seats and waited for Father Stanovich to come back so we could get on with Katie's funeral mass. The fire and smoke event had apparently been an icebreaker, as people were now having jolly conversations among themselves in the pews.

A few minutes passed.

Still no Father Stanovich.

Still no mass.

Bruno sat in the front pew chatting with his doctor friends, telling everyone he was all right. Eventually, Bruno stood up and walked through the altar rail and went back to the sacristy. A few minutes later, he reappeared. I could see the bruise on his forehead glistening over the lump. The cut still wept. Nevertheless, he wore a sly smile and walked arrogantly down to where he had been sitting, leaned into the huddle of his friends and began whispering. Next, he came over to us.

"May you rot in hell. All of you." With military precision, Bruno pivoted and walked over to fetch his sister and her husband and take them down the aisle and out of the church. Some of Bruno's friends and colleagues, Dr. Helfer included, followed.

Both my brothers stood up like they were ready to take Bruno outside and settle things, but Da said, "Sit down, boys. Sit down."

They actually obeyed. I heard Matthew mumble, "They're all leavin'? Good riddance t 'em."

Then I heard a small voice, it must have been Aula, her chirpy trill clear as the whistle of a bird, "My daddy said yer a feckin' gobshite."

51. Funeral Mass

FATHER STANOVICH TOOK HIS TIME returning, and everyone, except those who left with Bruno, remained in the pews. We were like passengers on a broken-down bus, waiting patiently for a replacement. But when Mitchell, now out of his altar boy robes, came back to us, we knew something was very wrong.

"Why are ya here?" Da asked him.

Head down and hair covering the tops of his eyes, Mitchell mumbled, "Father said the mass is over."

Da shot to his feet. "Over? It never started."

Mitchell shrugged and climbed over his brother and sisters, sat down, and waited with the rest of us.

More mourners, unsatisfied and confused, began to drift off. Some of them came up and said good-bye to us before they left. Da, brooding like a storm cloud, continued to sit facing forward, arms folded over his chest. He only spoke when spoken to.

Finally, when there was practically no one left in the church but us, Ma stood up, turned around, and faced the family. "Well, if this poor priest can't say mass fer our dear Katie, then I think we should say a Rosary ourselves. Hmm? Later, we'll have a proper service at Mission Dolores. Father Mac'll take care of it."

We nodded.

"Shall we say tha Sorrowful Mysteries?" Ma said, looking around for some concurrence.

"No, Irene, we should say tha Glorious," Da said. "This is about Katie's entrance inta heaven. Let's say tha Glorious Mysteries."

"But this's a funeral, Mal. I think it should be tha Sorrowful," she said, looking down at her husband sitting like a good schoolboy in the pew.

"Katie always liked tha Luminous Mysteries," Susan suggested.

"Ah, fer godsakes," Matthew said, "who cares what flavor of Rosary i'tis? Just say any old damed Rosary, Ma, n' get on wid it. This place gives me tha willies."

"Go on, Ma," Mark added, "jus' say a Rosary. A naked Rosary."

Color slowly drained from Ma's face. For a fleeting second, I thought she might be angry enough to strike both her sons.

"Well, I suspect tha' we're 'n this fix, Matthew dear, because 'a ya. I donut know how 'r why, but I t'ink you somehow 'ad a hand 'n all this smoke business." Ma turned to face forward and I heard her grumble as she knelt, "A naked Rosary. *Indeed.*"

Ma's head swiveled to take another glance at Matthew. We all knew that if he were still a little boy, right after mass, perhaps in the parking lot, he would have been spanked. I heard Darcy giggle.

Ma cleared her throat and began in a loud voice, "We will say tha Glorious Mysteries and meditate on the Resurrection, tha Ascension, tha Descent of tha Holy Spirit, the Assumption 'a Mary inta Heaven, 'n tha Coronation of Our Lady." She turned around again and shot both Matthew and Mark a look that could have shriveled a brave man's testicles, then she turned toward the crucifix, looked up, and began the Apostles Creed.

For my part in this family pageant, I had trouble saying the Rosary. While everyone else repeated the litany, I stared into the side altar and regarded the frameless painting of the brown-eyed icon of the Black Madonna, her head the shape of a tulip bulb planted upside down. Mary seemed to wearily scrutinize the O'Neil clan, disapproval apparent on her stingy lips. This wasn't the benevolent Lady of the Font, or even the kind, but sickly, Our Lady of Dyspepsia in the dining room, or the hard-working Mary at the side of Mission Dolores, the one with a waffle on her head. This was a defeated Mary, a Mary I didn't know.

Outside the church, we had another surprise. The arson inspector and a couple of other men were waiting. They regarded all of us like we were a bunch of hoodlums. I threw my shoulders back, said a prayer to Marilyn Monroe, and walked over to the arson inspector.

"Do you remember me?" I gushed. He rolled his eyes. "When do I get my car back?"

He practically snorted. "Does arson run in your family?"

"There wasn't a fire," I said defensively.

One eyebrow shot up. "Oh, really? A fake fire is still a crime."

I took a deep breath and repeated, "How do I get my car back?"

"Call the number on the slip I gave you."

"I do call, but—"

"And if I were you," he interrupted, "I'd get a good attorney."

52. Help from Helfer

"ANNE! ANNE! GOOD TO SEE YOU," Dr. Helfer said, as he showed me through the long hallway and into his dusty office. The 1960s furniture now felt familiar and the combination of the musty scent, the paintings, and Dr. Helfer's hulking desk, oddly enough, were comforting.

"What should we talk about today?" the doctor said.

I didn't know what to say. I couldn't tell him how glad I was to see that his crusty scalp was better. I had to think of something else.

"The funeral?" he said, after a long pause. He shook his head. "A very unfortunate event. Humorous in a most unbecoming way. Sad, too. I've never seen anything quite like it. Your family... " He shook his head and said no more.

I sighed and nodded. I hadn't come to speak of my family. His eyes were on me, two deep watery-blue pools.

"How are you, Anne? How is your grief proceeding?"

I didn't answer.

Dr. Helfer kept the silence. He waited for me.

"There's no grave," I whispered.

"Ah, yes. The cremation." He nodded. "I could see how it upset your family."

"Yes."

He watched me while I silently drifted off remembering that morning, that hideous funeral morning.

"I'm glad you've come to see me, but I sense a reluctance on your part. Remember when we were standing on the steps of the church that morning? You saw me with Sheldon and I could see something in your eyes. I could almost hear your thoughts. Me, your doctor, with Sheldon, your boyfriend. Me, your doctor, knowing your sister's husband. I think it caused you distress. I want you to know that therapy is confidential. Strictly confidential. I would never tell anyone anything you said to me."

My face flushed. He had sussed me out.

"All right?" Dr. Helfer said, softly. "Do you understand?"

I nodded, but I didn't know if I believed him. Maybe, like Da said, I was rigid as a stone wall. Dense as one, too.

"Good. Now what should we talk about?"

"I brought Katie's death certificate and I'd like you to see it." I fished out the piece of paper, slightly wrinkled because I had been sleeping with it under my pillow. "I went to City Hall to get it." I reached out and handed over the certificate.

"Ah," he said. "She had a heart attack. That's what this *myocardial infarction* means."

I wanted to scream that beautiful Katie couldn't have died of such ugly words.

We sat in silence. The tick of his wall clock seemed like a time bomb.

"We all must die of something," he whispered, his wizened face, both sad and sympathetic.

"She was too young to have a heart attack," I said.

"I heard she was anorexic." Dr. Helfer set the death certificate aside. It was so wrinkled it wouldn't lie flat, but seemed to undulate across his desk as though Katie could be in that paper and fighting to get out.

"Who told you?" I asked.

"That she was anorexic? Dr. Stark told me."

"He would," I snorted. "Bruno would say that, but it's not true. I think it was something else. She wanted to eat, but food made her sick."

"People who have anorexia frequently do get physically ill when they eat. Their system is starved for nourishment and minerals. They can have irregular heart beat and this can end in a heart attack."

"Katie wasn't starving herself because she thought she was fat. It wasn't that way. Katie had a good image of herself. Except she was horrified about the changes to her body. She saw it wasting away. She tried to eat, but food gave her diarrhea and she grew paler and sicker and her hair began to fall out." I felt tears pushing up behind my eyes.

"That happens sometimes with anorexia. It's a slow starvation of the body by the mind."

"*She didn't have anorexia,*" I said, so vehemently Dr. Helfer twitched. "She kept eating, but it didn't do any *good*."

"Anne," Dr. Helfer said, "you must accept the fact that your dear sister is dead and it's not your fault."

"I never said it was." Tears teetered on my lower lids.

"Let's change the subject," Dr. Helfer said. "How is Sheldon?"

I was too embarrassed to say that I hated him, nor would it be true. I pulled a tissue from the box on Dr. Helfer's desk, daubed at my face and used the time to think.

"Are you still seeing him?" Dr. Helfer queried.

I shook my head.

"And why not?"

The truth weighed on one side of me, a big fat lie on the other. I decided to tell the truth. "I gave him up."

"Gave him up? What do you mean?" Dr. Helfer's jaw dropped to his worn necktie.

"I told him to go away."

"You don't like him anymore?"

I couldn't answer that.

"You gave him up... like a mother gives up a child for adoption?" he said, his cheerless eyes seemed to tilt down at the corners.

"Yes. Like that. You give up something you love... because you know they'll be better without you." My chin trembled, but I tightened my muscles so the twitching would stop and whispered, "You know it's the right thing to do."

"I see." Dr. Helfer played with his pen. "Did the Virgin Mary tell you to break up with him?"

"No. It was my idea."

"May I ask why?" Dr. Helfer waited. "I think you need to verbalize this, Anne. Take your time."

"Because..." Finally, in a giant blurt, I yelled, "We had sex the night Katie died!"

The doctor remained silent. "And?" he whispered.

I spread my hands palms up giving him the signal that I had already shown him the reason. There was nothing more to say.

"That's not a reason," he said.

I couldn't speak.

"Was he a gentle lover?"

I nodded. Tears started to roll down my cheeks and collect on the folds of my sweater.

"But now you've rejected him," he prompted.

I nodded again.

"Is Sheldon happy about this?"

"I d-d-don't think so," I managed to croak.

"But you rejected him because you felt guilty."

I gave him a half-hearted shrug.

"Guilty that on the night your sister died, you had sex with your boyfriend."

My nod was feeble, but perceptible.

Dr. Helfer's voice grew tender. "Was this your first time?"

I looked down to my lap and watched tears soak into my sweater. Slowly, I nodded.

"Anne, I'm not Catholic, but I understand orthodoxy. We Jews have our rules as well. The worst burdens in life come from dogma clashing with life events. Both our religions agree that lovemaking is a gift. A very beautiful gift. Perhaps for you, this gift came at the wrong time."

I thought about that while I swiped at my eyes. In the midst of my confusion, I began to hear an inkling of sense. I raised my eyes to meet the good doctor's.

"Have you been praying about this?" he asked.

My breath trembled as I pushed out the words. "Only for the strength t-t-to give him up."

"I think you shouldn't be so hard on yourself, Anne. You fell in love—a perfectly normal thing to do—and now you have mixed up your sister's death with your personal joy. Is

God so vengeful that He would want you to suffer because your sister died?"

I shook my head.

"Would Katie like it if you gave up your boyfriend because she's not here?"

I shook my head again.

"All right, then. I think you might want to have an open mind about this."

We were silent for a long time, then I looked up at Dr. Helfer. "Am I too rigid?"

Dr. Helfer paused. "Yes," he said, nodding his head. "Sometimes, I believe you are."

I needed to go home and think about this. I couldn't figure this out while sitting in front of him. "I still don't know why Katie died," I whispered.

"I told you—"

"No, you didn't," I interrupted. "You said she had a heart attack, but why wasn't there an autopsy?"

"Wasn't there?" Dr. Helfer absently scratched at the fringe of hair above his ear and I watched the white fleas of dandruff pop out.

"No. Bruno found a doctor to sign off. That's what he called it. *Signing off.*"

"Ah. Interesting." Helfer reached for the wrinkled death certificate again and examined it, then leaned back, his hands a tent across his sunken chest.

"Her hair fell out rapidly. All in a week. The night she died—when she fell off the chair—her wig fell off."

"Oh dear. What a shock for you." His head tilted to one side while he tis-tisked and frowned.

"Bruno never was nice to us, you know. As soon as the death certificate was signed, he arranged the cremation. No viewing of her body. Nothing. Boom. We never saw Katie again."

"Dr. Stark remains a very sad man," Helfer said.

I wasn't going to be dissuaded by Bruno's acting skills. I moved on.

"I know you never believed me. Not really. About that night at Katie and Bruno's house when he came after me. I'm not the type who would ever commit suicide, Dr. Helfer. Bruno made all that up. Now I think he did something to

Katie to make her sick. To make my family grateful that he took care of her."

The doctor stared at me and allowed me to ramble on.

"I've been on the Internet and I think he has a condition."

"Dr. Stark has a condition?" Now Helfer was amused.

"Yes. It's ah... um... it's called Munchausen by Proxy." I waited for him to respond.

Helfer nearly laughed. "Why would you say Dr. Stark has Munchausen by Proxy?"

"Because he took delight in Katie's sickness. She was completely dependent on him. My father always called him "Bruno-god-love-him" like it was all one word. That was his name: Bruno-god-love-him. Now my dad's furious about the cremation, mind you, but before, Bruno was a hero who watched after his beautiful daughter. And since Bruno was a doctor, no other opinion mattered.

"We could all see how Katie's health slowly deteriorated, especially after the last miscarriage, and we were all relieved that she had a doctor to take care of her. But all this time, Bruno was pressuring me to have sex with him. He was coming up to me at family functions, standing too close, calling me up, asking me out. Telling me he married the wrong sister. It was *disgusting*."

"Relax, Anne. Calm down." Dr. Helfer reached for his pad and began to scribble.

"You don't believe me, do you," I said, my voice a monotone.

Dr. Helfer looked worn out and I felt sorry for him, sorry that I told him these tales. It was obvious he didn't know what to say.

"Go ahead. Tell me you don't believe it. Tell me you think that Bruno is a wonderful person. That he couldn't possibly have done anything to Katie. That he couldn't possibly have ever been attracted to me. Go ahead, Dr. Helfer, *say it*."

Dr. Helfer put down his pad and pen, and touched his chin. "You're very angry today."

"Damn right." I stared at him for a while, then added, "I am rigidly angry. I also know, Dr. Helfer, I am rigidly right."

There was more silence between us. I listened to his breathing, the bong of the hall clock, the impatience of a distant car horn.

"Let's look at the other side, shall we, Anne?" Dr. Helfer said, breaking the silence. "You have quite a checkered history, you know. You converse with the Virgin Mary. You were brought to the hospital last month in hysterics, you just broke up with someone you love because of deep-seated religious-based guilt, and you want me to believe that Dr. Stark has ingratiated himself with his in-laws by purposefully making his wife ill and is also responsible for her death. You think he connived not to have an autopsy in order to hide a murder."

My face relaxed, my shoulders slumped back against the padded chair. "Yes," I said. "That's precisely right, Dr. Helfer. Thank you, thank you, thank you! Now you're getting it."

But his reaction wasn't so gleeful and I watched as he again scratched at the little fringe of hair above his left ear. Pop, pop, pop. Bits of dandruff leaped out.

"Don't you realize, Anne, how ridiculous this sounds?"

"No. I know Bruno poisoned my sister. The signs are all there. Look for yourself."

Dr. Helfer tucked a patronizing smile into the corner of his cheek. "And what poison would this be, may I ask?"

My face grew serious, my voice firm. "From my research, probably thallium."

"Thallium," he repeated. His eyebrows rose and remained like small gray mouse tails on top of his droopy eyes.

"It happens all the time in Russia," I said. "Read back issues of *Newsweek Magazine*. You'll see."

Dr. Helfer didn't look at me, his eyes had locked on the corner where the ceiling met the wall. I watched his eyebrows lower and begin to independently twitch, first the right one, then the left, then both. It was quite a show.

"Alexander Letvineko, 2006," I blurted. "Two Americans visiting Russia in 2007."

"We are not living in Russia, Anne," he said. The reproach in his voice saddened me.

"A doctor could get it, though," I said, trying to make a defense. "Couldn't he? It's a powder. They used to treat ringworm with it. It's an ingredient in some rat poisons. He could have mixed it in her food, a little at a time. Enough to make her not feel well. Enough to establish that Katie was sickly, always weak, always pale, always ailing. Everyone knew it. Then, when he was ready, boom!" I shouted, then I leaned forward over his desk and whispered, *"He gave her the lethal dose."*

Dr. Helfer breathed in through his nose. It sounded like he was sucking wind through a snorkel. "Anything else to add?" he asked. I couldn't tell whether he was being sarcastic or whether he was merely humoring me.

"Bruno insisted she eat her vanilla pudding, Dr. Helfer. Bruno made it with some extra spoons of protein powder. Katie even asked me to make it for her. And I did. The thallium was probably mixed into the protein powder."

Helfer's eyes were filled with doubt, but they didn't leave my face. I sensed an advantage and continued.

"The day after her death, we all came over to their house. We used the refrigerator. All traces of the pudding and the protein power were gone. If there was nothing wrong with them, why would he decide to clean his refrigerator the day after she died?"

Dr. Helfer's chin tilted left, then right. "So Bruno cleaned his refrigerator. That is not proof of anything."

"I know," I said. "But there is proof. A couple of weeks before, I took a sample of both the protein powder and the pudding." A devious smile crept across my face.

Our eyes engaged and I could see him hesitate, see a definite uncertainty play in his eyes.

"My goodness," Dr. Helfer said, "where did you put it?"

"I'm not going to tell you where I put it, Dr. Helfer. You might tell Bruno. And then he'll come for me and destroy it."

"Anne," he said, through an exasperated and wheezing heave of air. "Everything you say here is confidential."

I pretended not to hear him. "You know, Doctor," I said, looking around at the old prints on the wall, at the foxes being chased by the hounds, the horses jumping over stone walls, "this has been the first session I've had with you where now I actually feel better."

"You feel better?" Helfer squeaked.

"Yes," I said. "Getting it all out does do wonders for the soul. Sort of like a confession to a priest, but without absolution. There's just one more th-thing."

"There's more?"

I wanted to speak, but my breath wouldn't move in, nor would it move out. I felt like I was on the edge of a cliff and I needed to jump.

"Goodness me, are you all right, Anne?"

I had to do this. I had to make myself say it. "Yes, I'm a-a-all r-right," I stammered. Then I remembered the gush. "There's just one more thing I have to say—something I've never told anyone before. I m-mean, I've confessed it, sort of broadly, to a p-priest, but I still feel bad."

"My goodness," he said, blinking rapidly. "What is it?"

I inhaled and whispered, "It's about what happened the night of my Junior Prom."

53. Melancholy Standoff

TWO WEEKS INTO this fuming standoff between my family and Bruno, we still had no body to mourn, nor grave to visit. The grief amongst us burst forth in wild waves of anger and as sure as firing shotguns at each other, the snipes and broadsides left a poisonous melancholy on everything. Feelings were hurt, our resilience tested, saints praised, and Mary daily entreated for her intercession into Bruno's heart so he would give us Katie's precious ashes.

As for me, I had even more to think about than Bruno's stubborn withholding of Katie's ashes. I waited to either get my car back, or be charged with arson. Every approaching stranger seemed menacing. Every phone call promised doom. I rushed home before dark, locked my door, didn't answer my phone and cursed the day I had taken an apartment by myself. I hated being alone. I hated my life.

One night, gripped in this chokehold of misery, with everything funneling around my head in a giant tornado of emotion, I seized the small statue of Mary from my dish garden. *Let her experience darkness*, I thought. *Let Mary feel the pain of abandonment.* With all the strength I could muster, I pitched her out the kitchen window.

After I did this horrible deed, my head ached and I turned away and staggered to the living room to sit on the couch. But the living room was empty. The couch wasn't there. I had already rammed it up against the front door. I swayed over to it and let myself fall against the soft pillows. I lay there without thought, tears drying on my face, my heart empty and without hope.

The doorbell nearly gave me a heart attack.

"Who—who is it?" I said.

I heard a male voice. "It's me, Sheldon."

What was he doing here?

"I d-d-don't want to—" The words stuck in my throat.

"I have Mary," he said.

"Mary?" I croaked. I pulled myself up on one elbow and turned toward the door, which, since the couch was up against it, was only inches away.

"Mary who?"

"Geez, Anne, I don't know her last name. Uh—Mary David? You know, Joseph's wife. From the Bible. *Your Mary.*"

"Go away."

"Come on, Anne," Sheldon said, gently. "Open the door. I've got your statue."

I pushed the couch back enough so I could open the door a few inches. Sheldon stood there; the head of the Virgin Mary peeked out of the top of his clutched hand. My eyes roved from the statue up to Sheldon's face.

"I don't know. I was just driving by and I saw your lights on and—" He looked down at his feet and shuffled. "You know, I check up on you once in a while, to make sure you're all right. I saw your lights. Are you all right, Anne?"

I couldn't answer. The lump in my throat hurt too much to speak.

"So, I'm standing on the sidewalk and all of a sudden something came shooting out the window and landed on the lawn in front of me." Sheldon held up my small blue statue like it was a bowling trophy. He cocked his head to one side. "What happened?" he whispered. "Did you mean to throw it out the window?"

Disloyalty pinched my heart. I couldn't look at him, but he was at my door and in some strange way, I had hoped for him.

Sheldon's voice sunk to a whisper. "Anne, what's going on? Are you really all right?"

I nodded. Then snatched the Virgin Mary from his hand. "Yes, I'm f-f-fine. I've got to go." I started to shut the door, but his hand darted out and braced it open.

"Is that your couch in the hallway?" he said, peering behind me.

Embarrassed that I had opened the door too far, I shrugged as though it wasn't there and he must be hallucinating.

"Don't you feel safe?"

I shook my head. "No. I mean, yeah. I'm fine. Thanks. Thanks a lot, Sheldon. Thanks for...for my statue."

I started to shut the door.

"Look," Sheldon said, pushing the door back, "maybe we've moved too fast. If having sex bothers you, we can wait."

I looked up into his eyes. They were kind. Gentle.

"Really?" I whispered. Two tears dribbled aimlessly down my face. I quickly swiped at them.

"Sure." He nodded. "We'll wait."

I didn't know what to say.

"And Jude?" he said, pushing the door open a few more inches. "Is he all right? You didn't throw—"

"No! Of course not. At the m-m-moment I can't find him. But he's there... er... here. Somewhere."

"Want me to help you look for him?"

My heart fluttered. I thought I might pass out. I turned around, pushed back the couch and let him in.

54. Nothing's Good About Good Friday

IT WAS FIRST FRIDAY AGAIN and close to the end of Lent. In fact, today was Good Friday, two days from Easter Sunday. All Da had been talking about was interring Katie by Easter. This, however, was impossible. We still didn't have her ashes.

Ma and Da had purchased a niche at Holy Cross Cemetery. I couldn't imagine what a niche looked like, nor could I imagine my sister squished into a tiny square. I banished the thought. I also banished the vision of her sickly skin, her wig tumbling off her patchy bald head, and her pale blue lips darkening to indigo.

We all helped Ma prepare dinner under the gaze of Our Lady of the Scullery. I had never noticed how tattered the edges of the picture had become. A layer of dusty kitchen grime lay across the top of the scroll, and even the string holding the tableau looked sandy. It struck me that Katie, too, had turned into dust.

While Susan and Jennifer peeled and cut up potatoes, my sister Darcy helped Ma with the frying of the fish and chips. Fiona and I set the table in the dining room.

In the parlor off the kitchen, the men were watching TV, the kids played games at their feet. No one was in the mood for our usual raucous First Friday. There was no ceremonious mixing of fancy drinks, no peals of laughter, no piano playing in the living room. Even Uncle Jimmy and Aunt Lucy had begged off tonight.

When the fish-frying was done, Ma called us all to supper. Like androids from another world, we filed into the dining room. Da stood at the head of the table and made his blessing.

"Bless us O Lord 'n these, Thy gifts, which we're about to receive from Thy bounty. Amen."

That was it.

I had never heard him give such a short blessing. None of us had, and we remained standing behind our chairs to hear the rest of it, fully expecting a rendition of the previous month's tragedies, the botched wake and vigil, and the fouled-up funeral.

Da opened his eyes and looked around. "Quit starin' at me with yer berry pies. Eat."

"Such a short blessin', Malachi," Ma said.

No one moved.

Ma closed her eyes and said, "Bless 'ur daughter Katie, O Lord and keep 'er under yer wing. May all tha angels 'n saints welcome her inta yer Glory. May baby John be there ta welcome her inta Yer kingdom. We ask this 'n tha name of tha Father, tha Son, 'n tha Holy Spirit."

"Amen," everyone said.

Amid the scraping of chairs and the shuffling of feet, we sat down and began to help ourselves to the bowls and platters on the table.

There was no conversation, for I suppose we had nothing to say. It was Susan, whose middle name should be Perky, who spoke up. "How's Sheldon, Anne?"

A piece of fish stuck in my throat. I forced a swallow and coughed. "He's picking me up at seven."

"Ye still aren't seein' tha' sheeny bloke, are ya?" Matthew said. "Tha one wid adorable feet?"

"What a man does with his feet is none of your business," Fiona said.

Mark stuffed his mouth with a huge wedge of potato. "He prob'bly wears pink underwear."

"White jockeys," I murmured.

"Ooooooooooo," my brothers crooned.

My face caught fire.

"No-o-o-oo," Da said, the air totally out of him. "Not ye, Agnes Anne! Not ye! Ya shouldn't know these t'ings. Yer a good girl."

"First off, Da," Fiona snapped, "she's no girl. She's pushing thirty."

"I'm twenty-eight," I retorted.

"Twenty-nine in a month," Fiona said. "I rest my case." She screwed up her face like she did when she was seven and I was nine.

The table erupted into a series of short questions, all aimed at me. I wanted to defend Sheldon. And at the same time, tell them all to shut up and leave me alone, but Ma stood up and shouted, "I forgot! I 'ave tha Good Friday Holy Water!"

Ma flew to the sideboard and picked up the small bowl of Holy Water she always brought home from church on Good Friday. She would now use the palms from the previous Sunday's Palm Sunday service to dip into the Holy Water and bless each one of us. She started with the kids' table in the corner.

"Bless my grandchildren, O Lord 'n keep 'em safe from harm. Let no evil fall upon 'em." Ma dipped the palm into the Holy Water and shook the palm leaves. Water flew off and landed on the squealing and giggling children.

"Let m'children thrive in honesty 'n righteousness," Ma said, at the foot of our table. She dipped the palms into the water and flung droplets out across the expanse of food and drink. Everyone made the Sign of the Cross.

She came behind my chair and sprinkled me. "'N may Agnes Anne, who's 'ad a difficult year, Lord, while she maimed 'er face 'n moved out of 'r house 'n took up wid a Jew—may she learn ta find 'er footin' and regain 'er moral compass."

"Ma!" Fiona said. "That's not very nice."

"Well, it tisn't very nice wha' she did, 'tis it?" Ma said to Fiona. "'N how wud a nice girl know wha' sort of underwear a man wears?"

Everyone, except Da and me, laughed.

"'N bless m'sons, O Lord. Luke, who's never here." She dipped the branch and flung water to an invisible person. Ma next blessed Fiona and then Darcy and Domenic. At the head of the table, she blessed Da, then moved to my brothers and their wives.

"'N bless Mark 'n Matthew," she said in full voice. "'N forgive 'em fer what they did ta ruin tha funeral."

"I didn't ruin it, Ma," Matthew said.

"Yes, ya did," Ma said. Her eyes flashed fire. "'N fer tha', I can barely be civil to ya."

When Matthew protested, Ma's jaw locked tight and she stood ramrod straight behind his chair. "May this Holy Water 'n tha Intercession 'a tha Holy Spirit cure ya of your deceitful ways." She lifted the bowl, as though offering it to heaven. "I ask this in the name 'a tha Father, tha Son 'n tha Holy Spirit, Ah-men."

We watched agog as the entire bowl of Holy Water cascaded over Matthew's head, drenching him back and front.

"Ma! Fer godsakes!" Matthew cried, jumping up. "Are ya crazy?"

He grabbed his soaking shirt and stripped it off his back.

Fiona applauded. "You deserved that, Matthew. That smoke-thing had your name all over it. You too, Mark."

In the general hubbub, we had not noticed the visitor. As more people spotted him, the room fell silent. Bruno Stark stood at one end of the table, his face coiled back into a crooked sneer.

"Good evening," he said. "I see nothing has changed in the O'Neil household." Bruno brushed some blond hair from his eyes and gazed down at us with unconcealed contempt.

"Where's Katie's ashes?" Da said, pointing his finger at him. "I wan' her interred by Easter, damnit. Easter." Da rapped the back of his knife on the table several times.

"I would have brought them," Bruno replied, smoothly, "but I'm on my way home from the hospital. I don't drive around with Katie's ashes, you know. I've been calling Anne. Didn't she tell you? I keep asking her to come and get them, but she's never bothered."

"Agnes Anne! Ya knew 'e had th'ashes?" Da gasped.

Fiona picked up my distress. "I'll come with her, Bruno. We'll come together to get Katie's ashes."

"No, I'd prefer to see only Anne."

Frozen with revulsion, I managed to glance at Da. He looked quizzical, but not negative. Surely, I thought, he'd see through Bruno's evil intent. But Da seemed hypnotized. His desire for those ashes had addled his brain.

I glanced over at my brothers. Matthew still stood bare-chested, drying himself with his rumpled shirt.

"Will you do that, Anne?" Bruno said. His voice brought me out of my trance.

"No," I said loud and clear. "I won't."

All sets of eyes riveted on me.

"You wouldn't want anything... *bad* to happen to them, would you?" Bruno's lower lip jutted out in a fake down-turned pout.

I flashed on all the things he might do with Katie's ashes. Pour them down the sink. Flush them down the toilet. He wouldn't.

Oh my God. Maybe he would.

"Bring the ashes here, Bruno," I whispered. "You owe us that."

"I owe you? *I owe you?* After that crazy funeral mass? Embarrassing me in front of my colleagues? Is that what you people think? *That I owe you?*"

"I t'ink ya owe us a lot," Matthew said. Still shirtless, he cocked back his arm and I worried what might happen next: a scuffle, punches thrown, broken china, maybe Our Lady of Dyspepsia used as a club—a terrible example for the children.

"Hold on," Da said, rising to reach out for Matthew's arm. I couldn't believe Da was saying this, but I think he was afraid of losing the chance to get Katie's ashes. Maybe he thought this was our last chance. My stomach turned sour.

Bruno backed up a step. "Take it or leave it, O'Neils. Anne needs to come over and pick up the ashes. The ball's in your court." The next sound was the slam of the front door.

"Why is Uncle Bruno mad?" one of the kids asked.

Everyone ignored the question.

"Uncle Bruno didn't bless himself when he left," Colleen added matter-of-factly. She returned to slurping her milk.

"Hell of a nerve," Da mumbled.

Ma still stood on the other side of the table with her hands clasped across her breast. She looked down into my eyes. Her voice plaintive and a bit unsteady, she whispered, "Can ya go, luv, 'n bring yer sister home?"

55. Ashes to Ashes

THE TABLE HAD BEEN CLEARED and dishes done; the little ones were already at the TV watching old Tom and Jerry cartoons. Matthew's shirt came out of the dryer no worse for the drenching, and Mark, Jennifer and Susan were still doubled over laughing about Ma's special "blessing." It was going to go down in O'Neil lore as The Good Friday Soaking. It was a dialogue on the TV that got my attention... one cartoon character kept asking, "Are you a man or are you a mouse?" It made me wonder what I was. Would I always be afraid of Bruno? Would I always cower at the sound of his name?

Was I a man or was I a mouse?

It was then I knew I had to be the one to pick up Katie's ashes. Everyone seemed occupied. It was the perfect time to sneak out of the house.

I spotted the hedges by Katie and Bruno's and swung my car—my newly sprung from Impound car—into their driveway. The misty fog reminded me of that horrible night when Da said I couldn't stay at the house anymore and Fiona didn't want me either and I ended up here. I inhaled and exhaled slowly. So much had happened since then. I had to leave those thoughts behind. I had to stay focused. Easter was in two days and I knew how happy it would make Ma and Da to have Katie with us on the day of the Risen Christ. My plan was simple. Knock on the door. Ask for the ashes. Don't enter. Leave as quickly.

Still sitting in my car, I made the Sign of the Cross and said a quick prayer. "Dear Lord, protect me in all I do. Amen." Then I added, "Saint Michael the Archangel, protect me." Then I said, "Dearest Mary, ever Virgin, protect me." I rattled on and on like this, calling upon all the saints from all the Holy Cards I had in my collection.

I thought again of Saint Michael and his swift sword. Crossed myself three more times and kissed my first two fingers, the ones I'd made the Sign of the Cross with, and for good luck, touched the Miraculous Medal hanging from my rear view mirror. *"Hail Mary, full of Grace, help me to not screw up."*

I stepped out of the car and was startled to hear a car behind me. The door opened. Sheldon stepped out.

"Sheldon! What are you doing here?"

"Fiona said you'd left. She thought you might have headed here."

"You needn't have come. I'm fine." I turned away from him and walked up the path to the house.

"Are you here for Katie's ashes? I'll come with you."

I turned around. "No. Don't. Bruno's a bully and this is something just I have to do. I'll meet you back at Ma's, Sheldon." He didn't move. "Go on," I said. "I'm okay. Really."

"But you—you—"

"I have to do this alone, Sheldon. I have to prove to myself that I'm not afraid of him. Okay?"

Sheldon looked dubious.

"Okay." Sheldon drawled out the word like he was a southern gentleman or maybe thought I was nuts. "I'll wait out here for you."

"I'll catch up with you back at my parents'. OK?" Now I sounded dubious. I snapped out of it. "See you there."

Sheldon climbed back in his car, but I could see his reluctance. I watched him start the car, heard the rev of the engine.

I approached the front porch with bravado, turned and waved at Sheldon. I found the knocker that Katie had purchased on their trip to Europe. It was the shape of a hand clasping a brass ball. I lifted it and released, then banged it several times and listened for Bruno's footsteps. Soon I heard the dull thud of his shoes on the hall floor. Or maybe it was the drumbeat of my own heart. The front door swung open.

"Why, little Agnes Anne," Bruno said. "You're *here*. I wondered if you'd come." He grinned like he had won at a game of cards and stepped forward to give me a weak peck on the cheek. I retracted my neck.

"No need to be rude," he said. "Just because we don't have Katie, we're still related. Aren't we?"

"Actually, no. I don't think so," I managed to whisper. "We're not anything to each other. I'm just here for her ashes."

"Yes, of course you are." Bruno made a grand gesture as though we was guiding me down the hallway. When I didn't move, he added, "Your sister's in the kitchen."

My heart felt as though someone had wrung it out like a sponge. *Katie? In the kitchen?*

"I'm not coming in, Bruno. Bring them to me."

"Well, I'm not touching them. If you want the ashes, come and get'em."

"No. Bring them here."

"What's your problem? Oh, you think—" He crossed his arms over his chest and snickered. "Guess what? I'm not interested in you anymore, Agnes. I have no interest in you whatsoever because I can tell you've already given yourself to that nerd. I like virgins... and you're no longer in the club." The smirk on his face made me want to slap him. "Am I right?"

"None of your beeswax."

"What a waste." He snorted. "I'm done with you and your crazy family. If you want your sister's ashes, then march your ass in there and get them." He pointed to the hallway.

I still didn't move.

"Well?"

"Bring me Katie's ashes," I said, louder this time.

"Look, if you don't want them, that's fine. I don't want them, either. I think I'll just flush'em down the toilet."

"No!" I shouted.

Bruno's smile, as I look back on it now, was calculated and smug. I should have walked away, yet the thought that he might do that, that he *could* do that, made me not want to take the chance.

I bolted past him and headed for the kitchen.

Bruno pointed to a white string bag standing tall in the middle of the kitchen island, next to the salt and pepper shakers, a bottle of olive oil, and a crock filled with cooking utensils.

"I-Is that it?" I said, gulping air. "Katie's in there?"

"Yes. That's it. Ten years of marriage. Ten years of hoping for an offspring, ten years of my devotion, ten years of nursing a sickly wife, ten years of complaints and that's all there is."

Anger frothed through my brain. "You forgot to mention the abortions," I said.

Lightening flashed through Bruno's eyes. "Let's not go there, *Anne.*"

"How could you ask her to do that?"

"Don't bring up the past," he said, sharply. "It's over. Take your sister. Run out the freaking door like Katie's a football and your car's the goal post." His hollow laugh disgusted me. Still, my feet didn't move and my hands didn't reach out to clasp the bag holding the dust of my sister.

"What's the matter? Never seen someone's ashes before?"

When I caught my breath, I shook my head.

"We all boil down to the basic elements, you know. I hear we're only worth about $4.98 on the open market."

"You killed her, didn't you," I whispered.

I watched a flash of horror cross his face.

"How *dare* you say that. Prove it."

"Someday I will. I took a sample of that pudding, you know. Wait until it's analyzed."

"You what? *You what?*" Bruno's face glistened with sweat.

He grabbed me by the arm and shook me. His fury made his neck swell and all the veins in his face looked about to rupture. I hoped they would all pop. It would be so nice to have natural causes sweep him from this earth.

"Tell me that's not true. Tell me, Agnes," he said, shaking me until my brain rattled. "Tell me."

"You did it. I suspected all along, but I d-didn't act on it. I didn't want to b-believe—"

Bruno slapped my face so hard my ears rang. Before I could recover, he dragged me into the den and threw me in his desk chair.

"Stop it," I screamed. Dizziness spun my head in a dozen directions.

Bruno grabbed for some paper and gave me a pen. "Write what I say," he commanded.

My hand shook. "No," I said. I forced myself to stand.

Bruno punched me in the side of my head. I slumped over, my head throbbed with pain. I heard the sound of ripping tape. Then Bruno wound silver duct tape around my hands, arms, and middle. He taped my legs to the heavy chair. I was so groggy, I couldn't seem to fight him off, although my mouth worked. I yelled and screamed help. Screamed for Sheldon. For anyone. The prick of a needle made me go limp.

"I want you to sign this, sweetheart," Bruno crooned into my ringing ear.

I raised my head and tried to focus, but it was no use. My eyes were blurry. Besides, there was no way I would do anything Bruno wanted. Ever.

I felt the pull of tape against the skin on my right arm. He had freed it. Then he put a pen into my hand and squeezed my stiff fingers around it. "Sign this," he commanded.

"No," I muttered. "Go to hell."

"Agnes," he yelled, "I want you to *sign* this."

My throbbing head hung low. There was a letter in front of me. A typed letter.

"Do you hear me? Sign it." He rapped the desk with his knuckles.

"Maybe I could hear if you hadn't clobbered me."

"Stop being sarcastic. What's going to happen now is very simple. You are going to commit suicide. I'm going to help you and it won't be painful, I promise. I'll tranquilize you so you'll be out, then I'll put you in the bathtub, pour in nice warm water and slit your wrists. Painless way to go. Really. It is."

My head banged like a drum. I had to get out of there. At that moment, I regretted sending Sheldon away. But I was always sending him away, wasn't I?

"Take the pen," Bruno commanded. When I wouldn't, he put my fingers around it again and squeezed them into place. "Sign your name like a good girl."

"Go to hell," I muttered.

He slapped his letter opener down in front of me. The edges of the sword had been sharpened. That's when I noticed he was wearing blue latex gloves.

"Do you recognize this?" he asked.

I stared down at the letter opener. Of course I did. It was the "evidence" he had given the police that night he tried to attack me. Even that Clipboard Lady at the nut house had bought into it.

I tried to glance up at him, but the pain in my head crushed my intent. This agony was a monster. I needed Saint Michael to slay it. To slay him.

Please, Saint Michael, help me.

Bruno put the pen in my hand once more and again squeezed my fingers around it.

He had to be kidding.

I scribbled all over the note and dropped the pen like it was a snake.

"That's fine, Anne," he said, in his slippery voice. "Scribbling over it will only make you look crazier. Now sign the damn thing, Agnes. Now."

I picked up the pen and wrote BRUNO KILLED KATIE.

Another blow to my head. Everything went dark.

56. The Last Ride

THIN KNIVES OF PAIN sliced through my eyes and my skull. The agony in my head clashed with the ache in my heart. Somewhere in this painful fog, I knew I had to wake up.

Through the slits in my swollen eyelids, I came to realize I was in a car. A back seat. I thought Bruno had said bathtub.

I squinted and tried to understand where I was.

This was my car. My back seat.

Then I realized the head I saw was the back of Bruno's head. *Bruno was driving my car.*

Where was he taking me? Could he be taking me back home?

Instinct said, fat chance.

I was in trouble.

Katie's sort of trouble.

I pushed myself up on one elbow, as far as the seatbelt and duct tape let me. "Where are you going?" I croaked. "I thought you'd kill me in the bathtub."

"This is plan B," he replied. "More realistic than you committing suicide in my tub. That plan was too hasty, didn't have the ring of truth. But this one's great."

"Creep," I muttered.

His conceited laugh seemed touched with madness. "Tell me about Sheldon. Was your love-making fun? Did you enjoy it?"

I was too busy trying to free myself to say anything. I picked at the edges of the duct tape.

"It should have been me, you know."

I struggled against the seatbelt. He had me in there pretty good. I tried to see where we were. Looked like Portola Drive. The forest on Twin Peaks was on the left.

"Won't talk about it? You're used up, Agnes. You know that? You're now a fallen woman. You're finished." Bruno turned around. I saw his eyes. They were crazed with hate and fury, and yet touched with fear. He stopped yelling and drove. I struggled against the tape, against the pain in my head, against the damn seatbelt. He had turned onto O'Shaunessy and we wound down the hill. Would he murder me in the eucalyptus trees? It was uninhabited down there in back of Glen Park.

"You're no better than a whore. You know that, Agnes Anne?" he yelled.

I collapsed back on the seat, praying, begging God, Mary, Joseph, Saint Michael and my guardian angel to stop him. Again, I tried to see where we were. I didn't recognize anything. Now I saw industrial buildings. We went under a freeway. I glimpsed the lights of the ballpark in the distance. Oh no. We were down on the docks. It was dark. Old piers. Junky boats, weeds taller than the car.

"You're no better than a prostitute, you know that Agnes?" he yelled, again. "You're a trollop, a slut. Agnes Anne the nympho—"

The car bumped over something and bounced again and again. With every jolt, my head exploded in agony. Bruno gunned the engine, then abruptly stopped. My head bounced back against the seat. Pain throbbed though me.

I heard him take a deep breath. "Okay, end of the line, dear sister-in-law."

Cold air flooded in. He had opened the back door. "Tell me where the pudding sample is and I may let you go," he said. "Do you hear me?" Bruno forced my face around so he could look into my eyes. I spat at him.

Bruno jerked me out of the back seat and began ripping the tape off my hands and feet. Then he slammed the back door, opened the front door and threw me against the steering wheel. A blinding bolt of pain shot through my ribs.

"There you go," he said.

My blood ran to ice.

"Suicide. Pure and simple. You tried it before and now you'll succeed. Case closed."

He shoved my legs the rest of the way into the car and slammed the door. The car rocked. It didn't feel like the brake was set. My ribs practically screamed, they hurt so much. I couldn't get a decent breath. The dome light went out. Darkness surrounded me.

I felt the car move, rolling over something rhythmical and slotted, like big rough boards. Then the hood tipped down and I fell forward.

I heard a scrape and the car wouldn't move forward. It was stuck. From the back, Bruno seemed to be bouncing it, pushing from the rear. I heard grinding and groaning from beneath me, like the growl of a metal giant. I knew it was a matter of seconds before the car fell. But fell into what?

I heard someone yell, "Anne! Get out! *Get out, Anne!*" Was it real? Maybe I imagined it.

Behind me, scuffling. I pushed myself back and scrambled to find the door handle, but I was fighting against gravity, the car at a terrible angle. I thought my head might rip in two.

Why couldn't I open the door? I turned my body, but I fell forward and bumped against the steering wheel again, the forward pressure greater than I could fight.

I reached for the dashboard and found the car keys. Maybe I could start the engine and back up. But the engine wouldn't turn over. I fiddled with the shift. Park. It had to be in Park for the engine to start. I had to be pressing the brake.

The engine roared to life and I threw the gears into reverse, but nothing happened. Just noise from the front. Stupid me. Front wheel drive. My front wheels were spinning in space.

I glanced back. Saw shadows. Heard blows. Bruno was fighting with someone.

Again, the scream, "Anne! Get out!"

The car groaned and trembled and I was suddenly weightless and, for a beautiful second, I felt free, free of pain, free of everything. Then the car crashed into the water, bounced like a huge ball and floated in the darkness.

My fingers gripped the door handle and shook it. The door wouldn't open. Icy water touched my feet. I scratched around to find the window buttons. But they wouldn't operate. Fright shivered through me.

Freezing water surrounded my chest, paralyzed my breath. I thought of Katie. I thought of Sheldon. A profound sadness welled up within me.

I had let everyone down.

Katie? Are you here?

Thudding against my window.

Water at my chin.

I must hold my breath.
I must hold it.
And hold it.
Water came into my mouth... my nose... and I swallowed
and tried to find air, then swallowed bitter salty water again
and again. Salty water bit my tongue. Scraped my throat. I
had to float up and find the air bubble. Surely there would be
a slice of air where the roof curves to the window.

I floated, removed my shoes. I did find air, but before I
could get a good second gulp of it, the car rocked and moved.
I lost my chance. Was I upside down? Darkness everywhere.

Then I saw a light. A blue light. I floated toward it. *Mary?*
Are you here? I told myself to give in, to give up. I would not
be rigid. I would not fight. I would let the force grab me and
pull me onward.

Holy Mary, Mother of God, pray for us sinners, now
and at the hour of our death...

57. My Savior

HANDS SCRABBLED OVER my head, my neck. I reached
out to these hands. They pulled me forward. Shoved me
upward. "Here," the voice commanded. "Get on the roof."

Brackish grit spewed from my nose and mouth. I coughed
until I practically threw up. And coughed some more.

Nothing made sense. Roofs were high. This was water.
Gathering my senses, I realized I was kneeling on the roof of
my car, with water rising across my chest. I stood up slowly,
trying to balance. Sheldon stood up with me, water now at
our knees and climbing as the car sank below us. We were in
the Bay. The lights from the distant ballpark cast a slight
glow around us.

"Sheldon," I said, through a cough and another spit.

"Anne," he said. He hugged me as we rocked with the
waves and stood on solid, albeit shaky, ground.

"Thank you." My teeth were chattering now, my sweater
weighing me down. I slipped off the water-soaked garment,
as well as my draggy skirt. My feet bare and cold.

"Anne." Sheldon's voice sounded fearful in the dark.

"Thank you, Sheldon," I said again, hugging him. Clinging to him, clinging to this wonderful, wonderful man.

"Anne—"

"Let's swim over there, Sheldon. See that light? I think I see a ladder."

"I can't."

"Why not?"

"I can't swim."

Sheldon grasped me. Held on as the car sank further into the water, sinking, sinking. Water at my waist. Water at my chest. He began to flail.

I began treading water. Sheldon lost his footing, his arms flailed.

"Don't grab me," I said.

He went under. I pulled him up by the back of his collar. "Stay still," I commanded. "Don't turn around. Float on your back. Stop wiggling."

All those summers as a camp counselor came back to me, all those silly swimming rehearsal rescues. Because of them, I managed to haul Sheldon, the man who had just saved my life, back to the pier.

"Climb the ladder," I shouted at him, ignoring the splitting pain in my head as well as the pain in my ribs.

"No, you go," he said, through a shiver.

"No. You. Now. Climb it now."

Sheldon obeyed. The crash and crackle of dead wood blended with the sound of the waves lapping into the posts under the pier. I looked up. Sheldon dangled by one arm and tried to scramble to the next rung.

The sheer effort made him cry out, but he managed to clamber up the rest of the ladder.

I was next. I reached for the rung. It came off in my hand. The two rungs above it were also gone. Was there another ladder somewhere?

"Anne!" he shouted from above. "Where are you?"

58. Could This Be Heaven?

A KEENING SCREAM split my ears. Pain winced through me like I had taken Saint Michael's sword in the temple. Dizzy and perhaps delirious, I saw someone who looked like Sheldon sitting in a jump seat and wrapped in a sheet.

Maybe I didn't make it out of the water. Maybe I died. Could this be Heaven?

No. I was freezing.

Could I have become the frozen Holy Water?

"She's coming around," someone said.

I raised my head. There was a needle in my arm. The smell of metal stung my nostrils. I wanted to get it away from my face. I needed a good solid breath.

"This is oxygen," someone told me. "Let the mask alone."

Sheldon didn't have his glasses. He looked pale and strange without them, like he did that night we made love.

"Where's Bruno?" I whispered.

Sheldon shook his head. "Don't talk," he said, through a shiver. "Just breathe."

"Bruno killed Katie," I said, pulling the mask away. "The pudding." I tried to push the words out. "It was in the powder. All along... the protein powder."

"Don't talk. Just rest," Sheldon said, again.

"But if I die—someone has to know. Sheldon, listen to me. He admitted it. He told me. Tell the cops. Please, tell Luke."

"You won't die," he said. He looked at the medic between us. "She's not going to die. Is she?"

"Sit back down, sir. And buckle in. We don't want you to be injured if the vehicle stops abruptly."

"Oh, Anne," he said, coming across the ambulance to kneel beside me and take my hand. "I won't let you die. I love you." Sheldon started to cry and I felt the steady clasp of his hand. I didn't want him to let me go.

I'm not one for drugs, that I found out when I had my nose done, so what happened next is still a hazy blur. But I do remember the kindness of the nurses, being swaddled in warm blankets, Sheldon's hand stroking my cold head, and the moment Da and the boys burst into the hospital like a gang of roaring pirates. Through the ache in my skull, I caught glimpses of my brother Mark hugging Sheldon, throwing him up in the air like a cheerleader at a rally.

"The little muscles ye have there 'n what they did!" Mark shouted. Again, he tossed Sheldon. "Look a' that!" Sheldon came down in a great puff of air. I could tell Mark was making him nauseous.

"No. It wasn't like that—" Sheldon protested.

"So ye lost yer horses 'n asses, eh lad?" Da said, a smile covering his face.

Sheldon blinked like a fish in a bowl.

"Glasses, lad! Horses 'n asses. Glasses. Ye lost yer glasses."

"Oh yeah, I can't see. But it was Anne. Anne who saved me."

"No need ta see!" Matthew's shout made me wince again in pain. "It's wha' yu've done tha' counts! Ya saved m' sister's arse." He started to cry. Not a snivel or a quick wipe of his berry pies, but Matthew erupted in a real open-mouthed wail. "I lost one sister, I couldna' do fer another." Then Da started to sob. Then Mark. Soon the whole room filled with howling and bawling men.

Ma was beside me looking grim, crying and shaking her head while I seemed to be flying up and around the room, hypnotized by drugs and the warm, warm sheets. All the while, the pounding inside my head mimicked the beat of a gargantuan base drum.

"D'ya luv her?" Da squeaked between sobs.

I was too stupid at this moment to be embarrassed. This was akin to watching a play.

"Yes," Sheldon said.

Like he was the last of the toothpaste, Mark gave him another giant squeeze.

"Well, then, come inta tha family, lad!" Da yelled. "Propose ta my little bottle of water! I donut care if yer a

Jew. I donut care if yer ass is purple and yer tits light up. I've never heard'ov a little bean counter like ya havin' such power! Ya beat tha pulp out of tha' feckin' eejit. My god, yer an O'Neil if I ever saw one!"

"How in all heaven n' hell did'ja do it?" yelled Mark. "Givin' Bruno such a whack! Why he'll be out 'til Christmas."

"I don't know how. I just knew I had to," Sheldon said. "Bruno kept pushing the car so I picked something up and beat him off. I broke the wood across his head. Then we threw punches. Then the car fell off the pier. I jumped in the water and got over to it. Which is weird." He turned from one to the other and mumbled, "I can't swim."

"Then how did'ja—"

"I grabbed the door handle. It wouldn't open. God, it was dark! I kept trying and trying. It was sinking. I knew Anne was in there. The car went lower and lower. I nearly lost it. I couldn't see, but I dove anyway." Sheldon's voice shut off. "And then I saw the light. Thank God for that light."

"A light?" Da said. "In tha car?"

"A blue light. In the car. Around the car... I found Anne's hand and I grabbed it and she came out and we came up through the water and got onto the car roof." Sheldon huffed and wheezed and maybe he cried right then, I don't know. "And then, and then... " Sheldon said, between gulps. "I realized I couldn't swim and Anne—" He pointed at me and whispered, "Anne saved me."

"She cud always swim like a fish, tha' one," Da said.

About then, I sat up. I don't know how I managed it, but I did. "Where's Bruno?" I asked. I saw spots and nearly blacked out.

"Down tha hall. A right grand battalion of cops around 'im," Mark said. "He's sittin' tight. Don't ya worry. They won' let him go."

"Don't get out 'a bed," Ma said, trying to hold me back. "Ya 'ave a concussion and two broken ribs. The doctor said ya have ta stay still."

"I want to see him," I said.

"Ya can't. Yer attached t'all this." Matthew pointed to the IV drip and the oxygen.

I ripped the tubes from my nose and immodestly threw my legs over the side of the bed, then grabbed onto the IV stand. "I want to see him," I said, gasping for air. "And I want all of you to be my witness."

No one spoke. And no one stopped me, either.

I must have looked like a witch who had risen from the depths, hair stringy and eyes laden with revenge. Leaning on Sheldon and walking down the hall with the IV stanchion, we saw several cops, Luke among them, outside a door.

"Bruno Stark in there?" Da said. The men in front of his room stared at us. "He 'as a caller."

A couple of the police looked wary. Luke came forward. "Hey, gorgeous." Then he eyed Matthew and Mark and his voice changed. "Ya can't touch him. He's under arrest. D'you understand?"

Da spoke up. "Yer sister wants a word 'n since Bruno just tried ta kill 'er she deserves ta say 'er piece. That's all we want. A few words."

They let us all crowd around Bruno's bed. One of the cops said again to my brothers, "Behave yourselves. He's in custody."

Where Bruno's face wasn't bandaged, it was red, raw, and bruised. I couldn't believe Sheldon had done that.

"Tell them, Bruno," I rasped.

"What?" Bruno said, all groggy. He opened his puffy eyes. When he saw the O'Neil men, fear showed across his face.

My voice was even and without emotion. "Tell them how you poisoned Katie with the pudding."

Bruno looked up at me, but didn't speak. His eyes were slowly getting bigger, his anxiety palpable.

"We know it was thallium," I said. It was the "Royal We" I spoke, a total bluff, just like the police had bluffed me that day they told me to hire an attorney and made me worried sick that I would be charged with arson.

Bruno's eyes blazed with hate, then morphed into fear and confusion.

"You did it," I rasped. "You poisoned her to get to me."

I wobbled then, but steadied myself. I would not cower. I was rigid Agnes Anne, inflexible as a stone wall.

"Tell them," I said, sharper this time. "You might as well, because you know I know, Bruno." I leaned and tried to find his pupils inside those puffy slits. *"I know everything, and so do the police."*

Bruno wouldn't speak, but I heard a wheeze and saw his eyes tear up, his chest convulse. The first sobs broke through the ice in his veins, but still, he didn't utter a word.

"Thallium," I whispered.

He thrashed like he was on a hot griddle, but he couldn't go anywhere. He was tied to an IV and someone had secured one of his wrists to the bars on the bed. I stared at the handcuff.

I leaned in and came close to his face. *"Say it,"* I said.

Bruno's scraped and discolored face strained with the effort to keep from sobbing.

Matthew gazed at the IV lines and flicked one of the bags a couple of times with his thumb and forefinger. Bruno looked back to see what Matthew was doing, and then over to me. I leaned down again over Bruno's face so I was the only thing in his vision, a specter from another world.

"Tell them, Bruno," I rasped.

His voice was shallow and forced. "I want a lawyer."

"You'll need more than a lawyer," Mark said, holding his fist out.

"Thallium," I said, again, moving away so everyone could see him, gaze at his reaction. "It was thallium," I repeated. "Colorless. Odorless. And no one suspected that day and night, you were giving it to her a little at a time. It made her weaker and weaker, all the while Da praising you for taking such good care of his little Gaelic Princess. 'Bruno-god-love-ya,' he kept saying, 'we're so glad we have you in the family,'" I mimicked. "And there you were, smug and arrogant, delighted that we were impressed by the great Dr. Stark while we all watched Katie slowly dying." I choked back tears.

"Yes," he yelped, "I have thallium in the house. So what? So what?"

"So what? It means you murdered her!" My voice was shrill, and Sheldon reached his arms around me so I would calm down. "What did you have it in the house for? Ringworm? No one treats ringworm that way anymore."

While Ma was speechless, Da's lips trembled. Matthew and Mark began to blubber like babies.

"If you didn't want her anymore, why didn't you divorce

her?" I whispered.

Bruno shook his head.

"You liked all the attention, didn't you?" I said. "You got to play the Great Doctor Bruno and reap the sympathy of taking care of a sickly wife."

"Ya poisoned m'Katie?" Ma screamed.

Bruno couldn't speak. He shook his head. But tears ran out of the sides of his eyes and across the bandages covering the wounds on his left cheek. Bruno's body trembled, his chin chattering as though the room had fallen below zero.

I decided to strike again.

"Now tell them, Bruno, about the night of my Junior Prom."

Bruno looked confused. I know I was being petty, that Katie's murder was more important than what happened to me twelve years ago, but I couldn't help myself. I rode on a runaway rollercoaster fueled by adrenalin and pain killers.

"The night of my Junior Prom," I said, "you tried to rape me and then you told me that if I said anything you'd run me over in a crosswalk. Isn't that right, Bruno?"

I watched him flounder like a gutted fish.

"Say it, Bruno or so help me God, I'll rip this IV right out of your arm and strangle you with these tubes." *Oh my goodness, did I say that? Mother Mary, forgive me.*

Bruno's nod was big and exaggerated.

"How about telling them that you tried to make me sign a suicide note before you were going to kill me?"

The room erupted in angry shouts and expletives.

"Or that you burned down your parents' house for the insurance money?"

The cops tried to quiet my brothers. My brothers tried to hold back Da, but it was Ma who surprised us all. From the foot of the bed, she leaned forward and, as though she performed a graceful movement in a ballet, she spat directly at Bruno and hit him precisely in his unbandaged eye.

My head throbbed as I searched for words, but I was exhausted and completely spent. I could go no further, and began to cough uncontrollably. The shooting pains in my ribs rendered me speechless.

I knew there would be a day in court. I knew this story would not truly end for years, and the hole in all our hearts left by Katie's death would be something the O'Neils would have to deal with forever. I turned to lean on Sheldon. He hugged me and, for a few seconds, we rocked like we were still on the roof of my car and sinking. Then, with an arm around my waist, Sheldon gently led me back to bed.

The moment I left Bruno's room, it sounded like all hell broke loose. Luke was threatening to arrest his own brothers as well as his father if they didn't stop trying to harm the prisoner. When the three of them came back to my room, they shouted because they had been tricked, then wept for the senselessness of it all. If Bruno hated Katie so much, why couldn't he have just left her and let her live? They looked at me and asked why I'd never said anything about my Junior Prom.

"Too young," I said, not meeting anyone's gaze. "Too ashamed."

"Ya should'a said *somethin'*," Da said, his face a peculiar mixture of incredulity and mortification.

"I tried."

"What's thallium?" Mark asked, looking from one tearful face to the other. Luke explained how the poison hides from coroners, how it's odorless and tasteless, and causes weakness, nervous center disorders, fevers, gastric upset. The anorexia diagnosis actually fit her symptoms. In the middle of this, Luke's voice failed, and, head in his hands, he openly wept.

"Sheldon yer a he-man!" Da called out, his voice so loud, some of us twitched with the sound of it.

"Yer the only one who got ta give him what 'e deserves," Matthew said. After he dried his face with a paper towel, he lurched into the gleeful recollection of seeing Bruno's battered face, the cuts and bruises of a brawl.

Everything dissolved into shouts and for the third time, they went through it all over again, blow by blow. Finally, Ma told the boys and Da to go home and threw everyone out of the room. Everyone except Sheldon, who slowly crept up on the bed and lay next to me, his cheek and forehead plastered with bandages, his knuckles taped up like a boxer after a match.

"Agnes Anne," Ma said, as though her words were stepping stones and she was crossing an unknown river. "Ya never told us 'bout tha high school dance. How were we ta know?"

"I was too ashamed to speak of it, Ma." I heard the click of her tongue.

"All these years? He's been..." She searched for the next word. Nothing came.

I closed my eyes and didn't want to think of Bruno anymore. So I let the feel of Sheldon's shoulder next to mine and the warmth of his hand wash over me. He was here. And he had saved me.

"I'm sorry," Ma said. "I should'a noticed. I t'ought I knew all m'girls, but I—" her voice cracked.

"It's over, Ma," I managed to whisper.

"'Tis," she said. "He fooled us, that Bruno. Bein' a doctor, I always t'ought 'e was smarter than us. Why, we deferred ta him like he was some sort a' saint."

"I know, Ma."

"Oh, Agnes—I mean Anne—I let you down."

I opened my eyes and watched tears streak down her freckled face. "It's okay, Ma. It's over. And you don't have to call me Anne anymore. Agnes is just fine."

"Thank God ya have this lovely man ta stand beside ya," she said. "Even though he's... he's... not a our faith."

Sheldon squeezed my hand and the blush of a smile crossed my face, because the issue wouldn't be forgotten, this I knew. But even if our relationship didn't work out, from now on Sheldon had a new place of honor in our family.

I heard the wheeze of the door. "Agnes Anne?" Da croaked. He leaned over the bed while I gazed up into his red-rimmed eyes.

"I've na' done ya right, girl."

"It's okay, Da."

"No, 'tis not okay. A real man makes 'is peace."

I could tell Da was having a difficult time saying whatever it was he'd come to say, but I was too tired to make it any easier for him.

"I've been a bit of a bully and I'm ashamed of tha'. Ashamed a' m'self. I should'a known... I should'a guessed. That damn Bruno fooled us all."

Before I could make some sort of response, Da held up his hand.

"Agnes? I mean, Anne. I wonnut do it again."

Before I could say anything, Da kissed me on the forehead. When he straightened up, he gazed at Sheldon and bent back down to kiss him on the forehead as well. Not a tiny kiss, mind you, but a great big juicy smackeroo. I wish I could have seen Sheldon's face right then, but he was beside me on the bed and it hurt too much to move.

"As far as I'm concerned, Sheldon, yer a member of tha clan," Da said to him. "And from now on I'll treat ya like me own. Jew 'r not. Fish 'r fowl, yer one'a us."

Sheldon didn't jump at the chance to become an O'Neil. Couldn't say I blamed him.

"Thank you, Mr. O'Neil."

"Mr. O'Neil! Call me Da! I'm yer new Irish father, lad." Da's voice was so loud, I winced. "Whether ya like it 'r not," he yelled, "I'll be with ya for life. That's how we Irish are. Loyal to a fault."

"Oh..." Sheldon's voice sort of faded off while he probably contemplated a life with a friend like my father.

"Yer a lucky man, Sheldon Goldberg," Da said, waggling a finger above our heads. "I've been thinkin'. What you saw in that car tonight 'as nothin' short uv'a miracle."

Sheldon blinked. "It was?"

"Tha light! Tha light n'na car, lad! Leadin' ya to Agnes Anne. Leadin' Agnes Anne outov'a watery grave. Don't ya realize wha' happened?"

Sheldon sighed. "I don't know. It was just a light."

"And where wud'a that light 'av come from? Ya were under water. Tha electrical shorted out."

"I don't—"

"'N this light—it came ta ya! A Jew. I don' mean tha' in a bad way. We both agree n'a Old Testament. Right? Genesis 'n Ruth 'n Job 'n tha Psalms... that guy Ezekiel waz 'ad one wheel in'a sand, but no matter." Da lowered his voice to a whisper. "But lad! Ya saw a miracle!"

"The light has to have a logical explanation," Sheldon

mumbled.

"If it does, I'd like ta 'ear it."

"Maybe it was a short circuit, Mr. O'Neil."

"I'm yer Da!" Da shouted. "A short circuit wud cause total darkness, now wudn'it? What color was tha light? This magical light tha' enabled ya ta free m'bottle 'a water?"

Sheldon thought for a second. "Blue. A weird blue."

"Well there ya go! I think it wuz Mary sendin' tha' light so ya cud save m'daught—" Da's voice cut out and he stifled a sob.

Sheldon sniffled as well. "I don't—I don't know, Mr. O'Neil—er—*Da*. It's not logical. But—I could suddenly see her outline. The window opened. I reached through and got her." Sheldon began to sob. "How did... It's not... logical."

"Le'me tell ya something, Sheldon, m'boy. In this world, there's a time for logic 'n a time fer faith. Like your Hanukkah. Eight days 'a light from a single portion 'a oil. That's a miracle, boy. See?"

Sheldon kept rubbing his forehead. I heard another sniff. And then a cough. "I don't know..." he choked out.

"Ah, tha Festival 'a tha Lights, a lovely miracle, indeed. And now we had'r own miracle t'night, didn't we?"

Sheldon sniffed and shook his head. I could sense that he was far too upset to argue the point.

"Stick around, son, there'r little miracles everywhere. You'll see." Da bent down again and gave Sheldon another kiss and patted him on the side of his face.

"Okay, all right." Sheldon squirmed from either embarrassment or pain.

We both heard the wheeze of the door, but Ma still stood at the side of the bed.

"Good night, Sheldon, dear. Don't keep Agnes Anne up too late. Hospitals 'ave rules, ya know. Ya shouldn't even be lyin' on tha bed. She needs 'er rest. Oh, wait. Ya prob'ly need a ride. We'll take ya home."

"Yes, ma'am," Sheldon said through a snuffle. "Just a few more minutes, Mrs. O'Neil."

"After all this, Sheldon, I think ya should call me Irene." Ma crossed the room to leave, then at the door, she changed her mind and came back. "Mary must luv ya very much, Agnes Anne."

Ma usually said I made the Virgin Mary cry. Now it was me who blinked back tears.

"'N tonight, Agnes dear, if yer in pain—"

"I know, Ma," I whispered. "Offer it up."

"There's a good girl." I felt her lips on my forehead, heard the wheeze of the door as it settled back into the jamb.

"Anne?" Sheldon whispered, turning toward me. "I don't know what happened tonight. But I do know that I love you."

It hurt to smile, but I couldn't help myself. The grin that grew across my face could have illuminated all of San Francisco. Sheldon gently kissed my lips. I closed my eyes and said a silent prayer. *Thank you, Mary, for not letting me screw up.*

Acknowledgements

There are too many people to thank—from early readers
to late readers, to the San Francisco Peninsula branch of
the California Writers Club and all the friends I've leaned
on in the last few years. Special thanks to Bardi, Jim,
Ann, Chris and Lisa, all members of my critique group,
the LLBW—couldn't have made it without you!
Deep gratitude to editors Karen Edlefsen and Bardi
Rosman Koodrin. Thanks for seeing me through.

In the world of small press publishing it is sometimes difficult to get
books widely known. If you enjoyed this story won't you please tell
other readers by leaving a comment on Amazon, Goodreads or other
places where booklovers gather?

SHRP
Sand Hill Review Press